Ambassador for Life

Douglas K. Sanders

PublishAmerica
Baltimore

First printing

This novel is a work of fiction. Some of the settings, characterizations and the names of people have been changed. However, the author has used historical data and actual interviews. Please refer to the chapter notes and bibliography for more information.

ISBN: 1-4137-1669-5
PUBLISHED BY PUBLISHAMERICA, LLLP
www.publishamerica.com
Baltimore

Printed in the United States of America

Dedication

To my father, my mother and my wife, for helping me realize a dream of a lifetime.

Table of Contents

PART ONE

The Beginning

Anything was possible in 1964, the year the Johnson-Humphrey landslide was headed into the history books. It was also the year when Anthony Flint entered the fourth grade at the redbrick schoolhouse in Dalton, Indiana, to join his classmates, most of whom he would know and see through high school. There was time spent that first day learning assigned seats with the teacher, but this was the very beginning of everything he would ever come to know in his lifetime.

It was always intended for him to meet presidents, generals, the man who helped plan the Watergate burglary, a few country-western music stars, a national advice columnist, a starship helmsman, the king of popcorn, a women's tennis champion and the astronaut who walked on the moon and later searched for Noah's Ark.

No one else had quite the notoriety as Anthony Flint. His appearance on national television was a ratings booster on a Sunday night. It was arguable that anybody in America who saw the broadcast had incentive to go out and buy a newspaper and read his syndicated column. They would read for themselves what the fuss was really all about. It was also a matter of debate in everyone's mind to seek fame and fortune when opportunity knocks, and they all believed that Anthony opened the door.

What better example than the movie by Steven Speilberg? It created millionaires out of friends and neighbors and family, and the verdict was still out whether a stage producer wanted to buy the rights to put it on Broadway. None of it seemed impossible to produce or direct; this was a story of people, places and things more famous than Anthony Flint. Long before he was born, and even after his death, it was all part of America. But was anything by Flint actually true?

Remember that the first milestone had its origins in 1964 when, at the age of 10, Anthony Flint received a brand new science textbook in school. That did not begin to explain it all.

Chapter 1: First Man to Mars

During the 1960s the editorial staff of Scott, Foresman and Company was faced with its greatest challenges in the history of the company. Man was entering space for the first time, yet no one was really prepared for the new demand in science textbooks. School children could see Allen Shepherd, John Glenn, John Young and Gus Grissom on television in darkened classrooms across America. At the end of the day, they all clamored for more, and textbook publishers for the nation's schools were only too happy to oblige.

Anthony's science textbook was published in 1961. The complete series included nine textbooks and was published under revised copyrights in 1944, 1951 and 1956. He even took it with him years later when he moved to Orlando, Florida. But what he read and what he believed that day in Dalton was not a conflict. It was not yet even possible.

In all the years to come, Flint would hand the textbook to friends and family, and nobody would see it. Anthony did, clearly, and he could always remember the first time in Dalton. Again, it was not a conflict. More like a neat parlor trick—according to those who politely took the time to read it and then simply shrugged their shoulders and said they saw nothing.

Whether Flint accepted mysteries or miracles did not matter anymore. None of the editorial staff from Scott, Foresman and Company would ever meet Anthony Flint. It was highly unlikely if any of them ever visited any of the classrooms in Dalton. The editor and staff were presumed to be at their peak, having all the resources they really needed from their offices in Chicago, Atlanta, Dallas, Palo Alto and Fair Lawn, New Jersey.

It was a best seller in the world of school textbooks. Each and every series had escaped serious challenges from television and computer games— the kind of intellectual corruption that was not yet rampant in American classrooms in the Sixties. There was still time for students to read and fantasize about space travel and man walking on the moon. Or Mars.

Anthony Flint decided years later to write a letter to Scott, Foresman and Company. At that point it was anyone's guess as to the outcome of this truly remarkable situation. This was also an indication of what little options were still available to him.

Perhaps—because they were resigned to do nothing else—the editorial staff did not want to respond at all. They saw what they perceived to be a crank letter from Florida, but they were not blind. Looking outside their offices, the snow was blowing hard in Chicago, and it was a fact that the weather was decidedly warmer in Orlando. That, admittedly, probably tainted the opinions of everyone in the room that day.

Flint seemed to trust his own judgement. He had broached the subject enough times with others that he no longer wanted to push his luck. He never found another reference of it in his textbook. And in all editions, Scott, Foresman and Company proofed all the drafts the same way, looking for errors or omissions with great care and with success that was widely respected in the industry.

They never found the name of the first man on Mars.

No, it was not your typical story that could be expected from a small child in the fourth grade. Kids that age easily talk about baseball players or basketball teams and, yes, astronauts in space. Flint, however, was not a sports fan, and he was not yet so interested in the space program that he would know any fact from fiction. To name an astronaut who would walk on Mars, well, the teacher quickly offered to send him to the library. She told him to checkout the books on the Red Planet, future spacecraft and propulsion systems and anything else that could be used for a child obviously reaching out for something.

To do so, though, allowed the teacher to be in a position to explain to Anthony's parents what she thought was really going on. And because it takes a teacher time to know her students on a level that is different from the parents, or what is most measured by tests and national standards and the teacher's own expectations for the accomplishments of each student.

That year the fourth grade completed a class assignment that amounted to a science project—sort of. It was a homemade slide projector, and it was mostly a cardboard box with a lamp and a slot to fit the lens in. The lamp and the lens were not made by the children. Practically everything else was made or found by little hands with imaginations at work over a 2-week period. This was an excellent example of teamwork, class spirit and even old-fashioned praise. "Everyone did such a good job," the teacher told the parents. "You should be very proud of your son or daughter."

Like any member of the team, Flint made his contributions to the class project. For example, the film projector needed a long extension cord. By bringing his dad's to school one morning, the projector could be positioned in the classroom to make the projections on the wall big enough for everyone to see. Then someone else brought in the slides—a family vacation to Niagara Falls!

The general consensus of the teacher was this: Flint wanted much more attention in class than what he was getting for his part in the slide projector project. That was understandable. Nobody wants to be a face in the crowd or to go unnoticed when something big is really happening in school. As the teacher remarked: "What if Anthony said, 'Can I help on the slide projector?' We wouldn't say much more than simply to do this or do that. But what he chose to say is like a revelation from heaven—we just don't know what children are really going to do next."

His parents did find it a bit unusual in the very beginning, when it was first apparent to them that their son believed his book was very different. Anthony was the only one who had possession of such a textbook, and no one else could see what he would read in black and white.

Anthony's teacher even told his parents about the Indian who walked to the Dalton school in the 1920s. He often fought off bears and highwaymen to do it. The Indian was mighty handy with the bow-and-arrow, and the kids said he was "pretty doggoned good." Nothing escaped his eagle eye, which was worse than all the principals at the school who said they had eyes in the back of their heads. The Indian story found reasonable fascination with students each school year. This was, after all, a nation that still didn't have MTV or Jerry Springer.

Anthony Flint did come to school on some days to find his science textbook missing from the top of his desk. One of his classmates would always exclaim, "The Martians ate it!" or another student chimes in, "Jeff blasted it with his ray gun!" The truth was always pretty boring, even if the punishment was predictable. Inevitably it was a boy (never a girl!) with a sheepish grin on his face, finally rising from his seat and slowly walking up to the teacher still holding Flint's textbook behind his back. That resulted in no recess for the rest of the day for him, and it was also made in the spirit of no appeals.

Not that anyone was ever really mean about it at all. As soon as the laughter and all the commotion died down in the classroom, it was back to the multiplication tables or the reading or writing of something. It was like each one of them had his own internal clock and knew instinctively when the time was right to blow off stress and ease the burdens of learning in the classroom. The teacher also knew that nothing could keep their attention for very long. If it was only for a little bit, the diversion was acceptable and eventually helpful to get back to what she wanted to teach on the blackboard.

Everybody seemed to know what to do when Flint's textbook suddenly disappeared. Too bad they were not that good at getting in line for lunch or as efficient in going out the school doors during the fire escape drills. And in all the years to come, they no longer remembered the name of the first man to Mars.

Anthony's immediate instinct was to run his fingers across the black lettering on his textbook; he whispered to himself what it said: SCIENCE IS LEARNING. It was printed on a gray hardcover, and it was surrounded by various illustrations including a burning fire, a picture of two animals, and a little girl at her desk reading one of her schoolbooks. She had a large globe of the Earth on the table next to her.

The book itself comprised 128 pages and included the contents, index and five chapters. He opened it and began to turn the pages, and it was then that he happened to stop and read the following paragraph:

> From very, very far away we can see that the earth is round. It is a big round ball. We can see another thing about the earth, too. We can see that it turns. It turns round and round. All the things on the earth turn with it. All the plants and animals turn with it. All the people turn with it. You turn with the earth.

Then he read this:

> The sun shines on the turning earth. It is day when the sun shines on your part of the earth. It is night when your part of the earth turns away from the sun. Then you can see the moon. And all the stars. One of them is Mars. One day a man will go there. His name is Richard Crotty.

After Anthony Flint became a nationally syndicated columnist for *The Orlando Sentinel*, he did write the following:

NASA will make one of those decisions that make its job in manned space flight all the more difficult. The space agency one day is expected to announce the name of the first human to go to Mars.

And, ohmigod, I know who it is.

The debate is not over whether it is a man or woman in order to improve the success of the mission.

It isn't that we need to send an American astronaut to the Martian world. Now, as never before, we see nations with space programs that are "promising" or "on-the-cutting edge" of new technology.

NASA and the Congress are fighting over money. This is nothing new. The Apollo program used spare parts to get what it could done.

Three Apollo missions to the moon were scrubbed by Congress, not NASA, all because of funding. And who can forget all the congressional hearings for spending money on the first international space station?

There was no great public victory because America's space program was rebuffed in the attempt to launch more men to the moon. All this did was siphon the money for the Vietnam War and prolong our involvement in that terrible tragedy.

NASA attracts the attention of Washington, because public dollars are used in the name of science and in highly complex missions that take years to complete. Voters don't see any connections between sending a probe to Neptune or building a domed stadium for the local NFL team.

But the issue of public funding for these projects is the same.

Given a choice between the two, the majority of us would rather see the money go to the domed stadium. Watching a football team is more entertaining than watching thousands of scientists send a man into space.

This is what happens when you have a huge national budget and too many ways to spend it. It is used for so many things, big and small, that nobody would dare attempt to say it all balances out in the end.

The only way to have a proper debate on what to do with the money spent on NASA programs is to take away any obscurities on its use.

Then we can expand our options to include building a lunar

base, training more astronauts and increasing science education in our schools, as well as funding NASA or sending a mission to Mars.

Without that, NASA funding is not relevant in the eyes of the American voters

NASA will make one of those decisions that make its job in manned space flight all the more difficult. The space agency one day is expected to announce the name of the first human to go to Mars.

This mindset has to change. And, heck, why not? What else is there to do with the millions we spend now? That would have such a national good for America?

What this nation needs is for NASA to put the mission together, build the spacecraft and give us our "second small step for mankind." And send Richard Crotty to Mars.

Don't bother looking his name up in the phone book. He's not even born yet.

What's more, this will not happen in our lifetime. Try 50 years from now, when public funding for the Mars landing is finally in place. To ensure that this country won't become impatient, I add this bit of advice: we have had many frivolous spending programs approved by Congress. It's time for a good one.

PART TWO

Chapter 2: Watergate

Near the Santa Barbara channel in southern California, a small group, wearing suits and ties, walked to a bridge and over an inlet to the beaches on Aug. 14, 1974. No one with a 35 mm camera saw them. Except for a 20-year-old biology major from Ball State University. His name was Dwight Brill, from Alexandria, Virginia, a suburb of Washington, D.C.

Brill snapped several pictures with his Minolta SRT-100.

On the beach was Richard M. Nixon six days after his resignation as President of the United States of America. His daughter, Tricia Nixon Cox, and his son-in-law, Edward Cox, and the Secret Service agents formed a small contingent that walked with him.

They all stopped as Brill approached the former world leader during a very peaceful encounter. Brill certainly did not see any signs of illness, fatigue, anger or even depression on that sunny day in southern California. But within days Nixon would develop thrombophlebitis in his left leg while resting at a friend's 200-acre estate near Ventura, California, the home of Walter Annenberg, U.S. Ambassador to Great Britain. Doctors later announced it was an inflammation of a vein, accompanied by a blood clot.

In Long Beach, California, several days before the walk on the beach and the pardon by President Ford, there were medical tests at Memorial Hospital Medical Center. Then Nixon was wheeled out through the double doors of the Nuclear Medicine Laboratory. Kent Henderson, of the *Long Beach Independent Press-Telegram,* suddenly attempted to take a picture of the ex-President. The reaction was unexpected as the once leader of the Free World cursed Henderson abruptly, forcing hospital officials to rush him back through the double doors that morning and was not seen for the rest of the day.

The obligation of photographers and reporters in the news media was simple and yet not entirely fair. No media outlet had any pictures or interviews with Richard M. Nixon in the early days following the presidential resignation. The first sound bite on television or the first interview in print would be a world-exclusive. But the encounter in Long Beach was not very peaceful.

Back in college that fall, Brill carried in his shirt pocket the telephone message to meet Anthony Flint inside Emens Auditorium on the campus of Ball State University. Flint was a staff reporter for the *Ball State Daily News*, the campus daily. They found an empty room with tables and chairs. Here they finally got together and started looking through copies of *Time* and *Newsweek* magazines, each with published pictures of Nixon by Dwight Bill.

Brill told Flint: "I walked up and met them, and asked him if I could take his picture and he said 'sure' and posed for me. The whole time I was nervous. I was really surprised to see the former President of the Untied States.

"He seemed to be pretty friendly, and I shook hands with him. Then they began walking again on the beach and I walked along aside of them. And the Secret Service followed right behind us, and we walked up to his car and he got in.

"Most of the other newspapers have misquoted me, saying he looked terrible and had a long drawn-out look. But when I saw him, he looked old from the standpoint of having to go through what he did and he seemed just to have aged quite a bit."

Brill added: "If Nixon didn't want me to take his picture, I wouldn't have. I never thought those pictures would amount to this much. They were just ordinary pictures."

In 20 years the former President would be buried on the grounds of the Richard Nixon Library and birthplace in Yorba Linda, California. Dr. Billy Graham officiated at the funeral services on April 27, 1994, and was followed by Dr. Henry Kissinger, 56th secretary of state, Robert Dole, United States Senator from Kansas, Pete Wilson, Governor of California, and Bill Clinton, 42nd President of the United States. Local estimates said nearly 50,000 people viewed the Nixon casket in the library lobby, some waiting 18 hours in a line nearly two miles long.

The news of the Nixon resignation first reached Anthony Flint inside the break room at Chrysler Corporation's maching and forge plant on 1817 I Avenue in New Castle, Indiana. The latest game of euchre was suddenly halted as everyone in the room listened to the small transistor radio on the table. Richard Nixon had resigned as the 37th President of the Untied States of America. For Anthony Flint, a college student working that summer at Chrysler, this would prove interesting. For one thing, he would meet Dwight Brill at Ball State University in two months. And then another thing, in 10 years Flint would interview the former finance counsel to the 1972 Nixon re-election committee. He was also a former aide on the staff of John Ehrlichman, assistant to the President for domestic affairs. His name was G. Gordon Liddy.

ANTHONY FLINT: As a former FBI agent and having worked in the Treasury Department, did you have any idea how you would be portrayed in the press?

G. GORDON LIDDY: First place, one cannot, legitimately, take universal positions about the press, you know, all the press, anymore than you can say all Jews, all Catholics, all Protestants, all whites, all blacks. You know, the press contains within its body of many, many people the good, the bad, the indifferent, the competent, the incompetent. And I have never characterized the attitude of the press toward me in terms of harsh or lenient or what-have-you. I haven't said so. I think, certainly, some members of the press were upset that I wouldn't discuss it with them. Certainly, Bob Woodward and Carl Bernstein (laughing).

(Woodward was 29, and Bernstein was 28 in 1972 when they started writing their newspaper stories for *The Washington Post* about the early morning break-in of the headquarters of the Democratic National Committee in the Watergate office-apartment complex. Then White House Press Secretary Ron Zigler called it "a third-rate burglary attempt"; but the Post won a Pulitzer Prize, and actors Robert Redford and Dustin Hoffman played the two reporters in the 1976 motion picture based on their account of Watergate, *All the President's Men*.)

G. GORDON LIDDY: There was one man for whom I have a very high regard, and that is the late Stewart Alsop (a syndicated newspaper columnist), and he wrote to me and said very early on, all has been discovered, there's no point in you remaining silent, you owe a debt to history, et cetera.

Now I had a high regard for that man because he had been in the OSS (Office of Strategic Service—the secret espionage agency that antedated the CIA) during World War II, and when he wrote me, he was dying and behaving, I thought, nobly, in the process of dying. He had what I suppose one would characterize as a blood cancer. And this man would go into the hospital and, at the cost to him in great pain, get all of his blood removed and new blood pumped in, and then go out and practice his profession for as long as he was able and keep going through the process until finally he died. But when he wrote that letter to me, I knew that all had not been discovered. And so I took the attitude that, well, yes, I do owe a debt to history. I understand, having studied history, what a primary source is. But that did not mean his request was a demand note, payable at that time.

And so I waited until all the many statutes of limitations in several jurisdictions had run out—before I spoke on the subject (of Watergate). That way I could do so, candidly, without reservation and I did so.

ANTHONY FLINT: The House Judiciary Committee drafted three articles of impeachment against President Nixon in 1974. One of them said the President abused his executive powers when he formed the so-called "Plumber's unit," attempting to stop leaks in the White House to the media by using unlawful covert activities. You were a member of this group. Did you understand, fully, what was going on?

G. GORDON LIDDY: I have a doctorate in law, and I have post-doctoral studies from a law school in New York. And I generated the whole thing. I assure you I understood it thoroughly and completely. I was a big boy; I was forty years old; I knew exactly what I was doing.

The break-in that was done in 1972 was the kind of thing that was done every four years. If you will recall 1964, when Barry Goldwater was the Republican nominee for President, his place was broken into, wiretaps put in, documents taken out. Now the difference is, no one was apprehended that could be identified with the Democratic Party. So I cannot assert to your readers that it was the Democrats who wiretapped Barry Goldwater in 1964. But I do not suspect that Goldwater had his own office bugged.

ANTHONY FLINT: How has Watergate changed your life?

G. GORDON LIDDY: It has enabled me to get my first lecturing engagement. Of course, if I weren't a good lecturer, I wouldn't have had a second. But since then I've had books published—a number one best seller, another best seller. I've been published in English, French, Italian, Dutch—all over the world. Plus doing television and appearances all over the world. I appeared in Paris, in the spring, and on the 8th of December, I'll be going to Brussels for more appearances and then to France.

I've done very well, indeed. I'm sure that it will further disturb John Sirica (Chief Judge, U.S. District Court for the District of Columbia) that I've come up a winner (laughter).

(The Watergate burglary eventually led to the arrest and conviction of 40 government officials including, but not limited to, the United States Attorney General, White House Counsel, White House Chief of Staff, White House Special Assistant on Domestic Affairs and the five Watergate burglars.)

ANTHONY FLINT: There have been several books written on Watergate, including your own.
G. GORDON LIDDY: John Ehrlichman writes his own stuff, but to my knowledge, John Ehrlichman has not written a Watergate book. John Dean's book was not written by John Dean; it was written by Taylor Branch, who was an editor at Harpers when I was contributing to Harpers. Sirica's book was written for him by an employee of *Time* magazine.

I have no business relationship with any of them, but some of them I consider good friends. I consider myself a very good friend with Maurice Stans (finance chairman for the committee to re-elect Nixon). He's much older than I am, and he's retired now, but I have a high regard for him. I'm a good friend of Hugh Sloan (treasurer for the committee to re-elect Nixon), I'm a good friend of Bart Porter (scheduling director for the committee to re-elect Nixon).

The members of the break-in team are Mr. Howard Hunt, Mr. James McCord, Jr, myself, and then the Cuban fellows (Bernard Barker, Virgilio Gonzalez, Eugenio Martinez and Frank Strugis). I still hold the Cubans in the highest regard, consider them good friends, and would welcome any one of them anytime in my home. I cannot say the same for Mr. Hunt or Mr. McCord because they did not respond to stress as did the Cubans.

Mr Colson is now in the religious business. I'm not religious. The only contact I had with Mr. Colson occurred when I was in prison. And he had been freed, and he had a service, and I did not attend. I guess that offended him. At any rate, he said he wanted to see me. And I said I will see you but not in the chapel because I'm not religious. So I saw him outside the chapel, and he put his arms around me and he said "Gordon, have you seen the light?" And I said "Chuck, I'm not even looking for the switch!"

ANTHONY FLINT: Did Watergate tarnish America's image around the world?

G. GORDON LIDDY: Richard Nixon has always been viewed in Europe, Africa and Asia as about the most competent President we've had since Franklin Roosevelt. They go out of their way to tell you that. I've even had a reporter in France, a communist writer, say the same thing to me. If you recall, when the *London Times* reported on Richard Nixon's resignation, the headline was "HAVE THE PEOPLE OF THE UNITED STATES LOST THEIR MINDS."

ANTHONY FLINT: Do you keep in touch with the ex-President?

G. GORDON LIDDY: We live hundreds of miles apart, but it is correspondence that I would characterize as very warm, very nice, from him to me and, of course, respectful from me to him.

There was still another time when Anthony Flint wrote a story on what became known as the Watergate scandal. The speaker on the night of Feb. 6, 1975, was one of 38 members of the House Judiciary Committee that completed the historic impeachment hearings against Nixon in 1974. This had not happened since President Andrew Johnson and his impeachment crisis of 1868. For one thing, only 12 actual impeachments had been convicted on the Federal level and included senators, Supreme Court justices and district court judges. And the political process was usually very high-stakes. Many in the Student Center Forum Room on the campus of Ball State University that Wednesday night remembered the speaker as a former member of Congress. Only seven months ago, his re-election fund-raiser was held in Muncie, Indiana, by Vice-President Gerald R. Ford and the Indiana State Republican Party.

His name was David W. Dennis, a law school attorney from Harvard University with his own law firm in Richmond, Indiana. Dennis and ten other committee members voted "nay" to the three articles of impeachment. He told his audience: "I personally voted against the articles not because of personal defense of Nixon, but rather in defense of due process of law as I understand it. I think Mr. Nixon is entitled to the same constitutional rights as every other American citizen."

QUESTION: Did President Nixon have a constitutional reason to tape conversations in the White House?

DENNIS: (Laughing): Of course he doesn't! I don't know why he did it. It doesn't make any sense to me why the President didn't burn the tapes when he had the chance.

ANOTHER QUESTION FROM THE AUDIENCE: Is the former President banished as a world leader?

DENNIS: I feel sympathetic to Mr. Nixon. He must be going crazy sitting out there in San Clemente, out of politics that were so much a part of his life, but he did lie to the American people for two years concerning his knowledge of the Watergate break-in.

A FINAL QUESTION FROM THE AUDIENCE: What about Nixon's pardon by President Ford?

DENNIS: He is the first President to leave the nation's highest office in public disgrace, and I think that is sufficient punishment.

Chapter 3: Mr. Flint and the 40-Acre Farm

Keith and Beverly Flint, after 10 years as husband and wife, signed a real estate contract in 1962; and then, in May, moved the family of three young sons to the 40-acre farm not more than five miles from Hagerstown, Indiana. On the day it snowed. Anthony always remembered that.

He also recalled the old Pontiac in the big pasture that was not far from the banks of the tiny creek. For years the frame rusted away, the engine block rested sideways on the ground, and the dashboard was located at the foot of the walnut tree a few hundred yards away. Most of the coupe was still intact; but it, too, weathered the endless seasons of Indiana from its spot near a pair of locust trees. Sometimes it seemed that parts of that old car were found in the most unlikely places for years to come. It was the grandest scavenger hunt, ideal for Flint and his younger brothers.

In the very first years on the farm, before the bedroom renovations and the dining room addition, there was the "warm morning" coal stove. It was in the living room and almost centrally-located in the house as it radiated heat, garnished from buckets of coal briquettes, and wood left to burn long into the night. Flint did remember the bin in the old hen house as the source of the family's coal. He clearly remembered the walks in the woods on Saturdays with his brothers and father. The purpose of these missions, as the routines lasted into the mid-afternoons, was cutting wood with a chainsaw, marking each log equally, or as well as could be expected, and bringing the wood back to the house, finally, to last the winter and maybe a chilly spring. The sound of a chainsaw in the woods far away always seemed to make Flint feel colder than he actually was each winter. Or at least it seemed that way.

Flint, like his younger brothers, had more than one turn behind the wheel of the Farmall H tractor, usually in the month of July when it was always a hot day to drive the mounted cultivators down a row of soybeans. The dust would climb up slowly and settle like fine sand on the manifold of the tractor, and on the face and arms and neck. Hour after hour, going up and down the long field. It was not a very good environment for most young boys to pay attention to what was going to happen next. And it was always suddenly—in a matter of seconds, it seemed—for at least six yards of bean row to vanish from the face of the earth. Forever ripped out by the sharp shovels of the cultivator.

All three brothers admitted to this catastrophe. But it was Anthony who managed to flip the 2-bottom plow upside-down during one momentous time in the spring. One minute it was there in the furrow where it belonged, and one minute it was over the ground and dragged, ignominiously, by the tractor.

Even the oil change was a form of Russian roulette, on a 1950 Farmall H tractor, that consisted of 2 small thumbscrews located near the bottom of the oil pan. Flint could never remember if the direction was clockwise or counter-clockwise to open and close them. The penalty if you was wrong was a pool of gathering oil on the concrete floor to greet the next morning on the farm.

Anthony Flint was born on Sept. 2, 1954, at the Henry County Memorial Hospital in New Castle, Indiana. He was all of 5 pounds, 8 ounces at 4:35 a.m. that year. The family physician was Dr. Alfred Hollenburg from Hagerstown, Indiana. Then in 1956, there was Eugene, who grew to be the tallest; and Clark, who was born in 1958 and was named after his grandfather on his mother's side.

None of the birth announcements would ever reach the desk of the local Congressman from Indiana. This was an oversight caused by the headlines of a busy nation looking in every closet for Communists. It was also captivating to hear the scary "beep, beep, beep" sounds from the television and radio news reports, and that was all about a satellite in space named Sputnik.

The boys would be born healthy, and their lives would continue in a family that was one day designated by President Richard M. Nixon as a member of the "Silent Majority." This was very much a family that raised its sons and daughters in states like Indiana, who lived in rural counties that had cornfields or avocado trees or orange groves or apple orchards. It was really no difference among them primarily because most of the common denominators of Church and State were always the same.

Flint had early memories of the hen house on the west side of the lane to the house and barn. His father found an old train set inside a dusty room that surely hadn't been completely empty since the Great Depression. This particular room was small and was full of assorted items of junk. It seemed that none of it was ever really important enough to be moved out as yesterday's trash. Yet the room itself was very compatible as the future site for the coal bin—the first of several renovations to come—with the labor of the father and three sons.

The farm did have a log cabin that was once occupied by a man named Kennedy. This information was supplied one day to Keith Flint by a member of the LaMar family living down the road. His name was Vic LaMar. And for this to be true, LaMar probably stepped inside the log cabin when he was a small boy nearly the same as young Anthony Flint. That seemed a long time ago. Kennedy and LaMar, in the log cabin that was built and hewed with hand-tools in some forgotten summer. Later, a tin roof was added for better protection from the rainstorms. And windows with glass must have been a real improvement—for luxury as well as light.

Now the view must have been something to behold from inside the log cabin. Anthony imagined dense forests with wild game and no one around as neighbors. The house and the barn would not be built yet. And, for that matter, no telephone lines or electricity had reached the 40-acre farm. It was also a sure thing that LaMar Road was still a dirt nightmare that was not that much wider than a well-traveled footpath.

As the first year went by, the family would find the wood in the house so hard it was not easy to hammer a nail without drilling the hole first. Flint never did recall what kind of wood that was or whether this was any kind of sign that the farmhouse was really old and possibly historic. His family did learn that the barn and the hen house also had wood hard as steel. And when this subject came up with their new neighbors on LaMar Road, it was the same thing—wood that would last long into the senior adulthood of their children.

Anthony Flint often heard his father talk about a wood called "hedge" that was an excellent source for fence posts. His father knew early on that all of the fence rows on the 40-acre farm would have to be replaced. It would take years to do it. And nearly all of the work would have to be confined to the summer months. That was when they needed a steady supply of fence posts, preferably hedge. In the beginning they also used locust wood because it was plentiful and because it was easy to cut. But this was not hard wood, and that was one problem.

Flint was amazed how critical building a fence could be when everything was reviewed years later with perfect hindsight. Even the simple task of setting the posts into the ground proved harder than it looked. You had to account for the cold winters and the spring thaws each year and what that would do to the new fence row. If it the posts were not firmly tamped in the ground, it would work loose in the next couple of years. And this would lead to a sagging fence or even a downed fence line. That was also true with the kind of wood used for the fence posts. If a softwood like locust was used, then it was likely to rot away in ten years.

These were some of the problems that were worked out over time. They found solutions, and they even had agreements with the adjoining neighbors to split the costs for the new fence rows on the boundary lines. The neighbor on the north end even agreed to put a gate in for access between the farms.

It was always hard work, and Flint and his family didn't always have all the tools they needed to work with. On one occasion that meant using the family's Ford Falcon to pull out the saplings in the old fencerow along LaMar Road. This was a plan of action for 15 minutes, and then they had to stop when the car overheated.

Nearly all the fencerows were put up in the 1970s. The strange thing to Flint was how they would all come down by the turn of the century. It had nothing to do with fencing building but it was a matter of changing philosophy. A fencerow always had to be cleaned out, and it was a maintenance and cost factor. But if you no longer raised livestock and you didn't really need a fence to mark your property line, then it was no longer any use from any practical standpoint.

One by one the fencerows were gone each time Flint came home to visit in the future years to come. And the neighbors on LaMar Road did the same thing for the same reasons. It was a remarkable transformation to see the countryside change into endless wide-open spaces and as well kept as the greens on any golf course in Indiana.

There was once a mishap on the farm that happened to Clark and not his brothers or even his parents. It was an occupational hazard, sort of, but no one was ever obligated to write a report with OSHEA. There was a trip to see Dr. Hollenburg and the subsequent examination in his office. This resulted in stitches and a big white bandage on the back of Clark's head when he finally came home with his mother.

It was a long afternoon at the post office for his father. He was assuming more and more duties and responsibilities of the postmaster he would become in the next decade. But the news he was receiving from his wife was very reassuring to the point that it wasn't necessary to join her at the doctor's office. She told him it was not a serious head wound. That was not to say Clark wouldn't be the butt of those "hard-headed" jokes, she said, with a smile that Keith Flint was sure was growing on the face of his still-nervous wife.

Most neighbors knew a farmer who lost a finger in some kind of accident with a self-propelled combine, a corn picker, a grain augur, or some other kind of farm implement that sounded pretty dangerous to young sons like their own. Anthony certainly didn't forget seeing the first hand of a neighbor farmer who had only four fingers and no thumb. Farming was dangerous, and accidents could happen to anyone at anytime. But it sure seemed different with Clark.

Here's what happened: Clark proved that he was no "easy rider" when he climbed on the rusty seat on the old horse-drawn disk that for too long was left where it was—a small lot that was close to the house and was once used by the Taylor family as a garden on the 40-acre farm. And since Clark was too young to tell what happened to begin with, his parents had only their own speculations and imaginations as to what really transpired that day.

It was probably something like Clark pretending to "rein in the horse," and as he did so, the sudden movement broke his seat. Then he fell backward and hit his head on one of the disks that was almost completely sunk in the ground. Unfortunately, there was still enough aboveground to cut his head and produce a lot of panic.

Still to come would be the day when Eugene wrecked his dad's white Chevy truck near the new junior-senior high school. Eugene gripped the steering wheel tightly as it flipped over and walked away with only a bruise to his teenage ego. And when it was Anthony's turn, he cut one of his fingers on the sickle bar when he got in a hurry trying to cut the weeds along LaMar Road. That prompted a drive in his dad's old pickup to the ER at Henry County Memorial Hospital in New Castle, Indiana.

And still another time, when there was no mishap at all, Anthony led his younger brothers up inside the tall silo on the farm of their neighbors to the east, Homer and June Beeson. That was the summer when the Beesons watched the boys each day when Keith and Beverly Flint went to work in Hagerstown.

What was so surprising was the fear of heights that Anthony had and would have for the rest of his life. How did he find the courage to do this?

And how did he get Eugene and Clark to trust him? And what were they all thinking, anyway!? All good questions which no one who was involved remembers as being answered in the affirmative.

But one thing was for sure, and that was when Homer Beeson went to work, he would hear the boys in the silo. He had to walk to the garage to get his light blue truck. And when he had done this, and when he got out to close the garage door, it was luck on everyone's part that he could hear the voices of the Flint children.

Now who could forget a strong voice like the one Homer Beeson had when he said, from way down below them: "Anthony, come on down. Are your brothers with you? Come on down, now!"

Flint had relatives in Lynn, Indiana, who lived approximately 25 miles from the 40-acre farm. They had a shoe repair shop that was fun to play in on a Sunday afternoon. That was the best time when all the adults were in the house next door. Always in the large living room with the big framed illustrations hanging on the walls. One said "The Tree of Knowledge" and the other said "The Tree of Evil." It was a fine example of what one could really say was "food for thought."

From past experience, Flint or his brothers knew how much time they needed to "paint" as many of the wheels and grinders in the shoe shop with black stuff found in the small pots that were mounted on the sides. They easily did this with what looked like large tooth brushes in their small hands.

There was always time because the adults had too many issues of the day to openly discuss and disagree on. One of the hot topics was the new President who was also Catholic. Another good one was the spiritual implications of space travel itself. "Does God want man on the moon?" was never fully analyzed by anyone present and who really was honest about it.

Flint also had relatives near Carthage, Indiana, who lived approximately 40 miles from the 40-acre farm. Here it was the pure symbolism of a time when the future President of the United States was promising a "chicken in every pot." Flint and his brothers could still draw water from a well by cranking the lever of something that looked like a larger silver pitcher mounted on a table. They could also walk through rooms with 14-foot ceilings and examine more antique furnishings than all the museums combined in Indianapolis. They also saw the white clapboard sidings of the 2-story farmhouse when playing outside in the yard.

Over in the large barn was the best possible memories of rural life. Up in the voluminous hayloft were hundreds of bails of hay, and this was ideal for each boy to build his own fort and attack the other two without any fears of ending up in a body bag. And hanging high from the mounted track was a large claw that transported hay to the door at the end and then dropped it into waiting wagons for the cattle in the winter. But, in the ever-growing imaginations of the Flint brothers, this thing was always a jaw of some prehistoric dinosaur. It never moved while they played, but it sure looked hungry and threatening enough to eat everything in sight.

Chapter 4: James Warren Jones

Esther Coates, a fifth grade teacher in 1942, described him to Anthony Flint while Anthony was still a reporter working for the Indiana Bureau of *The Cincinnati Enquirer* in Lawrencebrug, Indiana. She said he was a very bight student, very mischievous, but also a loner who liked to play preacher at an early age and sometimes conducted funeral services for dead pets. "I remember Jimmy came out in the yard one day and came over and told me that President Roosevelt had died," she added. That was on April 12, 1945.

The prospects from a childhood spent in a small Indiana town never indicated the hell to come. Jones was the only child of James and Lynette Jones. They raised him up in Lynn, a community of 2,000 people in southern Randolph County. His father was a disabled veteran of World War I. He died while his son was still in high school. His mother was from Mt. Carmel, Indiana, south of Indianapolis.

The family was poor, living on the father's disability payments and what the mother earned working in a factory in Richmond, Indiana. They were really not that much different from anybody else on the block. One neighbor was plainspoken about it when she told Flint: "This is a small town. The Jones family settled here a long time ago, and we kids always played together, and he wasn't any different from any of the other boys and girls." A former classmate added: "He always dressed nice, but there really isn't anything outstanding you can say about him."

James Warren Jones, a.k.a., Jim Jones, transferred to Richmond High School for the last three months of his senior year. The school superintendent told Flint: "We were on an A and B semester schedule then, so he could have been graduating early or might have come to Richmond to make up a semester. The records aren't very clear on it, and nobody on our staff is left around who remembers him. All we know is that he was here from September 1948, until January 1949, when he graduated."

Jones married the former Marcelene Baldwin, of Richmond, when he was 18, a short time before he was ordained as a minister in the Christian

Church/Disciples of Christ. He founded the People's Temple in Indianapolis during the early 1950s. This was initially an inter-racial mission for the sick, homeless and jobless; and Jones preached a mixture of racial integration, socialism and faith healing. The church also predicted a racial war in the United States, but the faithful members were promised they would not die in the conflict.

The Founder of the People's Temple moved his congregation during the 1960s to California. Nearly everyone who worshiped with Jones had found the social climate in Indiana too racist. Also, a government investigation was challenging Jones' cures for cancer, heart disease and arthritis. Things were much better in San Francisco, a city with ultra-liberal beliefs on nearly every street corner. Jones once boasted there were 20,000 members during the early 1970s. He received public acceptance and went on to become politically active as well. That was when the People's Temple supported the election campaigns of California Governor Jerry Brown and San Francisco Mayor George Mascone. Then in 1975, Jones was named chairman of the San Francisco Housing Commission.

The year 1975 was also when Jim Jones visited Lynn for the last time. A neighbor who saw him then said to Anthony Flint in 1978: "Jimmy came through bringing his group of congregation members from San Francisco to Washington, D.C. He stopped in town just to see Myrtle Kennedy, the grocery store clerk who befriended him when he was a little boy." He also told Flint how loyal Jim Jones was with friends and how he remembered them.

Lawrenceburg, Indiana, was not far from the banks of the Ohio River. The flooding in the spring was sometimes too close for comfort whenever the rising waters reached the front steps of the office door. This was literally bringing the news to the Enquirer's Indiana Bureau. It was an exclusive that was never envied by *The Cincinnati Post*. The competition between the two newspapers had limits when there was something like this. The editors for the Enquirer and the Post did allow for most reporters to cover news in Cincinnati, but readers were always moving to the country in Kentucky and Indiana.

Flint did his part with feature stories, photographic essays and hard news reports from southern Indiana that included Wayne, Franklin, Rush, Union, Decatur and Fayette Counties. This was the area where his by-lines would usually accompany the stories he filed with the Indiana Bureau. It was where the teacher strike ended in Connersville and where landowners disbanded the $1.5 million Whitewater Valley Conservancy District; and where, in 1980, Chrysler Corporation dropped plans to build a $160 million transaxle plant in Richmond.

Driving home on weekends was a good opportunity to relax and get away from the office. Flint would travel and see beautiful settings that included the rolling hills south of Brookville, where the trees were most prominent when the leaves changed color in the fall. Then from Connersville to Cambridge City to Hagerstown, the land was flat. Hear the plantings and harvests in the fields played out in full view and seemed to beckon motorists to pull off the highway and watch from the side of the road.

Flint did allow for extra time one Friday afternoon to photograph the courthouse spires in Rushville, Liberty, Brookville and Greensburg. He always passed through these towns and looked for the large clock at the top of the building. Sometimes the clock face appeared to hover over the horizon like a small moon, still visible from distant roads leading into the city at night.

Flint was listening to the car radio on one return trip from Hagerstown to Lawrenceburg. His dial was tuned to a radio station in Cincinnati. The announcer said there was a train derailment early Monday morning along a section of track north of Dillsboro, Indiana. Authorities had ordered the forced evacuation of 12 families living in a 2-mile radius; six tanker cars contained flammable chemicals. It was a cold day in the month of January, but the ground was frozen hard enough that heavy equipment could come in with no problems.

The actual site of the derailment was a remote area that was covered with barren trees. When he arrived, Flint could see volunteer firemen, a state trooper and several employees of the Chessie Systems walking along the tracks. All together they counted 23 cars from the Baltimore & Ohio freight train that either turned over or simply plowed into the ground upright. The force of the derailment itself wrecked nearly a mile of track.

Anthony snapped several photographs and took care to stay out of the way. The work started slowly, as crews began to determine the extent of the leaking tanker cars and make sure no one was injured. Later in the day, the railroad equipment would arrive at the scene and be put to use to clear the tracks as soon as possible. By late Monday afternoon, there was little threat remaining to the area, and all but three families were allowed to return home.

Mrs. Frank Shaffer was a first cousin of Jones still living in Lynn in 1978. She was upset that news reports described Jim Jones as biracial. It was true that his mother was dark-complexioned. It was also true that Jim Jones was taunted by classmates in elementary school about his mom being an Oriental or Negro. "I really am angry about this," she told Anthony Flint. "The kids started that rumor 30 years ago, and there is absolutely no truth to that whatsoever."

Disgruntled members of the People's Temple told the news media about fake healings, extortions and beatings with death threats. In the mid 1970s, the magazine *New West* raised more suspicions of illegal activities. Then Jim Jones moved hundreds of members in 1977 from San Francisco to Guyana, South America. Here was plenty of freedom on 4,000 acres of dense jungle leased from the government. They would become "The People's Temple Agricultural Project," and they would raise animals for food and assorted tropical fruits and vegetables for consumption and sale.

For the rest of the world, it was known as Jonestown, Guyana, the last home on earth for nearly all of its inhabitants. They were far from the family and friends that were freely left behind, but they always had each other. Jones saw to that, with directions and certain admonitions that lasted nearly a year. Jonestown was really a society that needed no elected government or any real contact with the rest of humanity.

One of the lingering theories for the end of the agricultural commune in Jonestown was for the protection of CIA secrets. Some people believed that the People's Temple was an experimental laboratory operated for or by the CIA, and for the purposes to perfect mind-control techniques. These experiments were so vital to national security that anyone standing in the way would be assassinated in order to maintain secrecy.

Information obtained under the Freedom of Information Act has never implicated the CIA. Neither has the House Permanent Select Committee on Intelligence which announced in 1980 that there was "no evidence" of CIA involvement at Jonestown. The Committee on Foreign Affairs of the U.S. House of Representatives (now the Committee on International Relations) conducted a separate investigation on the deaths in Jonestown. This was never released to the public and was classified "for the intervening decades." Ironically, some 6,000 pages of information was obtained from the U.S. Department of State by an unknown hacker who posted it on the Internet.

Other assessments made by sociologists, researchers and think-tanks were based on the following:

- Mental illness of Jim Jones, aggravated by drug abuse.
- Intense fear of the imminent end of civilization.
- Extreme isolation of Jonestown.
- Anti-cult groups, news reporters and federal investigative agencies "hounding" Jonestown.

In November of 1978 the rumors of human rights abuses and the considerable number of defections from the People's Temple had attracted the attention of Leo Ryan. His congressional district included San Francisco and the former headquarters used by Jim Jones,which was obliterated by the Loma Prieta earthquake in 1989.

Ryan's strong motivation prompted him to visit Jonestown to conduct a personal investigation. After an uneventful first day, Ryan was approached by 16 members of the People's Temple who said they wanted to go home with him. The Congressman took them to the Port Kiatuma airfield and waited to board the flight back to the United States. They were followed, tragically, by heavily armed security guards sent by Jim Jones. In broad daylight there was the ambush and murder of Ryan, three members of the press, a Temple member and the wounding of 11 others.

It got worse in a hurry. Jones, his family and a large core of followers decided there would be retribution for this and quickly called it quits. It was the children who drank the flavored cyanide first, huddled in the embrace of their parents. Sipping the grape drink also meant consuming a number of sedatives like liquid Valium, Penegram and chloral-hydrate with what some sources say was Kool-Aid and others say was FlaVor-Aid. Many could not be persuaded and were injected with poison needles or shot down in cold blood. The luckiest few of all ran into the jungle and survived this hell on earth.

The Guyanese coroner found dead bodies in a state of extensive decay in the days to come. When the authorities arrived, they documented 638 adults and 276 children killed in the lost commune of Jonestown.

The death of James Warren Jones was a very violent end to a doomsday cult, having as its founder and leader, a man for all the wrong reasons. It was intended for human freedom, equality, and love; and this also included helping the least and lowliest of earth's human population. The end saw it become explicitly socialistic, and even communistic, in the only view that was ever forthcoming in Jonestown—none other than Jim Jones himself.

He held degrees from Indiana University and Butler University. But he did not want to become a Fundamentalist preacher. No way. Jones was too destructive and disastrous for membership in a mainline Christian denomination; he was preparing the People's Temple for new beliefs without the endorsement of organized religion.

Beliefs like Translation had become one of his favorites. All members of the People's Temple would die together in glory. At the end of the practice for mass suicide, they all pretended to drink poison and fall to the ground; and then they would be ready one day to begin a new life on another planet.

In one unique defection, a group called Concerned Relatives went public with numerous claims against Jonestown, describing a concentration camp and people being held in Guyana against their will. It was founded by Tim Stoen, the right-hand man of Jim Jones and the Temple attorney. His group was able to leave South America in time to save their own voices for protests of Jim Jones and the People's Temple.

This whole story would come out like shockwaves sent through the civilized world. There was generated enormous public support for the anti-cult and counter-cult movements. The sheer volume of media stories was nothing more than a juggernaut of impossible horror.

Even in Lawrenceburg, Indiana, Flint would find the connections of friends and family and the steady chorus of disbelief that seemed to come from Lynn, Indiana. Flint could surely appreciate this, for he could always remember his own family reunions and gatherings in that small town. Never a better example than the home of his aunt and uncle—a 2-story house that was white in color and with a detached garage that was converted into a shoe repair shop.

Whether Flint accepted his fond memories as typical was only part of the equation. None of the news events from Jonestown deserved to be something that tarnished any of the hometowns back in the United States. It was not fair if anybody blamed Lynn in the first place. The Jones family had lived among them and then they were gone.

The mass murders in South America were made into a television mini-series in 1980. Actor Powers Booth won an Emmy for his portrayal as Jim Jones. James Earl Jones, Ned Beatty and Randy Quaid also starred. And so Flint watched the broadcast and was curious to see if any local sights would appear on television—none, really, as he found out in the end. There was a brief moment in the beginning when the name "Lynn, Indiana," appeared at the bottom of the screen.

Chapter 5: Dickens at Dalton

Flint was a student at the redbrick schoolhouse in 1963, and where, in one moment, his principal came into the classroom with a grim look on his face. In the last few hours or so, in Dallas, Texas, and with the First Lady in the backseat of the open limousine, everything in the United States had changed forever. Now there would be no recess; furthermore, all the buses would be arriving early in the afternoon. In the meantime, the principal told all the students to have their books and coats ready to take on the bus. Even the outlook for the rest of the week was not good; the playgrounds and classrooms closed until further notice. And so on. Because everything had changed forever.

What happened next in Wayne County, Indiana, was this: more schools closed abruptly and City Halls passed resolutions of sorrow. The death of the President was met with open disbelief. The county was predominately Democratic, and so was the state. A well-oiled political machine as any found in Cook County, Illinois. It was operational for his brother's presidential campaign in 1968, and even in 1980, for the youngest brother who could not beat Jimmy Carter.

Indeed, the assassination of the 35th President of the United States, on that day in November, was not in the stars. Because of 1964. And the need to mend political fences in Texas as soon as possible. For one thing, the President had wanted a second term. In 1956, he did not become a vice-presidential candidate for Adla E. Stevenson. But there was hard work and national exposure, which he never forgot. In 1960, campaigning against Nixon, Kennedy had LBJ to win the vote in the South. He wanted the White House almost as much as his father.

So it was intended to be Kennedy and Johnson, president and vice-president, in 1964. They would end the escalation in Vietnam, see fit to put a man on the moon, and occasionally acknowledge Richard Nixon and his friends to keep tabs on that troublesome but ambitious politician.

Flint did have a memorable field trip in the spring of 1964. His class visited a 5-acre farm only 12 miles from the redbrick schoolhouse. This turned out to be the birthplace of Wilber Wright, the co-inventor of the world's first powered-flight aircraft. Yet it was also the site of an on-going restoration project—first started in 1956—with the labor of inmates from the reformatory prison in Pendleton, Indiana.

An archaeological dig was used to locate the original stone foundation of the house erected in 1845. Then they used lumber from an old building razed in the canal town of Metamora, Indiana, to rebuild the Wright farmhouse. And the antique pottery pieces found at the site during the restoration were included in the study by the Indiana Department of Natural Resources. Later, a crane was used to mount an F-84F jet aircraft from Bear Field in Ft. Wayne for public display near the new picnic shelter and restrooms.

Flint returned to the Wright farm in 1974, as a freshman journalism student at Ball State University and later as a married man in 1996. Each time he could see the hard work of committee members first-hand. They had access to money appropriated by the Indiana General Assembly and private contributions and the Lilly Endowment Fund and Henry County to set in motion a long-range plan for the Wilber Wright Birthplace and Interactive Center.

Since 1953, when the site became a State memorial, programs promoted the birthplace and attracted such dignitaries as Apollo 17 astronaut Engene Cernan, Ivonnette Wright Miller and Wilkerson Wright, niece and nephew to Wilber and Orville Wright, and Indiana governors Roger Branigan, Otis Bowen and Edgar Whitcomb. It was Whitcomb who corresponded with committee members on Aug. 16, 1973: "You may be sure that I will be watching with pride the progress being made in the restoration of this Hoosier landmark."

Not everyone in Anthony's class recalls that it was Orville, the youngest of the Wright brothers, who won the coin-toss and kept the Wright Flyer airborne for 12 seconds on Dec. 17, 1903. It was the first of four flights that day at Kitty Hawk, North Carolina.

Everything was always scattered across the 2-acre playground at the redbrick schoolhouse in time for the annual New Year's Day Sale. This brought families into Dalton with used refrigerators, clothing, hand tools, and plenty of home-cooked food. It was also when a very small community came together and all the children had a place to play at the same time. The schoolhouse seemed a logical choice for 15 years, beginning in 1951.

Driving through Dalton would take no time at all. There was a convenience store less than 20 houses and the home and barn of Cameron Dennis that was located across the street from the school. Flint did remember the barn in Dalton as the place to vote on election days. He clearly remembered the line of people in 1972 waiting to re-elect Richard M. Nixon and Spiro T. Agnew as President and Vice-President. The landslide from these neighbors, as voter precincts from across the nation would show, was one Presidential campaign with media savvy, totally out-flanking the Democratic candidate, George McGovern. It brought the use of television to new Presidential efficiency, finally, to suit the White House and rival even the National Rife Association.

Anthony Flint's boyhood memories of the Dalton schoolhouse were as clear as if he was still standing outside the front doors. He could still see the surrounding farms and pastures in the distance and the first of three yellow buses coming at the end of the school day.

Harold Pine was one of the drivers. His wife and son were also behind the wheel of a school bus based in Dalton. There was also a daughter that graduated with Flint, played in band with him and rose to the rank of drum major. She could also toot her fugal horn on the Pine farm, and Flint could blast his trombone in return. Because the two farms were not that far away and because it was a musical Morse code that no one else was using at the time.

At Christmas Harold Pine pulled his bus over to the side of the road usually toward the end of his route. It was time to open presents from all the kids. Here were some of them: the Bell, Heacox, Smith, Manifold, Beeson, Bowman, Messer, Burgess, Stockberger, Hendershot, Dishman, Lindley and Flint families.

With the absence of students packing weapons to kill, or waging war on their schools, this was truly a bygone era, made possible by Harold Pine, a farmer with a daughter on the bus. He never needed a video camera mounted in his bus to catch students committing horrible crimes. Everybody sat in their seats and liked each other.

Flint was also a witness to a production of *A Christmas Carol* put on by the 6th grade class. Under the direction of the principal, Marfield Cain, another farmer, the stage inside the redbrick schoolhouse was transformed into the Victorian times of London, England. For the year 1843.

On stage was the counting-house of Scrooge and Marley. The clerk was working in the outer office copying letters—trying to warm himself from the fire of one single burning coal. The heat in the main office was a little better but not much. Here the coal-box was kept under lock and key by Scrooge himself for good measure. It didn't matter that the whole warehouse was dark, bleak and cold.

Joel Davis had the role of Ebenezer Scrooge, the sole business partner who managed to do work even on the day of Marley's funeral, 7 years ago this Christmas. There were such stories about Scrooge that no man or woman would ever ask him how he was or the time of day. No beggars ever asked him to bestow a trifle; also, a blind man's dog would, somehow, lead his master away from Scrooge if ever there was a chance encounter on the streets of London.

With that opening scene, enter, stage left, Mike Smith, with a cheerful voice as Scrooge's nephew: "A merry Christmas, uncle! God save you!"

"Bah!" said Davis as Scrooge. "Humbug!"

"Christmas a humbug, uncle! You don't mean that, I am sure?"

I do. Merry Christmas! What right have you to be merry? What reason have you to be morose? You're poor enough."

"Come, then" Smith replied as the nephew. "What right have you to be dismal? What reason have you to be morose? You're rich enough."

The lead role that holiday season was only the beginning of things to come for the future Drama Club president from Dalton. First, as Ebenezer Scrooge, and later, as Emile de Becque in *South Pacific*—the high school production for the spring of 1970.

As for Flint, who later played in the pit orchestra for *South Pacific*, the best part from the Dickens masterpiece (for him, at least) was Marley's ghost, played by Steve Messer, visiting Scrooge in his equally cold and dark bedchambers:

> **MESSER AS MARLEY'S GHOST:** I am here tonight to warn you, that you have yet a chance and hope of escaping my fate.
> **DAVIS AS SCROOGE:** You were always a good friend to me! Thankee!
> **MESSER AS MARLEY'S GHOST:** You will be haunted by Three Spirits.
> **DAVIS AS SCROOGE:** Is that the chance and hope you mentioned? I think I'd rather not."
> **MESSER AS MARLEY'S GHOST:** Without their visits, you

cannot hope to shun the path I tread. Expect the first tomorrow, when the bell tolls One.

DAVIS AS SCROOGE: Couldn't I take 'em all at once, and have it over, Jacob?"

MESSER AS MARLEY'S GHOST: Expect the second on the next night at the same hour. The third, upon the next night when the last stroke of Twelve has ceased to vibrate. Look to see me no more; and look that, for your own sake, you remember what has passed between us!

Anthony Flint got a black eye one day when he was running in the basement of the redbrick schoolhouse. He was heading in a nearly straight line toward a destination that was lost in the mind of a 9-year-old. Then there was a monstrous steel door that was partially open. Actually, it was one of the latches on the outside that made sudden contact with him. He quickly fell down in pain, stars spinning around in his head.

On the floor he looked up—it was gray in color and as large as any door to a bank vault in the State of Indiana. Inside was the room for the boilers, hissing with steam and generating heat for the school that was built in 1924. As he turned to look out the basement windows he could see it snowing, and he was thinking how comforting it would feel on his throbbing eye.

With new schools today, no general contractor in his right mind would expect to find basements or boilers in the blueprints. It was ancient history. That, and the fact that the Dalton school—like all homes and barns in the area—was built for the ages. The building was over 40 years old when Flint was in the basement with one eye shut.

All of the children in Dalton Township considered the redbrick schoolhouse a home away from home. You could hang your things on the coat rack in the center of the main hallway, which was accessible for everyone. And you could stand in line for a drink of water from the water-coolers at the north and south walls. This was such an everyday habit that the floor around the coolers was warped by years of water droplets from the mouths of youngsters.

Next to the school was the old horse and livery stables. Always a building in a rundown condition for many years. The children would play around it the entire school year; but it was the wintertime when you could make a racetrack circling the building, packed firm in the deep snow by all those little feet.

But it was the Rathbun family who managed to convert the schoolhouse into the largest home in Dalton. That was in 1974, when most of the remolding was done and which saw the removal of several blackboards, 70 strips of fluorescent lighting fixtures and the old heating registers. Then, with the old horse and livery stables razed, a large wood beam was preserved as the mantel to a reconverted fireplace. This was also made possible by using an old classroom ventilation duck that leads to the roof.

Even the classroom for the 6th grade had changed. The original 13-foot ceilings were lowered by five feet to accommodate the petitioning walls. This made plans possible for two 1-bedroom apartments in order to use the 4,000 square feet of floor space still unoccupied by the Rathbuns. The stage itself was gone. A site of more productions than any off-Broadway theater and, most certainly, those famous Christmas plays and even the eighth grade commencements.

The past, then, was transformed in the formation of the Dalton schoolhouse as a family home. Often by the hands of neighbors who were once students at the school. It was good that the Rathbuns could count on them for help. Fred Pope was also there in a pinch. It was Fred Pope who was the school's custodian the day it closed, and later, bringing lumber and supplies to the remolding.

So it was to be that Flint went to school in Dalton, then a year at the old schoolhouse in Millville, Indiana—not far from the birthplace of Wilbur Wright, it turns out. The middle school years were spent at Greens Fork, where sometimes the surrounding countryside reminded Flint of the farms and pastures around the Dalton schoolhouse.

It was the way it was before the school consolidations and the completion of the new Hagerstown Junior-Senior High School in 1972. Flint was a trombonist in the band that played for the dedication ceremony that year. A school for the next half-century, and one that had an in-door swimming pool and an orchestra pit for the new stage. But also a school that had no annual New Year's Day Sale.

Ledona Henderson was the third and fourth grade teacher at the Dalton schoolhouse. She made a trusting admiration that found no prodigy in Flint. But also no good reason to forget his high school graduation in May of 1973. She presented him a card with a shinny silver "A" taped inside; she hoped this would make up for the one he never got from her!

Henderson had a memorable event that probably kept the name of Anthony

Flint in her mind long after her retirement. Anthony was the "lookout" one day for two friends, Jeff Vanderbilt and Marvin Heacox, who appeared to be very adept at what they were doing. The objective was some form of revenge, and none of them would get caught in the act. Being in the fourth-grade also was a great hindrance—no money. Thus it had to be something they could get their hands on with no cost and minimal trial and error.

It was decided early on to examine the light blue car out in the school parking lot. This required a through examination, much like the deliberations of young ghosts and goblins who are indecisive as to what Halloween trick was most appropriate for the occasion. Certainly, a car was a good target for anytime of the year. And when one considered all the facts, which they did, it was proof to them how something so handy and available was really the best target of all. And it was the teacher's car.

So what could they do? Cut the brake lines? Pull one of the spark plug wires? Again, no easy consensus, and especially when no one in the group knew how to do either one in the first place. Still, a statement had to be made. They also agreed to break no glass or scratch paint or damage the car in any harmful way. A realty check indicated they were never that mad at their teacher (or for what reason as they tried to remember many years later).

The simple solution was to get down on your hands and knees and let the air out of the tires—as much as possible. This was really good. Nobody used a knife. And, of course, Mrs Henderson could easily have her tires inflated in time for supper.

This was immediately a dark secret with the young suspects as they returned to class and took their seats behind the old wooden desks—the ones with a small circular opening on top to hold a bottle of white school paste. But Flint was too young to remember how much apprehension was building on the faces of his unindicted co-conspirators. When Mrs Henderson walked to the window to look outside, this, then, became the moment for psychological climax. It made no difference if she was looking at her car—or the birds in the tree. The inevitable confessions suddenly had detailed remorse. And no way to take them back.

Flint always remembered the six weeks with no recess. He realized the sound of classmates playing outside each school day was punishment fit for the crime. At least it was a time when he wasn't dizzy or out-of-breath from swinging on the maypole.

This was how the school day usually ended for Anthony Flint and his classmates at Dalton: a story read to the class by Mrs Henderson. The imaginations of the students seemed to orbit the earth with the Gemini astronauts; and she could see the looks on their faces every day. They would be bundled up for the winter or wearing jeans and short-sleeve shirts in the spring. They would be waiting to get on their school bus to go home. This was her best time to read to the class. The kind of stories full of human interest, guaranteed, for the most part, to last a lifetime.

Chapter 6: The General at Stones River, Tennessee

Hazy mists from the river were rising slowly in the early evening air north of Murfreesboro, Tennessee. Nearly all the trees along the banks and in the woods were barren of leaves. The bark and the branches still glistened from the late-afternoon rain, which was less than an inch. Nearby the rows of identical white markers make up a solemn recluse that is a military cemetery. The battlefield itself comprised most of the 400 acres.

Across the opening in the field, Anthony Flint could see the picnic pavilion and the restrooms. The pocket camera he left behind on the table had escaped the detection of the other tourists during the day. He was right to come back and see if it was still there. The pictures on this roll of film included a memorable afternoon at the Hermitage, south of Nashville; it was the home of Andrew Jackson, seventh President of the United States and the hero of the Battle of New Orleans.

Walking back to his car, he heard the first sounds of horse's hoofs, advancing evenly over the cover of damp leaves and through the wet thicket of saplings. Flint stopped and turned back to look at the pavilion. It was empty. So was the parking lot, and surely the sounds were not coming from the small restrooms.

Then he saw a pair of translucent figures approaching the restrooms and the picnic pavilion. He also realized there was no film left in the camera.

A man and a horse had come out of the forests.

This was the spring of 1980, and the year of the Reagan Revolution. It was also the time that Anthony Flint went to Tennessee with his father. To visit Eugene, then a basketball coach at the Christian School in McMinnville. There was still time that first day for the Wednesday evening service at the Church of Christ, but it would be a full day at Stones River National Battlefield on Thursday.

At the visitor's center and at the museum, the story of Stones River: two armies of the American Civil War fighting to a draw in late December of 1862, and in early January of 1863. Braxton Bragg's Army of the Tennessee and William Starke Rosecrans' Army of the Cumberland, each approximately equal in strength.

Within five days, Bragg withdrew his soldiers and left the area. Union forces then entered Murfreesboro on the fifth day of January, yet Bragg would defeat Rosecrans later that summer in the Battle of Chickamauga.

Bragg was a graduate of West Point and had severed in Florida's Second Seminole War. He was also a military advisor to Confederate President Jefferson Davis in Richmond. At the end of the rebellion, he became the chief engineer for the State of Alabama.

In many ways, he served the Confederate States of America with honor and dignity. Just like his commanding officer, Robert E. Lee.

The man, appearing to be in his late fifties, was nearly six feet tall, with gray hair and a trim silver beard. He had a broad forehead, prominent nose, thick neck, big shoulders and a deep chest. He was wearing a double-breasted grey dress coat with gilt buttons. Around his waist was a deep red silk sash, and over that was a sword belt of gold braid. At his side hung a dress sword in a leather and gilt scabbard.

A grey horse carried the man. The bridle held by one gloved hand, the other hung down at the side of the erect rider in the saddle.

Flint was not sure if he was in any real harm. What he saw and what he believed was a conflict but not a threat to his life. It was not possible that these images would ever appear again in the State of Tennessee, the Volunteer State.

Even in the light of dusk, the man and his horse could be seen moving through the walls of the restrooms and then to the site of the picnic tables under the shelter of the pavilion. Flint could see through them, and he could clearly see the white illumination of the images themselves. Again, it was not possible.

Whether he accepted ghosts or spirits was purely academic now. Stones River was a memorial to the Battle of Murfreesboro and nothing more in the way of the supernatural. It was not known to be haunted. The soldiers' souls were presumed to be at peace, having accepted the South's surrender and the end of slavery.

Stones River, in fact, was well-suited as a final resting place for its Civil

War dead. Each and every tombstone had escaped serious vandalism, graffiti or forms of desecration not known a century ago. There was enough preservation here for young oaks to become large trees and for graves to be shaded for endless afternoons to come.

Anthony Flint decided to walk away from the car and watch the images as they emerged from the shelter. At this point the pair of white illuminations came to a stop in the parking area. This was only a few yards from where Flint was standing.

Perhaps as a gesture of goodwill, the man removed his dress sword and proceeded to drop it to the ground. Flint saw the weapon gleam in the growing darkness; but he also saw the man pull back his coat to show the absence of any pistols or knifes in his possession.

Somehow, this show of disarmament was not needed. There was a purpose that was not dangerous. For his part, Flint seemed to trust the man on the horse. After all, he had no weapons of his own, and he had walked far enough from the car that he was no longer in a position to safety return to it.

Not that he wanted to walk—or run away. Flint had found a sudden appreciation for Elvis sightings and UFOs in Roswell, New Mexico. If this was not an aberration or a vision, what would be the implications on this night? This was something that had to be more than merely finding one's self in the right place at the right time. A juxtaposition of never-seen and never-told, this would be two of the most infrequent components for any writer or any story.

Could it be that one of the most important figures in American history was still alive? Honored and revered by both the North and the South?

By now the darkness at Stones River was only interrupted by the white illuminations of the man and his horse. The silence of the evening was ended by the voice of the man; by way of introduction, he commented on the weather and the need for more rain.

This was a hot and mostly dry summer. It was a lingering drought condition that was not favorable for the ranks of advancing armies, the man observed. Nor was it too kind for horses, livestock or the crops in the field. This, too, was instrumental for a military victory or even a successful retreat from the region. Also observed by the man who said he was Robert E. Lee.

Flint would make a second trip to Tennessee, this time with his mother, to visit the 1982 World's Fair in Knoxville. Admission was $9.95 apiece, including tax. But nothing happened there.

At Stones River, on horseback, at a moment in time when Flint could not recollect any other sight or sound, the General said this would be the only meeting possible. It was not necessary to know anything else. The General offered no explanations, and none was plausible that night.

Still, it was clear the General had purposefully sought out Flint because he was a writer. He was always looking for ways to tell people about the campaigns he had engaged. "I want that the world shall know what my poor boys, with their small numbers and scant resources, succeeded in accomplishing."

This was not a vindication of himself, or to promote his reputation. In fact, the writing of memoirs was rather a painful subject to Lee. His father, Henry "Light-Horse Harry" Lee, authored a two-volume work on the Southern campaigns of the American Revolution. But he did it while in the confines of prison—a debtor, who was 50-years-old when Robert E. Lee was born.

But the son was always keenly interested in the subject of combat and the future prospect of war. He brought up the name of Gen. James Alward Van Fleet, a 4-star general who died at the age of 100 in 1992. Van Fleet was honored in his hometown of Polk City, Florida, only weeks before his death. Flint was there that day to write a column. He counted many politicians and a few military leaders. Even head football coach Steve Spurrier, of the University of Florida.

Like Lee, Van Fleet received many high military honors from several countries around the world. He had distinguished himself in World War II. He then served as head of a U.S. military mission that aided the Greek Army in their successful campaigns against Communist guerrillas. He was also a consultant to the Secretary of the Army on guerilla warfare during the Kennedy Administration.

Lee said he admired General Van Fleet because of his ability to fight war as guerrillas and thus make the conflict end sooner. Something he did not see as an option for his own troops. In the hours before meeting Grant, Lee told Flint: "My men would be without rations and under no control of officers. They would be compelled to rob and steal in order to live. They would become mere bands of marauders, and the enemy's cavalry would pursue them and overrun many sections they may never have occasion to visit. We would bring on a state of affairs it would take the country years to recover from."

Lee never mentioned Stones River that night, or whether he even visited the site during his lifetime. He did say he changed the command of the Army of Tennessee from Maj. Gen. Pierre Gustave Toutant Beauregard to Gen Braxton Bragg. It was his opinion that Beauregard had sometimes been egotistical in planning military operations too ambitious for supplies and transportation to be practical.

Nevertheless, Beauregard was one of Lee's generals who stayed in America after the war. Others departed the South for new military roles in Egypt, Rumania and in Korea. Then there were the Confederate generals who saw a new life in Mexico, Cuba, Canada, England and even in Brazil. It was in South America that offers of free land in exchange for experience in handling slaves was very tempting.

And it was Beauregard who asked Lee after the Civil War if it was honorable to regain U.S. citizenship in the South. Lee told Flint he used Washington as an example in his reply to his former general.

"At one time he fought in the service of the King of Great Britain; at another he fought with the French at Yorktown, under the orders of the Continental Congress of America, against him. He has not been branded by the World with reproach for this, but his course has been applauded."

He was, in the end, the general in command of all Confederate forces. Including four family members. A son, Major General W.H. Fitzhugh Lee, a cavalry commander. His nephew, Major General Fitzhugh Lee. His oldest son, Major General Custis Lee, and his youngest, Captain Robert E. Lee, Jr. And all the more reasons to cease the War Between the States.

Years later, having moved to Orlando, Flint remembered what Lee said about the General's visit to Florida. Traveling down the St. John's River aboard the Nick King steamer where, at some point, the General's party stopped near Palatka and he picked an orange from a tree.

Lee said the farms of north Florida provided much of the food for confederate armies. And Florida sent more soldiers than registered voters to fight in the war. He was speaking not as a tourist. After all, he had visited only parts of Virginia, Washington and Baltimore since the surrender at Appomattox.

Flint had visited Gettysburg National Military Park in 1976 and again in 1993. That was the formal extent of his Civil War training. But Lee was there before the grounds were consecrated in a world-famous speech by Abraham Lincoln. And before the scenic tours and the monuments and the gift shops for every generation to come.

With 75,000 soldiers of the Army of Northern Virginia in 1863, Lee lost 3,500 men in three days. Another 18,000 wounded, and another 5,150 POWs. All because this great army was looking for shoes to put on the feet of its men. The stores were open for business in Gettysburg that summer in July, but nobody remembers it.

"This has been my fight, and upon my shoulders rests the blame," Lee said to Anthony Flint that night.

Lee had no objections to anything he said ever appearing in print. It was interesting to note that Lee was the first in the world to propose "press scholarships" for "young men intending to make practical printing and journalism their business in life."

As President of Washington University, later Washington and Lee University after his death in 1870, Lee received several men of the South who attended classes for a degree in journalism, and who worked 1 hour each day at the printing plant of Lafferty and Company in Lexington, Virginia.

Lee's intentions were to "give them as through a training as possible in the ways of their profession and to give them as good an education as possible that they may make better and more cultivated editors."

Nearly 10 years after his interview with Lee along the banks of the Stones River, Flint ran this column for *The Orlando Sentinel*:

When soldiers dug trenches and fought hand-to-hand combat, they meant to kill the enemy. They didn't know war would become so impersonal and high-tech.

Today, when nations go to war in some distant corner of the world, soldiers know cruise missiles and computers will do the dirty work.

Yet, as the mass exodus of Iraqis continue to flee the burning streets of Baghdad, we know there is still something too personal about the face of war.

Why? Because nations are great powers which isolate the people from the tragedies of war.

Like our nations, we citizens make an art form out of ignoring our neighbors for the good of the family, no matter what.

We extol universal rights for freedom of religion and the right to bear arms and pretend the domestic hell next door has no consequence in our own lives.

The more we are impersonalized, the more conflict is a part of our society. Nowadays, that's a one-way ticket to war. Not good.

Some time ago, this writer traveled to Stones River National Battlefield, a place not far from reality, really.

This area is little-known outside the great State of Tennessee. With a little luck, it proved to be a favorite countryside of Robert Edward Lee. You know, Robert E. Lee, the great Civil War General. In the flesh, or something like that. You can add your complete disbelief now, and I would understand.

Whatever your persuasions, it would be prudent to hear me out. It would be a shame to waste such an opportunity by allowing any prejudice to degrade the matter. Whether he was real, or a statue in the park, that kind of integrity and insight can be good for every generation.

Who among us cannot imagine, to some degree, the faces of 83,000 Civil War soldiers fighting at Stones River? Or that 23,000 died?

"I fear we are destined to kill and slaughter each other for ages to come," said Robert E. Lee, on that night at Stones River. "May God help the suffering and avert misery from the poor."

If Lee is joined by a nation of people who personalize the face of war, our elected leaders will find it exceedingly difficult not to look it straight in the eye.

Chapter 7: LaMar Road

The 40-acre farm included the house, barn, hen house, one or two small hog sheds and the old log cabin. The lane to the house was never paved. In the winter, this was one of the first places that drifted shut by the winds of a Hoosier blizzard. Off the side of the lane near the barn was the future site of the basketball court. The demolition of the hen house made that happen. By 1980, when all three sons had left the farm for college, the basketball court was more than ideally converted as the concrete floor for the new red poll barn. And that project was not complete until the name FLINT was erected near the top of the barn and easily visible from La Mar Road.

What happened to the Taylor family was equally important: husband and wife moved from the 40-acre farm to the Flint home on 20 Woodlawn Drive. The Flint home was the finest residence they would ever own. It was built in 1958 by the Flints for $14,000.00. It wasn't that far from the farm, but it was in Jefferson Township and where Hagerstown was incorporated in 1832. It was a home that needed no wood-burning stove for heat. And no longer was it possible that they would live in jeopardy of crop failures.

Yes, the real estate transaction between the Flints and the Taylors was a win-win situation, a deal that was good as any handshake and as relevant as any business in the nation. There were many reasons, to be sure. In 1962, the Flints needed a bigger home and yard to raise three sons. There was plenty of room on the farm, and for expansions to the old farmhouse completed by the Newton Brothers Construction Company.

For the Taylors, it was Woodlawn Drive for the retirement years, and the care and concern of animals and farming to the Flints. Both families would see and visit each other in the early years, yet the decade of the 1960s was fraught with change.

Flint had a DVD copy of the old 8mm home movies shot by his mother in the fall of 1962. This included three little boys waving to the camera at the end of the lane. Where else could the brothers wait for the arrival of Harold

Pine and his Nettle Creek school bus? There was room to make a turn-around off LaMar Road, the boys stepping up into the bus, and Beverly Flint to stand and wave back at her sons and to film the whole episode at the same time. Not captured on camera were three little bikes resting against the fence row. Yet it was important to recall that none of them were ever stolen during this time. At the end of the day, the boys would return to their bikes and ride up the lane to the house.

As the years went by, the "bus-stop" at the end of the lane was severely tested on several occasions. Flint remembered most of those times as due to everyone in the family oversleeping. Whoever got up first could always see the bus backing up the lane slowly, with all the red lights flashing and the horn honking. Now there was really little time left to get the boys ready for school. It usually meant a ride in with mother because she was one of two librarians at Hagerstown Elementary School.

On the same reel of film was Homer Beeson with his International M tractor and a bulky combine. He was heading into the field, carefully looking back to see that farmer and machines had made it through the small gate. The film would jump in the projector from time to time, but Flint could see the combine stopping to unload grain into the waiting wagon. Often, his father appeared on the screen as he turned and waved back at the camera, standing in the field of his first harvest. He was all of 35 years of age, with no farming implements of his own, a young family now living in the country and a 40-acre farm pretty much the way it was since the Great Depression.

In 1967, he purchased the Farmall H for $800 from a member of the church. He drove it home through two counties on a day of sunshine and high expectations. It was the same day that he took it next door to the farm of Homer Beeson. It would be the first of many conversations on farming in general.

Flint always remembered the long friendship between his father and Homer Beeson. Farming was still a business, and it required each of them to keep records on hours worked, seeds purchased, and everything else that they had accomplished together during the past week. The accounts were good and paid-in-full for over 30 years.

The Walnut Grove grain elevator off Jacksonburg Pike was a frequent farmer destination. This was the place where the farms around Hagerstown bought their grains of harvest, where the tall silos gleamed together in the autumn sun to hold the bounty of the season, and the dusty offices were always busy to sort, weigh, and sell to a hungry world. It was a place of records and a source of information to the local Farm Bureau, the Wayne County soil and water conservation board and even the United States Department of Agriculture in Washington, D.C.

Driving to the grain elevator each time would take a few hours for Anthony Flint. There was a road gear on the International Farmall H which allowed the tractor to travel at speeds up to 25 mph—even when pulling a wagon full of heavy corn. Flint did allow for extra time to negotiate all the intersections, dirt roads and curves on each round-trip. He always took the less-traveled route which ended up being the most scenic part of the trip. The leaves from the trees in the fall—a sure sign of winter months approaching—was one memorable sight from the seat of the tractor; then, later, turning off Jacksonburg Pike and waiting in the line.

The grain elevator was surrounded by tractors and wagons, new and old, big and small. Flint could see the loads of grain pulled slowly up on the large scale and the man in the office then waving the drivers to move inside to unload their wagons.

On this day Flint was hauling soybeans. His turn was next as he shifted gears behind the wheel of his tractor to come to a complete stop. There was a moment inside the office when the man recorded the total weight of the tractor, wagon and driver. He looked up and motioned that he was finished; Flint could drive on and stop again, this time for workers inside to unhitch the wagon from the tractor. And attaching chains to lift it, and, at the same time, opening the long wood doors on the floor; this revealed the turning auger that was suddenly awash by the rush of crop from the tiled end of Flint's wagon.

As he looked up, Flint could hear the family's grain travel up the pipes in the grain elevator itself. All his crop and subsequent loads to be stored in the tall silos outside. And there to remain until market conditions were high enough or the grain was dry enough to sell, which was easy to do when the time was right; there was always a half-dozen empty box cars on the rail spur nearby, ready to go in no time at all.

Not done yet, Flint and the other drivers returned to the scale and waited on the man in the office. This enabled the grain elevator to subtract total weights from net weights, and to determine the weight of each load brought in. Usually that was it. Other times it was the mechanical failure of a driver's tractor or some piece of elevator equipment that tested the long-suffering patience of all the farmers present. But not today—an afternoon filled with the autumn sun of Indiana and one that was really no different than the bright blue heavens of Florida.

Keith Flint and his sons herded the sheep on the farm into the barn on the coldest nights of the winter. They could keep track of the newborn lambs and, at the same time, guard against the harsh realities of very cold temperatures. It was still possible that they would catch their deaths even while wearing coats of thick white wool. Here was also a good opportunity to inspect the flock for injuries, disease or for any oral medications that were necessary according to the medical charts that were kept in the barn.

With the absence of winter storms in the summer, it was other forms of death that needed attention the most. To be safe, dunking the sheep in chemical baths for protection against maggots in the spring, or shearing the wool to sell for profits and to keep the animals reasonably cool for summer days ahead. But it was the summer nights which were the most dangerous because of the threats of roaming dogs, attacking the sheep in packs and leaving bits of blood-stained wool and dead ewes for the light of morning to reveal.

The best moneymaker for the sons of Keith and Beverly Flint was making hay while the sun still shined. Under no other conditions than what the area farmers needed most of all: plenty of muscle for the summer of 1972. Plus a willingness to go to work with only a few hours' notice.

On the flatbed wagon in the field was Anthony Flint. He was always working in the hot sun—taking each bale of hay from the bailer and stacking them from the back to the front of the wagon. Each row was four bales across and five bales high. He could get almost 80 bales of hay on every wagon and, in fact, stack them as well as any builder of the ancient pyramids of Egypt. It didn't matter that Flint was allergic to hay chafe, so long as he worked outside in the open air.

Eugene and Clark Flint handled the bales of hay once they reached the barn. The main qualification to manage this work was a matter of default— neither brother was allergic to hay chafe. There was also the long hours in the hayloft. The two brothers unloaded hundreds of bales of hay, in a very dusty environment that was hot as hell. No water break was ever long enough; also, every now and then, a bale of hay would contain a sharp thistle on the outside, surely cutting teenage fingers if either brother forgot to wear his gloves.

The work was the same on each farm all summer long. No matter who answered the ringing phone in the kitchen, it was always another job that was referred to the three Flint brothers by the last grateful farmer. First, in Wayne County, and later, in Henry and Randolph Counties—adding new meaning to greener pastures on the other side of the proverbial fence. This was especially true if there was a "second" or "third" cutting of hay in anyone's field.

As for Flint, who was able to save $300 after 10 weeks of stacking hay on wagons, the best part was the purchase of a brand new 10-speed bike at the Schwinn store in downtown Richmond, Indiana.

There was one time when Keith Flint turned to the Old Testament of his Bible and searched for a name to his first black angus heifer. Wearing a long-sleeve white shirt and narrow black tie, but standing straight in the light breeze of a Sunday afternoon, he found it in the passages from the second book of Samuel, Chapter II:

> And it came to pass in an evening-tide, that David arose from off his bed, and walked upon the roof of the king's house: and from the roof he saw a woman washing herself; and the woman was very beautiful to look upon.
> And David sent and enquired after the woman. And one said, Is not this Bathsheba, the daughter of Eliam, the wife of Uriah the Hittite?

It was King David of Israel himself, none other than the author of the 23rd Psalm. The same king who slew Goliath as a boy but now killed for the love of another man's wife. Anyway, it was the name of Bathsheba that Keith Flint bestowed on his unsuspecting farm animal that day many years ago. And, indeed, it was a name that Anthony Flint never saw listed in the membership records of his 4-H Club or, for that matter, among the many animal tags visible each year at the Wayne County Fair in Richmond, Indiana—or the State Fair in Indianapolis.

Nor was the name of Lylocks something that veterinarians used most often to write down the name of some sick animal on the farm. But the Flints had one when they bought the farm and the cow that came with it. She had her own stall in the barn with her name etched in the wood overhead. As it turned out she also had a lasting impression with the boys. At breakfast the family used her milk for the cereal and put real cream on top—the brothers didn't know immediately if they liked that or not.

Lylocks and Bathsheba became the first of many livestock (with and without names) to be raised and sold for market. This usually involved a very early Wednesday morning for the three sons and the father. Whether it was sheep, cattle or pigs, Cameron Dennis from Dalton would bring his International truck to the barn on the 40-acre farm. This was always accompanied by noisy protests and near-escapes before the animals were finally secured for the 20-mile ride to the marketplace in Centerville, Indiana.

Dennis would drive his truck back down the lane to LaMar Road, just as the sun was rising above the line of trees to the east. Flint, like his brothers, had stopped to catch his breath and walk slowly back to the house. Always a good workout when it was market day on the farm. The brothers would shower and dress for school, but there was always more physical conditioning after school.

All three Flint brothers participated in sports: Anthony and Clark in cross country and track, Eugene in basketball. But it was running in the winter that proved to be the best training for Clark. That was in 1977, when he found the most time to run in the back fields of the farm, covered by a light snow and stems of the soybean crop still visible in the long rows. The ground would be frozen and hard, a patch of ice here and there and even droppings from the livestock that were now hard as rock. This was a far cry from the green golf courses in the spring and usually the site of a high school cross country meet.

A regional track meet in Indianapolis was not as audacious as running on the farm in the dead of winter. The desolation in the early morning hours was not complete without breathing the cold air into your lungs and hearing only your footsteps in the snow. You could see cars and trucks moving on LaMar Road and not hear a thing. This environment was great for total concentration, something Anthony knew was achieved by some professional athletes in Florida when hypnotizing themselves before a professional tennis match.

The snow was seasonal and did not last forever, giving way to the transformation in the spring. Often by the budding leaves in the trees or the chirping of birds who had gone south for the winter. It was good that all the farms on LaMar Road would come to life again and see a new crop in the fields. Keith Flint and Homer Beeson were no longer seated around the kitchen table to plan the summer months ahead. It was time to plant as soon as the ground was dry enough.

So it was to be that they tended to the soil on the 40-acre farm. A surface once deep and stretching across many of the early farms of Indiana; a black humus rich in plant-supporting minerals indiscriminately used by the settlers in the time of Abraham Lincoln. The trick was always to use the right mixture of fertilizers, crop rotation and tillage methods to keep the ground alive for the next generation.

Another thing about making hay in the summer of 1972 was the weather. Somebody had to bring the wagons in when it started to rain. The fastest way was to simply drive the tractor, bailer and wagon into the barn. This was not, however, an option always available. Often times the bailer was covered quickly with a tarpaulin and left in the field; then the tractor was hitched to the wagon and the load of hay was pulled to the barn. Now you had a difficult task if there was only room for the wagon: back it in with the tractor. And none of the brothers could master it from the seat of the Farmer H tractor. Was it turning the steering wheel right in order to turn the front wheels of the wagon left? Or was it left for right?

Chapter 8: Mr. Sulu, Ann Landers and the Rev. Rex Humbard

H. Wayne Huizenga, at one time or another, built Waste Management into the world's largest waste collection company, managed Blockbuster Videos to reach annual revenues of $4 billion, and, at one time or another, owned the Miami Dolphins, the Florida Marlins, the Florida Panthers and Joe Robbie Stadium in Miami. But Anthony Flint never got any closer to this south Florida billionaire than the Blockbuster Video store on 2211 Edgewater Drive in Orlando on June 4, 1985. That was the day actor George Takei came to town late but apologetic to dozens of fans waiting to see him and get his autograph.

His apology included his frustrations over the primitive form of transportation he was using to reach Orlando. It was nothing like the starships and the transporters he was used to using as Mr. Sulu on the starship *Enterprise*. Indeed, he would play the part of Sulu in some form or manner for 30 years; and nobody wanted to believe it was only science-fiction.

ANOTHY FLINT: When you first started the series, did you think it would last as long as it has?

GEORGE TAKEI: Of course not. As a matter of fact, back in 1965, when I did the pilot show and when we were on TV every season it was always the 'Perils of Pauline.' Are we going to make it? Are we going to be renewed? Are we going to be cancelled? You know, do we have life after this season. And at the end of each season, the threat of cancellation was very, very strong. After the second season, they did cancel us. But, bless those Trekkies out there, they wrote those letters in such volume and such quality that they (NBC) gave us another season. We had three seasons. And finally after that it was cancelled. The reason why it was cancelled, I think, was those Klingons at NBC! They didn't know what they had, and they didn't know where to program a show like *Star Trek*.

I always considered *Star Trek* an intelligent, hip, with-it show. And Friday nights at ten o'clock, that kind of audience is out. Being hip and with-it. And they weren't home watching television. So, when we finally did get cancelled and the syndicators took over, and the local TV stations, then they put it on at a much more rational, reasonable hour for a show like *Star Trek*. Seven o'clock, seven-thirty, eight o'clock. And that's when our audience finally discovered us. Alas, it was after cancellation. But that's when the ratings started skyrocketing.

The reason why it's lasted so long, I think, is because *Star Trek* has a lot of dimensions to it. On the surface, it was a rip-snorting space opera. Beyond that, *Star Trek* made some very profound observations about the human condition. You know, we dealt specifically with the Vietnam war, the Civil Rights crises, or the hippie movement, or the generational alienation, you know, the important social issues that, in many respects, were tearing the country apart at that time.

It was disguised as science fiction, but those who had the intelligence to see it, you know, were able to find that message there. So, that intrigued one group in the audience. Another group was interested in the technological speculation. Some of the kinds of devices that we had on the shows. Those people found, you know, the speculation on our future technology in *Star Trek* was done with a great deal of care and rooted in the legitimate speculation of the scientists and the writers of the 1960s.

On another level, I think, *Star Trek* had characters that the audience could identify with. But also, admire and respect. *Star Trek* characters personified some ideal and noble qualities of humankind. They were heroes in the truest sense and this, at a time when the country was talking about anti-heroes. You know, the small man, the failed man, the sympathy for the tragic figure. Rather than to see someone heroic; someone who had courage and grace under pressure; someone who had extraordinary intelligence and the qualities that people could be inspired by and try to emulate in their own lives. That, I think, was one of the key elements.

Star Trek also had a positive vision of the future. To see the future not in terms of gloom-and-doom and fear. But as a challenge for the human potential. And for all those reasons, I think, over the years our audience has grown and grown and grown. And here it is, our audience covers the whole spectrum—from senior citizens to youngsters who were born after *Star Trek* was cancelled, from West Cost yuppies to Appalachian blue-collar workers. As a matter of fact, our audience is international. In Europe, Asia, Australia—it's a very, very big and popular show.

ANTHONY FLINT: How long will all of you continue to make the *Star Trek* movies?

GEORGE TAKIE: Well, the attitude at Paramount studios is, you know, we'll keep making them as long as the audience is out there. And so they haven't made any commitments beyond the next film. I think that's a foolish attitude because I am absolutely convinced that we can be doing *Star Trek* 24, and all of you will still be lining up at the box office!

ANTHONY FLINT: Back in 1966, there was a desire for an international cast on *Star Trek*. How did you get the part of Mr. Sulu?

GEORGE TAKI: (laughing) It was an undeniable talent that they all saw on camera! There was no other choice they could make!

ANTHONY FLINT: And in August the 4th film. What can you tell us about that?

GEORGE TAKI: We were actually hoping to start shooting in March of this year. And then we had some script difficulties, so they pushed the start date to December. But Paramount still has plans to release the film in the summer of 1986 which is, of course, our 20th anniversary.

The director will be Leonard Nimoy. The approach this time will be a little different than the first three films. It's going to be a little lighter, more frolicking, along comedic lines. Beyond that, I don't think you'd want to know, would you? Because you want to be able to enjoy the plot twists and turns and discovering them for yourself in the theatre.

The first *Star Trek* motion picture was directed by Robert Wise and premiered on Dec. 7, 1979. It was called *Star Trek: The Motion Picture*. The film was nominated for an Oscar for special effects as it portrayed a revamped *U.S.S. Enterprise* on a mission to discovery the source of an unidentified energy cloud deep in space. It was also a box office smash that was not popular with film critics. And even though Flint did not keep the letter he sent to *Time* magazine, he did file the response he received one day at the Indiana Bureau of *The Cincinnati Enquirer* in Lawrenceburg, Indiana. It said, in part:

> By now you will have seen the several letters on Richard Schickel's review of *Star Trek* that were published in the January 7 Letters column. They were fairly representative of the more than 500 we received—some (a few, we must admit) liked it, but most felt as you did the review was extremely unfair. We are sorry we weren't able to publish you letter too, but thank you for a frank opinion.

Ann Landers visited Orlando and *The Orlando Sentinel* during a brief visit in the spring of 1983. The Sentinel was one of 1,200 newspapers that carried the Ann Landers column and that reached a world-wide audience of 90 million readers at the time of her death in 2002. The column, she said that day, was often written at home, sometimes in the bathtub. Flint had these additional notes:

> I am just not smart enough to know all the answers to all these questions that are put to me. So I need the advice of the experts. And I have access to, I would say, the best brains in the country. There isn't anyone I can't pick up the phone and call, and I do call a great many people. And this is another part of the job—I have to do this. You can't have a secretary call the chief of cardiology at Harvard Medical School, for example, or the head of the dermatology department at the Mayo Clinic. These calls I have to make myself. It takes a great deal of time to do this but I do it because I feel this is what gives authenticity to my column. My advice has got to be correct. Approximately seventy million people are reading that column every day, and there are a great many people who are experts out there, and I use them because I better be right.
>
> I get about a thousand pieces of mail a day. But, mercifully, approximately one-third of those letters is requests for my booklets. And I don't have to deal with that. I have two people who do nothing but open the mail and separate the reader mail from the booklet mail. So that leaves about six hundred letters—most of those letters are from people who need referral services.

I cannot untangle a life that has been messed up for twenty years—I cannot do it with one letter. Or two inches of newspaper space. These people need continuing help, and many of them have no idea that there are agencies, and they need to know the hotlines and the addresses. And I am able to provide that because we have in our offices in Chicago, probably the greatest referral system in the world.

I think problems in marriage have always been the number one problem. Women, particularly, write more about it than men. And now that women are out there in the work force in greater numbers than ever before, and they're going to be out there in greater numbers than ever before; we're going to see more women who are getting divorced, who are having children later, who are meeting men more interesting than their husbands; and the men are meeting these same kinds of women. Well, after ten or twelve years, it's not difficult to find somebody more interesting.

The Marlboro Country Music Tour in the fall of 1983 included Merle Haggard, Hank Williams, Jr., John Anderson and Ricky Scaggs, and a concert at the Orange County Convention Center in Orlando, Florida. Also appearing that night was the Rev. Rex Humbard, the pioneering radio evangelist who started out in Akron, Ohio, and was later seen on 200 TV stations in the 1980s with his weekly "Cathedral of Tomorrow" broadcast.

Anthony Flint joined the press conference after the sold-out performance:

QUESTION: Are you encouraged with the response of someone like Ricky Scaggs on your programs?
REV. REX HUMBARD: I think we're going to turn back to the middle-of-the-road music in all kinds of music, myself; and, particularly, the people want something with a moral fiber to it. They like to see guys like Ricky Scaggs; I do. Because, see, I'm supposed to preach. I've been an ordained minister for 45 years; but he is not. And he just lives his life and goes to church when he gets an opportunity. And tries to be an inspiration to someone else. Sometimes this means an awful lot to fellows like me. And I really appreciate his dedication to faith, but also to be willing to help on this prime time special for Thanksgiving.
QUESTION: What has been the biggest source of inspiration through the years in music to you?

REV. REX HUMBARD: Well, back in the Forties I was doing local programs. My mom and my dad and all of us traveled. We had, really, a country band in those days doing gospel music. See, I've been in radio for 53 years, 33 years in television. And one day in Nashville, Tennessee, Eddie Arnold walks up to the same microphone that I used just 15 minutes before, with his Oklahoma Wranglers, and he did a nationwide program on radio on the old Mutual radio network. Well, this just blew my mind. Here I was with the same microphone, and I only had one radio station. So, finally, I was on the Mutual network. So, fellows like that have been a great inspiration to me down through the many, many years. Then when TV came on there were no preachers on TV. And I pioneered that across America because I felt God ought to be there. And I don't criticize the other things on TV, they all have their place. But my thing has its place, too. And we try to keep our place there.

Chapter 9: Newspaper

Snow was falling on a late Friday afternoon in Hagerstown, Indiana. Anthony Flint was seated at the typewriter, waiting for his next inspiration. He looked out the large windows and saw Roy Johnson from across the street. Johnson was greeting every driver who pulled in slowly at Johnson's Texaco Service. The snowflakes in the direct illumination of the headlights gleamed the brightest on the large windows. So did the service station sign that was just as bright, and the Texaco star at the very top was much more a beacon than it was anything else.

People were walking past the large windows and crossing the street. They had parked anywhere they could in this small community of 2,000 citizens. The destination for this pilgrimage was Guy Welliver's Fabulous Smorgasbord. Named after Hagerstown's most famous chef, a businessman who successfully expanded his business on the same block since 1946.

Looking back at his typewriter, Flint knew that inspiration was not a problem for very long. In fact, this was the best place to beat writer's block when seated behind the big desk of the editor. It was like walking through the attic of your grandmother's house. Always something new to see, yet, inexplicably, never finding the same artifact twice. Anthony examined bits and pieces of souvenirs from the local piston ring factory—notes from the school board meeting; schedules for the football team; and, yes, another piece from his wife, a writer on local historic things.

Anthony Flint was the only one in the building of *The Hagerstown Exponent*, a weekly newspaper with a stationary shop in the front and printing presses and supplies in the back. And large windows to always see the town.

In 1981, there was a typewriter and desk jammed in a corner at *The Hagerstown Exponent*. People entering the stationary shop could easily see the editor at work. It was the pipe and a lingering haze of blue smoke that was usually the first impression of Floyd Lacy. Also, his straight-legged, wheat-colored jeans, ankle-high suede shoes and a purple nylon jacket with the face of a golden tiger on the front. This was the mascot for all the athletic teams up at the high school.

The editor—affectionately known as "Old Lace"—had no need for the kind of hard news that made the pages of a large daily newspaper. Those who read *The Exponent* never saw a headline for a murder or rape. Families living in Hagerstown did not fear crime; they knew friends and relatives in the big cities that did.

Local hard news, such as it was, seemed relegated to the only daily newspaper published in Wayne County: the *Palladium-Item* in Richmond. Readers expected it to cover the misfortunes and the misadventures of neighbors, politicians and the world at large. But Floyd Lacy was responsible for publishing the name of a child who made straight A's, which was never more newsworthy than in the Nettle Creek valley of Hagerstown. He would see dozens of high school football games and photograph hundreds of local young people achieving something under the age of 21. This was a remarkable achievement that the journalism schools cannot teach; nor was it ever easy to reconcile the long hours associated with the duties of a weekly newspaper editor.

How he served as editor for *The Exponent* was best revealed in letters from the Indiana Republican Editorial Association; Chapter 1501, UAW Retires; the Governor of Indiana; the Hoosier State Press Association; the American Heart Association and President Ford who, on April 8, 1975, wrote: "During these years you have served with distinction and dedication, channeling the local news through your community and stimulating community involvement. *The Hagerstown Exponent* has carried the vital information that has affected the life of your community and has built a record of outstanding service. You have my best wishes for continued success in the years ahead."

Ralph R. Teetor was a man blinded by accident when he played with a knife at the age of five. The mishap was particularly remorseful to his parents, John and Kate Teetor. They lost their 4-year-old daughter, Eva, 11 months earlier when she died in 1889. Then it was later that John Teetor was diagnosed with Parkinson's disease.

Yet it was the Teetor family that would help to start the Railway Cycle Manufacturing Company in 1895. And it was Ralph who registered patents in his lifetime for lock mechanisms, fishing rod holders, luggage, an early power lawnmower and speed control devices now used in nearly every car manufactured in the world.

It would take editors of *The Exponent* and over 100 years to report on the Teetor family. First, it was the local factory that made cycle cars that operators could pedal down the railroad for visual inspections of the tracks. This was something that sold in 38 countries for $50 each. Then, in 1907, it was a bigger company, making cylinders, pistons and a revolutionary process of individually casting piston rings.

The headlines and stories of 1914 included news of engine manufacturing. This was needed for such automobiles as the American, Pilot, Westcott, Auburn, MacFarlane and the Empire. All of them were made in Indiana. Most of the factories were less than 40 miles from Hagerstown.

It was not until 1918 that the assembly lines in Hagerstown made only piston rings, now under the name of the Indiana Piston Ring Company. And it was such a curious piece of the engine itself, a circle of iron polished like a mirror for perfection as much as possible. It was mass-produced by the millions, and from additional plants built in Richmond, New Castle and Rushville, Indiana.

Ralph R. Teetor was Hagerstown's most famous citizen, a lifetime resident. He served as vice-president of engineering and later president of the company with the new name: Perfect Circle Corporation. It was a brilliant era, from 1946 to 1957. Teetor developed many design improvements for production, thus helping to establish Perfect Circle's reputation as the leading manufacturer of piston rings.

His death was a story that needed half of *The Exponent*'s front page for Feb. 17, 1982. It was all about a blind man who became an inventor and philanthropist; the one who built a gasoline-powered motor car with a cousin in 1902; and, with his graduating class, constructed the town's first electric sign for the 1908 commencement exercise at the Odd Fellows Hall.

During World War I, he was the assistant to the superintendent of the New York Shipbuilding Company at Camden, New Jersey. There it was his genius that found a way to dynamically balance turbines for torpedo boat destroyers. This was a feat that had baffled engineers for weeks. Even with America's entry in World War II, the turbines were removed from storage and shipped to England for the greatest war effort in the history of the world.

A weekly edition of *The Exponent* always included pictures and did what a hometown newspaper does best. Here that would be photography of the latest retirements from the piston ring factory, newcomers to the community and, on a very good week, group photographs of the Junior Girl Scout Troop

85, the Brownies of Troop 225 and the Boy Scouts of Troop 3.

A good week was also one without misspelled names or, worse, names inadvertently excluded from the accompanying pictures published in the newspaper. Flint knew how important it was to get all the names right. As, for example, the group photograph of the Hagerstown Swim Club, one coach and 26 members on the team.

Flint setup his tripod and mounted his camera at the junior-senior high school. He chose a spot that was out in a hallway and against a white wall. This way he could use as much available light as possible. He would not need any flash photography that might make this young team blink their eyes more than once.

It was true that he had never covered a swim meet or interviewed Coach Bill Ennis. It was also true that he did not know any child present that day in a swimsuit. But that was not the most important thing to know for the moment. He needed first and last names, and he needed them yesterday.

Coaches can be helpful when it comes time for the team photographs. Boys and girls will stand still when ordered by the coach, even in times of championship wins, when the parents are there and the photo opportunities are loud and often crowded. So it was Coach Ennis who got this club together and told them to settle down and be quiet. Those who were the tallest found themselves standing in the back.

They had their moments of laughter, still fidgeting, of course. Flint identified each child, and none was left out: Kevin Thomas, Aaron Thomas, Ryan Herold, Shane Benedict, Mike Powell, Stacy Walther, Leah Inman, Kristina Weaver, Sally Henley, Jane Mendenhall, Bill Powell, Courtney Sherwood, Kin Tibbetts, Angie Bryant, Shannon Gillespie, Debbie Hines, Matt Sherwood, Lisa White, Farron Landreth, Jimmy Bryant, Chris DeVinney, Sonya Otteson, Kim Monaghan, Kerstin Grimes, Stacey Cornils and Stacy Mendenhall.

The editor of *The Exponent* was the first writer that Flint had ever known. It was his job to put all the stories together for publication on most Tuesday nights for 17 years. And there seemed to be a lot to do in those days. His sports statistics were as official as the records maintained by the coaching staffs, counting every final first down or the last free throw shot.

Up at the high school—in the teacher's lounge—his mailbox was stuffed with the names of students who went to school in the community. There was a story behind each name, and it was everything from the prom queen to the soil judging champion.

The editor also kept active with his column on the back page. He would never admit this in public, but this was, in fact, the editorial side of things for him. It was where comments could be made on current events of the day and even matters of greater importance. That would be 9-digit zip codes, the metric system, government bureaucracy, the Democrats and the big daily newspaper in Richmond. There was always a gentle jab in all of it, but it still was a way to absolve any suggestions of problems in his town.

Flint read all the stories in this newspaper and continued his subscription when he moved to Orlando, Florida. At least he was still in contact with his hometown. These were times when the smallest article was important enough to read again and again, as if he were looking for clues of some kind—anything that might tell him how it was back home. Then there was the editor's own obituary that was read by all *Exponent* subscribers on Sept. 24, 1986.

During his last stay in the hospital, the editor continued to read many newspapers as he always did. This produced a series of observations in notes to friends, complete with stories or pictures clipped together. And to the family (wife and son) all instructions directed them to cut more stories and pictures from newspapers and mail them to a longer list of people that the editor of *The Exponent* had come to know over the many years.

Flint completed 22 paragraphs on the school board meeting at 6:25 p.m. The headline for the story read: SCHOOL BOARD OKAYS MASTER CONTRACT, BUT DELAY ON ARCHITECT.

This was important to 86 teachers, their principals, all seven members of the school board and even the school superintendent. It meant that nine months of bargaining negotiations were over. All the salaries from top to bottom were now set for the next three years. This included pay hikes for major medical coverage. Then the board also approved one-year salary advancements for the retirement funds of six teachers. And they approved contracts for new coaches, fund-raising projects with magazine subscriptions and sausage and cheese sales; plus an expense account for a business education workshop next month in Indianapolis.

In the same meeting, the board was undecided on which architectural firm to hire to design a new roof at the junior-senior high school. These expenses have to include contingencies for future maintenance problems. That was the vision of the school board president, who said: "We don't want to pay all our money on the roof. You have to be prepared for something else." The board would need to review the cumulative building fund and make a decision at the next meeting on December 23.

But this story proved to Flint how the biggest and most consistent source of news for a town the size of Hagerstown, and its weekly newspaper, was, unquestionably, the schools of the community.

Obituaries were usually the first work that entry-level journalists did on the larger daily newspapers. Yet this, too, was the job of the editor of the *Exponent*. After receiving each notice from the funeral homes, he would always double-check the information on the services, the survivors and the memorial contributions requested in honor of the family.

Flint submitted three obits to be published during his week behind the editor's desk. One was for a woman, a native of Hagerstown, who was 90; another was for a man from Texas who spent most of his life here, age 73; and another man, 57, from Eaton, Ohio, who lived here and died at Reid Memorial Hospital in Richmond.

This was a milestone in the lives of three people in the small community of Hagerstown. It affected neighbors, friends and, of course, all the survivors from the three families. Flint counted a grand total of 3 sons, 3 daughters, 10 brothers, 9 sisters, 7 grandchildren, 5 great-grandchildren, and nieces and nephews.

The time was now 9:15 p.m. The snow was still falling outside the large windows at *The Hagerstown Exponent*. All the lights were off at Johnson's Texaco Service, except Johnson's sign with the bright red star on top. Within the hour, Flint had called home and told his parents he was still running late, unavoidably. They reminded him that the lane would be slippery when he did make it in for the night. Whenever that would be, please drive carefully, they said.

This was the last time he would sit behind the desk of Floyd Lacy, where he had learned so much. He would never become editor of any weekly newspaper for the rest of his life. It was not to be. In this case, he was only substituting for the editor. Lacy had called him to fill in while he went into the hospital for a series of tests and consultations with doctors. Then it was nothing serious; he was probably lectured to take it easy and find a way to loose that pipe. Yet he still worked long hours for the town's sesquicentennial in 1982 and did just the same thing for the newspaper's centennial celebration in 1975.

On Dec. 9, 1981, Flint ran his first column on the front-page of *The Hagerstown Exponent*:

$8,685.00.

In plain dollars and cents, that's just how much it costs to run the Nettle Creek School Corporation, for a typical day.

It's an amazing feat of decimal points and dollar signs from the desk of assistant superintendent Lyle Bonnell. Where everything has a price. Charts. Graphs. Percentages. Even for a single day.

Since the entire corporation budget is now before the Indiana State Board of Tax Commissioners, according to Bonnell, school money is always important this time of year. The complete budget amounts for the next school year are approximately $2,546,935— as they now stand before the state board completes its work early next February. But the following short look at the money numbers demonstrates it plainer.

Probably the next time your children go to school (and even if they don't), 19 Nettle Creek buses roll at roughly $1,700 per day. This includes insurance, fuel, drivers, and whatever else it takes to move that yellow fleet of vehicles.

When the lights go on in the classrooms, about $200 keeps the bright ideas alive among the school's 1,550 students most days of the week. That's everything electrical.

Hungry at school? Noontime lunches cost $1,234. But that is not part of the school's typical one-day expense. Federal funds and student dollars make the cafeterias self-supporting, Bonnell admits.

As for the weather, $501 for fuel on a winter day—not too cold.

By the end of the day, pay $7,572.00 for teacher, custodial and administrative salaries, which include school trustees, coaching duties, teacher substitutions, nursing, guidance, corporation aides and librarians.

For a typical day.

Chapter 10: The Fire on Merritt Island

Midnight and a light breeze in Orlando, Florida. It seemed to add a chill in the night air despite a temperature of 85 degrees, and with no rain in the 5-day forecast. *The Orlando Sentinel* building seemed deserted on 633 North Orange Avenue as Anthony Flint walked to his car. He stopped and looked up at the stars shining dimly in the heavens. The light of the moon, however, was much more reassuring. Even with the security lights surrounding the parking lot, Flint could see the bright rays fanning out from the larger crater rims. Someday, he promised himself, he was going to learn the names of some of the most prominent features on the lunar surface.

He knew traffic would not be a problem at this hour as he headed south. In fact, he made good time when he reached his next exit in only 10 minutes on the John Young Parkway—so named after Orlando's own space hero, a *Gemini* astronaut, one who walked on the moon and was the first space shuttle pilot.

Slowing down, he took a left turn on Highway 525, a toll road better known in Orange County as the Beeline Expressway. It leads past Sea World and Orlando International Airport and on to the east coast of Florida. Here Flint would spend the next 45 minutes heading to the John F. Kennedy Space Center. It was plenty of time to play Elton John's "Rocket Man" on the cassette player.

In 1962, there was once a large mural of the solar system on a wall at Hagerstown Elementary School in Hagerstown, Indiana. Students entering the library could easily see how the planets orbit the sun. It was the mural on the wall that was Flint's earliest memory of space travel. Maybe, also, a Sunday night after church. His mother bought him a small book on space flight next door at a drug store in Richmond, Indiana.

Robert A. Heinlein's *Orphans of the Sky* was probably the one book of science fiction that he could never forget. It was not famous like *Starship*

Troopers or *Stranger in a Strange Land*, also by Heinlein. But it was the story of a spacecraft five live miles long on a mission to Proxima Centauri. The journey would take generations of human life onboard the ship. Families lived out their lives and knew less and less about themselves until there were only myths.

Those who survived best in the centuries to come were the scientists. They relegated themselves at the highest decks of the ship. Others became a race of freaks and cannibals who lived on the low gravity levels and who had lost the most.

One man discovers the truth that their word is moving through space. He can see the stars from the "control room." This is something the current generation cannot believe or even hope to reconcile with the past. The truth is scorned as heresy, and the man is sentenced to death

How generations decide truth is a major theme of this 1941 science fiction classic. It is also a premise for certain groups of people who blame NASA for the greatest hoax in history. That man had ever landed on the moon.

At the end of the Beeline Expressway was when the view changed dramatically. Through the night hundreds of people had parked their cars bumper-to-bumper along side roads arid makeshift campsites and waited for the shuttle liftoff. Others spent the night inside RVs of every shape and size. One sign on the back of a minivan said it all: FLY HIGH DISCOVERY!

Businesses stayed open with launch parties and spaghetti specials. Also, the local homeowners charged fees for parking vehicles in their driveways and front yards. It was always better this way than to leave your vehicle unattended. Usually no questions were asked.

Flint continued across the Indiana River to Merritt Island and the 140,000 acres that contain wildlife refuge and space flight center. Then it was a left turn and heading north on Highway 3 to the space shuttle press badging center at Gate 2.

The block walls inside were covered with insignia of 25 space shuttle missions. All abbreviated with STS for Space Transposition System. Flint had covered six shuttle flights since 1981. He signed his name now for press credentials to cover the STS-26 mission. He would have access to the launch press site and briefings by companies flying payloads onboard the shuttle. Only military missions would be strictly limited.

Anthony continued north on Highway 3 to the intersection with NASA Parkway. A left turn took you to the Visitors' Information Center, less than a mile east. It was home of a Skylab replica, a Viking Mars lander and an outdoor rocket park with some of the nation's earliest spacecraft on exhibit This was a popular place. In 1983, some 14 million tourists came to the space center, making it the 4th largest attraction in Florida.

Tonight Flint would drive on to the Vehicle Assembly Building ahead. At 525 feet tall it was visible from a number of locations off Florida's space coast. Known as the VAB, it was the shelter for America's space shuttle fleet. Flint read a NASA booklet that said the eight-acre site was built to withstand winds at 125 mph.

In minutes, the VAB filled his view as Flint turned right and drove the short distance to the press parking area. Getting out of his car, he looked back at the VAB and remembered the rollout of STS-26 on the Fourth of July.

Two months ago, the giant Crawler-Transporter took the *Discovery* space shuttle out of the VAB and into the night air. Then a journey to the launch pad for seven and a half hours, moving along a strip of river gravel approximately 130 feet wide.

To do that, NASA needed 20 people, two 2,750-horsepower diesel engines, four 1,000-kilowatt generators and 16 traction motors: a mobile launch pad weighing eight million pounds total. And to do so was historic because STS-26 was the first manned space light in the United States since the *Challenger* explosion 33 months ago.

On a good day there is a vantage point in literally dozens of counties throughout Florida to see a manned liftoff into outer space. Flint knew a reporter with *The Tallahassee Democrat* who videotaped a shuttle launch from a rooftop at Florida State University. He did the same thing on the rooftop of the Sentinel building on the cold morning of January 26, 1986. This was as good a spot as any in Orlando as he setup his tripod and mounted his video camera.

Anthony was not covering the flight or the shuttle crew that included Sharon Christa McAuliffe, a school teacher with an 8-year-old son and a 5-year-old daughter. But he did a column in 1985 on President Reagan wanting a teacher to be the first member of the general public to ride the shuttle. And so NASA received and reviewed 80,000 applications. Those eligible to apply in America at that time included 2 million full-time elementary and secondary teachers.

NASA had others from all walks of life who wanted to fly as a space shuttle passenger. They had their reasons, of course; but they included, and were not limited to, John Denver, Bob Hope, Tiny Tim, James Michener, Hugh Downs, Malcolm Forbes, an entire fifth grade class from Weehawke, New Jersey, plus a bright high school senior who lectured on the stars n Fullerton, California.

There were letters also, 5000 of them:

If you sent me up, a 12-year-old student, that would make Russia think that our whole country is ready for war, not just the military...

I have multiple sclerosis, and since there is no cure, I was wondering if some day NASA would take a person like me that has the illness to see what weightlessness would do to my body....

We would like to have six applications. We are New York City workers and would like to know, if we are chosen, would you pay us for the 200 hours in training?

NASA's pubic affairs director in Washington told Anthony Flint: "Actually, people have been writing since the Sixties for a chance to be rocketed into space. The big boom began in 1982 when a task force was asked to look into putting passengers on the shuttle, but some of those letter-writers we've heard from haven't even asked to go themselves. They nominated someone else."

Really? Who?

"Walter Cronkite."

The first time he saw the orbiter *Challenger* was high in the sky on February 11, 1984, at 7:12 a.m., EST. The shuttle appeared as a tiny gray triangle at just 9,000 feet altitude. It didn't seem big to the press at the shuttle landing strip or the 75,000 spectators along the highways and riverbanks. The shuttle, however, was as large as a DC-9 aircraft; each of its three main engines would easily dwarf the first *Mercury* space capsules.

Up on the press mound, with a few minutes more to go, photographers adjusted cameras for the moment when the first shuttle would land—not mounted with a 747 carrier aircraft—in the State of Florida.

Discovery kept turning and did a U-turn to line up with the southbound end of the runway. The shuttle cropped with astounding speed until it was at the start of the 5,000-foot-long landing strip. It nosed up to lightly touchdown and slip through the thin morning fog.

Then, at 7:16 a.m., the chase plane roared ahead into a steep incline. And *Discovery* whisked by the press mound at 215 mph without any sound of its own. It was a big, bulky bird with ungainly fat aft.

Flint watched the recovery convoy form on the runway where the shuttle finally came to a dead stop. At least 20 vehicles accompanied by the safely assessment team. These were technicians who exchanged places with the astronauts and connected the orbiter with electricity for air conditioning. They also moved into place a large fan to disperse any lines from the space shuttle.

On his way back to Orlando, Flint listened to his car radio and the interviews of the crew members by James Beggs, NASA's chief administrator. Mission specialist Ron McNair took his turn and said he always played his saxophone when he came home late at night to relieve stress. He thanked his wife who was six months pregnant with their third child.

McNair would fly aboard the *Challenger* again in two years, with Sharon Christa McAuliffe.

The time was 4 a.m. on the morning of Sept. 29, 1988. A large launch clock on the grassy field was running at 03:47:07 at the LC-39 launch press site. From here, Flint looked at shuttle launch pad 39-A, three and a half miles away. Then he turned and looked at the press grandstand with seating for 350 people. Some of those in the stands were photographers; indeed, some of them had set up tripods near the launch clock and weighted them with water jugs for stability.

Others, from a practical standpoint, would form groups of photo pools for the best still pictures possible. One group of 150 photographers form the survey photo pool. They depend on remote locations outside the perimeter fence at the launch pad. Each camera has a motorized mount, a sound-unit and a shutter that opens at four frames per second. The roar of the liftoff activates the camera.

Still other groups included the 75-member pool for the astronaut departure from the Operations and Checked Building on launch day. This was a large pool assigned some 12 hours before launch for the sunset photo opportunities at pad 39-A; and another 40-member pool was escorted to the VAB roof for coverage of a potential launch abort.

The last time Flint saw the space shuttle *Challenger* was hours after it exploded over the waters of the Atlantic Ocean. After a long day in the newsroom, he suddenly remembered his camera was still on the roof. He made a hasty climb to the top of the building and ran over to the tripod and camera. It was still pointed east to the space coast and just was as he had left it.

As he played the tape back, he could see two bright trails of fire and smoke edge away from each other. A third, smaller band was faint and quickly disappeared. Later, at home, and with the repeated use of his VCR, Flint soon enough determined that the pair of bright trails were, in fact, the solid rocket boosters. They were always attached on the right and left sides of a shuttle stack assembly and could be used again after the recovery from the ocean waters.

On the videotape, each solid rocket booster was soaring away as an independent space vehicle and then detonated by Mission Control. The faint band in the middle was the space shuttle *Challenger*—seconds after it exploded into history.

The time was 7:15 am. The moon was still visible over the VAB. All the lights were on inside the studios with large windows used by ABC News, CBS News, NBC News and Mutual Broadcasting. Within the hour, the astronauts would pass by the press parking area, stopping briefly. They would travel in what looked like a silver RV Airstream. Whatever it was, the vehicle moved on with the astronaut crew and support personnel to the space shuttle out on the distant horizon.

This was a big day in the life of any astronaut—male or female. It was the culmination of life-long dreams and heroic training. In the case of Richard Truly, it was also patience. He was once America's youngest astronaut, at age 27. Then came a proficiency totaling 6,000 hours in jet aircraft: the F-8, F-9, F-I I, F-101, F-I 04 and the F-106. Yet he waited with mounting frustration as one manned space shot was cancelled, a second trimmed. A third mission was with John Young as the co-pilot on the first space shuttle flight. This was 16 years of patience. It was also time enough to see his kids become adults, moving the family three times and becoming the first grandpa in the space program, twice.

After the *Challenger* explosion, a nation stopped to reflect. Beverly Flint was one of them. She sent a short note to her oldest son in Orlando, Florida:

An Epitaph to the Challenger

A rocket liftoff in the Florida sky;
with experiments onboard for you and I.
A crew of six, a school teacher, too;
got onboard in the whole world's view.
It didn't go far on that fateful day;
they'll find out why, the experts say.
A sky of blue filled with disaster;
the souls of the crew on the way to their master.
Why did they choose to make this flight?
leave their homes where all was right?
Rigorous training, hard work, a pioneer to be;
to open space doors for you and me.

The time was 11:35 a.m. Flint could see NASA employees gathering on the staircase outside the Launch Control Center, a 4-story structure east of the VAB. It was close to the launch of the space shuttle *Discovery* and its crew of five astronauts. The liquid hydrogen tank was pressurized for flight. Very soon the flight instrument recorders would start, and the control of the launch itself would switch from Mission Control to the computer sequences on the space shuttle.

The countdown is carried by dozens of loud speakers at the LC-39 press site. The announcer is the voice of Mission Control: Hugh Harris, who was there for the first shuttle countdown five years ago. And so were many of the reporters and photographers gathering around Flint as the countdown continued to the closing seconds.

Harris announces the start of the hydraulic power units on the solid rocket boosters at T minus 20 seconds and counting. Then the nozzles on the solid rocket boosters are moved to start position. And in the last ten seconds everyone at the press compound can see Pad 39-A slowly engulf in billowing clouds of light gray color. Not seen is 900,000 gallons of water flooding the launch pad at the same time. It was a cushion to the acoustical shocks of liftoff and the intense heat.

Discovery clears the tower, bringing with it a dazzling shower of orange fire and a growing column of smoke tracing the path of the spacecraft into the blue skies over the Atlantic Ocean. The orbiter quickly surpasses Mach 4 as it enters space after only two minutes of flight. NASA calls this juncture in space flight "Max Q," for surviving a dangerous combination of wind and speed shears at the most critical point. And the sound of *Discovery*'s liftoff is delayed by mere seconds before it thunders across the press compound like the stomping feet of one billion children.

Chapter 11: Band

The outdoor stage facing the grandstand was not Clews Hall, where the Indianapolis Symphony Orchestra preformed each year. Nor did the orchestra ever have to compete with the likes of one exhibit billed as the largest in the world. It consisted of one hog weighing in at 1,000 pounds. Next to that was a large stand selling buttered popcorn to lines of starving fair-goers of every age. The scene was merely an indication of all the sights and sounds not really far from the stage.

Everything in the grandstand was festival seating. But the best seats in the house required only two things. One, climbing the stairs quickly. And two, running hard through the ground floor tunnel that leads to the stage from the grandstand itself. Now the front row was immediately available to the people choosing to stand, or sitting cross-legged in the dirt of the oval track. Of course, teams of horses had been known to gallop past the grandstand during the past week. The judges were not to blame for anything still left behind. Fortunately, today's events saw marching bands in state competition from across Indiana; this was never a mess.

This was the dirt track used for harness racing and demolition derbies at the 1975 Indiana State Fair. It was also August, and the weather was hot and hazy in the state capitol. To get to the seats in the stands, nearly 50,000 fans pass through gates opened by the Indiana State Police about an hour before the concert. There was still time in the Communications Building next door to go over tonight's total gate receipts.

No matter how many tickets were sold, this rock group was phenomenal and a done deal with the Indiana State Fair. "You never know exactly what a rock group is going to do," says one official inside the Communications Building, watching fans outside his windows for nearly two hours. "We're not always sure they'll even show up!" It was intended by the state fair to attract the headlining entertainers of each generation. This band had its origins in Chicago where all but one of the eight members were born and raised.

They completed a 12-city tour with the Beach Boys earlier that summer. It was the brainchild of James William Guercio, 29, a former guitarist with the Mothers of Invention. He was the group's manager that year; yet, occasionally, he sat in on bass with the Beach Boys. Guercio toured with both groups and saw the stadiums fill with SRO crowds. Attendance reached 700,000 people in concerts, totaling $7.5 million. It was also reported that the combined record sales of both groups was over 65 million by 1975.

This was interesting to the record company that easily marketed the rock group by the name of its hometown, Chicago. Most fans did not know the members in the band. Names like James Pankow, Terry Kath, Lee Longname, Walter Parazaider, Daniel Seraphine and Laudir de Oliveira. America saw them all last summer during a network television special, at the band's own Caribou Ranch near Nederland, Colorado. Another appearance was on a Bill Cosby special in 1977. In the 1980s, vocalist Peter Cetera would make it big on his own.

But tonight, 50,000 fans saw the stage lit in blue light. Anthony Flint was one of them. "Are you ready?" It was James Pankow, the trombonist. "It's great to be back in Indy!"

Four of Chicago's members studied at music schools; this was Flint's fascination with the group. The brass instrumentals behind such classics as "25 or 6 to 4," "Saturday in the Park" or "Does Anybody Really Know What Time It Is." Pankow as trombonist for Chicago was also a role model. Flint played trombone in high school. He practiced in the barn on the 40-acre farm for his senior solo in 1973, with the north doors wide open.

The trombone can be a loud horn to blast away without much thought to the other musicians in the band. Good examples of this were the flute, clarinet, and even the piccolo. Many of them together could never equal the volume of one trombone in a marching band. Flint's parents could always hear him on the football field during a halftime show. It took hardy lips and lungs to pull this off. He ran cross country and track after school, and that increased his stamina each year. But what he really liked the most was concert band and the chance to play in brass quartets whenever possible.

In his junior year, he did play in a quartet of two trombones and two trumpets. The first time they played in public was the fifth annual Community Christmas Concert at the United Church of Christ in Hagerstown. Their selection in the candlelight service was "Alleluia!" from *Christmas Oratorio* by Saint-Saens. Four churches participated with vocal and instrumental numbers that cold Sunday night.

Then this mixed brass quartet from Hagerstown practiced for the 1972 solo and ensemble contests at Ball State University in Muncie, Indiana. This was sanctioned by the Indiana School Music Association for the central southern division, a Saturday in January for 3,250 young musicians playing an instrument. All the band directors, parents, and students had worked too many hours for this single day in the spotlight.

It was, in fact, a sponsorship of not only the Indiana School Music Association but also the Indiana Music Educators Association, the National School Band, Orchestra and Vocal Association and the Music Educators National Conference. And, after 25 years, this coalition worked as well as any labor union in the country.

There was also plenty of help from the university's School of Music at Emens Auditorium. They provided the classrooms for the contests and, most important, the judges for students competing in piano, woodwinds, brass, percussion and the small and large ensembles. Also, hot dogs, potato chips, candy, donuts, coffee, hot chocolate, milk and soft drinks were sold as refreshments by Sigma Alpha Iota, Mu Phi Epsilon (women's music honoraries) and Phi Mu Alpha (men's music fraternity).

The judges that day provided musical and technical scoring for five groups. Each was selected for their professional competence and the understanding of school music programs. The awards to each group ranged from first to fifth—with gold medals to the first place winners. With time permitting, the judges also provided written comments and suggestions.

At 11:51 a.m., the Hagerstown mixed brass quartet appeared before Judge Bernard G. Pressler in Room 123. This guy had done it all—soloist with the U.S. Marine Band and the Atlanta Symphony Orchestra; a Baroque recitalist; a graduate of the Eastman School of Music and had also toured with the Jimmy Dorsey Orchestra to France, Belgium, Spain and Switzerland.

No member of the quartet had seen or heard of Pressler prior to that moment. It made no difference because they had only 15 minutes to play in Room 123. There was no time for apprehension of any kind.

Flint could not recall what piece they performed for Pressler. That was all right. It was a good time for them and a first place award in Group Two. And all the students with a first place in Group One went on to the state competitions at Butler University on February 19, 1972.

At Civic Hall in Richmond, Indiana, the stage was inside the auditorium and faced the court used by the Richmond high school basketball teams. It was also the setting for a 12-piece orchestra outfitted in black dress trousers, black bow ties, black dress trousers and red jackets with black trim and a maple leaf emblem.

It was, after all, the Royal Canadians in concert with Guy Lombardo as conductor. At 71 in 1973, Lombardo on stage was still magical like he was on New Year's Eve at the Waldorf Astoria ballroom in New York City. He always rehearsed, adding new music; but he was careful to arrange melodies that fit his style. It was called "the sweetest music this side of heaven" by Ashton Stevens in the old *Chicago Examiner* newspaper. "It just sort of evolved, and my men—they're all polished performers; they know what they're doing and don't need much direction," Lombardo said that night during intermission backstage.

This was not a rock concert, but it was the good old days when the big bands toured the country. The women that night wore long dresses, and the men wore suits. To make things more complicated, teenagers were present that night in the company of their parents. One of them was Anthony Flint and his mother, Beverly.

It was not a trip down memory lane for him, but, rather, another appreciation for the sound of brass, perfect harmony and rhythm. And because the sounds of a big band captivated him. Lombardo's crowd pleasers included "Frankie and Johnnie," "Spanish Eyes," "Mack, the Knife" and the perennial favorite, "Auld Lang Syne." That was a Scotch tune he began using in 1928 as a traditional closing song in Ontario, Canada.

Another big band was especially liked by Flint while a senior in high school. The conductor was a trombonist and a major in the Army Air Corps when his plane disappeared on a military flight from England to France on December 15, 1944. But the music of the Glenn Miller Orchestra lived on, in 1956, under the leadership of Ray McKinley, who retired and passed the baton to Buddy De Franco in 1966.

"Glenn had the knowledge of how to impinge on everybody's nervous system," McKinley said 17 years later. "He made it pay, and he made people love it. In the movie (*The Glenn Miller Story*) they kind of made it seem an accident. That's so stupid. He mapped it out. I resent it when the storytellers make it sound as if he fell into this sound. Anything that pays off like the Glenn Miller music did, you work for.

"I don't like rock music," he continued. "That's not to say there isn't good rock music being played by groups like Blood, Sweat & Tears and Chicago. Some groups are good musicians."

Flint had two band directors while in his middle school years at Greens Fork, Indiana. One of them drove a motor scooter to work each day with the weather permitting. He had three band directors in high school. In his freshman year he was in the pit orchestra for the last musical in the school's history, *South Pacific*. It was held on the stage in the old high school gym on Sycamore Street.

But it was the band director in his junior and senior years that made a lasting difference in his life. This was the one who was the source of encouragement to enroll at Ball State University in the winter of 1973. Student and band director followed the progress of careers and families of each other over the intervening years. Flint became a nationally syndicated columnist with *The Orlando Sentinel*. And Joseph W. Backmeyer became superintendent of the Nettle Creek School Corporation.

One day at Dalton school, Flint spotted a trombone for the very first time. He had made it through those squeaky song flutes in music class; now for the good stuff—real musical instruments that came in cases with handles, with names like the saxophone and the sousaphone. He did find it a bit unusual in the very beginning, when it was first apparent that the slide goes up and down on the trombone. And no other horn could do or sound just like that. This, and nothing else, was what he wanted to play; and in the years to come, play he did.

Beginning with the middle school band in Greens Fork, then the high school concerts in Hagerstown. And one summer each at Butler University in Indianapolis and at French Lick in southern Indiana. He was one of the band camp counselors for the next generation of the Hagerstown Golden Tiger Marching Show Band. Other events in the music world were duly noted in 1975 and in 1976; most conspicuous, however, was any mention of all that music echoing from the hills of southern Indiana.

All three brothers had played a musical instrument; Eugene and Clark played the trumpet (Clark also played the violin). But it was Anthony who managed to audition for the Ball State University Varsity Band and make it in 1974. The winter concert was January 24 at the University Hall, and the spring concert was May 2 at the Arts Terrace.

Flint did not know many names of the students in the Varsity Band. The music was also unfamiliar: a "Chorale and Variant" by Victor Del Borgo and a "Sketches on a Tudor Psalm" by Fisher Tull. In high school he could play the theme song to the TV show *Hogan's Heroes* or Tommy Dorsey's theme song by heart. As first chair in his senior year, his impromptu repertoire included *The Dick Van Dyke Show*, *The Jetsons*, *The Andy Griffith Show* and *The Donna Reed Show*.

But the eventual realization was he would not be needing a Senior Recital in college. He would not be making a living as a trombonist like Jimmy Pankow in the rock group Chicago.

So what. He did memorize musical notes for nearly half of his senior year in high school. A long time spent with the band director and the young lady seated behind the upright piano. Objective? As he looked out into the crowded room at Ball State University, Mr. Robert W. Messer, both music professor and music judge. Three minutes to play for Mr. Messer but not having to do it all, because the judge waved to him to stop.

With musical competition being what it always was, the decision by the judge should be considered here more closely. He did not give a reason. No comment. No penalty. No danger. No real precedent. Not even a clear expression on his face. The part Flint played had a few high G notes, which he missed pretty much in full view.

So it really was a surprise to go to the lobby, standing in line with music students from across central Indiana and read the comments of the judge, and to suddenly know and feel the victory of a superior rating in Group II competition.

Flint took his trombone with him when he moved to Orlando, Florida. It always ranked near the top of his list of prized possessions. In time, it was placed on the top of his wife's cabinet grand piano in the living room. It was difficult, if not impossible, to relocate the piano anywhere without contracting a moving company. Yet it was always important to discuss the horn with Flint before any handling or any cleaning, and so it remained where it was and treasured like an Oscar statuette until the end of time.

Chapter 12: Jimmy Carter and George C. Wallace

Jimmy Carter was on the Presidential campaign trail in 1976 at the University of Notre Dame in South Bend, Indiana. Nearly 500 people were seated inside the university's center for civil rights to hear the former governor of Georgia. This was also a fall campaign ritual for Notre Dame—since 1952—to invite presidential candidates and their running mates to address the election issues of the day. Last month, for example, it was the turn of the Democratic candidate for vice-president, Walter Mondale.

It was a sunny afternoon for the scattered protestors on campus with anti-abortion signs waving in the air. They were also waiting to see Carter and were part of what the candidate described in South Bend as a "beautiful mosaic." Or, in other words, just a sample of the total resources of 215 million Americans standing up for their country.

Flint read one of the signs. It said: "Save Those Little Peanuts!" He arrived that day with a good friend from Ball State University—Pat Herrmann, who was now a general assignment reporter for *The Berrien County Record* in Niles, Michigan. They rode together to Notre Dame and watched the Rev. Theodore Hesburgh introduce Carter. Hesburgh would serve as the university's president for 35 years and would become as much a Man of Peace as Jimmy Cater. Hesburgh was the former head of the U.S. Commission on Civil Rights. He also served on a dozen presidential appointments, received over 140 honorary degrees and was awarded the presidential Medal of Freedom in 1964 and the congressional gold medal in 2000.

Hesburgh's introduction included the announcement that the University of Notre Dame would hold formal hearings on abortion after the November elections. Carter's speech began with "renewed commitments" in civil rights around the world.

He also said: "Any nation, if they want our friendship and support, must treat their people with basic human rights. We cannot look away when a country tortures its own people. We must speak out forcefully when there is torturing in the world, even in the most totalitarian countries.

"Americans pride themselves on the ability to achieve unity through diversity. The question, I think, is we have been too pragmatic, too cynical. I know of no other nation in history that has extended itself abroad the way we have. We have become the arms supplier to the world."

Carter was critical of past administrations for dragging America into the "quagmires" of Cypress, Chile, Vietnam and Bangladesh. He further described it has having "tough realism on the one hand, and idealism on the other." The Democratic candidate for president was also restating what he said during the second nationally televised debate with President Gerald Ford.

Gov. George C. Wallace of Alabama was one of the 10 Democratic candidates for President in 1976. That year a small jet brought the candidate and members of his campaign to Weir Cook Municipal Airport located northwest of Indianapolis, Indiana. The jet was escorted during taxi by state police cruisers. Secret Service agents and Indiana State Police provided tight security as Wallace entered through Gate 11 shortly after 2:30 p.m. to greet about 55 people and reporters.

Flint drove from the State Capital Building to the airport to cover the hour-long press conference for the Ball State Daily News. He saw that Wallace was seated in his wheelchair behind a dozen or so microphones set up on a table. It was from there that Wallace announced he would enter the May 4 Indiana Democratic Presidential Primary. He also would appear on the same ballot as Indiana's Senior Senator, Birch B. Bayh, a former Speaker of the Indiana House of Representatives and a friend and political ally of Sen. Edward M. Kennedy. Bayh had announced his candidacy on October 21, 1975, from the family farm near Shirkieville, Indiana. Of Bayh, Wallace said: "Our political views are not all that compatible."

What was compatible was winning his party's nomination and not running as an independent. "A great number of people are registered as Democrats," he said. This probably included some members of the press who also covered Wallace as a candidate for President in 1964 and in 1968. The Alabama Governor got more than 40% of the Hoosier primary vote in 1972. He expected to receive at least 75 delegates from Indiana for the 1976 Democratic National convention in New York City.

Wallace said American agriculture was a "bright spot" in a sagging national economy and said busing was "one of the most asinine experiments ever." He also told his cheering crowd: "I wish I had my positions copyrighted.

They all sound like they come from Evansville, Indiana." But they were not as unrelenting on issues like abortion or gun control or even the Equal Rights Amendment.

He did not apologize about anything related to the old segregationist views of the Deep South. Wallace would live long enough to say it was wrong. When he saw the new political realities of the 1990s—and how easy it was to delete anything on the emerging laptop computers.

Nettle Creek School bus driver Harold Pine was a major influence on Flint. All those mornings and afternoons riding the bus tended to add up by the junior or senior year. Such discussions between schoolboy and bus driver developed more with each passing year—which could only be politics, since neither was ever excited about watching a professional athlete make $80,000 on a typical Sunday afternoon.

To be sure, Flint new that Pine was a loyal supporter of George Wallace, the perennial candidate for President and one of the longest-serving governors Alabama had ever seen. This political affliction became a real problem when Flint came home from school one day and turned on the family television set. Usually it was the parents who watched and then pontificated on the news of the day. Other times it was the teachers who tested the students with pop quizzes on current events. Such as it was, the Wallace rally in Indianapolis was news that evening on the local television station. But Flint was never entirely sure that he saw Harold Pine wearing a Wallace for President hat on the front row with a Wallace campaign sign in each hand.

Flint interviewed Father Theodore Hesburgh years later when he was the commencement speaker for the graduating class at the University of Central Florida in Orlando. Here was part of it:

> **ANTHONY FLINT:** What is your opinion on the morality in our schools today?
> **REV. THEODORE HESBURGH:** I think it's true that there are such a variety of schools in America, that we've got schools as bad as any in the world. And we've got schools that are better than any in the world.
>
> And I have to say that, from where I sit, at least at the university, there must be some good schools, somewhere, because we get students from some 2,000 different high schools across the land

and foreign countries. And the quality of our students today is better than it was before.

I think the problem is we have a lot of terrible ghetto schools in America today. We're turning out four or five hundred thousand minority students every year who are still in schools that are not integrated at all. And they are in terrible neighborhoods, many of them. And the quality of education there is bad. Because the quality of everything there is bad. Bad housing. Bad streets. Bad unemployment. It's hard to educate youngsters at that age—you know, elementary and middle school—when all around them they are surrounded by failure.

ANTHONY FLINT: Are we living in a society that is more indulgent than it was 50 years ago?

REV. THEODORE HESBURGH: well, some of the things that go on are just absolutely terrible. One the one hand, people have been so hardened by some horrible things that have happened, like school kids killing each other, you know, or older people picking on little people or people abusing women just because they're women. These are things that we should never lose our ability to get outrage about them. We can't become so passionless that we say this stuff happens and then don't do anything about it.

ANTHONY FLINT: Is there a role for religion in our country today?

REV. THEODORE HESBURGH: I think so, because all my life I've been a priest. I never thought I was a priest just to give sermons and work in the church, and hear confessions and marry people, bury people and so forth. Everything we live and do is human in nature. I suppose I've spent more time on human rights, for example, not only in this country, but throughout the world. And I've seen the results, and it's marvelous what people will do when given a little bit of encouragement. And around the world, we still have enormous problems, but we're working on them, and we're making some progress. I mean, peace, well, the President of the United States is in the White House working on this most of his time. And we have a part in this, really, to see that all people have a decent life.

On March 15, 1977, *The Ball State Daily News* ran this story by staff reporter Anthony Flint:

> Billy Carter stood outside the family business grimacing at the downtown sights, congested with out-of-state motorists, and quickly returned inside the Carter peanut warehouse. The incident went unnoticed in hectic Plains, George, now booming with assorted Presidential spin-offs.
>
> Plains is an interesting proposition for American enterprise since its number one citizen, Jimmy Carter, became President of the Untied States.
>
> The tiny town has more people on its streets than in its homes.
>
> At the White Plains Baptist Church the green lawn has become trampled from daily tourists taking photographs.
>
> Old red brick general stores and clapboard restaurants are full with Carter postcards, copies of the inauguration speech, prints of the President and his family, even anastigmatic shots of townsfolk with Jimmy or Rosalynn or Chip or Miss Lillian.
>
> Carter Country tours go through the flat lands where Jimmy once raised the family peanuts or where Billy steered a tractor into a ditch.
>
> Down at the depot a big green and white banner says: PLAINS, GEORGIA, HOME OF JIMMY CARTER, OUR PRESIDENT. The word "NEXT" was eliminated after the November election.
>
> Billy's rundown Amoco station is constantly flooded with Yankee motorists who spot the "Billy Carter's Service Station" sign above the faded white business establishment. Big RVs and sporty compacts drive by the Carter home that is now guarded by the secret service.
>
> The water tower with Old Glory painted on it hosts television relays for national networks which are assured news events until at least 1980.
>
> The luring qualities are certainly no mystery in Plans, Georgia. Here Jimmy Carter slept, farmed, campaigned, and probably lusted here, and that brings together the capitalist and the curious amidst a national notoriety too tempting not to sell history with hustle.
>
> And Billy tried to stop it. He was the one who said the town is going to hell, and with much gusto, ran for mayor to stop it.

Anthony Flint was 25 years old in 1979, the year of the Islamic Revolution in Iran. That was when the Shah of Iran, Muhammad Reza Shah Pahavi, fled to the United States as militants toppled his government and put in a new leader who was in exile, the Ayatollah Ruhollah Khomeini. But when the U.S. refused to extradite the Shah, the U.S. Embassy in Teheran was seized, and 66 American citizens were held as hostages.

President Jimmy Carter ordered a secret mission in April of 1980 to rescue the hostages with a daring military operation. It involved the use of helicopters to fly more than 400 miles over the desert at night. Secretary of State, Cyrus Vance, opposed the mission and resigned before news reached the White House that aircraft had crashed into the sand and lives were lost.

The hostages would be released on Inauguration Day for Ronald Reagan in 1981—eight months later. But from his desk at the Indiana Bureau of *The Cincinnati Enquirer*, Flint sent a letter to the President on April 26, 1980, which said, in part:

Please accept these brief words on my behalf for your administration's gallant attempt to free our American hostages held in Tehran. As a print journalist in the great state of Indiana, I can only express my gratitude, admiration and respect in the hard realities of this rescue plan.

Our allies here and abroad may contradict such humanitarian action, and the Communist bloc nations may misconstrue an aggressive military posture here in American. I believe your willingness to face the many great risks, uncertainties, and geopolitics was a terribly harsh and yet necessary response by you and your top senior advisors.

Although there were lives lost in the Iranian sand, we can now know that Americans will still come to the aid of their countrymen in times of urgent international stress. And I feel I have witnessed a most impressive statement of the American spirit in my lifetime.

The reply from President Carter was this:

The White House
Washington
April 30, 1980

To Anthony Flint:

Thank you for your message of support following the mission which was going to rescue our fellow Americans held hostage in Iran. I deeply appreciate your understanding and your kind words of encouragement.

The unity and the prayers of the American people are important to me as I carry out my manifold responsibilities to all our citizens. I was pleased to hear from you.

With best wishes,
Sincerely,

Jimmy

Carter became the first elected President to lose his bid for reelection since Herbert Hoover in 1932. In 2002, however, he won the Nobel Peace Prize for what he accomplished after leaving the White House.

Chapter 13: Church

In 1966, Donald Hamilton made his first drive up the lane on the 40-acre farm in Dalton Township. He was a student from David Liscomb College in Nashville, Tennessee—not far from Vanderbilt University. That summer the backseat and trunk of his car were nearly full of Bibles, commentaries, lessons, audio cassettes and other religious materials from the Southwestern Publishing Company, also in Nashville.

It was intended by Southwestern to enlist young college students like Donald Hamilton to sell the Word of God north of the Mason-Dixon line. But this was always different with the Flint family that easily befriended Don and supported everything he did. At his wedding in 1970 to the former Ann Crittenden, of Madison, Tennessee, the invited guests from Indiana included Keith and Beverly Flint and the congregation from the Southside Church of Christ.

Most book sales for the Southwestern Publishing Company were not followed by home-cooked meals on the dinner tables of grateful customers. Or even home-made ice cream for dessert. The company also didn't expect its sales force to attend church services with customers on a regular basis. But the Flints saw Don Hamilton as an older brother to their three young sons on the Indiana farm. They made sure he could hang his Sunday best with closet space always available for him.

He was a Son of the South who stopped at each home on LaMar Road to closeout a good week in Wayne County, Indiana. Everything was by the book. Hamilton had proper accounting records as far as Southwestern was concerned. Good selling techniques. Timely inventory. A tendency to make friends with people who answer the door.

This was his last stop for the day. He saw the weeping willow trees, a tall Chinese elm and a pair of maple trees with beautiful canopies providing an abundance of shade for the house on the farm.

His decision was made behind the wheel as he approached the mailbox on the side of the road with a small red reflector and the name K.D. FLINT on top. He looked up the lane and noticed the fresh-cut grass and the fence rows free of tall weeds.

As he rolled his window down, Hamilton could still smell the hay chaff in the fields on either side of the lane. All of the alfalfa was recently cut and bailed and stacked away in the barn for the winter. No doubt he looked north and saw the rows planted with soybeans which, at that time of the year, always shined with a golden brown color under the afternoon sun.

Nobody in the Flint family remembers who greeted Don first at the front door. It had to be one of the boys. Keith Flint was in the barn, working on something that had to fixed on the Farmall H tractor. Soon enough he would spot the small white car parked in the driveway with a rebel license plate from the State of Tennessee.

Beverly Flint on that day was on one of her trips to town that were usually combined with stops at the dry cleaners and buying the groceries. It was also after school. The boys were watching television in the living room. To make his introduction, Donald Hamilton gently knocked on the screen door and smiled when he spoke. The boys heard a southern drawl nearly typecast from Hollywood. It was welcome, friendly and disarming as it was supposed to be. This was a good start. The 40-acre farm would not see a home security system for the rest of the 20th century.

Now halting his repairs on the tractor in the barn, Keith Flint headed to the house and joined his sons to meet Don Hamilton. They all ended up standing in the driveway, and where they could begin by talking about the weather. What else? The past summer was not too wet and not too dry. It was a good year for seeds, fertilizer, pesticides, and the whole cycle of farming.

Keith Flint said it was all very much like an intricate puzzle that each generation of farmers would study and worship fervently for the crops to be harvested. Hamilton agreed and said no one would ever have all the pieces all the time.

Hamilton also gave every growing indication that the Flint's of Hagestown, Indiana, would not be a family that he would have to write down to remember. Hamilton wouldn't need to refer to his sales receipts. He also said he didn't need any maps of Wayne County to find them, either.

Flint and his brothers were baptized at the Southside Church of Christ on February 22, 1972. It was on a Thursday night, with no one else in the church except the brothers, their parents and the minister. With the congregation absent, there was also nobody present that night to sing the song of invitation.

What happened to the brothers the next morning was nothing at all. Flint remembers sitting in band and wondering if he were now a new creature like the minister often described in his sermons. A creature that was free of sin. Flint hadn't even thought about it, but the baptismal certificate linked his name with Jesus Christ. It was a union that was mysterious with every reader of the Bible. No one with a baptismal certificate understands it fully. Yet the baptisms of Anthony, Eugene and Clark were not unexpected. Keith Flint was an elder at the Southside Church of Christ. The father of Beverly Flint, Harold Clark, was also a Church of Christ elder. There was also Jason and Agnes Brown, the aunt and uncle who were lifetime members of the Church of Christ in Lynn, Indiana.

Keith and Beverly Flint were always ready for the baptismal year and the doctrine and Sunday worship and Wednesday night prayer and even the Gospel meetings hosted by a visiting minister. Years later both parents attended church on vacations with Clark in Kentucky and Anthony in Florida. But not Eugene, a Southern Baptist in Houston, Texas.

Don Hamilton walked to the pulpit at the Southside Church of Christ on a Sunday morning during the last verse of "Faith of Our Fathers." He asked the congregation to be seated. His sermon, as Flint could remember it decades later, was about man's ultimate preparation to meet God.

The Bible describes the Christian's work much like the labors of a man in a vineyard. Vines that produce fruit are frequently trimmed, always maintained. Other vines that are impotent are cut and summarily cast into the fire. No greater analogy than this exists that best describes any man who is not preparing to meet the Almighty.

Don quoted other Bible verses to show unprofitable servants who disobeyed God for not using their talents and time in a vineyard that is the world itself, and which was created to show the power and glory of God. The Prodigal Son was also used to show how a man who had no plan in the beginning—except to spend his inheritance as he liked it—returned to his home and father with a heart full of repentance and sorrow.

It would be like a minister who comes to Sunday services and hasn't prepared a lesson to preach. What would that be like? There was silence as Don paused for untested emphasis at the pulpit. Then he stepped down and walked back to the pew where he sat down next to his wife, Ann. She suddenly had an alarming look on her face. The congregation became very still now. No one knew what to do or say next. Don remained seated.

97

The song leader decided to get up and lead the congregation in the invitational. Flint couldn't remember if anyone came forward that day to accept Jesus Christ as their personal Savior. He was only 14 in 1968 and was actually formulating plans of his own to ask Carey Wheeler to sit with him in church next Sunday. However, the sight of the preacher stepping down after speaking for only 10 minutes—why, that was truly a powerful point to ponder. It lasted longer on the minds of most people that day than Don's continued employment as the minister of the church.

He always considered himself a lecturer, but he moved on to a Christian school and became superintendent. It was a plan of action that proved practical as evidenced by the letters the Flint's received from Don. This was new work in the vineyard.

Everyone in the Flint family wanted to see God someday. This was a message that was reassuring, for all of its profound implications. Flint seemed to trust his own curiosity. After all, he had not died and gone to his maker, and he could not realize how the abyss between earth and heaven could be traversed, and in such a way that he really wanted his number to come up.

Not that he wanted to be left behind. Flint had images of a burring hell in his mind ever since he was a little child. This was not the place to spend eternity, so heaven was it. This didn't take a rocket scientist to figure it out.

In church Flint would hear family and friends talk about seeing God in heaven with the angels and with Abraham and Moses and the Apostles. Flint could picture it, somewhat, and he could also see a reunion with loved ones who died a long time ago.

Again, it was not a desire that was easily definable. Money could not buy it. And it most certainly was a one-way trip—that, according to those who took the pulpit on Sundays to preach from the scriptures and verse of the Holy Bible itself.

Whether Flint accepted heaven as being up in the sky was only part of the problem. The misunderstandings about the kingdom of God seemed rampant 2,000 years ago, when a majority of Christ's disciples wanted a powerful revolt against the Roman Empire. They saw Jesus Christ as the new Emperor of the Jewish world.

But a spiritual kingdom was a concept that was easily lost during the teachings of 1st century Christianity. Each generation and most believers had God in heaven with infinite power and wisdom—the source of the Universe itself. Yet a power that was not yet ready to call all the children of Man to the

Judgement Throne. There was still time for people to read the Bible and wonder about the image of God and walk in his footsteps.

Anthony Flint decided years later to try the pulpit for himself and present a sermon to the congregation that worshiped with his family in central Florida. At that point, it was anyone's guess whether Flint was any good as a preacher. This was also a very tiny insight in the awesome responsibilities and accountability of a church minister.

Donald Hamilton married Clark and Cyndi Flint in the summer of 1984. The Hamiltons now lived in Kankakee, Illinois, but made it in time to attend the rehearsal dinner at the old Ryan's Steakhouse. Nobody in that reunion had seen each other in 15 years. The wedding and reception were both held at the Southside Church of Christ in New Castle, Indiana. Clark brought his own stereo speakers, cassette deck and selected music from the rock group Chicago just for the ceremony.

But it was the only wedding in the Flint family that saw one of the boys take a bride from the home church. This was the one that was the source of four male heirs to the Flint family name. Everything was done on schedule. Bride and groom exchanged their vows, and the best man made his toast audible enough for all the family and guests to hear. Earlier that week he wrote it down between classes at Indiana University. The newlyweds then proceeded to head west to honeymoon in California and visit the sites of the summer Olympic games in L.A.

Keith and Beverly Flint celebrated their 50th wedding anniversary at the Southside Church of Christ, on June 8, 2002. The day, also, when their oldest son pulled out in front of a car and was suddenly another traffic incident report for the Henry County Sheriff's Department. He was slammed on the driver's side of his silver 1999 Mercury Sable SL. The force of the impact pushed him across the road into a large muddy field. A wreck that happened in front of his home church, and where his wife was still decorating the beautiful cake inside the new fellowship hall.

There was no pain at all in the very beginning, when he pulled himself out on the passenger side and began to limp toward the couple in the second vehicle. No one was hurt badly that day. That was a miracle and, if nothing else, was what he wanted to tell his daughter when she was older.

Beginning with the anniversary in the fellowship hall in New Castle, then the family group pictures that included his wife and daughter. And Clark and his wife and four sons. There was also Eugene from Houston and Dee Anne Jackson from Gilbert, Arizona, a cousin and a genealogist who found 400 years of family ancestors all by herself.

Anthony's family made the trip with his parents to the airport in Dayton, Ohio. They said their goodbyes and then encountered a lengthy check-in because of the heightened national security from all the terrorist acts against the United States in 2001. Other airports around the world were no different, with many one-way flights and passengers with multiple pieces of luggage receiving the most inspections.

Flint flew home with his family to Orlando after a connecting flight in Atlanta. The car was left in Indiana for the work estimates and the repairs that lasted for six weeks. It was all fixed for $6,878.55. This included, but was not limited to, new headlamps, fender panels, wheel fronts, tie rods, steering column, door trim, mirrors, tail lamps, rear bumpers, sheet metal and refinish.

In 1966, the only grandmother Flint had ever known had died in Spencer, Indiana. Madeline Clark was the mother of Joan Hines and Beverly Flint, and a telephone operator who once worked in Hagerstown. The phone numbers she was responsible for had only four digits; and there was not a single area code in the whole country to dial. She also had an apartment at one time. This was where Flint watched *Bonanza* with her on a Sunday night. One episode was all about Hoss Cartwright finding a real leprechaun on the Ponderosa ranch. Flint remembers watching the program on grandmother's color television set.

The members of the congregation of the church brought food to the small kitchen on the 40-acre farm. Enough to feed the Twelve Tribes of Israel. It was probably the oldest memory of the church that Flint has to this day. Everyone was bringing covered dishes through the house and setting them on the table and all the available counter space. Everything, it seemed, under the sun.

Chapter 14: The Bellamy Brothers

Howard Bellamy was late for the press conference scheduled that morning on the 2,500-acre cattle ranch northeast of Tampa, Florida. He was, in fact, attending to the birth of a new calf—something the Bellamy family has done on this land in Pasco County for over 100 years. But the press conference was about the music thing with his brother, David; and Anthony Flint was there.

QUESTION: The Bellamy Brothers join Alabama, The Oak Ridge Boys and the Statler Brothers as nominations for vocal group of 1983.

DAVID BELLAMY: There is no real criteria as far as song writing is concerned. As a matter of fact, we're not even choosy if we write it or not. If we write a good song, we try to record it. If we run across a good song, we try to record it.

HOWARD BELLAMY: You know, I think after you've done it so long everything comes so gradually to you in this business. It did to us, anyway. And there have been groups that actually hyped into the situation pretty fast. But in our situation, it's been quite gradual, and it was a shock the first time they told us, you know, that we had more number one country songs than any dual in the history of county music.

DAVID BELLAMY: We generally decide all our singles and all of our album cuts and all of the album covers. We have input from Warner Brothers and from Nashville, but it's usually down to me and Howard. They let us do it so if it doesn't work out they can blame us.

QUESTION: You wrote "Spiders and Snakes" for another native Floridian—Jim Stafford.

DAVID BELLAMY: Me and Howard came in one night, and Howard woke up with a chicken snake in the bed with him...

HOWARD BELLAMY: (laughing) First snake I ever woke up with!

DAVID BELLAMY: ...and I thought it was real funny because it didn't happen to me. That's basically where that song came from. I wrote it totally and then got it to Jim, and Jim wanted to rewrite it for himself. We recorded it on our *Sons of the Sun* album, and that's pretty close to the way Jim and I ended up doing it. Only, it's a little bit more swampy, musically, I think, than his version was.

("Spiders and Snakes" sold three million copies worldwide for Jim Stafford. That was a mega hit. The Bellamy Brothers moved to L.A., where Howard worked as the road manager for Stafford and lived in his home with David. They had access to Stafford's basement studio; but, even better, they were playing with other musicians including the drummer and a roadie with Neil Diamond's Band. It was then when the Bellamy Brothers first heard the song, "Let Your Love Flow.")

QUESTION: "Let Your Love Flow" was number one in ten countries in Europe.

DAVID BELLAMY: Well, in seventy-six, things took off real well for us in Europe. We never had the slumps in Europe that we had here. We had a couple of slumps here. And although now they don't seem like much, at the time they were pretty bad, and we didn't have that problem in Europe. Everything was so good there, we considered moving there and signing a record deal.

Now we haven't been off the road in seven years. And we don't ever really stop. I don't go over to Howard's room in the hotel, and we don't ever sit down and say, "Hey, have we made it yet."

QUESTION: You record your albums here on the ranch?

DAVID BELLAMY: We have a little studio here. We recorded two of our albums here, the *When We Were Boys* album and the *Strong Weakness* album. The new stuff we're recording in Miami just because they have the new technology there that we don't have available here. But when we record here, we bring in remote trucks with a complete studio. Obviously, you know, there's three or four million dollars worth of equipment in a 24-track recording studio, which for one artist to use that, you know, is crazy. And we record for two or three weeks with the remote truck here, and when we're through, they pull away and we keep the tapes.

QUESTION: What is your favorite song by The Bellamy Brothers?
DAVID BELLAMY: I would say that "You Ain't Just Whistlin' Dixie" might be the best song by me—I've been trying to top it ever since, and I doubt I've done it.
HOWARD BELLAMY: Probably a song called "I'm Making Music, Mama." It was never released as a single, but it's on one of our albums. I like that song a lot.
DAVID BELLAMY: You don't find that many good ones. Every time we come home, our office is full of tapes. We do try to listen to them because you really don't know where you will find a good song.

Chapter 15: Post Office

Keith Flint was postmaster for Hagesrtown, Indiana, from 1953 to 1988. In the beginning, he was only part-time help and still holding down a full-time job with the telephone company. He was always willing to work at the local post office on holidays and even greet the sheer volume of mail in the last weeks and days before Christmas. It was literally stacked to the ceiling. This was also mail that had to be sorted by hand without the advent of zip codes.

He made his own letter slots at home on 20 Woodlawn Drive to practice sorting the mail. The easy deliveries included the local piston ring factory, the high school, the elementary school and Hagerstown's most famous citizen. This was one way to assure himself that he would not always remain as part-time help. And he would come to know almost everyone with an address in town over the next three decades. He also learned about next-of-kin, birthdays and whether or not a family on Sycamore Street was away for summer vacation. So it was the kind of customer database that would make Sam Walton proud. Not to mention the Postmaster General of the United States of America.

The post office itself was one of the largest buildings in Hagerstown ever since its dedication in 1932. It was built under the WPA of President Franklin D. Roosevelt with plenty of limestone, tile roofs, marble floors and a customer service counter with a large marble countertop.

All patrons could hear the echoes of their footsteps as they walked across the marble floor of the lobby to the customer service counter. The frequent "bang" from someone hand-stamping mail would also produce a loud echo throughout the building. And from the counter, one could see the post office carriers sorting the mail or stacking the mailbags on carts to be taken out through the double doors in the back of the room.

There were also a series of small rectangular slots near the ceiling. They were openings used by postal inspectors, but Anthony Flint thought it was something more diabolical than that when he was still a little boy. He made sure he didn't lick his stamp first until his money was safely in the hands of the clerk at the counter.

The southside of the building had large steps leading up to the front entrance, and there was sufficient room surrounding the main doors to place tables or loudspeakers for public events. This was quite versatile as a stage that was elevated enough for judges to review the Jubilee Day parades, or citizens to sit down and hear the piston ring factory band in concert on Main Street.

It was really the center of attention when Hagerstown placed its time capsule at the base of the flagpole in 1976. Main Street was closed along a 2-block area adjoining the post office building. Patriotic streamers in red, white and blue decorated the stage at the top of the post office steps. And the dignitaries each stepped up to the microphone to honor America's bicentennial celebration. One of them was Keith Flint. He always remembered how quiet the town had become in that moment of time.

During the week leading up to his father's retirement, Anthony Flint wanted to take his video camera and film from the roof of the post office building. This was his idea to create a dramatic opening; and it would show the town as it was when his father was still postmaster. But getting to the top of the building was an interesting proposition, to say the least. First, he followed his father through the mail room and up the stairs to the second floor. Then there was another flight of stairs leading into a large area where one could see the wood rafters of the roof itself.

They followed a short catwalk above a deep layer of insulation to the end, and Anthony waited while his father pulled on a chain to open the small door that was above their heads. Now they could see the blue sky. It only remained for Anthony to climb up the metal ladder and make his way through. But it was like emerging from the hatch of a submarine after surfacing in the North Atlantic Ocean. The cold March air seemed more of a reality than it was when he was on the ground. And he buttoned his jacket because the wind made him feel like he was standing on the peak of an iceberg.

Under these conditions, he began a panoramic sweep with his video camera on the roof of the Hagerstown post office. He saw the Hagerstown Public Library, still nestled with the brown trees of winter, and then the building where his grandmother once answered the calls as a telephone operator. He could also see the pharmacy, the furniture store, the dentist's office, the savings and loan and even the empty lot that was once the site of the circus tent used by the Nettle Creek Players. And so he could see his hometown like he could never see it before.

Keith Flint backed his tractor out of the barn one very cold morning and headed down the lane with snow blowing across the 40-acre farm. He looked both ways before inching slowly on the drifting LaMar Road and then he was careful not to steer far from the center of the road. And he never saw any on-coming traffic for five miles as he traveled mostly to the south and through a white world of endless nothing.

Flint's Farmall H tractor should be considered here more closely with all the tractors in the fields today. It did not have a cab. No heat. No CD player. No radio. No power steering. Not even a geographic positioning system. So it really was a hard journey in the blowing snow, dressed in the heaviest garments he could find to survive the arctic air, and to open the lobby and clear the counter for the first customer of the day at the Hagerstown post office.

Dedication was surely something that was a special part of Keith Flint. It was a challenge to him to do his job as well as he could under any circumstance that was documented in postal regulations that often created great postmasters. Of course, no where was it written that you had to use your own tractor to arrive at work in the worst weather on the planet. And no where was it written that a postmaster was ever supposed to accept challenges—no matter how dedicated—from the local newspaper editor.

There are positions in local towns that are role models—the police chief, the school superintendent, the postmaster and the local newspaper editor. It was entirely possible that any one of these could have accepted the challenge and even become the hero of the hour. But it was better that the postmaster do it and in such a way that the outcome would never be in doubt.

The challenge was made in the editor's own column of *The Hagerstown Exponent*. And only after the editor was a guest of the postmaster to see how mail is sorted with modern automation in the bigger post offices like the ones in Muncie or in Indianapolis. The bigger offices handled the mail from the smaller offices, and it was all efficient as clockwork, really. This made a good impression with the editor. He wrote his first story and said so, and his pictures on the tour were the kind of public relations that corporate management could hardly get for free.

Then there was another story about the editor and the postmaster and the friendships that prevailed between them for many years. And like any good thing, there is opportunity, more often than not, to push the envelope to see what really happens, which was literally the case here. And so the editor agreed again in print how efficient and orderly the mail-sorting system was on the day of his visit.

And now came his challenge: What would happen if a letter was mailed in an envelope with only a 9-digit zip code? With no other forwarding address? And no return address? And would the envelope make its way through the mails at all?

The editor concluded by asking the postmaster if he was willing to see this thing out. He could use the editor's own column to comment, one way or another. And if the envelope reaches its destination, then all is well in the universe. The system works fine, and for that, everyone should be thankful. But if the letter never sees the light of day?

Anthony Flint couldn't remember what the consequences were to his father if the editor's letter was never delivered. But he did know that he accepted the challenge and the editor's determination that the letter not be mailed from anywhere in Hagerstown. The editor didn't trust the local post office because he knew the postmaster might interfere somehow and deliver the piece of mail himself. It had to be dropped off somewhere else, somewhere in the great American network that was the United States Postal Service. Keith Flint knew this to be true, but he also would bet that the editor mailed his letter not that far away, simply because he knew the editor's dislikes for long trips in the car.

Thus there followed a sequence of events whereby employees of the United States Postal Service handled the letter and sorted it through the automated systems. Their comments, if any, were not known. But it would be curious to see a plain white envelope with only the following numbers on the outside: 47346-0111. Yet this envelope would be part of the mail volume for that day, and it was really not that conspicuous. After all, there were no flammable or hazardous contents. The postage was also correct. And so were the numbers that matched the 9-digit zip code assigned to *The Hagerstown Exponent* in Hagerstown, Indiana.

Police Chief Carl Allen drives down Main Street in Hagerstown, Indiana, on the night of March 13, 1988. This was not a typical evening that saw people standing in line outside Guy Welliver's Fabulous Smorgasbord. One of the banquet rooms inside was filled with postal employees who wanted to wish a fellow colleague well in his new role as a Federal retiree.

Allen had read the front-page story in *The Hagerstown Exponent* that told its readers about the retirement of postmaster Keith Flint, who wanted to go while the stamp was still 25 cents! *Good for him,* Allen thought. The police chief would go on and serve as town manager in a new city hall and retire in the next millennium. But his job tonight was to keep his department alert on the limited parking. This was almost like dealing with race fans during the month of May. They always made their way to Hagerstown and the Smorgasbord before heading on to the Indianapolis Motor Speedway.

Between Carl Allen and Keith Flint, they had more than 60 years in total service to this east-central Indiana town. Both were veterans who served their country in times of war. And both men were interviewed by Anthony Flint. For the police chief, it was a story in the *Exponent* on June 26, 1974, with pictures featuring Allen's extensive scale-model railroad in the basement of his house. And Anthony's father would have recurring roles in his son's novel published in the first half of the next century.

TOM FETTY, NATIONAL ASSOCIATION OF POSTMASTERS: I did think "What in the world can you say enough about Keith Flint?" He's been "Mr. Everything" to us. Mr. NAPUS. Mr. Postmaster. He's been a Mister by almost any title you can think of. He's been nothing but a gentleman, a scholar—in his work, with his family. He's been a real swell fellow that's just done a lot. I envy you. I really do. You really retired at an age that you can enjoy it. I do wish you the best.

(Applause from the audience).

BEN GRIFFIN, POSTMASTER, MARION, INDIANA: I remember first associating with Keith and his wife at the 1983 national postmasters' convention in Puerto Rico. I think we rode clear across the island in the same van from San Juan to Ponce. Right warm day, as I remember.

(Applause from the audience).

BETSY POLK, WIDOW OF THE FORMER POSTMASTER: The Hagerstown post office has always been very, very dear to me. I came in 1950 and married my husband then, and he was with this post office for 45 years. Keith came in 1953. His family is very much a part of my family. When Anthony walked in tonight with his parents, I couldn't help but remember Keith's three sons. They were our post office kids. I would see them come in and wait on their dad, and I watched them grow up over the years to come. I want to wish Keith and Beverly the very best, and I'm glad that you are here tonight, Anthony.

(Applause from the audience).

DON BOXER, POSTMASTER, MUNCIE, INDIANA: In addition to all of you being good managers, you are also good friends to me. I recall the day when Keith was sworn in as postmaster in 1953. Among the many accomplishments he's done, the energy awards, the wellness awards, the efficiency awards—what I will remember most of all is your friendship and your loyalty to the United States Postal Service.

(Applause from the audience).

JOHN NEWCOMBE, POSTMASTER, RICHMOND, INDIANA: Keith, I think your retirement has shown us all how well we worked together as a team. Seventy people here tonight is just wonderful. We have this book here that we want to present to you. We know you are a great Civil War buff. Everyone has signed this book—it's Harper's Pictorial History of the Civil War. It has a lot of reading in it. It also has dozens of illustrations and pictures about the war. We all want you to have this.

(Applause from the audience).

JOHN NEWCOMBE, POSTMASTER, NEW CASTLE, INDIANA: You started in the post office before I was even born!

(Laughter from the audience).

PART THREE

Chapter 16: USS *Cony*

John Fitzgerald Kennedy was not yet President of the United States of America. At the naval shipyard in Boston, and before a crew standing at ease in dress whites, he was still only a young but rich congressman from Massachusetts. The speaker who would commission a Fletcher Class DDE warship on November 17, 1949. He was, however, a former Navy officer in World War II. His PT boat was rammed by the Japanese destroyer Amagiri, in the early morning of August 2, 1943. Then there was so much force in the collision that the surrounding waters were suddenly covered by flaming fuel in a matter of seconds.

What happened for the next 30 hours was this: Kennedy swam in the Blackett Strait off the Solomon Islands, bringing his men from the floating hulk of the PT boat to the shores of an island. Then he plunged back into the water and swam for miles in an effort to intercept another PT boat on patrol.

It was a great war adventure that would recruit an Admiral. Certainly it played a part in the career plans of one man who joined the Navy nine days after his honorable discharge as a U.S. Marine. After first enlisting with the Corps in July of 1946, he began his 11-week boot camp training at Paris Island, S.C., and then served as a Marine for three years. But something was still missing.

So it was that Keith Flint was assigned to the USS *Cony* DDE 508, a destroyer commissioned by Kennedy that would do combat in the Korean Conflict. The ship measured approximately 300 feet in length and was, in fact, close quarters for the crew of 250 men. Each sailor was scheduled for the firing line for 15 days with six hours on duty. They spent the time off duty doing other jobs on the *Cony* like storekeeper of the ship—that was Keith Flint. He was responsible for the books and ordered supplies for the recruits.

Much of the time on the ship was spent in surveillance to help protect U.S. battleships in the area. This was often dull, even mundane work. The *Cony* also happened to be typical for ships of that time: there was no air conditioning, and the crew had to find a place up on the deck just to sleep in some comforts. Yet it was the adventure of a lifetime, and Keith Flint traveled the globe on the USS *Cony* to see Singapore, Colombo, the Persian Gulf, Marseilles, France, Gibraltar, the Azores and northern Italy. As the years went by, Flint served in the Pacific Theatre in Japan, Guam and Korea. He could see the makings of the Cold War firsthand.

Naval forces of the United Nations moved into battle positions off both coasts of North Korea in late October of 1951. This was nearly 16 months since the invasion of South Korea by North Korea, and the UN's historic first use of military action to repel an aggressor. To do so, however, required a coalition of armed contingents from South Korea, the United States, Australia, Belgium, Luxembourg, Canada, Colombia, Ethiopia, France, Great Britain, Greece, the Netherlands, New Zealand, the Philippines, South Africa, Thailand and Turkey, with medical units from Denmark, India and Sweden.

All of the participating ground forces from these nations were grouped in the U.S. Eighth Army. This created part of the unified UN forces headed by the United States Commander-in-Chief in the Far East, General Douglas MacArthur. It was MacArthur who was ordered to fight a limited international war involving the combat readiness of the United States and 19 UN allies.

Bad weather for three straight days cleared on this Saturday for the air operations of Task Force 77. This began with navy pilots from the USS *Essex* and the USS *Antietam* blasting railroad cars and knocking out four gun positions north of the City of Hungnam. Hungnam was once a small fishing village until the 1920s, and then it was developed by the Japanese into a large port and industrial center in the South Hamgyong Province. The city was a major UN target because of the manufacturing of petroleum products, primary metals, chemicals and textiles.

Other flights from the carrier Sydney bombed and destroyed buildings at Yonan and near Haeju and strafed troops along the north bank of the Han River. The air battles on this day would be tailed to the total war effort and the ultimate loss of some 900 aircraft. This was especially true in the so-called MiG Alley over the northwestern skies of North Korea.

The Communist pilots flew MiG-15s, jets built by the Soviet Union. Supersonic aircraft was used for the first time in the Korean Conflict. The MiG-15 was generally regarded as the best jet aircraft to fly over the Korean peninsula, superior even to the formidable F-86 Sabres. This American aircraft was only available after a crash program was put together in the United

States to make them.

Hungnam was on North Korea's east coast, along the Sea of Japan. It was systematically pounded by UN air power and devastated by the end of the war. Many North Korean coastal points were instrumental in the support of North Korea's ground forces. Either they were primarily supply lines using airfields to reach Communist troops or they were industrial centers using hydroelectric plants to energize war factories.

Now one of the first to unleash its firepower from off the coast today was the USS *Helena* and the destroyer *Eversole*, both shelling marshalling yards in the Sinpo area. Next they steamed to Songjin to blast bridges, shore batteries and enemy troops. Another unit followed and was led by the cruiser HMS *Belfast* to shell enemy infantry positions between Sogwanni and Monggumpori on the Changsangot peninsula.

Other west coast Communist targets were blasted by the HMS *Blackswan* and the New Zealand frigate, *Taupo*. They fired on eight large groups of enemy troops camped near the Han River. And the destroyers *Storme's* and *Reinshaw* joined in firing through fog and mist at targets in the Wonsan area—south of Hungnam—while the Thailand frigate *Bangpakong* patrolled off the other harbor.

The USS *Conway* hit hard at vital railroads and highways leading into Hungnam. Other Task Force 95 ships bombarded similar targets at Songjin, Chuuronjang, Tunamdong and near Nanam. The destroyer escort *Moore* picked off a railroad bride south of Songjin and the USS *Cony* battered a concrete bridge and shelled a troop headquarters in the northern sector.

Some of today's bombardment could easily have been redirected to the city of Kaesong, which was not far from the South Korean border. But Kaesong was the site of the intermittent peace talks between the UN representatives and the Communist commands. The preparatory talks began in June of 1951, at the urging of the Soviet delegate to the UN, but open discussions started on July 10. There was mutual suspicion most of the time and a major stumbling block: a prisoner of war should not be returned against his will to his respective army.

Negotiations at Kaesong would break down completely a year from now. Not until April of 1953, in late spring, did both sides finally agree that POWs unwilling to return to their own countries would be placed in the custody of a neutral commission. This was good for 90 days following the signing of the truce agreement and it gave each nation time to persuade its nationals to come home.

When the final peace accord came in July of 1953, it was not signed and sealed soon enough to save the lives of 157,530 casualties suffered in the U.S. ranks. It also did not save the lives of an estimated 2 million Communist soldiers. No one was even able to calculate the economic or social damage to the Korean nations.

None of the missing or dead were ever known by the crew of the USS *Cony*. They all would live to see their ship fire its guns into distant horizons, survive tempests at sea, and speed endless days in far corners of the world. This was often done with the realization by each sailor that America was the greatest military might in the history of the world.

They never did know how much power they really had on deck—more so than a thousand chariots of Pharaoh's or even a million foot soldiers in the Roman Empire. As an amateur historian, Keith Flint had no trouble studying military history and coming to terms—with the power to wage war—of what even one ship can do. Examples came to mind like the Civil War ironclads, *Monitor* and *Merimack*; the German battleship *Bismarck*; or the USS *Enterprise*, America's first nuclear-powered aircraft carrier. The crews that manned them could certainly attest to that.

There was significant change in firepower for the *Cony* when the forward 5-inch gun mount was removed during the Korean War. This was replaced with a Mk 15 trainable anti-submarine warfare (ASW) hedgehop projector and was fired from circular portals in the midships deck house. Also installed were triple tube Mk 32 ASW torpedo launchers that fired either the Mk 44 or Mk 46 ASW acoustic homing torpedo. But only three Fletcher Class ships actually completed the FRAM program updates: DDE 446, 447 and 449. And besides the Weapon Alpha and other ASW weapons upgrades, they had a Variable Depth Sonar (VDS) hoist on the stern along with the VDS array itself.

But the *Cony* was still a ship afloat, vulnerable to any attack. More than once, the lookout on the bridge of the *Cony* spotted a mine. This prompted the sailors on the 20-MM guns to immediately blow it up. The North Koreans were known to use fishing boats at night as a ploy to lay mines off shore where navy ships were patrolling. The next day the *Cony* went to a nearby fishing village. The crew at Keith Flint's battle station opened fire from the three-and-a-half-inch mounted guns and destroyed the entire fleet of fishing vessels.

It was no contest. And radar showed no enemy aircraft approaching the scene. The *Cony* also did not expect much resistance, if any, from the targets.

Flint and the crew of the *Cony* could only imagine the havoc this bombardment was making. They remained safely off shore. But they could see the orange hue from their shells exploding on impact. Then the debris of small boats and the surrouding water suddenly gushed high into the air. And it was scattered over a wide area. It looked much like the aftermath from an angry child—stomping his toys to pieces on the floor of his bedroom.

The sound of the blasting itself was deafening enough to leave bystanders on shore sometimes unconscious. Or suffering a sever or complete loss of hearing. And any North Korean solider hiding in one of those tiny boats, possibly to ambush a UN patrol, was surely a dead duck by now. It didn't seem possible that anyone could survive this kind of attack.

More rounds of shells were fired and the explosions and debris and water shooting up like geysers was repeated over and over. It was inevitable that there would be nothing left in the end. Not even for salvage efforts from the local villages trying to earn a small profit. It had to be destruction so complete that the moral of the North Korean solider was as low as any of these sinking boats.

Today reminded Keith Flint of General William Tecumseh Sherman and his decisive Civil War campaign through Georgia in 1864. Sherman led 60,000 Union troops from Atlanta on a march to the Atlantic Ocean. Each man had tacit license to plunder, maraud and pillage. Nothing useful was to be left for the Confederate enemy along a 50-mile-wide path of destruction. And when concluding his dispatch that announced the capture of Atlanta, General Sherman added:

We have, as the result of this quick, and I think well executed movement, twenty-seven guns, over three thousand prisoners, and have buried over four hundred rebel dead and left as many wounded. They could not be removed. The rebels have lost, beside the important city of Atlanta and stores, at least five hundred dead, two thousand five hundred wounded, and three thousand prisoners, whereas our aggregate loss will not foot one thousand five hundred. If that is not success I don't know what is.

During the early 1960s, many Fletcher Class DDEs were sold for scrap, with only a few being retained with the Naval Reserve as training ships. These vessels would remain in active duty well into the 1970s. However, by the end of 1979 all of the U.S. Navy Fletchers had been retired forever.

All guns onboard the USS *Cony* were silent on Armistice Day, November 11, 1951. Yet all hands on deck were still ready as the warship crossed the Equator. This was not battle stations for any ship at sea, but many moments of frivolity and camaraderie that give credence to the old saying "boys will be boys." The orders for that day simply included a strict slate of events not that dissimilar from any initiation to a fraternity back in the States—except, of course, no one was actually killed.

The idea here was to keep the sailors alive long enough to face a mock court, a water dunk tank, and the "trumped-up charges" levied against 175 men of the *Cony* crew lowly enough to be called Pollywogs, and because none in their ranks had ever before crossed the Equator. That included Keith Flint, of New Castle, Indiana. This would all change late in the day when King Neptune himself ordained them officially as Shellbacks; and now and forever they too were veterans of the crossing of the Equator.

Keith Flint's many medals in honor of his military service included his United Nations Medal, Sharp Shooter Medal, Korean Medal, the Good Conduct Medal from both the Marines and the Navy, World War II Victory Medal, and two stars for serving in operations on both the East and West Coasts. He also was presented with a bronze medal by the Republic of South Korea that marked the 50th anniversary of the outbreak of the Korean War.

On Veteran's Day, November 10, 2001, Keith Flint told the *New Castle Courier-Times*: "Today's military are well-trained professionals. The armed forces now emphasize safety. They have corrected many of the problems aboard ship that sailors encountered during World War II and the Korean War. I guess my military career wasn't anything really heroic to some, but Veteran's Day always means so much to me."

PART FOUR

Chapter 17: At the Indiana Statehouse

Anthony Flint walked to the Indiana statehouse on his first day as the temperature hovered around zero on November 6, 1976. He made it inside from the parking lot and shook the snow off his coat. Then he looked again at his map to locate the small news bureau on the second floor. This was jointly shared by Gannet News Service, the *Louisville Courier-Journal* and the *Ball State Daily News*. There was room enough inside for the tables, chairs, typewriters, a water cooler and a secretary who answered the telephone and posted all the daily messages. A second room across the hall was used by the Indianapolis television stations as a studio for interviews with legislators or other news makers.

From the news bureau, Flint learned where to find offices and committee rooms used by the Indiana Legislature. So it was here where Anthony would spend the next three months working at his desk or attending journalism classes at the *Indianapolis Star and News* building. Flint had made arrangements to stay with a fellow journalism student who lived in Danville, Indiana. He would commute with Pat Herrmann each weekday to the statehouse in downtown Indianapolis. It was certainly "on-the-job training" for them, with real enough course studies in human nature.

This day was also an organizational meeting for the 99th session of the Indiana General Assembly. The Indiana Senate was very busy when it referred 355 bills to committees before adjourning at 2:30 p.m. One of them called for the repeal of the Indiana Higher Education Commission and was sponsored by the President Pro-Temp of the Senate. He said: "They are not accountable to the legislature or the Governor or any other consistency and therefore do not serve the entities for forming policies and allocating funds."

Over in the House of Representatives a child abuse bill was proposed by Dennis Avery, a Democrat from Evansville, and which would setup a statewide register to trace negligent or abusive parents. The bill would also allow public health officials to hold an abused child in emergency protective custody until an official protection order was obtained. And another bill sponsored by Robert D. Garton, a Republican from Columbus, would provide a hearing and a review process for each teacher in Indiana whose contract was not renewed by the local school corporation.

It was hard to imagine that inside the statehouse were all the people who passed the laws for the people of Indiana. Here were state senators, state representatives, career staff, lobbyists, the Lt. Governor and the Governor himself, who was also a medical doctor from Rochester, Indiana. Nevertheless, Otis R. Bowen was Governor of Indiana in 1976. He would go on and serve as United States Secretary of Health and Human Services in nine years. But his job now was to convince a joint session of the Indiana General Assembly to pass a "no-frills" budget. This was highlighted in the annual state of the state address when the Governor said: "This budget is not one which will woo friends with 'fast and loose' spending. It places a moratorium on new state spending."

Bowen's remarks covered property tax relief, unemployment, welfare and a warning that he would veto a budget package from the state legislature if it exceeded his recommendations. "I cannot accept more total spending than is projected by this project. If one is appropriated for one area, it must be subtracted from another or the entire budget is in danger. The question before all of us as responsible elected state officials, is whether or not we can maintain the prudent self-discipline that it is going to take to spend 'only a little.'"

Later, it wasn't hard for Flint to find a legislator who found fault with the Governor's conservative fiscal restraint. He was told by State Representative Leo A. Voisard, a Democrat from Muncie, how several economic factors over the last three years had created a state surplus of half a billion dollars. This was the result of numerous funds including, but not limited to, the property tax replacement fund, the general fund and the tuition reserve fund.

Voisard told Flint: "The Indiana Board of Tax Commissioners have continually cut city, county and township requests for budget surpluses with a philosophy being if it is there, then somebody will find a way to spend it." Voisard then used his own heating and oil company as an example of increased expenses without tax relief. He could show that his customers paid $17.50 for 100 gallons of oil in 1973. The State collected 35 cents for each gallon sold. But in 1976 the same purchase costed $40.50, with the State collecting $1.62 as sales tax per gallon.

Democrats like Voisard were not opposed to having a rainy day fund for Indiana that would be good for emergencies or other unexpected expenses.

But they didn't want to see surplus accumulating from state income, to be locked up in several state accounts. This was money that wasn't being spent any time soon and should go back to taxpayers in some form of tax refund.

The first sports story that Flint ever wrote in his life was on March 24, 1977, while a reporter for the *Ball State Daily News* in Indianapolis, Indiana. Inside the statehouse that day was 6'11" redhead, All-American center Kent Benson, the second all-time scorer from Indiana University, but first a Hoosier from New Castle, Indiana. He was a prolific athlete, something like 98 winning games during his collegiate career, totaling 1,740 points, and he was named the most valuable player in the 1976 NCAA men's basketball tournament.

Outside the office of Gov. Otis R. Bowen, Benson told Flint: "I didn't know how I would play my first year at IU, but the student body, the fans and everybody seemed supportive of me, and I worked hard for Coach Bobby Knight." His mother added: "There were so many things. I guess the NCAA championships is the best memory we have." His parents were standing with him, and so were his sisters: Kathy, 21; Karen, 17; Krista, 16; and younger brother Kim, 6'8", 210 pounds.

Earlier, as he was honored with a signed resolution, Benson told a joint session of the Indiana General Assembly: "What I am is the will of God. And what I do with myself is my will to God."

Arnold Miller was president of the United Mine Workers of America in 1976. He brought a group of miners to the statehouse in Indianapolis. Several miners were wearing yellow hard hats as they stood outside the television studio and watched Miller's press conference. It was some kind of protest, but Flint never had a chance to do a story on the Hoosier miners. What he did know about Miller and the UMWA was all about standing up for the rank-and-file. Miller himself was quite a fighter and won the presidency of the UMWA in 1971, after a bitter and costly campaign against the incumbent president, W.A. "Tony" Boyle.

No doubt Miller and the UMWA had traveled to Indianapolis on behalf of the Indiana coal miners and to keep the union membership very happy. More than a dozen counties in west-central and southwestern Indiana had coal mines and large numbers of local people who were members of the UMWA. What they felt was wrong or right was what Miller wanted to hear. And if they voted to shrike, then the picket lines would go up, and the mines were surely shut down.

Flint was always amazed at the number of groups who came to the statehouse to protest or lobby. Even the most veteran legislators were probably not completely at ease with the whole political process and would privately agree that anything accomplished in committee was a surprise to them. And who can forget the opening day as senators and representatives take their seats? The large floral arrangements, boxes of candy, pen and pencil sets, framed pictures, and whatever awaiting them at each desk? Each gift was some form of thanks from last year's political victories.

And remember when the Equal Rights Amendment was a rising protest of the 1970s? The ERA was supposed to be the 26th amendment to the United States Constitution, but only if it was first adopted by the legislatures in 36 states. It never happened. And it didn't stop a protest in January of 1976 when people arrived at noon on a Friday and marched around the liberty bell in the center of the Indiana Statehouse rotunda. They were holding signs and singing chants in front of the television lights and cameras.

This group had planned to lobby while the Senate was in session. They were too late as the upper chamber had recessed earlier in the day. Sen. Thomas Teague, a Democrat from Anderson, Indiana, met briefly with them and introduced himself as the minority caucus chairman. He explained to the group that the legislature's 30-day short session in 1976 was not enough time to debate any passage of the ERA.

This was not something that was acceptable for women like Kathy Wagner. She was a member of the NOW chapter from Ball State University. She told Flint that most state senators in Indiana were "very, very hard to talk to" and "hard to hold their attention." Wagner said the prospects for those who supported the amendment was something that would "castrate themselves politically" if they even tried to send the ERA proposal to the Indiana House of Representatives.

George Strycker was a male member of the NOW chapter from Indiana University. He joined the discussion when he told Flint: "I don't think that they can keep freedom from more than half the people in the country. It's appalling that over half the people in this country are kept under the male finger. There's quite a resource of talent that is not being used, like leaders to bring the country out of the depression it's in."

The only kind of civil protest Anthony Flint ever did occurred on April 21, 1975. As the City Editor of the *Ball State Daily News*, Flint voted with the editor, managing editor, night managing editor, campus editor, arts editor and sports editor to do the one thing that always found headlines in Indiana, a state with factories and unions. They had decided unanimously to go on strike. The editor said it was due to "massive equipment failures." She also said this: "When we made the (strike) decision Friday, we were not sure that we could even put out a newspaper with the large number of breakdowns we have been experiencing."

Yes, the strike was all about money. There was not enough of it to replace non-operating typesetting equipment. In fact, more would be needed soon enough to replace the entire equipment systems of the campus newspaper. Things had gotten so bad that only a single sheet was published to carry all the advertisers who bought space in that morning's edition. The director of student publications and chairman of the journalism department said the strike was news to him: "I don't know how they could strike against themselves. It is the decision of the editor to publish the newspaper."

That year the *Ball State Daily News* was subsidized by $80,000 in student fee allocations, $100,000 in advertising revenue and printing job work that amounted to $18,000. But if student fee allocations were raised 50 cents per student per quarter, as requested by the student editors, that would mean an increase of $20,000. That amount should be sufficient over a three-to-five year period to replace or buy new equipment as needed.

There was also an emergency request earlier in the year to replace a broken printing press. But no amount of money was approved by the vice president for instructional affairs. Even though this was supported by the director of student publications and chairman of the journalism department. And, believe it or not, a request for increases was turned down in 1974, the year of Watergate and a protest of a different kind.

Student fees, at Ball State University, had not been increased for several years, the director went on to explain, and "if there is no more money, there is no way to give the newspaper more money."

Lt Gov. Robert D. Orr of Indiana visited the news bureau in the statehouse one day for an interview with Anthony Flint. It was a chance to meet the State's second-highest official and to find issues that were relevant for the readers of the *Ball State Daily News*. And so Flint began with the decriminalization of marijuana. He knew Orr had served as a state senator on a committee five years ago that studied proposals to make possession of marijuana a misdemeanor of the first offense. But the study was never acted on.

Orr said: "I certainly recognize the use of marijuana is more prevalent today than what it was before. But it is too simplistic to say let's decriminalize marijuana. This is an easy use of words—allowing it to be too easily abused." Orr's primary concern was the possibilities of adverse health affects that need to be studied further. And Government has a responsibility to protect the individual as well as society, Orr explained.

In other issues, Orr said he was opposed to abortion on demand. In a case of rape victims, the Lt. Governor said it should be a nullifying position. If the mother's health is placed in jeopardy, the abortion should be allowed. And in national politics he would support Gerald R. Ford in a second term as President of the United States. But, as everyone knows, Ford was appointed to the Oval Office, and he did pardon former President Nixon. Orr predicted Ford would have trouble with voters on this troublesome period of U.S. history.

Indiana was no different than any other state when it came to putting back money in the general fund for public education. The moral reasons to do so are never up for discussion; but then there are economic ways to do it that are more political than others. And yet none of them are more controversial than using a percentage of the proceeds from legalized gambling.

In 1976, the debate inside the Indiana statehouse centered on the pari-mutuel betting bill, and was legislation sponsored in the House by Speaker Pro Temp Craig Campbell, a Democrat from Anderson. Specifically, the bill created a 5-member Indiana Racing Commission with the power to issue licenses, supervise pari-mutuel pools and to set dates for the horses to race. There was also a special local adoption process that included a public referendum before any county could be approved for a pari-mutuel wagering system.

To a young college journalism student like Anthony Flint, this seemed to cover all the bases. Wrong! Remember that all statehouses in America are composed of "citizen legislatures." And some of the citizens are ministers who have constituents attending their churches on Sunday mornings. This is not altogether a bad thing, really, when one considers that it was at least one segment of the population that wasn't politically apathetic.

But it did mean a long night at the statehouse for Flint as he found out the hard way. There were simply too many protestors who found a way to have a turn at the microphone. Some of them had visions of Indiana going to hell in a handcart, and then there were others who compared this bill to the end of time itself. And like Daniel Huff, a legislator and minister from Indianapolis, any extra money from pari-mutuel wagering was simply not worth it.

Huff said this: "I enjoy seeing a horse in motion. But this bill would create a climate for more gambling and would legitimize something for nothing. I know that every state that has adopted pari-mutuel wagering has seen its industry suffer. Nevada, for example, is the lowest ranking state in the west when it comes to the establishment of commerce."

Then there was Ray Richardson, a Republican from Greenfield, who wasn't so sure the math was right. He figured out individuals would have to lose a total of $140 million annually at the tracks just to produce $20 million in profits for the state's general fund. The bill's sponsor agreed on this: the funding formula was complex and admittedly confusing. But each county still had the option to pass or reject a public referendum for a local horse track.

Another minister, Mendell Adams, a Democrat from Marion, found fault with the pari-mutuel bill on grounds that it was adopted first in the Senate—which it was. Adams' argument was that all revenue producing bills are to be sponsored first in the House, and this was according to the Indiana Constitution.

Finally, in the tense moments before the House vote, a little humor was added by John Flanagan, a Democrat from Indianapolis. He said he was advised by his mother that she would no longer go to Kentucky to gamble. "It's too damn far to drive to Louisville!" she told him.

So how did it end that Wednesday evening inside the Indiana statehouse? The vote was 52-45 in favor of pari-mutuel wagering. And as he did so in 1975, Gov. Bowen vetoed the measure faster than any prescription he scribbled as a medical doctor in Indiana.

Chapter 18: Orville Redenbacher

This icon of Walt Disney World has a futuristic A-frame design and the monorail service that passes directly through the 15-story atrium. It is the Contemporary Resort Hotel in Orlando, Florida: a total of 1,041 guest rooms with standard accommodations for five people and a child sleeping in a crib. And it was here on October 25, 1985, that Anthony Flint interviewed the King of Popcorn.

ANTHONY FLINT: October is National Popcorn Month. And I'm assuming popcorn is distinctly an American treat?

ORVILLE REDENBACHER: Yes, Anthony, popcorn is American. It originated here, originally, we thought, with the Inca Indians. Then in 1955, we discovered in the bat caves of New Mexico (evidence of popcorn), which pre-dates the Inca Indians by some 4,000 years. So it's been around for some 5,600 years, and it's really the oldest food item we have, and it originated somewhere in the southwestern part of the United States.

ANTHONY FLINT: Popcorn is low in calories, sugar-free and high in fiber. And it has various tastes. Has popcorn changed that much in the last 200 years?

ORVILLE REDENBACHER: The big change came about when we hybridized popcorn. The actual hybridization took place at Purdue University in 1930. And so the first popcorn seed was allowed to be produced away from Purdue in 1941. I started breeding hybrid popcorn seed that year and breeding it ever since. As a matter of fact, we have a nursery at the wintertime at Homestead, Florida, and we do that in order to get two generations of popcorn each year. We have one in Valpraiso, Indiana, in the summertime, and we have one in the wintertime at Homestead, Florida. And we're still trying to make a better hybrid. We have two men working full-time on the breeding of the hybrid popcorn seed.

ANTHONY FLINT: How did you get started in popcorn?

ORVILLE REDENBACHER: I'm living now in southern California, and the main reason I'm out there is because the TV commercials are made in Hollywood, and I moved out there from Indiana. However, all of our popcorn is practically grown in northwestern Indiana, and it's all processed and packaged in Valpraiso, Indiana, and shipped to all 50 states and Canada from there.

I got started in it because I grew up on a farm in southern Indiana. My father and I always liked popcorn, but we actually didn't get started in the breeding of it until I graduated from Purdue University and then following ten years as a county extension agent in Terre Haute, Indiana.

The one thing the people at Hunt and Wesson foods have done is they have spent more dollars on advertising than all the other popcorn processors combined. You see, we started out producing strictly hybrid popcorn seed, and we became the world's largest producers of hybrid popcorn seed. Then we made the breakthrough on the gourmet variety in 1965, and I have tried to sell this to every company that you can name. All the various processors and they said it wouldn't work because we were asking two-and-a-half times the price of regular popcorn. And the main reason for that was that it doesn't yield as much, and so we had to pay farmers $50 a ton premium to grow this gourmet variety.

We gave them a chance, and they turned us down, so we decided to come out with our own brand. There were only two brands on the market back in 1971 when we came out. It took us five years to go from zero to number one.

You see, popcorn is recommended by the American Medical Association and the American Dental Association. A cup of lightly buttered popcorn contains only 40 calories and is much cheaper than most of the snack items on store shelves. College students think it's great to have a popper in the dorm room—much cheaper than going out to get a pizza, potato chips or pretzels.

ANTHONY FLINT: How is popcorn sold and consumed in other parts of the world?

ORVILLE REDENBACHER: They grow popcorn in any country where they can grow corn. For example, they grow popcorn in the southern part of Europe, they grow popcorn in Israel, they grow popcorn in south Africa and in Argentina. They don't raise any popcorn in England and they don't raise any popcorn in the northern part of France or Germany. Most of that was introduced by our soldiers during World War II.

ANTHONY FLINT: How do you see yourself today as the most famous spokesman for popcorn in American?

ORVILLE REDENBACHER: I get a lot of telephone calls asking if I am for real. They don't think you're Betty Crocker. But this is the same name I've had all of my life. People stop me all the time, and that's the reason I developed these little stickers that say 'I've Met Orville Redenbacher!' It doesn't take long to pass out a thousand or so stickers.

Another frequent misconception is that popcorn is made from corn. And that is not true. There are several kinds of corn. One corn is the big crop that we grow in the Midwest for hogs and horses and to make Cornflakes and corn meal; there is sweet corn that we eat as corn-on-the-cob; and then flint corn is this multi-colored corn that we hang up for decorations. But only popcorn will pop. It has a real hard starch, and when the moisture and temperature is just right, it will explode and pop.

It took us over a year to catch up to the demand when the microwave oven took off in the marketplace. Our sales people sold five times as much as our marketing people had anticipated. It is so convenient. Its so quick and easy to clean up. There are also so many things that you can do with popcorn. Like caramel corn, chocolate, cheese or cinnamon additives. You can also do other things with popcorn. You can make art work out of it. Some schools have contests with their students on this and have a lot of fun with it.

ANTHONY FLINT: The tie we see you wear on your commercials is probably as famous as you are!

ORVILLE REDENBACKER: I've been wearing bow ties ever since I was in high school. Actually, making a bow tie is very simple. You're making a square knot. They teach you that in Boy Scouts. You're making a square knot and it's straight-across and in the right proportion. If you make it into a granny knot, then it will be at an angle. So it's fairly simple at times.

Chapter 19: Monticello

Monticello was the first plantation in Virginia to have a homestead on a mountaintop. It was first cleared in 1769, and later became a prime spot for brickmaking, nail manufacturing and numerous plantings of peaches, pears, cherries, plums, apricots, almonds and pecans. It was also the home of Thomas Jefferson, a 35-room mansion with a Greek portico capped by a Roman-style dome. A terrace on either side concealed the icehouse, servant's quarters, wine room, stables and laundry room.

When living in France, Jefferson made notes from the Hotel de Salm and the Halle aux Bleds in Paris, and Madame du Barry's Pavilion de Louveciennes, outside the city. All of these locations ultimately influenced Jefferson's vision for Monticello. On a piece of land that was inherited from his father in 1757. It is still mostly isolated from the world in rural Albemarle County, Virginia, as Jefferson wanted.

But it would vividly reflect the personality and lifestyle of its owner, and unique in ways that befitted the great kings and queens of Europe. It was not just the home of an American President who was also a plantation owner and the master of many slaves. Monticello had endured as well as anything in Jefferson's life. As well as any quotation or document of Jefferson's writings. It was symbolic of Jefferson and Virginia and a young America.

It remains a great house, filled with paintings, sculptures, bones, minerals, maps, Native American artifacts, and even collections from Lewis and Clark's expedition of the Louisiana Purchase in 1803.

On September 25, 1993, the 250th year of Thomas Jefferson's birth, the humid air at Monticello was easy to associate with a time when there was no air conditioning found anywhere in America. When the United States had elected only three Presidents. It certainly seemed real enough to Anthony Flint, his brother, Clark, and his wife and children. Altogether they formed part of the afternoon groups to tour Jefferson's Monticello.

First they were led into the Jefferson Bedroom just off the entrance hall.

Left as it was, on July 4, 1826, the day Jefferson died in his bed at the age of 83. Large mirrors in the room increased the amount of light and the sense of spaciousness. Then they walked into the parlor, one of the largest rooms at Monticello. It was, by 1809, the location of at least 48 of Jefferson's finest hung paintings. The parquet floor of 10-inch cherry squares with beechwood borders was Jefferson's design. So, too, was the room itself, in the form of a semioctagon, and west of the entrance hall, separated by glass doors.

Flint was one of many in the group that appreciated the mechanical dumbwaiters in the dining room. Jefferson had them on each side of the fireplace. This permitted the drinks to be sent up from the cellar below, to the guests and the family seated at the Chippendale dining table. This, as Jefferson had intended, reduced the number of servants needed in the room at any one time.

Across from the dining room was the north octagonal room. The tour guide said it was the only one in the mansion with wallpaper. The pattern was known as the "Lattice and Treillage," a reproduction of the one purchased by Jefferson in Paris. Next was the north square room. It was often used by a Portuguese scientist and diplomat who visited Monticello. By looking out the window, one could see the weather vane in the ceiling of the portico.

The second and third floors were not open to the public, so the group found itself outside again. They stopped along the north terrace walk with the white Chinese railing, and the commanding view of the south pavilion across the west lawn.

The tour guide brought them together for the last time. "Jefferson built his house on top of a mountain for the view. He said, 'How sublime to look down into the workhouse of nature, to see her clouds, hail, snow, rain, thunder, all fabricated at our feet! And the glorious Sun, when rising as if out of a distant water, just gliding the tops of the mountains, and giving life to all nature!'"

The next voice was not that of the female tour guide. Nor was it anyone around Flint.

His first impression was similar to the one experienced in church one Sunday morning. The sermon was abruptly cut-off by a frequency problem with the wireless microphone. A second voice was actually being received from a cell phone transmission. Flint remembered it was nothing too personal or too obscene. The minister switched the microphone off in time to conclude his remarks and extend the invitation to the startled congregation.

But Flint was not using a cell phone. He was not wearing any sophisticated hearing device or carrying a portable cassette player with headphones, the kind found commonly at some historic sites with pre-recorded messages, allowing visitors to walk freely from one location to the next without a tour group or tour guide.

There was nothing on his person that could act as a receiver of any kind.

Yet, from the very beginning, the identity of the voice was no mystery. It was a man who said who he was; he also said he knew what Flint was thinking. With an introduction and then with an explanation, the voice said he was never a part of any group tour in the history of the Thomas Jefferson Memorial Foundation.

Until now, he had been content to let issues stand by themselves. There was no need to intervene at any level with any generation. All had seemed as it should be, in his opinion. Of course, things change. He has changed. His country has changed. It was not one issue but many issues. The voice said he waited for decades to decide when the time was right to speak his mind.

He knew the world had not expected to hear from him again. Ever. There were also the historians and the scholars with questions that only he himself could rightly answer.

Flint was not at all clairvoyant. But this all happened to him.

Somehow, he took a deep breath. He had the program guide and a pencil to take notes. All that he had. Except for the voice.

Unlike the Lee encounter in Tennessee, 13 years before, there was no vision, or aberration—only the voice. It came from many directions, each perfectly mixed in tone and volume. As Flint stopped walking, he looked around as if to find the source of the voice. The rest of the group continued on the path to the Jefferson family cemetery ahead. None of them were listening. None of them were surprised.

There was no attempt at introductions in the very beginning. He was too anxious to talk. Finally, as Flint secluded himself near one of the outbuildings, Thomas Jefferson announced himself as someone who was nearly 300 years old.

He found no interest in the triumphs, tragedies, or even the scandals of any American President—before or after him. He also expressed little about his years in the White House. Not surprisingly, he was interested in building things. That was something that was held passionately and dearly to his heart. "Architecture is my delight, and putting up and pulling down, one of my favorite amusements," Jefferson said to Flint at one point that afternoon.

Flint knew the former President spent 40 years building Monticello and never finished it. Visitors in his time were equally impressed with the home near the village of Charlottesville, Virginia. The Marquis de Chastellux, after leaving Jefferson's plantation in 1782, said: "Mr Jefferson is the first American who has consulted the Fine Arts to know how he should shelter himself from the weather." Jefferson readily agreed. "All my wishes end where I hope my days will end, at Monticello," he said.

The President did more than talk about his Monticello. He was more than concerned and equally impressed with the rebuilding of south Florida after Hurricane Andrew in August of 1992. Most remarkable was the adoption of stringent building codes for electrical, mechanical, plumbing and energy efficiency. It was his opinion that every state in the Union should follow the example set by the Florida Legislature.

Thomas Jefferson said weather-related events like Hurricane Andrew caused untold economic hardships in the New World. As a child he heard stories from his father, Peter Jefferson, about the hurricane of 1622 off the Florida Straits. That year the Spanish gallon, *Nuestra Senora de Atocha*, the *Santa Margarita* and 26 ships of Spain's Terra Firme Fleet were lost or heavily damaged at sea.

The Archives of the Indies in Seville, Spain, contain copies of the manifest that listed the *Atocha* has having onboard 24 tons of silver bullion in 1,038 ingots, 180,000 silver coins, 582 copper ingots, 125 gold bars, 350 chests of indigo, 525 bales of tobacco, 20 bronze cannons and 1,200 pounds of worked silverware. Not on the manifest—no doubt to avoid taxes—another 70 pounds of emerald contraband.

Salvage attempts the next morning found the *Atocha* in 55 feet of water with the top of its mast in plain sight. The divers were unable to break into the hatches but marked the site and hastily returned to Havana for recovery equipment. It was later that a second hurricane ravaged the area, tearing the upper hull structure and masts from the ship. All signs of the wreck had vanished when the skies were clear again. And more than $60 million of precious cargo would lay undistributed for the next 350 years.

Jefferson said he visited the Mel Fisher Maritime Museum in south Florida and saw the glittering treasures on display that were salvaged from the *Atocha* and the other shipwrecks. It was more than enough to rebuild Solomon's Temple.

Since 1931, the Empire State Building has towered over the skyline of New York City. Jefferson said the building's design for the 2-acre site in midtown Manhattan was excellent. At a cost of $41 million—during the Great Depression—it contained more than 2 million square feet of office space. And at a height of 1,472 feet, thanks to the addition of a television transmission tower in 1950. The Empire State Building was the brainchild of Shreke, Lamb & Harmon, a firm whose reputation soared as high as the building itself. But no thanks to the World Trade Center, which dethroned the Empire State Building in 1971 as the tallest building in the world.

Jefferson's review of the greatest collection of skyscrapers on earth was incredible. It sounded to Flint like Jefferson had actually visited the Observation Deck on the 86th floor of the Empire State Building. The former President said he considered the impact with weather and with metals and the prospects of tall buildings standing for each generation to see.

Certainly one of the tall buildings in Jefferson's time was Independence Hall in Philadelphia, although he was much too busy in 1776 to remember anything but the growing storm clouds of the American Revolution.

At one point in his life, he had total land holdings of nearly 6,000 acres with Monticello as the centerpiece. That was in 1794, and included five farming operations, several overseers, work forces and animals. Close to home he had access to nearly 600 acres of cleared land, although the hills were numerous and the soil had seen its share of seasonal plantings for Indian corn and tobacco. "It is still, however, very strong and remarkably friendly to wheat and rye," Jefferson explained.

The former President was more than interested in modern agriculture and especially the overall emergence of the fast-food industry in the United States. But Flint wondered if Thomas Jefferson had ever been curious for the taste of a Big Mac? "I have lived temperately, eating little animal food, and that not as an aliment, so much as a condiment for the vegetables, which constitute my principal diet," Jefferson answered.

As the master of 115 slaves in 1796, Thomas Jefferson informed Anthony Flint that history did not give credit to the slave owners who successfully cared and housed and fed what amounted to be a small village of black people living on a large plantation. One must also add to the equation the severe agricultural depressions of the 1820s and an economy based on slave labor.

It was truly a monumental risk on both sides of the Atlantic, according to Jefferson. He said Europeans discovered the best buys on West Africa's coast, and where they could barter with pewterware, weapons, cloth, iron bars, glass beads and spirits for ivory, pepper and slaves. But a prospective buyer was obligated to inspect his investment more closely when it came to the latter. This was often done by prodding the bellies, poking fingers in the mouths and checking the teeth of slaves. It was an informal means of guaranteeing that each one was fed earlier that morning, and cleaned, shaved, oiled, and any wounds finally attended in preparation for the public sale.

Every auction, however, was still affected by the outcome of transporting the slaves from across the Atlantic Ocean. A voyage of three months was normal, with good weather. The ship's huge copper cauldron boiled up two meals a day—usually beans or yams. This was served to slaves sitting, crouching or lying on their sides, but not occupying more than 18 inches of floor space and five feet of headroom.

Under the best of circumstances one in five perish before the final destination is reached, or 20% of all salves onboard ship. Some became seasick but were flogged into submission. Many were deprived of fresh air or were weakened by dysentery or fouled by excrement. Many times the infections or disease claimed the lives of captives and crew alike. Anyone who died was thrown to the sharks that swan in the ship's wake.

Jefferson emphasized again that the risks of running any economy in the world with slave labor would always be high. A good example was the English merchant-slaver, *Henrietta Marie*, which sold 190 captive Africans in Jamaica and then sank 35 miles off Key West in May of 1700. In two voyages the 120-ton, 85-foot vessel delivered some 450 Africans to lives of servitude. It was human chattel worth more than $400,000. Yet the vessel and the crew were lost under unknown conditions, and with it a ship's registry of sugar, cotton, wood, indigo—among other things.

Once in Paris, Jefferson told Flint he purchased an initial stock of 59 bottles of Bordeaux at a cost of 200 francs. That was approximately the equivalent of three months' wages for the average French worker. He also bought a grand total of 2,000 books for himself and as gifts to George Washington, Benjamin Franklin and James Madison. He also found it necessary to buy 63 paintings, seven terra-cotta busts and a chariot with green morocco leather that cost 15,000 francs for all the repairs.

Jefferson made it clear that he recorded every purchase and that he kept voluminous farm records when he was at home in Virginia. However, he did not say if he ever made a profit in his whole life. He sold his private library of 6,707 books for $23,950 to replace the collections destroyed at the Library of Congress when the British set fire to the capitol. But he died with debits exceeding $100,000, more than the value of Monticello, the land and all of his possessions. Even a state lottery established on his behalf was unsuccessful.

Jefferson saw his estate change owners and rise and fall at the hands of fate for nearly a century. During the Civil War the Confederate government seized Monticello as alien property and sold it at public auction in 1864. Not until 1923 did things really turn out for the better and that was when the Thomas Jefferson Memorial Foundation organized and charted as a non-profit organization with the goals of purchasing Jefferson's home, preserving as much as possible as a national monument.

That night they traveled I-95 back to the Red Roof Inn at Richmond. There was talk in the rental car of the day's events at the Jefferson estate. Clark and his family enjoyed themselves, no doubt. Especially Clark, a 10-year mechanical engineer with Westinghouse in Baltimore. It was Clark who admired how the double doors between the entrance hall and the parlor operated in Thomas Jefferson's day. He saw how a wheel, or drum, was positioned at the base of each door below the floor. Joined by a small chain, the figure eight arrangement allowed both doors to move when one was opened or closed.

At Mt. Vernon a year earlier, both families had visited the home of the nation's first President. That was a wonderful vacation, too. But Anthony Flint (as he remembered to himself) was not so sure: Washington had not said a word to him.

Nearly five years after his insights with Jefferson at Monticello, Flint ran this column in *The Orlando Sentinel*:

If you are bewildered or amused about Thomas Jefferson and Sally Hemings, this may help clear up the confusion:

Thomas Jefferson was the third President of these United States. Sally Hemings was his slave.

Thomas Jefferson authored the Declaration of Independence and founded the University of Virginia. Sally Hemings was the mother of six children, two sons and four daughters.

Now, it gets a little complicated. First, the DNA study was conducted, and the results are valid. This comes from the Thomas Jefferson Foundation and its website on Thomas Jefferson and Sally

Hemings. But this report, with its conclusions, also says many aspects of this likely relationship are, and may remain, unclear, such as the nature of the relationship, the existence and longevity of Sally Hemings's first child (Madison).

It makes sense to explore the implications of the relationship between Jefferson and Hemings. Both are part of history.

To see for myself, I went to the home of Thomas Jefferson. It seemed the answer came from the apple trees in the orchard, the east front columns of the mansion, the vegetable garden terrace, even from the library where 6,000 books once filled the shelves.

"I am so much immersed in farming and nail making (for I have set up a nailery) that politicks are entirely banished from my mind," I thought I heard Jefferson say.

Jefferson, the progressive farmer, has survived more than 200 years, and not a few calamities along the way. His wife, Martha Wayles Skelton, died in 1782. Daughter, Maria, in 1804. There was also the fire in the North Pavilion in 1819.

In 1827, a year after Jefferson's death, there was a public sale of his slaves and household furnishings. His home and gardens would not see responsible ownership until 1923.

So, don't let bewilderment or amusement make you think you will lose another American Icon. Not this time. Thomas Jefferson is here to stay.

Chapter 20: Houston

Moving to Houston was always the best thing for Eugene Flint because he never felt the need to look back. It was especially true when he was still coaching boys' basketball teams in Murfeesboro, Tennessee; and where and when the pressure to play sports in a parochial school was really no different than the stressful toll found in public school. Winning would always be everything with any program that wanted to be first all the time. But to do that, and to do it well, Eugene had to contend with problems both on and off the court.

Just ask the coach or even the owner of the team that won an NBA championship. But with the star forward arrested for aggravated spouse abuse in the off season. Or was it attempted murder? Then there was always the sick or injured and the prayer of every coach to keep his team healthy. When sin entered the picture, the coach always found more time to talk to the owner. And did the mother name any of the teams' multi-million dollar players?

Eugene didn't have players on his team that made six figures and saw product endorsements out the ying-yang. He did have parents and school boards and the fans on any given day. One thing was really as bad as another thing. It didn't seem to make a difference if anyone was under contract or not.

That's why Eugene left his coaching position and joined the ranks of underwriters with Drexel-Burnham in Houston. This was a company of the 1980s that soon collapsed under the enormous fraud of a zillion high yield bonds that were less than investment grade. They were not widely held in investment portfolios and mainstream investors and investment dealers did not deal in what became known as "junk bonds." And because very few people would actually accept the risk of owning them in the first place.

But Michael Milken led a major investment charge at Drexel-Burnham into junk bonds in the late 1980s. His financial researchers began to observe how the returns of junk bonds were quite high. It was the advent of the modern portfolio theory that suggested the credit risk was more than compensated by the higher interest payments.

Eugene had no part with the scandal or the collapse of the many lower rated issuers with Drexel-Burnham. He did find it necessary to accept a new job with Prudential Stock Securities, which was a better neighborhood for himself as well as all his faithful investors. People like Keith and Beverly Flint. And his brother, Clark. And he was so certain about this that he saw to it that he never saw a school locker room for the rest of his life.

His brother lived in Houston, and Anthony wanted to spend a week in Texas. Not enough time to go to Dallas and Dealey Plaza, the site of the Kennedy assassination, or the Alamo in San Antonio. Eugene suggested the local sights of Houston and primarily because he was the one that was not on vacation. He really wanted to be with his brother when he went to places like Gilleys' in nearby Pasadena, where the *Urban Cowboy* film was shot with John Travolta. Eugene also made it possible for Anthony to see the Astrodome, the Galleria and a forest of oil derricks at a time when that industry was in a deep economic slump.

Not that his brother couldn't find his way around Houston. He went it alone a few times and quickly learned that Interstate 610 didn't have enough lanes for the heavy traffic. This was the bypass around Houston, and it was never the time or the place to safely read a road map. This was so true the first night that Anthony was convinced he wasn't going to find the right exit. He must have driven around the city four times. He also couldn't remember how he got off and slowly made his way to the apartment of his brother. It was such a nice and neat place for any bachelor in the first place. So how could Anthony every forget that?

Despite the junk bond saga, and because of it, the variety and number of high yield issues recovered fully to thrive in the 1990s. Many mutual funds have been established for investments exclusively in high yield bonds, which continue to have high risk-adjusted returns.

If you asked Anthony Flint, it was strange enough and not altogether scientific (was that the right word?) how the stock market really worked. His brother was a part of it. But did Eugene understand it any better? Did he really trust it? That was the key thing with Anthony. How could the market go up and down if the CEO of some company slipped on the floor in the executive washroom and banged his head? Better yet was the example of the occupant in the Oval Office at any perceived time of gloom and doom. If it was reported that the President of the United States did cut himself shaving in the morning, well, then, the stock market fell 800 points at the closing of the bell.

It reminded Flint of a story he once read in college about Frank Sinatra. It was all about the Chairman of the Board and what happened to his whole entourage when the singer caught a cold. All hell broke loose—and nothing much else was accomplished.

Eugene was quite aggressive to make it in Houston and to survive even the first job he had here as an employee of Honeywell Security Systems. The Houston economy was sluggish, and this was reflected by the sharp decline in crude oil stocks on the New York Mercantile Exchange and even on London's International Petroleum Exchange. And this was a time when Osama Bin Laden and his Al-Qaeda terrorists began looking seriously at pictures of the World Trade Center, the Pentagon and the White House as targets for destruction.

So it could be summed up this way: to sell in this town you had to think big. And you had to be bold enough to sell anything, even if it was security systems in times of economic recession. And to do this one had to create a need even in the most unlikely of circumstances.

This opportunity came to pass when Eugene drove his brother down to the Johnson Space Flight Center. It was off Interstate 45, southeast of Houston, and it was late in the afternoon when Eugene just got off work. They both agreed this was the best way to show Anthony the route to the space center so he wouldn't get lost when he came the next day with as much time as he liked.

When they arrived at the main gate in Clear Lake, it was Eugene who wasted no time asking the personnel if NASA needed a new security system. Or at least modifications and upgrades that would make a new account very lucrative for the next couple of years for Eugene Flint. He then left a few business cards with them and—as was said before—Eugene was quite aggressive.

Houston was famous as the home of Mission Control and the Johnson Space Flight Center. After visiting the NASA facilities in Greenbelt, Maryland, and Huntsville, Alabama, Anthony Flint sure didn't miss this opportunity to see where America's fleet of space shuttles got the go-ahead for lift-off. He even took the time to sit down and see Mission Control from behind the glass partitions inside the public viewing room. Although a few people were seated the day he was there, Flint knew it was a different story whenever there was a manned space flight in progress.

Perhaps the most famous time was when man landed on the moon and the place was packed as Neil Armstrong told Mission Control: "Houston, the Eagle has landed." No doubt there was not a seat in the house as the Apollo 8 astronauts read from the book of Genesis as man orbited the moon for the first time in December of 1968.

By the time Apollo 13 headed to the moon in 1970, it was already old hat to the world's public that NASA could do this thing and do this thing right. As it turned out, the mission was aborted before the planned lunar landing. And when Commander James A. Lovell, Jr., said: "Houston, we have a problem," it meant that three men in space would have to survive the explosion of one of the on-board oxygen tanks and come back to Earth as soon as possible.

But Anthony Flint was in high school when the United States sent its astronauts to the moon. Then when he was in college, it was a 9-month test program to see if the world's first reusable spacecraft could fly in the atmosphere and land like an airplane. This space vehicle was also very popular in 1977 with the viewers of the popular *Star Trek* television show. Many of them started a write-in campaign urging the White House to name it the *Enterprise*.

So NASA called it the *Enterprise*, and it was used in a series of test programs. The first part included releasing the orbiter from the 747 carrier aircraft and the orbiter's free-flight landings at Edwards Air Force Base in California. Next came the vertical ground vibration tests in Huntsville and then the launch tests in Florida. Anthony knew that years later the Enterprise was put on display at the Smithsonian's National Air and Space Museum annex at Dulles International Airport in Washington, D.C.

He saw some of the flights of that spacecraft on television like the rest of the nation. Flint wasn't any closer to the space program than the next available TV. Yet that was all about to change in the spring of 1981, which was the year he won an internship with *The Orlando Sentinel* in Orlando, Florida. And this was a newspaper that was purchased in 1965 by the same company that owned *The Chicago Tribune* and *The New York Daily News*. In 1971, this media group had 5.8 percent of the total national weekday circulation and 9.5 percent of the total national Sunday circulation.

Flint's internship allowed him to move to the Sunshine State and learn more about the kind of things most Florida travel brochures failed to elaborate on up north. Things like the "love bugs," the Mediterranean fruit fly, citrus canker, droughts, wild fires, crowded schools, excessive growth and so on. On the positive side, this state was immerging as a great place for college football fans, and the weather was internationally famous. And there was also the Kennedy Space Center.

He didn't see any bylines on any of these stories that year, but he knew that his day would surely come. Flint would have to learn the hard work of being an intern before anything else could really happen for him. He did attend enough media days at the area theme parks to know Mickey Mouse, Indiana Jones and Shamu on a first-name basis!

Mission Control was still relatively quiet on the second day of his visit. Very few people were seated at their computers and there was hardly anybody in the viewing room to watch them. Even the large map of the world did not show any orbital paths by the space shuttle to be closely monitored by Mission Control.

This, however, was an excellent time to reminiscence about the time when he saw his first shuttle launch and his experiences on November 4, 1981. Everything was going just "bang, bang, bang" for the scheduled lift-off at 7:30 a.m. These were the exact words of Deke Slayton, manager of NASA's shuttle test program. And inside the spacecraft was Air Force Colonel Joe Engle, 49, and Navy Captain Richard Truly, 44, both ready for the ride of their lives.

On the pad was the *Columbia* space shuttle, ready for its second trip into space after the first historic launch in April. The weather forecasters at Patrick Air Force Base predicted 30 to 40 percent chance of overnight showers. That was no problem. Neither was a slight drop in pressure inside the large external fuel tank.

Hurricane Kartrina was also on the minds of Mission Control that year, 350 miles south of Miami. Yet it was clear in Florida. And flight director Neil Hutchison gave the go-ahead for the final countdown. Hutchison was one of many flight directors for NASA who would see many delays in countdowns in the years ahead: everything from freezing temperatures to increased security for possible terrorist attacks. Yet the launch clock always stopped during pre-planned holds, and that was not always something to worry about.

Flint was somewhat curious to see several parked cars covered with plastic sheets. This, he was told, guarded against a thin particle residue that could drift across from the shuttle launch. Flint was not sure if there was enough time for him to cover his car. The count stood at T-minus nine minutes and holding.

Now NASA noticed another loss in pressure and told the computers to ignore it. Flint remembered the count at T-minus 31 seconds. The problem didn't seem serious. But why the moans and cries coming from the grandstand? He couldn't hear the loudspeakers very well, but there was, soon enough, more information about two oil filters than anybody wanted to hear. *Columbia*'s hydraulic devices used for orbiting and landing were suddenly questionable.

Somebody forgot to check under the hood, and the mission was off. Then whole place became a massive traffic jam. NASA security police were left dealing with the quick scrub as best they could. Which was no greater headache than the one facing the astronauts after five hours strapped to their backs. That's why John Denver told *The Orlando Sentinel*: "Sure, I'm disappointed, but I'm not as disappointed as those two guys in there." Denver and Robert Redford were the only celebrities in the special viewing block that day in 1981.

The near-launch convinced Flint how the space shuttle was still an experimental spacecraft. It proved to be an elusive flight for another seven days. After that, the launches would number over 100 missions in the next 20 years. This included flights into space to release the Hubbell Space Telescope and to build the International Space Station. And it was so that man was posed to leave Earth like no time in the history of the world.

Chapter 21: Billie Jean King and Julian Bond

Wesley Chapel is 30 miles north of Tampa and two hours west of Orlando. It is a thriving community of west-central Florida that is neither city nor county. But it is the home of the Saddlebrook Golf and Tennis Resort, which, in turn, has been the training facilities and home to such world-class athletes as Pete Sampras, Jim Courrier and Jennifer Capriati.

The Saddlebrook Golf and Tennis Resort was also the site for the 1983 Lean Cuisine Women's Legends in Tennis tournament. One of the legends who played that year was Billie Jean King. She was the first female athlete to win over $100,000 in prize money in a single season. King won a record 20 Wimbledon titles, was ranked No. 1 in the United States seven times and No. 1 in the world five times. In 1973, she even defeated Bobby Riggs, the 55-year-old men's champion in what was called the "Battle of the Sexes" at the Astrodome in Houston, Texas.

But 1983 was the year Anthony Flint interviewed Billie Jean King in Wesley Chapel, Florida.

ANTHONY FLINT: You've brought eight superstars to compete here, all legends in women's professional tennis. Do you feel pressure to win every time?

BILLIE JEAN KING: Life is pressure. And I think we all have stress in our lives, and I think how we react to the stress is very important. And if a child is going to be a champion, they love that pressure. That daily pressure of waking up and wanting it. You will find that when a child becomes eighteen, and when their parents no longer have as much say in their lives, if they really don't love the sport and don't want to be in it, they usually drop out. You kind of look at that age to see if they will be responsible for themselves. But most of the youngsters in the game (tennis) today, they really want to be there. And I have talked to all of them, and they all seemed to be very keen on playing and wanting to be there. They feel their parents don't have anything to do with it. The parents are supportive, and they think they wouldn't be where they are today if not for the parents; but they definitely wanted it.

I just feel bad when I see parents who force their children into anything they don't want to do. You see the stage mothers—why is it always stage mothers! I've seen stage fathers, too, especially in sports, where they have a huge influence.

Let's face it. Men have always been in sports. Sports have always belonged to men in the past. I always figured that the sports page should be called the men's page. I think that's finally changing. But it's taken a long time, and you find that many fathers are their children's coaches, or at least the ones behind them when it comes to sports.

I think there are individual cases where I must feel that it's too bad that the person was in tennis—probably because the parents pushed their children into tennis and not something else. And that's just something that you feel bad about. It's not something you can do anything about.

ANTHONY FLINT: How are younger players handling pressures in professional tennis?

BILLIE JEAN KING: Most of the children you read about—let's take Carlene Basset. She just won her first professional tournament. She loves tennis. She wants to be out there. Her parents could care less if she plays tennis. She just loves it. I mean, she has guts. This kid just thinks it's great being there.

Julian Bond was a state senator from Georgia and a future chairman of the National Association for the Advancement of Colored People (NAACP). Bond attended Morehouse College and was elected to the Georgia House of Representatives in 1965; yet the Statehouse in Atlanta denied him a seat because of his policies denouncing U.S. military action in Vietnam. He was, in fact, reelected twice and still refused entry by his fellow legislators. It took the U.S. Supreme Court in 1967 to rule that his exclusion was unconstitutional.

Flint covered a 1987 speech by the George legislator at Valencia Community College in Orlando, Florida.

(Introduction followed by standing ovation)

JULIAN BOND: Thank you for that kind introduction! Thank you very much! I must say I particularly appreciate the many kind words in that introduction. It reminded me of something that happened to me just this afternoon. My wife was driving me to the Atlanta airport, and because the expressway was so busy, we decided to take the service streets. We came to a railroad crossing, and as luck would have it, when you are in a hurry, you know, the bar is always down. So we sat there and watched this train go by— it seemed to have a thousand cars.

As we were sitting there, we looked over to the side of the road and saw this man trying to stand up. He looked like he slept in his clothes for a couple of weeks, and he looked like he had a liquid breakfast, lunch and dinner.

As he got to his feet, he pulled himself into an open boxcar and let his legs hang over the side. And I could see he was going to look into our car. And I could see he was going to look at me because I'm such a big shot. So I flashed my cufflinks, and I straightened my tie, and as the boxcar pulled by, sure enough, he did look inside our automobile and said: "Hey, Alice, how's it going?"

(Laughter.)

So I said to my wife, "What's that all about?" She said, "If you must know, that's the man I was dating before I met you."

(More laughter.)

She said, "When we became engaged, he took it so badly he took to drinking, and that's what happened to him." And I said, "Alice, that is a big day for you. You could have been married to this bum. And, instead, you've been married to man whose been in the Georgia Legislature for 20 years, a man whose got 14 honorary degrees, and a man who was nominated to be Vice President of the United States." And she said, "Shoot, if I married him he'd be the Vice President...."

(Interrupted by more laughter.)

I'm just very pleased to be here. I can see there are those of you my age, but for the younger people here today, you probably wonder how the civil rights movement came to be. Who cannot understand how a group of people let another group of people beat them? Who cannot understand how people once had to sit in the back of the bus and couldn't eat at the lunch counter?

I'm reminded that if Martin King had been able to celebrate his birthday this week he would have been 58 years old. Had he lived until today, there's no serious doubt that our world would be a very different place than it was for him in 1968. We live in a better world because he lived what he did. I wonder, had Dr. King lived until now, how he might look at this world with continuing alarm.

The movement he led now appears to be in some disarray. And the gains he can claim some credit for achieving now seem in danger of being destroyed. History should record that this man and the movement he led were the premiere factors in the struggle of the 20th century for economic and political justice. When Martin King was born, the world was rigidly segregated by custom and by law as is South Africa today. Most black people in the American South were just two generations away from slavery. Most of us then and some of us now are a paycheck or two away from poverty. As a people, we were political impotent, we were educationally improvised, and we were economically bankrupt.

But among this man's marvelous contributions was to give a voice to the dreams and aspirations of black Americans. And most importantly, to help develop a method of participation in the struggle for equal rights so that every man, every woman, student, housewife, minister, everyone, could become an agent of their own deliverance.

Now the movement King led and the movement which preceded him have passed through a series of climaxes. These were years of great legal struggles in the courts complimented by extra legal struggles in the streets. In this period, we won gains at lunch counters, movie theaters, bus stations, polling places, and the fabric of legal segregation in the United States began to come undone.

What had begun as a movement for elemental civil rights is now today largely a political movement. And an economic movement. And today black men and women are holding office and power in numbers and in places we never dreamed of before.

But despite this incredible increase in the number of black people holding public office, and despite the ability we've now got today to sit and eat and ride, and vote, and go to school in places which used to lack black faces, in a very real way, in 1987, we find our condition unchanged.

A quick look at all the statistics which measure infant mortality, medium family income, life expectancy, these will demonstrate very clearly that while our general condition has improved a great deal, our relative condition has actually managed to get worse.

Not simply because the towering leadership figure of the era was struck down by an assassin's bullet, or because another man was elected President of the United States.

It's not that so many of our fellow citizens are not aware but that so many are aware and simply do not care. Recreating that care and rebuilding that old coalition of conscience ought to be first priority for all of us over the next several years.

One of the great gifts that Dr. King gave us years ago is seldom remembered by most of us today. This was a message not original with Martin King, but no leadership figure in the struggle for human rights has expressed it so well before and since. For him, it began with Rosa Parks and her refusal to stand up so a white man could sit down on the bus. That's when mass participation came to the movement for civil rights. That kind of mass participation is badly needed in today's movement as well. Fortunately, there is ample opportunity for all of us.

The country's oldest human rights organization, the 76-year-old National Association for the Advancement of Colored People, has seen its membership relatively level over the last several years. But the country's oldest terrorists organization, the 127-year-old Knights of the Ku Klux Klan, has seen its membership inch every so slowly and surely up.

Now doesn't it make ordinary common sense that if the people dedicated to death and destruction are growing in strength and power, that you should do the same?

(Standing ovation.)

Chapter 22: New York City

Thomas Jefferson said the Empire State Building in New York City was a grand design. This being said, it was important to remember the home of the former President and the buildings designed by Jefferson at the University of Virginia. They represented what Jefferson admired the most in architecture when he was still alive. It was also noteworthy to most Jeffersonian scholars, who would not have any good reason to believe Jefferson liked anything else as much.

It was one thing to see the mountains, the valleys and the trees of rural Virginia from the north terrace walk at Monticello. But the view from the observation deck on the 86th floor of the Empire State Building was more than just impressive. It was also historic. It was a glimpse into the past and an era that saw a rush for taller buildings that would really serve as public statements to the men who wanted them in New York City. And if you could afford it, you could have completed something like the Gothic-inspired F.W. Woolworth Building in 1913, which was paid for in cash by Mr. Woolworth himself.

Yet the best example of all was the building commissioned by Walter P. Chrysler that was 1,048 feet high—even taller than the Eiffel Tower above the streets of Paris. This was not supposed to be the headquarters for the Chrysler Motors Company but, rather, a monument to Chrysler himself. It even had a small museum inside that housed the tools Chrysler used when he began building cars by hand.

But it was less than a year after completion of his building that Chrysler found himself looking out at the Empire State Building. It was the tallest building in the world for the next 46 years. And one of the best views of its construction from anywhere in New York City was from the observation deck at the Chrysler Building. They could see in the beginning how there was no room on the surrounding streets to store construction materials to build the Empire State Building.

The steel, prefabricated at the mill, had to arrive at the precise moment it was needed. The beams were quickly hauled up to the top of the rising frame and the truck that brought them to the site moved away to make room for the next load. And the new construction methods allowed workers to finish the building 45 days ahead of schedule and $5 million under budget. At one point, Jefferson told Flint 3,500 workers were on the job, and in one 10-day period, a staggering 14 stories were framed!

Jefferson viewed the Empire State Building preferably from the Rainbow Room, the top floor restaurant on the 65th floor of Rockefeller Center's RCA building. It opened in 1934 and set the standard as the most elegant tower dining and dancing spot in the city for decades to come. And it was here that the former President read a story in *The New York Times* in 1954, the year Flint was born, about the visit of England's "Queen Mum" Elizabeth to the Empire State Building. And in the evening he could see the lights at the top levels of the building and a special kind of beauty that was not seen during the day.

Jefferson was knowledgeable on how the skyline of New York City had changed constantly since colonial times. There are no traces at all of the buildings the Dutch built in the 17th century, nor of the improvements England brought to the cityscape. Many of those buildings, some 493 of them, were destroyed in a great fire in 1776, which leveled a third of the city. Disaster hit again in 1811, when fire once again swept through lower Manhattan, destroying 102 buildings and crippling business for months afterward.

Yet there was a time when New York City had no skyscrapers and only church steeples as the tallest structures in the city—like St. Paul's Chapel in 1789. The year George Washington attended a special service after his inauguration as America's first president on the steps of City Hall nearby at Wall and Nassau Streets. He also became a regular Sunday worshipper during the years that New York was the nation's first capital.

Jefferson came with Washington to New York City as the nation's first Secretary of State. He did so not because he wanted to but because Congress liked doing business in New York City. So did Alexander Hamilton, Washington's Secretary of the Treasurer. Hamilton was a delegate to the Continental Congress, a highly successful lawyer, and a founding director of the Bank of New York—the only one in the city at the time. And it was in Hamilton's best interests that he lobbied successfully for the nation's government in this city shortly after the Revolutionary War.

But Jefferson and Washington wanted the nation's capitol in Virginia. Jefferson told Flint he never saw New York City as a seat for national government but as a center of international commerce. The first stock exchange was established there in 1792. Then the Erie Canal was opened in 1825 after 8 years of construction and $7.5 million in costs. It allowed tons of goods from America's heartland to travel through the wilderness of upstate New York from Buffalo to Albany for 350 miles, and where it connected to the Hudson River and on to the harbor of New York City in an amazing 9 days total. By 1869, the Port of New York was the richest in the world and full with sailing vessels, steamboats and even transatlantic ships. It was handling a third of all the export business in the entire world. And the Erie Canal had more traffic than the whole Mississippi River system put together.

All of this, then, was confirmation that New York City would have as much impact on the United States of America as the nation's new capital surveyed in the District of Columbia. And which was created by Congress in 1800 from land formerly in Maryland and Virginia.

After his own visit to the Empire State Building in 1994, Flint and his wife, Candy, continued on the Grayline bus tour through lower Manhattan. Earlier that day they had walked past the Ed Sullivan Theater and saw people in sleeping bags waiting in line to get tickets to the CBS Late Show with David Letterman. Then it was on to Harlem, the United Nations, Madison Square Garden, and a stop at the world's largest gothic house of worship at the Cathedral Church of St. John the Divine.

At one point, with traffic jams in both directions and lights flashing and sirens wailing from emergency vehicles trying to move, it was a bilingual sign in Chinatown that said it all: Don't Even Think of Parking Here. Flint was certainly glad he left the driving to others who made their living behind the wheels of tour buses and taxicabs. He saw more of these vehicles on the streets of New York City than he could ever count in one day. Nothing seemed to faze them.

Along the way was a seemingly endless display of what you could quickly buy in the Big Apple. Outside the dozens of stores and huddled over boxes, bins and crates, people searched for bargains, souvenirs, watches, jewelry, produce, poultry, fish, meat, and, as they say, "the sky was the limit" to what could be brought and sold here.

Even the McDonalds Restaurant on 620 Broadway exhibited a male pianist in a tuxedo and tails behind a grand piano on the second floor. Once inside, you could place your order and then dine to the music of Broadway show tunes. You could also glance up at the moving band of illuminated stock prices and checkout your portfolio at anytime.

And so slowly but surely the bus tour was making its way to Battery Park, where they would get off and then wait on the Staten Island Ferry to take them to the Statute of Liberty and on to Ellis Island. Jefferson said a strong English fortress was once located at Battery Park and, for that matter, so was the Dutch fortress built in 1663 to protect the colony from the English and the Native Americans. This area was enclosed by a wall and is known today as Wall Street.

But it was at Battery Park that Anthony Flint first realized that Thomas Jefferson had connected with the Grayline tour. It was when the ex-president told Anthony about the house he leased once on Maiden Lane in the Big Apple. Jefferson did point out that he knew the city was not expected to be the capital of the new nation for very long. This was not important to him, and it did not stop Jefferson from immediately planning major renovations for exterior and interior improvements. It was also part of the plan to put James Hemings in the kitchen. Hemings was a mulatto slave who had become quiet proficient in the art of French cookery. Jefferson even wrote a letter to Paris to ask Adrien Petit to come to the New York home as soon as possible. Petit was a French courtier with good looks; he was highly recommended to the former President by John and Abigail Adams.

Jefferson was in New York City when Benjamin Franklin died in Philadelphia on April 17, 1790. Anthony listened as Thomas Jefferson complained about George Washington and his refusal to order an elaborate public homage for Dr. Franklin in New York like the one staged in Philadelphia. The House of Representatives voted to do one, but the Senate disagreed. That was when Jefferson went to Washington to see if the office of the President would still follow the example of the House. Washington said no, Jefferson told Flint, because Washington did not want to set a precedent for future presidents whenever a death of a notable person had occurred.

The voice of Thomas Jefferson still sounded bitter about this to Anthony Flint. Somehow, Thomas Jefferson thought George Washington could have done more toward the memory of Benjamin Franklin. Jefferson clearly was not happy about Washington's decision. Perhaps Jefferson's attitude on the whole thing was too personal to be objective now. A month before he died, Jefferson made a brief stop in Franklin's home before his journey to New York City. Franklin was gravely ill. Jefferson instinctively knew he would never see Benjamin Franklin alive again.

The ruminations on Franklin included a theory by Jefferson that Washington may have actually been jealous of Benjamin Franklin and on how history would regard him as a principal in the American Revolution. A sentiment, apparently, that was not shared by George Washington alone. Jefferson said he read a letter sent by John Adams to Benjamin Rush, a friend of Adams and the most esteemed physician in all of Colonial America.

Adams wrote:

> The essence of the whole will be that Dr. Franklin's electrical rode smote the earth and out sprung General Washington. That Franklin electrified him with his rod and thence forward these two conducted all the policy, negotiation, legislation, and war.

As the Staten Island Ferry pulled away, and as the long line of tourists waved to the passing ship, Flint remained the sole audience of Jefferson, and he enjoyed every minute it lasted. While everyone else was looking ahead at the approaching sight of the Statute of Liberty, Flint was more and more attentive to Thomas Jefferson.

For a number of reasons, he didn't tell his wife. He also wasn't filming anything with the video camera. Especially in the beginning when the World Trade Center was so prominent to see. The skyline on this sunny day in New York City was as spectacular as any postcard mailed from the Big Apple in the last 50 years.

Once they reached Liberty Island, it was late in the day, and the line was too long to wait to go up the statute. There was only time in the next hour or so for sightseeing around the 12-acre national park setting that is Liberty Island. The statue itself is resting squarely on what is mostly original masonry still intact of Fort Wood. It was built in preparation for the War of 1812, but the 11-pointed-star shape of the fort is nearly perfect as the distinctive foundation for the Statue of Liberty.

After a third request by his wife, who was growing impatient now and becoming a little worried about her husband, Flint walked back far enough that he could turn around and video his wife and the Statue of Liberty in the same shot. She wanted to do the same thing with him and was met again with blank stares that she interrupted as being mental thoughts somewhere else in time and space. He was certainly not thinking about the Statute of Liberty. What was more frustrating was she could never get him to open up when he was like this.

He stood still long enough that she was sure she got a good view of her husband and the statue even if he was not smiling. She felt this was also not fair to her. This was a dream vacation. It came at a very good time in their lives when they were still talking about the adoption of a baby girl. She had also argued successfully more than three months ago that they had the time and the resources to do this and there wasn't any good excuse on his part to say no.

She managed to lead him along the brick walkway that fronted nearly half of the island. From here the panoramic views of the Upper New York Bay were almost as exhilarating as the views from the Empire State Building. Yet it didn't seem to change at all Anthony's behavior on Liberty Island. Unknown to her was this unbelievable notion that Anthony Flint was both friend and confidant to Jefferson, Lee and God knows what else.

Jefferson was silent during the time spent at the Statute of Liberty, when Anthony and Candy Flint boarded the ferry again—this time heading just a few hundred yards north to Ellis Island. Anthony spent this time standing at the railing, thinking; he was much quieter than expected. When considering his surroundings, this should have been a non-stop "did you know" on how the Statute of Liberty was built—or something to that effect.

His wife asked him again if he was okay. Anthony changed the subject, like he always did, when he was seeking refuge from those things he could not explain. Flint did it this time by skillfully pointing out how beautiful the fully restored main building was on Ellis Island. It was also hard to believe that 14 million immigrants were processed there, seeking freedom, a better life, and fleeing religious or political oppression. But this all ended up sounding like another history lesson from her husband, which was a reassuring sign, because he did this frequently. Flint was used to the research he was required to do as a columnist for *The Orlando Sentinel*; he usually had a reserve of facts when he wanted it.

Her husband's love of history was always interesting to Candy, who always said she would rather see the home of so-and-so than to sit at home and watch it on the History Channel on any day of the week. And so it was that her husband liked to talk about history—what he really liked doing on any day when things were going right. This seemed good enough for Candy. She didn't know what was really going on, and besides, who could stay mad or worried for long on a dream vacation?

In a two-week period, they also visited family in Baltimore, a good friend in Boston, walked across Harvard Square and journeyed to Niagara Falls.

They even took the time to put on yellow rain suits and stand in the spray from the falling water and wonder repeatedly how anyone would want to go over it in a barrel.

There was no real answer to that. Neither was there any enlightenment in 1994 for Anthony Flint in New York City. He would never return here again. Yet his memories would surprise any historian of any age. Flint understood fully what he heard. Anthony was in a predicament that was becoming all too familiar to him. And to him only.

By the time the ferry stopped at Ellis Island, Jefferson began speaking about the Declaration of Independence to Anthony Flint. After all, here was a man who had the site of his grave marked for the whole world to read that he was the author. Other accomplishments—President, governor of Virginia, commissioner to France, apparently failed to make the final cut.

Now Jefferson could forgive the delegates to the Continental Congress that summer long ago that, more or less, secluded him in his upstairs parlor at Seventh and Market Streets in Philadelphia. To write and cherish words even more than his love of architecture, and to find a spirit and tone that was indeed proper for the occasion.

Needless to say, Jefferson referred to the Declaration of Independence as proof that a great republic had emerged from its principals. And from the Staten Island Ferry—somewhere—Jefferson remained quite pleased with America.

Chapter 23: Pope John Paul II

Villa Vizcaya Museum and Gardens in Miami was originally 180 acres when completed in 1916 as a typical Italian villa, completely self-sufficient, with a dairy, poultry house, mule stable, greenhouse and staff residences. The museum has art and furnishings that exhibit 400 years of European history. And in 1994, President Clinton hosted the historic Summit of the Americas here with 34 leaders of the Western Hemisphere. Other world leaders visiting Vizcaya have included President Reagan, Queen Elizabeth of England and King Carlos I and Queen Sofia of Spain.

In September of 1987, it was an overnight stay at Vizcaya for Pope John Paul II. It was all part of his Papal visit to Miami. The Pontiff was rapidly becoming the most traveled Pope in the history of the Papacy. The Holy Father first came to America in 1979, and he would again visit the world's only super power in 1995. And the Vatican was behind all of this, which was no small feat, and which included a watchful eye on the world's most troublesome war zones or the politically unstable countries. Later it would be the increasingly frail health of the Pontiff himself. Yet the Holy See was never really comfortable with the thought of curtailing the globetrotting head of the Roman Catholic Church.

So the Vatican arraigned and announced the next Papal journey of Pope John Paul II. And so it was that the Archdiocese of Miami issued press credential No #572 to Anthony Flint, a columnist for *The Orlando Sentinel*. Flint traveled to Miami the day before for extra time to prepare his column in his hotel room and to ensure he got an early start the next day at Miami International Airport. He was warned by his editors that everything would be hectic in this proud city of cultural and ethnic diversity. Even a stop for a pizza that night proved how right they were; it was time-consuming and frustrating, and the place was loud and boisterous and filled with the excited talk about John Paul II.

It was also times like this that Anthony Flint always regretted never learning a second language. It was not conceivable that he would need to know Spanish some day while still a young boy in Hagerstown, Indiana. He would never visit Mexico, Spain or Cuba; but here was the nation's 11th largest metropolitan area, and here the population was 65% Hispanic. And most of the journalists that year in South Florida knew the large Cuban heritage had infused Miami like no other city in Florida.

The headlines here were world famous for the overthrow of Fidel Castro and his Communist Cuba. And sometimes the headlines came from the most disenfranchised areas of Miami like Liberty City, where the neighborhoods survived riots, joblessness and despair. However, the image of Miami that was remembered the most was the ones on its beaches and 5-star hotels. Flint saw this years ago as a child at home watching the *Jackie Gleason Show* on television. The opening scene was shot from an airplane approaching the city's skyline along the sandy beaches, and all the hotels, pools and palm trees gleaming in the bright sunshine.

And it was a sunny day when Flint drove to Miami International Airport and then was escorted to one end where a large crowd was listening to a military band playing marching tunes. He was headed to the press site, a roped-off area in back of the VIP section. This consisted mostly of seated parishioners with tickets provided by the Archdiocese of Miami—and the others with a ticket as lucky as any that could be bought under the State's new lottery. But with the arrival of *Air Force One*, it was the crowd in the stands behind the press that cheered and applauded the loudest.

The plane taxed past the podium and stopped not far from the press site. It had the distinctive blue and white colors selected by President Kennedy when Boeing built the aircraft in 1962 as model 707-320B. Kennedy also directed that the words "United States of America" appear prominently on the fuselage and that the American flag be painted up on the vertical stabilizer. And 707-320B would go on and fly six presidents.

But President Reagan stayed inside *Air Force One* until the papal plane landed and taxed to a stop on the other side of the podium. It was a larger aircraft than Air Force One and was dubbed *Shepherd One*, although it was a chartered flight with the Italian national airline, Alitalia. Someone inside was waving hand-held flags of America and Italy extended through an opening along the top of the fuselage.

Pope John Paul II was the first to deplane. Then followed a long line of priests and cardinals and lay people nearly all dressed in black. They gathered on the tarmac and watched as the Pope greeted a waiting President Reagan. Now both men stood at the podium under a small cover and heard the national anthems played by the military band. The crowds in the stands then cheered and applauded at the end.

At Miami International Airport, President Ronald Reagan said:

It was my hope that one day you would return to the United States. Today, your Holiness, you begin just such a return visit. And, today, all America applauds.
(Applause and cheers from the crowds in the stands.)
In freedom, we Americans in these last 200 years have built a great country of goodness and abundance. Indeed, your Holiness, it is precisely because we believe in freedom and because we respect the liberty of the individual and the economic and political spheres that we have achieved such prosperity.
We are justly proud of the Marshall Plan—the 40th anniversary celebrated earlier this year in Europe. We continue to place our might on the side of human dignity. In Latin America and in Asia, we're supporting the expansion of human freedom. In particular, the powerful movement toward democracy.
(Applause from the crowds in the stands.)
Yet we Americans admit freely to our shortcomings. As you exhort us, we will listen. With all our hearts, we yearn to make this good land better for all.
(Applause from the crowds in the stands.)
Florida. South Carolina. Louisiana and Texas. Arizona. California and Michigan. Tens of thousands of Americans and more than 50 million Catholics will greet you. They do great works— America's Catholics—in the name of their church. Here in the United States American Catholics put their faith to work in countless ways. Maintaining parochial schools that give under privileged children in our inner cities the chance to receive a good education.
(Applause from the crowds in the stands.)
Supporting the AIDS hospices established by Mother Teresa's Missionaries of Charity.   (More applause from the crowds in the stands.)
And perhaps helping to put on a fund-raising dinner for the local parish. The American Catholic seeks to translate faith into deeds. Supporting missionaries in distant lands or helping America's

Knights of Columbus restore the facade of St. Peters in Rome.
(Cheers and applause from the crowds in the stands.)
Welcome back!
(Cheers and a standing ovation as President Ronald Reagan
shakes hands with Pope John Paul II.)

Hundreds of people sat in their lawn chairs along Biscayne Boulevard in downtown Miami to see the Papal Parade. It was here that the TV crews interviewed those who waited to see John Paul II. Also, they happened to be the best seats in the house, and they were free. It was never the intention of the Archdiocese of Miami to charge admission to help defray the $1.8 million it cost to bring the Pope to South Florida. And it was the same thing all over again for the Archdiocese of New Orleans, which was hosting a youth rally at the Superdome that weekend with the Pope.

But Miami was the first stop, and it attracted enough souvenir stands and vans with pictures of the Pontiff to fill the Superdome. One man was selling hand fans with pictures of John Paul II; he stopped and smiled and gestured for Anthony Flint to take his picture. Then he walked away, still clutching a dozen or so fans in each hand.

This whole area was a captive audience for things religious with crucifixes and all things on the life and teachings of the head of the world's largest church. This area was also heavily secured more than three hours ago by the Florida National Guard and Miami police. They even joined forces by having their men standing on the sidewalks every ten feet or so, creating a human fence along Biscayne Boulevard. But this wasn't all of it. The helicopters continued to fly overhead to sweep the area and look for any possible signs of trouble. And Flint saw the Florida Highway Patrol frequently send a vehicle speeding by him to fetch some idiot who had just climbed the fence to jump over.

To the south, Flint could see the historic Freedom Tower building. Then he could see the flashing lights of the law enforcement vehicles and motorcycles at the head of the parade. Then followed a vehicle with a boom that hoisted a platform for aerial shots directed at the Pope; and then followed a Mack truck pulling a flatbed that was used by photographers and TV camera crews for close-up shots. Then followed the white 1981 Mercedes-Benz popemobile, accompanied on both sides with dark sedans. Now the people along Biscayne Boulevard could see John Paul II waving to them from the rear of this vehicle.

The Pope was accompanied by another man standing next to him, and there were two people seated inside the small cab below. Then the parade came to an end with more law enforcement vehicles and motorcycles with flashing lights. And all of this passed by a huge billboard across the street from Anthony Flint. It had a picture of the Pontiff and large lettering that said: Miami Welcomes Pope John Paul II.

At Miami International Airport, Pope John Paul II said:

Mr. President, dear friends and the people of America, it is a great joy for me once again to be in your country. And I thank you for your warm welcome.
(Applause from the crowds in the stands.)
I come to proclaim the gospel of Jesus Christ to all of those who really choose to listen to me. To spell out once more the message of human dignity with its inalienable human rights and it's inevitable human duties.
(Applause from the crowds in the stands.)
I come as a pilgrim in a cause of justice and peace and human solidarity.
(Applause from the crowds in the stands.)
I come here as an apostle of the Catholic Church to speak and pray with the Catholic people. The theme of my visit: "Unity in the Work of Service."
(Applause from the crowds in the stands.)
It also enables me to experience evermore keenly the hopes and joys. I come as a friend of America and all Americans, Catholic, Protestant, Jews, people of every religion and all manner of goodwill.
(Applause from the crowds in the stands.)
I come as a friend of the poor and the sick and the dying, who are coping with the problems of each day. Those who are rising and falling and stumbling with the drama of life. Those who are seeking and discovering and those not yet finding the deep meaning of life, liberty, and the pursuit of happiness.
(Applause from the crowds in the stands.)
Finally, I come to join you as you celebrate the bicentennial of your great document, the Constitution of the United States of

America.

(Applause from the crowds in the stands.)

I willingly join you in a great thanksgiving to God for the Providential way in which the Constitution has served its people for two centuries. I join you in asking God to inspire you as Americans, who have received so much in freedom and prosperity and in human enrichment, to continue to share all this with so many brothers and sisters throughout the countries of the world. They are still waiting and hoping to live according to the standards of the Children of God.

(Applause from the crowds in the stands.)

With great enthusiasm, I look forward to being with you in the days ahead. Meanwhile, my prayer for all of you, the people of America, is this: "Let the Lord bless you and keep you; and let the Lord shine his face upon you and be gracious to you; and let the Lord look upon you kindly and give you peace."

God bless America!

(Cheers and a standing ovation as Pope John Paul II shakes hands with President Ronald Reagan.)

The Archdiocese of Miami expected half a million people to attend the outdoor mass at Florida International University. And it was the largest gathering of people that Flint had ever seen in his life. It wasn't something that he would ever see again. Many were holding hand-painted signs welcoming John Paul II to South Florida. Some were dressed in costumes, to perform on the large stage that was in front of a giant 2-story cross made of white steel.

Tower platforms scattered throughout the area with mounted speakers played background music as everyone filed in. From time to time, the announcer came on and asked the growing crowd where everyone was from. Cheers went up for Fort Lauderdale and Miami, and there were so many more.

Flint could see the local stations broadcasting live morning news shows from where he was standing. Earlier that morning he walked through the back areas and saw dozens of satellite trucks set up, with miles of cables running on the ground. He also saw a long line of law enforcement vehicles, their engines running, and the hoods partially up, to keep vigil against the rising temperatures of a typical South Florida afternoon in September.

Now in the distance Flint could see the Popmobile slowly making its way to the stage. His line of sight was hampered by the people running alongside it to wave to the Pontiff. This continued for several minutes and with an intensity that mesmerized the young, the old, male, female, Catholic and non-Catholic. It was also the kind of star power that was the dream of Hollywood's biggest names and the envy of the most famous rock bands. Not even the office of the President of the United States of America could have this.

Soon ancient rituals of the Roman Catholic Church played out on the circular stage that was lined by hundreds of potted yellow and white plants. Here composer Aaron Copland's "Fanfare for the Common Man" played as many men, women and children circled the base of the stage, dressed in white shirts and pants and holding tall banners with crests of different colors. Then it was the strains of "Hallelujah!" as the beautiful music played on and on as bishops in their white robes ascended up to the stage and surrounded the Pope dressed in a green robe.

John Paul II held his hands over the altar and proceeded to bless the people as far as he could see. His prayer was suddenly interrupted by a loud crack of thunder. That was a warning to Flint, whose instincts about Florida weather were as good as any Florida Cracker, which is a true native of the Sunshine State. So he needed no divine intervention to know he had to get out of the press area as fast as he could.

Flint made it to a stand under a tent selling refreshments, probably as a fund-raiser and maybe even for a local parish. He didn't remember who they were, but he couldn't forget the mass exodus of people walking in the pouring rain. They filed past the tent, and Flint could see a resigned look on their faces. It was universal, really. How this was a downpour and they were getting drenched big time.

Some had umbrellas, and some used newspapers to hold over their heads. It made no difference what they used—just getting to their cars to go home was tough business. And the rain seemed to last forty days and forty nights.

Nearly 20 years after the Papal visit to South Florida, Flint ran this column for *The Orlando Sentinel*:

Poor Rome.
Somewhere in the Vatican are the files kept on all the priests or
bishops who ever resigned because they were really pedophiles, or

worse.

The local parish is supposed to be a safe haven for the most fundamental members of any spiritual family on earth—the children of the world.

But once again, a priest in central Florida has been arrested for allegedly abusing dozens of altar boys over the last million years. I know we have read these kinds of stories before. We seem to be used to it.

But where did we go wrong?

God is usually not mentioned by the media, by the U.S. Catholic bishops or even by the people who work under the vaulting shrine of Catholic faith that is Saint Peter's Basilica in Rome; and where it has always been a struggle to move a church steeped in medieval ways into the modern world.

Before the current headlines, it was the infallibility of the Pope or the Vatican's long-awaited words on contraception. And believe it or not, the last edition of *Look* magazine was published on October 19, 1971, with a cover story on this besieged institution. One paragraph said this:

"Once a Mass was the same, sound for sound, sign for sign, whether in the center of Brazil or the hamlets of the Great Plains. Now there may well be drumbeaters at one, folk-rock singing at the other, and at neither can a worshipper be sure that the priest isn't planning to marry—if he doesn't already have a wife."

And you can't miss the heading to this article: "The Power and the Glory Are Passing." The story explores how Vatican Council II changed the church in the winter of 1965, much like the U.S. Supreme Court changed America with its legalized abortion ruling in 1973.

At first, even those outside the faith praised what was the work of 2,400 bishops to bring the Catholic church up to date and to overcome internal resistance. It was called a miracle by many.

But if you read the *Look* article further is says this: "The prospect now is that the Vatican Council the Catholics were no proud of may have accomplished little more than the trivialization of their beliefs. The liturgy of the Mass, shorn of its Latin, has degenerated in places into speech and song at its most primitive, crying out for the noble cadence of a Dominus vobiscum."

Pretty heavy stuff even if it was published more than three decades ago. The article goes on to describe a steady flood of defections from the clergy in the first six years after Vatican Council II. Their numbers included two U.S. bishops and at least 11,000 priests worldwide by the Vatican's own admission.

But nobody had any numbers on the people who gave up on the church but not their faith in God.

Now the cruelest thing about today's headlines is the millions of dollars being paid to settle all those lawsuits against the Catholic church. This basically requires any affected parish to dip into church funds, sell church property to raise funds or spend funds on lawyers and stonewall the whole thing.

And God is usually not mentioned. If an institution ever needed God, it is Roman Catholicism that has been in search of a new identity ever since the crucifixion of Christ.

It is time for Rome to wise up and get over this delusion that it plays any higher role in the church than God does.

You might say this is none of my business because I'm not Catholic.

Years back, when some of the television preachers of the 1980s were found to be sinners, and some even bilked their own followers to build a theme park, congregations rolled over like whipped dogs and looked the other way.

Society did not become part of any lasting solution. It kept to itself.

The ultimate act of apathy is claming you're not apathetic.

I have a better idea.

Mention God always.

Chapter 24: Dave Thomas in Lakeland, Florida

Anthony and Candy Flint, after the wedding in their home in 1992, adopted a little girl on January 20, 1999. She spent the first two years of her young life in one of the best foster homes in the state. They saw fit to raise her as one of their own; but, for many reasons, they knew she could not stay. This was always a big problem for any foster home, always acknowledging love to the needy child and still knowing that a permanent family may find her someday. It was especially so for this foster home because they had done it so many times in the past.

She was born on August 31, 1996, at the Orlando Regional Medical Center. She was all of 6 pounds, 6 ounces, at 8:29 a.m. that year. Her Final Judgement of Adoption listed the full name as Alanah Beverly Flint; her middle name was from her grandmother on her father's side. This was done primarily because Keith and Beverly Flint had four grandsons and no granddaughter. It was also neat to buy Barbie dolls at Christmas and her Easter dress in the spring, and it was all about a new home for a very deserving child.

Alanah was a healthy child, and her life was center stage in a home that was trained to have her by the Florida Department of Children and Family Services. This was very much a child who came with stuffed animals, toy racing cars and a big Winnie-the-Pooh diaper bag. It was also a memorable ride home for everyone in the car. The emotions present included joy, fear, surprise and apprehension. And Alanah cried all the way home. Anthony always remembered that.

Flint, like the others in his training group, had more than one turn "acting" out the role of a parent who had just adopted a small child. Usually under the direction of the counselor and when it was meant to be a stressful moment. The dishes were still in the sink, and the dog was barking at something, and on the face and arms of the imaginary child was peanut butter and jelly. Frustration becomes impatience, with everything else going wrong. It was not unlike a situation for parents who had a biological child. And it was always Monday—with your spouse away, it seemed—for the temptation to lose your temper and hit the child. Suddenly. And then it was all too late.

Everyone in the group admitted to these feelings. But it was Anthony who said he'd put the dog in time-out before anything really got out of hand. It was his way of handling the problem, even if he had no experience as a parent, and the group was quick to point this out.

Even the counselor agreed it was only part of the solution. And on any day, when things got wacko, you needed to stop and count to ten. The time would even come to count to 50, 100, 1,000, and this made everyone in the group laugh. Flint said he would also try to remember to pet the dog and hug the child. Or should he hug the dog and pet the child? And the smile on his face was another indication that he had no real experience as a parent. None whatsoever.

Wendy Thomas was the second youngest child of Dave and Lorraine Thomas. She was the little girl with red hair and pigtails and whose image appeared on the sign with the first opening of her father's new business in 1969.

In January of 1994, her father was the keynote speaker for the annual Chamber of Commerce banquet in Lakeland, Florida. He said this to 1,000 people at the Lakeland Civic Center: "We have so many children with special needs who have no homes. They really need our help. It's just the right thing to do."

His second book was published that year when his business was on track to becoming a $5 billion global company. This information was merely a minor point when Dave Thomas really wanted to tell his audience how proud that he was an adopted child. It amazed many others who assumed his start with Colonel Harland Sanders and Kentucky Fried Chicken was his biggest break. Nor did he consider Wendy's Restaurants his greatest achievement.

Thomas donated all the proceeds from his second book to the Dave Thomas Foundation for Adoption. He met with representatives from local adoption agencies that week in Lakeland. Thomas urged business owners to set up adoption incentives for their employees. It was especially important at a time when nearly 8,000 children lived in foster homes throughout Florida.

"You can do anything within the laws of God and the laws of man," Thomas told the chamber banquet that night.

Seven years later, Thomas died of liver cancer at his home in Fort Lauderdale, Florida. The next morning, a Wendy's executive arrived at company headquarters in Dublin, Ohio, at 6:45 a.m. This was when he noticed a second car in the parking lot. When he got out of his car, a woman got out of her car and walked up and handed him a sympathy card for the family of Dave Thomas. She was an assistant manager of a Sunoco gas station where Thomas stopped once in awhile. "He always contributed to the community, he was a good father and husband, and he was just a terrific man," she told the executive still standing in the parking lot.

There was a day at Moss Park in Orange County when the district office allowed several children up for adoption to run and play in a neutral environment. It was a chance to show them off—sort of—to perspective parents and a life in a home of their own. Here were teenagers and small children and boys and girls and the inevitable comparisons that the adults would have to make. This resulted in confusion and some introductions on the part of the counselors; a child would stand still long enough to say their name and how old they were and then run off to play.

It was a weird afternoon at the park for Anthony and Candy Flint. They had been on the waiting list as parents approved for adoption since 1995. But the children in the park attracted the adults in such a way that it was uncomfortable to find the courage to talk to a child. Candy told her husband she thought this whole thing was unfair. She told him it was like picking someone to be on your basketball team. That would be the tallest; or maybe it was the best runner or jumper? They both agreed about some kind of attraction that would make the adoption move forward. And just like a married couple, a time would come when a smile leads to friendship and then love, and the rest was history.

Yet most of the children seemed oblivious to what the adults were doing and seemed to be more interested in what they could find on the playground. Like a big tube slide, a rope ladder or some other kind of play station that looked pretty exciting to young people running around as free as the wind. Anthony certainly didn't forget seeing the first little girl riding the merry-go-round in endless circles. The district office said that was limiting the field and they would have to open their options if they wanted a real successful adoption. But Anthony always wanted a little girl.

A blond-headed one of six or seven was very popular that afternoon. She wound up on local television as "Wednesday's Child," when there was a special time for her to have a walk with the news anchor in Moss Park. Now she was allowed to talk about herself; in her own words, she really wanted a home of her own and even some brothers or sisters. The news anchor held her hand, and they walked to the swing set, and he pushed her in the swing until it seemed that she was as high as the birds in the trees. And since she was pretty and intelligent to begin with, the television director and his staff had only to count to five and then see the phones ring off the hook. They knew it was the power of television and hundreds of parents wanting to adopt this one child.

It was probably something that had all the right intentions and was meant to be a big draw for the adoption of all children in Florida. The objections from the Flints that day was how it all seemed to be a popularity contest. Nowhere was a runway used to model the girls in their evening gowns. And the boys had no bats to hit a home run out of the park. Unfortunately, however, there was still enough competition in other areas to produce a lot of heartaches.

Still to come would be the day when Anthony and Candy adopted Alanah despite all the odds. Candy called the district office one time in desperation and told someone in July of 1998 how the whole process was slow as molasses. Her husband wanted a little girl during his lifetime! And when it was Anthony's turn, he took the telephone from his wife and heard the very words for himself. That prompted a drive west to New Port Richey, Florida, and the foster home of Alanah. It was not far from the Gulf of Mexico.

And still to come was all the benefits of finally adopting a child in the State of Florida. Anthony learned that his new daughter was eligible for a college tuition waiver and it was good for up to four years of undergraduate study. It did not cover room and board or other expenses such as books and supplies. But who cares about that? This was a wonderful start to a seat in any college or university in Florida. That was when it was decided by her new mother that Alanah was going to be a cheerleader for the University of Florida—in the year 2015!

What was so surprising was Alanah also had her own Medicaid card, and that covered everything from coughs and fevers to open-heart surgery. Her new parents also received a monthly adoption subsidy. How they spent it was entirely up to them. But it would all be for the good of the child. All of the clothes and daycare and birthday bashes that could be bought when needed.

But one thing was for sure, and that was when Alanah Flint went to bed that first night, she would be safe. Anthony bought a monitor to set up in their house. And when he had done this, and when he turned it on, it was reassuring to hear the sounds of a small child asleep in her new home.

Alanah's first Halloween in Orlando found her wearing a pumpkin costume with matching green slippers and a cap on her head. Her parents took her up and down the streets of the neighborhood early that evening; they let her ring as many doorbells as possible. It was also the best time before all the bigger kids got involved. And always in groups ready for a blitzkrieg. There was also a flatbed truck every year with a portable generator for the floodlights and the boom box to blast music to the stars. It was always fun, and everybody enjoyed it.

After the first homes on the block, Alanah and her parents learned she only had to smile, and she didn't have to remember to say "Trick or Treat." The neighbors said how cute she was and unloaded enough treats to empty a Russell Stover candy factory. Even the home of Alanah's adoption judge was a popular stop in this neighborhood. Nobody had to worry about a Halloween trick tonight.

Other neighborhoods in Orlando and Orange County were different. Where some of the kids dropped rocks from the overpasses on cars and trucks, another one was all the fire departments, police stations and hospitals checking the bags of candy. Flint wondered if it was all part of the nation's War on Terrorism—the growing price to live one's life without the fear of death. And in Florida, it was law that these same places receive newborn babies from the hands of those who give them up. There would be no questions and no arrests.

She also got to see her first snow during the week of Christmas on the 40-acre farm. It was falling with the holiday beauty made symbolic by Norman Rockwell and Bing Crosby. Alanah and her cousins played in the white stuff while always under the watchful eye of their grandparents. They could remember a time when three little boys stood in the back porch, cold, stomping the snow off their boots, fumbling to get out of their snowsuits, and all the while, the strong demands for something warm to eat.

Now the oldest of them was over in the barn with his wife for a ride on the Farmall H tractor. Backing out into the snow, and heading to the field in front of the house, and where hundreds of bails of hay were gathered last summer. Flint wanted to drive past the house and wave back to the kids with his wife. But even though the snow was falling around them, it still wasn't could enough to freeze the ground. So it was that the tractor got stuck in the mud. The big tires on either side of him flipped the muck on top of the fresh snow; and Flint watched the whole thing as he shifted gears to go forward and then to go reverse. He just forgot how it really was to be in a winter wonderland.

Chapter 25: Death Row

Long ago the native Indian tribes of Florida named it the "Withlacoochee" for "crooked river." This accurately describes a waterway that makes a winding 100-mile journey through west-central Florida to the Gulf of Mexico. And the view from a canoe or small boat hasn't changed that much in a hundred years. Visitors can still see standing timber of all kinds, the slash pine, the longleaf pine, or a mixture of oak, maple, southern magnolia, gum and hickory. There were also the famous bald cypress trees that live to be centuries old. And the river itself was a great place to fish for largemouth bass and panfish. And in the springtime the goldenrod, thistle, blazing star and other colorful varieties of flowers bloom along the banks of the Withlacoochee River.

But here it was that authorities found the dead body of a young white woman. She was tied to a tree, with extensive burns and overwhelming evidence of great trauma. She was found in the Richloam Wildlife Management Area and that was a part of the Withlacoochee State Forest. Her discovery was nothing short of a miracle. This was, after all, the second largest state forest in Florida. A vast area of over 150,000 acres that was managed by the Florida Division of Forestry for lumber, wildlife, ecological restoration and outdoor recreation. It was also patrolled by sheriff's deputies in four counties. This was necessary because the number of tourists who came was 300,000 each year.

Even though two men were arrested and later convicted for the crime, no one in the beginning would know who the woman was except by the name of Tammy. Then witnesses for the state attorney's office recanted their testimony in 1983. A federal judge issued a stay within 16 hours of execution, and defense attorneys argued there was coercion and intimidation used during the interrogations of suspects and witnesses. When the body of the poor victim was finally identified in 1986, it was seven years after the brutal slaying. And so it was that Anthony Flint traveled to Starke, Florida, to the prison that housed Florida's electric chair, and to interview William Riley Jent, 35, and Ernest Lee Miller, 29. Both men half-brothers and both on death row.

ANTHONY FLINT: Did you see the broadcast by ABC News on its 20/20 news magazine?

WILLIAM RILEY JENT: We both seen that on TV back in our cells. The show was real good. It told the things we're up against and the things that are turning in our favor. In other words, it's just bringing out the truth.

ERNEST LEE MILLER: Everybody on our floor watched that TV program. It showed what the State was doing, mostly. It gives the national attention that it deserves.

ANTHONY FLINT: If you did not kill Linda Gail Bradshaw in 1979, who did?

WILLIAM RILEY JENT: As far as I know, a man named Bobby Dodds. He's in prison in Georgia right now.

ERNEST LEE MILLER: Elmer Carroll told me Bobby Dodds did it. He told me who the girl was and told my lawyers who she was.

ANTHONY FLINT: The Second District Court of Appeals in Lakeland ruled this year that law enforcement agencies must open the complete files on this case for public inspections. And the Eleventh Circuit Court of Appeals in Atlanta has returned your case to U.S. District Judge George Carr in Tampa.

WILLIAM RILEY JENT: We hope! That's all we're trying to get done. Somebody to listen to everything, you know. Two or three things could be overlooked, but not all of them. There are so many different versions of what happened. I mean, everything points away from us. So why are we here?

ERNEST LEE MILLER: The way they have it now, the State can hide evidence. And that's what we feel has happened to us. If they did, that's a violation of our rights.

ANTHONY FLINT: Robert "Bobby" Dodds, Junior, appears to be central to your defense. He has been convicted on charges of forgery, auto theft, child molestation, armed robbery and selling drugs. Dodds has been declared an habitual felon. He's serving two 10-year sentences. Now I want to ask you how you know this man?

WILLIAM RILEY JENT: The first time I ever even laid eyes on the boy was when 20/20 showed his face on TV. I've never seen him in person and never even heard of him before I was arrested.

ERNEST LEE MILLER: I might have met him one time when I went over to that trailer they talked about to see a friend of mine. Dodds and Bradshaw might have been there, but I'm not sure about that.

ANTHONY FLINT: Your attorneys consider Dodds not only the prime suspect in this case but also in the murder of Ida May Mockaba in Dalton, Georgia. Her 1979 murder has never been solved. Mockaba and Bradshaw both dated Dodds, and they both died the same way. Now let's talk about Elmer Carroll. He's in prison now serving five years for child molestation. In a sworn statement filed in 1980, he said Dodds and Bradshaw went with him to the Richloam National Forests in Florida. He says he saw Dodds pour gasoline on Bradshaw and then set her on fire. How do we know he's telling the truth?

WILLIAM RILEY JENT: They checked his story out. Everything he said can be substantiated. He had the right name and address for Bradshaw. Dodds had the motives, and we have none.

ERNEST LEE MILLER: The fingerprints identified Linda Gail Bradshaw, for one thing.

ANTHONY FLINT: The State's star witness was Glena Fry because she remembered the most details when she took the stand and testified against you. But she recanted her testimony in a sworn statement filed with the U.S. District Count in Tampa. Is she telling the truth now?

ERNEST LEE MILLER: Yes.

WILLIAM RILEY JENT: Yes.

ANTHONY FLINT: Fry testified in your 1979 trials that you both beat, raped and burned to death Linda Gail Bradshaw, of Cleveland, Tennessee. But in her 1986 sworn statement, she says she was coached in her testimony by local law enforcement agencies.

WILLIAM RILEY JENT: Every time something new would come up, they would have her change her story. And tell her what to say.

ANTHONY FLINT: Another witness was Carla Joe Hubbard who says she lied on the stand in 1979. She has filed a sworn deposition with her foster mother in Kansas City, Donna Huffman, a police officer.

WILLIAM RILEY JENT: I knew she said she lied back then,

DOUGLAS K. SANDERS

but I didn't know she gave a statement. If she's saying we didn't kill Bradshaw, she's telling the truth because we didn't kill anyone.
ERNEST LEE MILLER: She said she only said what the police wanted her to say. And that's the truth. She's telling the truth now.
ANTHONY FLINT: What would you say to these people who have recanted their testimony?
WILLIAM RILEY JENT: Thank you (laughing). I don't hold no grudges because I understand how all the pressure was put on them.
ERNEST LEE MILLER: I would thank them and probably hug their necks.
ANTHONY FLINT: Glena Fry told the *Tampa Tribune* this year, and I'm going to quote here, "I think I most scared now than ever. I look for Bill and Ernie to come after me. Those two scare me more than anything else in the world." Does she have any reason to be afraid?
WILLIAM RILEY JENT: No. None whatsoever. Even if I did hold a grudge, which I don't, there's no way I would risk being locked up again for anything! (more laughter) Besides, she was a young girl then, and she was scared. People in big offices was telling her she was going to prison if she didn't do what they told her to do. Who knows, anybody might have done the same thing.
ERNEST LEE MILLER: She doesn't have anything to fear from us. We're just happy she told the truth now. And basically, when we get out of here, we're getting out of this state. I mean they have shown what they can do to us. And we don't want to hang around in this kind of state. I mean, this is a police state. Period.
WILLIAM RILEY JENT: (laughing) We'll move back somewhere in Ohio!
ANTHONY FLINT: You know, recanted testimony rarely means much in court. The thinking being, if they lie on the stand, they most likely will do it again. But Elmer Carroll apparently knew about Dodds and Bradshaw and the story he wanted to tell for months—back in 1979. He was afraid that Dodds would harm him or his girlfriend at the time—Tina Marvin Parsons—or the baby she was carrying then. Parsons was a neighbor of Dodds and Bradshaw.

Did the both of you know there was a letter from one of the assistant state attorneys commending local law enforcement agencies in central Florida for, quote "breaking Carroll" and getting him to testify against you.

WILLIAM RILEY JENT: Not until our attorneys advised us of it. We didn't know nothing about it until then.

ERNEST LEE MILLER: I heard it from my lawyer, and then I saw it on 20/20. That's the kind of stuff they pulled. That just goes to show more of what they were doing at that time.

ANTHONY FLINT: Investigators assigned to this case denied during a 1984 Federal hearing that they improperly pressed Carroll for information. And one of them told the *Tampa Tribune* this month, quote, "I knew Elmer Carroll for a long time, and, in fact, they did break him from telling a false story to telling the truth."

WILLIAM RILEY JENT: I don't think the investigators know what the truth is. If they can look at our cases and not come up with some doubts in their minds, then they don't have a mind. That's just about it.

ERNEST LEE MILLER: The investigators don't what to be found out for what they are. They don't care about justice. They just care about the points they get for winning this case. Because that's how you move up in the justice system now. To win cases and that's all they care about....

WILLIAM RILEY JENT: (interrupting) They don't care if you are innocent or guilty. All they want to do is win. They'd send their own mothers to prison if they felt it would help their careers out.

ANTHONY FLINT: Tell me what happened on the night of July 12th, 1979?

WILLIAM RILEY JENT: We did have a party down by the railroad trussel behind Ernie's house. There was nine people there. We went down and swam for about two hours, and then we went back up to Ernie's. I went in and lay down on the floor and went to sleep because I was tired. Next thing I know, they woke me up the next morning about ten o'clock to take me to Tampa. They dropped me off, and I stayed there until Sunday. Then I came back on Sunday, and when I got to Ernie's house, they told me a dead body was found down by the river. It was about four or five miles away in the Richloam game preserve.

ANTHONY FLINT: We know the body of Bradshaw was found in the Richloam forests by horsemen chasing loose cattle. Did you see Bradshaw and Dodds at your party?

WILLIAM RILEY JENT: I never laid eyes on either one of them in my life.

ANTHONY FLINT: Did you see him beat her, rape her, douse her with gasoline and set her on fire to burn up alive.

WILLIAM RILEY JENT: How could I do that when I've never seen them before? Period. I mean, never in my life. I don't know them. I've never seen them—I have never even heard of them until we were arrested.

ERNEST LEE MILLER: A police officer came down to the river that night, and that was the only one besides the nine of us.

ANTHONY FLINT: Why did the officer come down to the river?

ERNEST LEE MILLER: It was his patrol area. We were swimming and goofing off, mostly. It was a hot night. We were just trying to keep cool. I spoke to him once.

ANTHONY FLINT: How did you two get involved in this? Your party was five miles from the murder scene.

WILLIAM RILEY JENT: I had two cuties with me, and we were standing in front of their house, and I was trying to talk with them. A detective and another guy pulled up and said they wanted to talk to me. I went over, and they said get in. But first he said, "Wait a minute" and he handcuffed me and put me in the backseat of the car. I said, "This ain't necessary," and he said, "Yes it is." They took me in and kept me for about four or five hours and kept telling me I was guilty of something I didn't know anything about.

ERNEST LEE MILLER: One day a detective came down and was showing a picture around—it was a sketch of a girl. He was asking everybody if they knew this girl. He asked me, and I told him she looked familiar. He started to ask me where I was that week, and I said I was at the river partying. About a week later, a fried of mine said his girlfriend was missing, and so I took him down to the police station. I saw Carla Hubbard there. Then they took me into this room and questioned me. They asked me if I would take a lie detector test. And could they search my car. I did everything they wanted me to. I didn't have anything to hide. Next thing I know, these girls were coming up with this stuff that we did it. I took the lie detector test, and it showed I had nothing to do with it, but they said I know something about it. We have since taken other lie detector tests, and we passed them. We have copies of it.

ANTHONY FLINT: Do you think the outcome in all of this would have been different if the two of you had come from wealthy families?

WILLIAM RILEY JENT: If we had come from wealthy families, yeah, if would have been different. We would have been able to hire people to help us. Our lawyers did a good job, I guess. But every time they tried to get help, the judge would rule against them. The judge wouldn't let them get their own forensic experts or an investigator of our own. We had to depend on what the police gave us. That was nothing.

ERNEST LEE MILLER: We would have used private investigators, and maybe we could have found out some of this.

ANTHONY FLINT: You have been on death row for seven years, and perhaps over the years, the public's perception of Miller and Jent has become apathetic. They're probably saying you're guilty of something, prostitution, drugs, outlaw bike gangs. And let's leave them there.

WILLIAM RILEY JENT: They mentioned on 20/20 about us being bikers, and they throw it up that a bike club came into the county and had done something before. I think they're using that against us. Just because we're bikers, we're guilty. That's it.

ANTHONY FLINT: The investigation mounted by your attorneys did not make any headway until April of last year. At that point the *Washington Post* uncovered a fingerprint match that positively identified the body as that of Linda Gale Bradshaw. Why do you think it took so long?

WILLIAM RILEY JENT: Because everybody was fighting against it. Nobody wanted to cooperate with nobody else. Florida didn't want to cooperate with Tennessee. The prosecutors didn't want to help the lawyers. The cops didn't want to help nobody. Nobody wanted to know except us.

ERNEST LEE MILLER: When the *Post* came to see us right here at Starke Prison, they got involved in it and checked into it.

ANTHONY FLINT: What's it like being here?

WILLIAM RILEY JENT: Well, you get up for breakfast, and then you watch an hour or so of TV, eat dinner, watch another couple of hours of TV, you eat supper, and then you watch TV until you fall asleep. And then you get up the next morning and do the same thing.

(Laughter from all three men.)

WILLIAM RILEY JENT: The cell is six foot wide, nine foot long; it's got a bunk, a footlocker, a sink, a commode, and a little shelf in it. There's probably enough room to fall out of you bed, and that's it. It's a single cell.

ERNEST LEE MILLER: I do a lot of pacing in my cell. So I pace back and forth a lot. And usually it's so bad I don't eat lunch. I exercise. If I'm lucky enough to get a letter, I will answer that. I watch TV most of the night until I fall asleep. A typical day.

WILLIAM RILEY JENT: I get a letter from mom every now and then. A girl will write me every two or three months, or a friend or something. Nothing on a regular basis. I mean, when I first got here, we were getting letters and money. (Pause.) Now we don't even need stamps because I don't have anyone to write to anymore. We get two free stamps a week, and I don't even use that.

ANTHONY FLINT: What did you think when you first saw this place?

WILLIAM RILEY JENT: I'm in a lot of sh— now!

ERNEST LEE MILLER: They have two fences about 18-feet tall with barbwire on top. They got that razor wire in between the two fences, so if you get past one fence, you have to through that razor wire. They have a guard tower at each corner.

(The air conditioning suddenly stops, and the lights dim briefly.)

ANTHONY FLINT: What's happening?

ERNEST LEE MILLER: They're checking the generator that goes to the electric chair. They only check it on Wednesdays. They turn it on at one-thirty and then turn it off at two-thirty. That way they keep it in good running condition so when they electrocute someone, it's running right.

ANTHONY FLINT: What has been the biggest adjustment?

WILLIAM RILEY JENT: Being away from my boys. (Sigh.) I have two sons, and I love them, and I ain't seen them in a long time. Marilyn, their mom, is taking care of them.

ERNEST LEE MILLER: Getting used to being locked up in that confined cell all the time. It's really rough. I'm used to spending a lot of time outside. That little cell will drive a man crazy.

ANTHONY FLINT: If your appeals are successfully, how will you put your lives back together again?

WILLIAM RILEY JENT: It won't be easy. It's going to be hard to hold a job anywhere. It's going to be hard to even find one.

ERNEST LEE MILLER: We hope to start over in Dayton, Ohio. We definitely got to get out of this state. Especially if we're proven innocent. The police won't like that. It will prove they framed us, and they did.

ANTHONY FLINT: You received a stay of execution in 1983.

WILLIAM RILEY JENT: It's kind of strange. You get nervous and everything.

ERNEST LEE MILLER: You can't do nothing about it. They control everything. They watch you 24 hours a day. They don't want you to commit suicide. They search your cell every time you leave it. They don't want you to have something that can hurt them or yourself. I had butterflies in my stomach. I'm not going to say I was not nervous. They done asked us what we wanted for our last meal. They measured us for a suit. Made out a Last Will and Testimony. Asked us where we wanted our personal property sent. I was really glad when our lawyers called and said we were granted a stay.

ANTHONY FLINT: Have you seen the electric chair?

WILLIAM RILEY JENT: I haven't seen the electric chair except in pictures.

ERNEST LEE MILLER: I saw it on TV. That's it.

A federal district court threw out the convictions of Miller and Jent in 1987 and said prosecutors had withheld evidence and acted with a "callous and deliberate disregard of the fundamental principles of truth and fairness." The following year the two men were allowed to go free on time served and in exchange for guilty pleas to second-degree murder. This allowed Miller to return to his hometown of Dayton, Ohio, where he got a job as a roofer. Jent moved to Arizona and became a ranch owner with his wife, Patricia. And the half-brothers won a wrongful-arrest lawsuit in 1991 that paid them $65,000, most of it going to lawyers' fees. Miller told the *St. Petersburg Times* on July 4, 1999: "The $14,000 I got bought me a nice Harley-Davidson motorcycle."

Chapter 26: Deed to Daniel

Downtown at the courthouse in the City of Danville, the countyseat for Boyle County, Kentucky. The room Anthony Flint was in had access to marriage records, divorce proceedings, vital statistics, probate, liens, tax records and real estate transactions. It was all a part of the history of Boyle County, and even when Kentucky was still a piece of Virginia.

A light overhead seemed to illuminate things pretty much like it did 60 years ago. The room was reminiscent of a time and place when the temperature wasn't all that different from the weather outside. This was important only if you wanted to search the records during the bitter winter or in the steamy summer. And the people who worked at the courthouse knew this would always be solitary work and not very glamorous at any time of the year.

Even now it was at infrequent times that a staff person entered the room to put a new record on file. Each one of them performed the task quietly and did not speak. Of course, none of them could ever recall the last time someone from Orlando, Florida sat in this room. One insight was the remote possibility that Anthony Flint was really a developer looking for property to build a Wal-Mart Supercenter. This was something that Danville and the Boyle County Economic Development Council wanted more than they wanted to admit in the newspapers. However, the courthouse staff was not sure about this and they decided early on to leave him alone.

Thus accessing the records in the very beginning was not a problem at all. In fact, Anthony Flint found what he needed when he saw the legal description to his brother's new farm on Kentucky Highway 590. It was then that he plugged in his laptop computer. This would allow him more productivity than all the typewriters or adding machines ever used in the Danville courthouse.

He began by downloading software from his office in Florida that was used by the advertising department of *The Orlando Sentinel*. It was very helpful in listing and sorting real estate sales; the user was also able to search for the date of construction, lot size, square footage, roof structure, plumbing, mechanical, electrical, permit history and, yes, even the date when the warranty deed was recorded. Now Flint was able to type in his request and wait for his reply.

<My footsteps have often been marked with blood. Two darling sons, and a brother, have I lost by savage hands.>

Flint was surprised by the response, but he also knew his link on the Internet was about as private as a billboard advertisement on Interstate 75. He also wasn't worried about security because he was working with records that are usually public anywhere in America. So Flint proceeded to re-type his request in the data fields that appeared on the screen of his laptop.

<No man before has ever dared to call me a coward.>

Now he knew something was wrong. This had nothing to do with a legal description and everything to do with some kind of prank by a computer hacker. He decided to reboot his computer and try again.

<Too many people! Too crowded! Too crowded! I want more elbowroom!>
Flint tried a fourth time.

<A man needs only three things to be happy: a good gun, a good horse, and a good wife.>

>Who are you?< Flint typed back on his keyboard. He was frustrated more than he was angry.

A pause.

<DB. 1773.>

Communications had come a long way from the days when a dedicated phone line was installed from Hagerstown to Richmond for the 1949 high school boys' sectional basketball tournament. That was when a missing link was made possible in east-central Indiana. It was done by Anthony's grandfather, Harold Clark, a telephone repairman, with his youngest daughter in the senior class. Beverly Flint would be a mother three times over in nine years; but that night she was joined in the gymnasium by her classmates. And with the absence of satellite trucks or network television, everybody sat in the bleachers and listened to the large speakers on the basketball court. They could hear the sound of the game in Richmond, and that was 24 miles away.

Now things were so different, and news organizations often got together and hired an outfit suitable to investigate vulnerable computers and fend off stalkers using cyberspace. In a lot of ways, securing safety in this world was as fundamental as obtaining a social security card. Yet one could always have his number stolen on the Internet even with protection.

So it was not the first time that *The Orlando Sentinel* called a computer data retrieval company for help. Within the hour, it was Omnitrac Data in Sarasota, Florida, online with the editors and beginning a complex search to find any mysterious e-mail correspondence linked to Flint's computer in Danville, Kentucky.

First, Omnitrac sorted the memory cache on Flint's laptop from their offices in Sarasota. All computers keep a log of websites visited by the user and, in turn, a trail for any cyberstalker to copy and access for himself. However, Flint's computer had cache-deleting functions, and he always used a dummy e-mail account with a false name. It was only his friends and people he trusted who had access to his primary account. But was DB a friend or foe?

There was still no answer to that question after the first two hours. Each time Flint sent or received e-mail, he also checked his browser. It displayed a symbol—a lock—that confirmed that the communications were secure and encrypted. Whether or not that meant there was enough scrambled to prevent unauthorized access, only DB would know for sure.

It was a farm with a seasonal pond off a hilly road that was for sale in Boyle County, Kentucky. Anyone stopping to park in the driveway could easily see how the place was perfect for Clark and Cyndi Flint, and their four sons, Bryan, Brandon, Eric and Nolan. And at the end of the lane was where you reached the barn that was big enough to hold all of Clark's antique tractors. Maybe, also, his own tobacco to hang and dry inside and then sell when the market was good as it got. No different, really, than the farm's owners in the past when they wanted to make a profit.

How families in each generation make such a change in life usually winds up as a sociological study at the nearest state university. It is also understandable even in many households where a choice to live in Baltimore, Maryland, or on a bluegrass farm in Kentucky was no contest at all. And Clark changing jobs from Westinghouse Corporation to Hitachi Corporation was just the beginning.

Then there was the unrelated fact that this was the first Kentucky farm that Anthony and his wife had seen up close. This was something that the hacker—"DB"—was really interested in, and when he immediately began to exhibit a remarkable knowledge about the state of Kentucky.

<It was on the first of May, in the year 1769, that I resigned my domestic happiness for a time and left my family to wander through the wilderness of

America, in quest of the country of Kentucky.>

When DB said he first saw Kentucky, he realized that everyone in his party could become rich like Boaz, the wealthy Bethlehemite first described in the Old Testament book of Ruth, and "having the cattle of a thousand hills." DB filed at least 29 claims to nearly 39,000 acres of land. He wanted it all for his eight living children. However, he was cheated out of some of it by unscrupulous speculators. And in order to pay the taxes, he had to sell a great deal of his land holdings in Kentucky.

Then there was the time in 1780 when he stayed overnight in a rural Virginia inn. He carried in his saddlebags $20,000 in cash to buy land warrants for the Transylvania Company, the very same group that started the settlement at Boonesborough in 1775. DB said he was entrusted with a great deal of money. But he had no cash in the morning and wasn't even able to pay the lodging bill. There was nothing else to do except to return to Kentucky and tell what he suspected had happened to him: that the innkeeper drugged and robbed him. Yet there was no way to prove this. And he was neither bitter nor remorseful about it.

But now he urged Flint to continue the research into the warranty deed on Clark's farm. It seems DB was deputy surveyor of Fayette County, Kentucky, in December of 1782. He also had an uncle who was a surveyor in Berks County, Pennsylvania. But it was his own son, Nathan, who admitted that his father's "knowledge of surveying was limited." DB agreed and explained that many property lines in the greater Lexington area showed how inadequate he was for that job.

There were other ways and many suggestions from Omnitrac in Florida to Anthony Flint in Kentucky. He kept his cell phone on with Sarasota and continued his e-mail with "DB" at the same time—all in the hopes of tracking down who or what this thing really was. So the things Omnitrac investigated included, but were not limited to, computer worms and viruses, accidental downloading of spyware, freely available hackware online and the websites used by Flint in the last 24 to 48 hours. The later was checked out to see if any information by Flint was shared with third parties.

It was also noteworthy that Anthony Flint used an anonymizer like www.anonymizer.com to hide his identify with every website he accessed. Most websites kept a record of each visit, but Flint's name would not be there. All of his uses were encrypted. Most important, his Internet service provider would also have no record and any potential hacker would have this obstacle as another hurdle to overcome.

Omnitrac also reviewed all of Anthony's e-mail accounts, his personal home page and any acceptance of unnecessary cookies—code stored on his laptop computer that identified him. All of it had password-protected access, and Flint could confirm each cookie listed in his browser preferences. And it was very much a dead-end. It didn't help any when a company employee with Omnitrac shook his head shortly after lunch and made this terse observation with Flint: "Remember, every idiot knowing how to press buttons is able to take control over you computer if you're not careful."

Flint was not impressed. "If I've got a secret, I don't put it on a computer hooked up to the Internet!"

There was no time for Sarasota to apologize for this on the cell phone. Flint had just received another e-mail from DB: >I can't say as ever I was lost, but I was bewildered once for three days.>

The hacker said he knew Flint lived in Florida. Then DB began to describe his own travel through South Carolina and Georgia to St. Augustine in the fall of 1765. The government was offering free land for those who wanted to settle in the Florida panhandle. But DB found little opportunity to hunt, and the landscape and climate was not what he was used to. He found Florida to be a land with high water and hordes of mosquitoes and crawling bugs he had never seen before. And at one point, the whole group became lost in a large swamp. They were lucky to be finally rescued by a party of Seminole Indians, who took them to their camp and fed them venison and honey.

Everything DB e-mailed to Flint could be attributed to Daniel Boone, the great frontier legend of America. It could also be found easily enough by anyone using the Internet like Omnitrac did when they verified the historical accuracy of the last e-mail that afternoon. It was all about a group of 100 settlers moving into Kentucky in September of 1779. This was the largest group ever to migrate to the Bluegrass State. Most walked during the trip, but a few women and children rode horses. Among the settlers was the family of Abraham Lincoln, whose grandson and namesake would one day become the 16th President of the United States of America.

DB said the party made its way across the Blue Ridge Mountains and continued north and west around several hills to the Holston River. They crossed a series of ridges and valleys of the Appalachians, and then it was on to the Clinch River and over Powell's Mountain. Then they followed the Powell River south to the Cumberland Gap, the most famous mountain pass in North America. Then after passing through the gap, they traveled through what is now the Daniel Boone National Forest in east-central Kentucky. The whole trip took more than five weeks.

This was a famous story, that was true, and was as much a part of the enduring legacy of Daniel Boone as anything in the history books. Yet DB was fully aware of U.S. Highway 25E, nicknamed "Massacre Mountain" by the drivers who once followed the 3.2-mile stretch through the Cumberland Gap. He cited numbers from the National Park Service that said 18,000 motorists crossed the mountain daily. With that was also a death statistic that saw an average of five people a year killed in traffic accidents there.

The road had been paved across the mountain to carry automobiles in the early 1930s. It was an engineering feat at the time. But it had some pretty sharp curves, and that's what made it dangerous. The National Park Service lobbied Congress to close the deadly old road and to build twin tunnels in a construction project totaling $240 million.

DB even read the old journals and the maps that were used by the Federal Highway Administration to restore the landscape to its natural contours. The workers hauled in dirt and planted grass and trees to grow a countryside once more like it was in 1775. And to do this restoration project it cost $5 million to complete.

The hacker seemed proud that not one fatal crash had occurred since the opening of the tunnels.

There does come a time in nearly everyone's adult life when the following philosophical question is asked in groups of two or more people: If you could talk to three people in history, who would they be? Whether he was in high school, college, Sunday school, on vacation or behind his desk at work, it was always the same answer for Anthony Flint. For him, he would most like to meet Jesus Christ, Adolph Hitler and Abraham Lincoln. It was funny that the names of Thomas Jefferson, Robert E. Lee and even Daniel Boone never came up for family discussions; it was especially so if Anthony Flint was ever a part of it.

Chapter 27: Astronaut James B. Irwin

Astronaut James B. Irwin was one of 12 Americans who walked on the surface on the moon in the 20th century. He was the pilot of the Lunar Excursion Module *Falcon* for Apollo 15, a 12-day mission that lasted from July 26 to August 7, 1971. He then spent the rest of his life relating his experiences with schools, civic organizations, scientific institutes, universities and word leaders. During one trip Irwin included stops at several churches in central Florida, and on September 11, 1985, he found time that afternoon to meet with Anthony Flint for nearly an hour at the First Baptist Church on Church Avenue in Dade City.

ANTHONY FLINT: As you approached a 1,200-foot deep gorge near the base of the Apennine Mountain range, you told David R. Scott, the Apollo 15 flight commander, to watch the road!

JAMES B. IRVIN: Mission Control was a little concerned. They thought we might tumble off the edge and go down into the gorge. We didn't have any extra oxygen.

ANTHONY FLINT: The low gravity on the moon made the journey on the lunar rover difficult.

JAMES B. IRVIN: It was very rough. Many times we would skid, and several times we almost turned over as we tried to avoid a large rock coming into view. It was a very rough surface. We used our seat belts—it was impossible to stay in the rover without them. My seat belt was so tight I had difficulty fastening myself in. In fact, Dave had to fasten me in. But I could unfasten myself.

ANTHONY FLINT: Do you see only black-and-white, or are there any color definitions on the moon?

JAMES B. IRVIN: Sometimes it's difficult to get the right color. It varies so much with the sun angle. I thought it was more tan and brown than the gray you seen in photographs of he moon. But again it depends on the sun angle. You can look into space—the absence of sky on the moon—it was somewhat difficult to see the stars, but if you shade your eyes for just a short time, you can begin to see the bright stars. The sun is out, and yet you can see stars—it was an unusual experience. We could see the Earth directly overhead us at this time. But it was about the size of a marble, and it was only a half-earth. But extremely beautiful, a blue jewel in the blackness of space. And we knew by its size that we were a long way from home.

ANTHONY FLINT: You spent 67 hours on the lunar surface, covering 21 miles. Apollo 15 was the first mission to use the $8 million, 400-pound lunar rover. You and David Scott collected about 200 pounds of moon rocks, including core samples, and brought back to Earth in sterile nitrogen containers to be analyzed by the lunar receiving labs in Houston. One milk-white rock was dubbed by the press "the Genesis rock," because it was believed to be part of the original lunar crust.

JAMES B. IRVIN: I think it must have been. It confirmed their theories about white rocks in the mountains of the moon. That was our purpose of our exploration, to explore the mountains of the moon, and we were the only mission to do so. We found only one, and it was sitting on a larger rock (sample #15415 was believed to be anorthosite, a crystalline piece of the moon approximately 4.6 billion years old). We only had to drive over to it, and we announced where we found it. Scientists were very surprised that we could find that white rock so far down on the slope. If we had the time to go higher, we probably would have found more.

And when we brought the rocks inside Falcon, we then pressurized our compartment with 100% oxygen because that was the environment we were living in. And when we did this, immediately—the lunar rocks oxidized: first time they were ever exposed to oxygen. And so you had something that smelled like gunpowder that had just been detonated. I was wondering how we could live in the LEM and sleep with such a strong odor all around us.

ANTHONY FLINT: Seismographs from Apollo 14 and 15 were set up to determine if there is any molten rock at the core of the moon.

JAMES B. IRVIN: There is still a lot of heat coming out of the moon. We were surprised about that. We also had heat-flow experiments that contributed more information—where it was determined that the heat flow was twice what was expected. About half the heat flow that we would find on Earth.

ANTHONY FLINT: Your training included astronomy, navigation and geology.

JAMES B. IRVIN: We spent many years trying to understand the geology of the Earth so we might relate it to the geology of the moon. We became skilled geologists so we could report what we were seeing on the moon. We found a great variety of rocks, probably the greatest treasure of any Apollo lunar mission. We also saw things that had not been seen before—like the layering that existed in the mountains and along the walls of the canyons. We were far north—26 degrees north—on the moon, in this beautiful valley with high mountains on three sides. It was Hadley Base, named for the British mathematician and astronomer who invented the sextant (independently invented around 1730 by both John Hadley and the American inventor Thomas Godfrey). There were prominent features around our landing site named after Hadley—Hadley Crater, Hadley Canyon, Mt. Hadley. So we thought we were in British territory!

ANTHONY FLINT: What have we learned from the lunar rocks?

JAMES B. IRVIN: Well, the study of the moon continues. The analysis of the moon rocks continues. When I was in Houston earlier this year, there are small fragments left of the Genesis rock. Pieces have been taken from it to be sent to laboratories for analysis from people around the world. So I think our knowledge continues to increase about our natural satellite; there are annual symposiums where the scientists combine information. Apollo 15 contributed quite a bit from our three days on the moon. We spent another two days orbiting the moon and photographing the lunar surface to provide information where future missions could land. There is a meeting in Houston later this year to discuss a future lunar base.

ANTHONY FLINT: What other tests were part of the Apollo 15 mission?

JAMES B. IRVIN: We had solar wind experiments to measure the energy from the sun to the moon. Then we did some soil mechanics where we did such things as dig ditches, to understand the soil characteristics and to know what has to been done to construct buildings on the moon. We put up another scientific station where data has been sent to earth for a number of years.

ANTHONY FLINT: Your command ship *Endeavor* mapped 20% of the lunar surface, producing moon photos never seen before on the far side.

JAMES B. IRVIN: Al Worden, our command module pilot, felt very satisfied in his task observing the moon while in orbit. In fact, he feels like he probably contributed more than we did because we were limited to a very small radius on the surface. He could circle the moon many times.

ANTHONY FLINT: What was your first reaction when you stepped foot on the moon?

JAMES B. IRVIN: It was magnificent scenery. I've always loved the mountains. I've spent a lot of time on Earth climbing mountains with my mother and father and even with my own children. And here I was in the mountains of the moon and looking up at their grandeur. They towered about 15 thousand feet above us. I was reminded of a favorite ski resort, and I thought, *Boy, this would make a great ski resort!* Maybe in the future people will try moon skiing. It would be a new sport introduced on the moon.

ANTHONY FLINT: What are the best memories you have with Apollo 15?

JAMES B. IRVIN: The most exciting moment of the mission was the lift-off from Earth. Tension builds up waiting for that moment, wondering if it will ever happen. So many things can happen—someone can take your place on the flight. I never knew until that moment of truth that it's all going to happen. And to sense all that power—7.5 million pounds of thrust directed very precisely to get us the right direction as we clear the tower and leave the Earth. I had tears of joy coming down my face as I realized—man! I'm on my way! I'm going to the moon!

ANTHONY FLINT: You suffered irregular heartbeats on the moon.

JAMES B. IRVIN: I was certainly overheated and hot. Really dehydrated. We had no water to drink or food to eat while on the surface of the moon. For almost eight hours at a time. And working very hard. And as a result, I paid the price for that. I did develop heart irregularities. And I've been plagued with heart problems ever since the flight. But it was worth that. Just to go to the moon, to visit another world and to come back with a new appreciation for the blue planet—just a new appreciation for things I've taken for granted.

ANTHONY FLINT: Let's talk about the spiritual impact of your flight.

JAMES B. IRVIN: I came back, and I vowed that I would do my utmost to preserve the Earth and to, somehow, help the people come to a similar awareness. We're all crewmen on this spacecraft Earth. We're all hurtling through space at a tremendous speed to an unknown destination. If we're ever to reach that destination, we must take care of the blue planet and take care of one another.

I really did sense that God was with us as we traveled out, and he allowed us to see the Earth, as he might view it. He was with us while we were on the lunar surface. He was there to answer prayers, to guide us to this white rock and to inspire me to quote scripture. I never quoted scripture before. So I came back, and I've been sharing these things, you know, ever since. I'm hoping others will be more open and more aware of God and inviting God to be a part of their life and to bless them.

To make all of our flights work, yes, I believe God is with us. It had to be a part of God's plan. Of course, he uses men and women to accomplish his purpose. He has really blessed us in our efforts to explore the universe. Here is the Universe—go and explore and learn more about it. And in the process, I think, we come to appreciate God more and to worship him and to praise him for the abilities he's given to us. He's certainly expanded our horizons, given us a new vantage point, and he's the one who gives us hope.

ANTHONY FLINT: After your return to Earth, you became equally famous for your search for remnants of Noah's Ark on Mount Ararat.

JAMES B. IRWIN: We've found some very interesting things in eastern Turkey. We have found some large stones with holes in the center that have been referred to as sea anchors; these were at the base of the mountains. We also found a boat-shaped object that certainly has the right dimensions to be Noah's Ark, and it's in the right area. But I'm not convinced it is Noah's Ark. I'm continuing to look high on the mountain itself, up in the ice, about 25 square miles, for what has been reported to be Noah's Ark. There have been many reports over the last couple of hundred years, and we're trying to follow up these reports. And I usually take a team with me. Sometimes archeologists, geologists, certainly, skilled mountaineers; it takes a team effort to climb any high mountain. We've been trying to get into one particular region that is more dangerous than the other areas of the mountains.

ANTHONY FLINT: You had a dangerous fall off Mount Ararat.

JAMES B. IRWIN: I recovered from the 1982 fall. I do not know precisely what happened, but I suspect I was probably hit by a falling rock and knocked unconscious; and I tumbled down through the snowfield into the rocks below. I know I was unconscious for about six hours; then I awakened in the late afternoon and found what my predicament was and tried to move out of that area. But I was too weak to move. Fortunately, I still had my backpack with my sleeping bag inside, and I was able to get into that and spend the night.

I made a mistake by traveling alone on the mountain by going from the high camp to the base camp to coordinate our move off the mountain. The others were so busy looking for the Ark I decided I wanted them to continue that and I would go down. But I made a grave error by traveling by myself, and I know I won't make that mistake again.

I did receive deep lacerations in my face, my head and some puncture wounds in my body. But I was taken good care of by the Turkish military. They put me in one of their finest hospitals, and five days later, they released me and I came home. I did have a chance to go by in Ankara and visit with the president of Turkey and thank him for his hospitality to us. He must have felt sorry for us. He said, "Colonel Irwin, any time you want to come back and look for Noah's Ark, why you come back as my guest." So I've taken advantage of that offer several times; I hope I'm not wearing out his gracious hospitality.

ANTHONY FLINT: You have taken five expeditions to Turkey. What makes you think the Ark is still there?

JAMES B. IRWIN: We did do an aerial search in 1983 and flew around the mountains several times, took hundreds of photographs and didn't see anything that looked like the Ark. But there is one particular area—and most of the evidence points to this area—and that's where we really want to get into and search it out. If there is nothing there, we'll be convinced we did everything we can that's humanly possible to find the Ark. But we just want to find what it is that people have reported seeing at the foot of the mountains, about 15 miles south of Mount Ararat. Teams are looking for evidence of any man-made activity—petrified wood, perhaps—in this boat-shaped object. But, to my knowledge, they have not found anything yet. But it's certainly interesting.

I'm going on reports from others, things that they've seen and that they claim might be Noah's Ark. I've not seen it yet, and so I continue to climb and continue to search. And I'll probably be going back. Whether I'll be going back next summer or not, I don't know. I promised my wife that I would take her backpacking in the mountains of Colorado, as a change, rather than deserting her in the good climbing days and going off to Turkey. So next year I might reserve for my own family.

ANTHONY FLINT: You're also searching for the Ark of the Covenant.

JAMES B. IRWIN: Several years ago I went over to the Middle East and went into Jordan to look for the Ark of the Covenant. And we opened up a new cave on Mount Nebo, but in that cave we didn't find the Ark of the Covenant. The only thing we found was an old German newspaper. And when we brought the newspaper outside the cave, the wind caught it and carried it off. So we don't even have that evidence. I would've loved to look at the date on that newspaper—this all happened before that move came out: *The Raiders of the Lost Ark.*

How important it would be to the world, I don't know. I just think, you know, the Lord has been so good to me and has allowed me to travel into space and to travel to the moon. He allowed me to find the so-called "Genesis Rock." Well, perhaps he will use me to find something more important from the book of Genesis here on the Earth.

Astronaut James B. Irwin died from a heart attack in Glenwood Springs, Colorado, on August 8, 1991. He was 61 years old.

PART FIVE

Chapter 28: The Treaty of Versailles

President Woodrow Wilson and five delegates represented the United States of America at the Palace of Versailles on the outskirts of Paris. More than a thousand people crowded inside the Hall of Mirrors to watch 72 delegates seated at a long velvet-covered table. Nearby was a small table raised on a dais. Resting on it were the official documents entitled: *The Treaty of Peace Between the Allied Powers and Germany.* It was, in total, a treaty of 426 pages, a summary of 13 pages, an additional 27 pages for *The Treaties of Saint-Germain and Trianon; The Treaty of Neuilly; The Treaty of Sevres;* and including 4 pages of maps, 11 pages for signatures and a covenant to establish the League of Nations. This was all bound into cloth-covered volumes and transported in black leatherette satchels.

What happened next was this: Herman Muller and Johannes Bell signed their names as the two delegates from Germany. As soon as they had done that, the great water fountains of Versailles were turned on. This was the first time since the Great War ravaged Europe in 1914. Then 50,000 people assembled on the grounds surrounding the palace roared with cheers and applauded with laughter. This was the first day of international peace that came on the heels of the "War to End All Wars."

Indeed, at three o'clock in the afternoon, the United States delegation signed the Treaty of Versailles. Next came the five British delegates, including Prime Minister David Lloyd George and Foreign Secretary Arthur Balfour. Then the delegates from the other 30 nations lined up next, including New Zealand, Australia, South Africa, Canada, France, Italy and Japan. But something was still missing: a spirit that was still thinking of all the military campaigns to come.

So it was that Robert E. Lee was present that summer day on June 28, 1919. He was not a signer of the Treaty of Versailles and was, in fact, not seen by any of the people inside the Hall of Mirrors. It was not possible that they would know he was even there. Lee spent his time reading the articles of the treaty and was very impressed with Part I—the formation of the League of Nations. This was based on the principles advocated by President Wilson but shunned by Congress; and the United States never joined as a member. The League of Nations was to preserve the peace and improve the world with specialized organizations dealing with labor and health, among others.

Wilson's tireless efforts won the admiration and respect of Lee. The first time he saw this determination was when Lee and his wife, Mary Custis, spent 24-hours on a train to Augusta, Georgia. It was all part of a long vacation that lasted two months and four days and ended up being a farewell tour of the South. Thousands of well wishers saw him for the very last time, and some saw him only once, like the 13-year-old boy at the Planter's Hotel in Augusta. Lee watched him make his way through the crowd that morning until he stood next to him, to admire the general in his own silent but unabashed way. When this boy became President 44 years later, Lee immediately remembered the encounter in Georgia and the name of Woodrow Wilson.

The hovercraft crossed the English Channel on November 21, 1995, to reach its final destination at Calais on the coast of France. This was nearly three days after all the sightseeing was completed in London, and the start of Anthony's first trip to the continent of Europe. To do so, however, required a 2-hour flight from Orlando to Washington, D.C., and then eight hours to Heathrow Airport. He was glad it was only a vacation. The day would not come when this form of travel would ever become routine for him. Even with feature-length motion pictures showing onboard the aircraft and the round-trip tickets in his briefcase, the realization that he was flying overseas did not really seem conceivable. It was war correspondents who flew to London, he reasoned, and not columnists from central Florida.

All of the cars and trucks transported by the hovercraft were unloaded and parked. People also stepped down and faced the brisk winds coming in off the English Channel. It was Candy Flint who accompanied her husband and who was now clinging dearly to her bags. She had the same look on her face the day she married Anthony, and that was a combination of pride and trepidation.

It was a ride straight to Paris on the group tour bus. This was very comfortable and very convenient for Anthony and Candy Flint. The group tour did it all. They even double-checked the currency rates in London and in Paris. It was also no problem with all the registrations for the accommodations, and there was free time to go ahead and get into trouble on your own. This was satisfactory with the group traveling with the Flints. Beginning with those who also came from Florida and then the teacher from Chicago and the young man and wife on their honeymoon from South Bend, Indiana. There was also the CEO from the oil company in Midland, Texas, traveling with his wife. The last couple in the group tour had just opened a new Chinese restaurant in Camden, New Jersey.

Many times the members of the group would look out for each other when things were not a part of the official itinerary. The net result was that all bases were covered. This was true one afternoon when Flint left his hotel room in London and was quickly spotted by the new entrepreneurs from New Jersey. They noticed that Anthony did not have his camcorder strapped on his shoulder. It was a calamity that was quickly resolved without any help from the American embassy.

Paris was reached at nightfall when there was a light rain in the air and when the group saw the Eiffel Tower in person for the first time. It was beautifully poised above everything else in the city. Many generations and a few invading armies had come down the Champs Elysees to gaze up at, arguably, one of the greatest engineering feats the world has ever seen. The Eiffel Tower was visible tonight in a light that was yellowish-brown in color. Everyone got off the bus to stand in the rain and see it before heading to the hotel.

In the morning, the tour started early with a drive around the Arc de Triomphe and then a stop at the Louvre for the next couple of hours. Now this was a palace that became one of the largest museums on the face of the earth. The celebrated collections include the Victory of Samothrace, the Venus de Milo, Michelangelo's Slaves, the antiquities of Egyptian, Greek, and Roman civilizations, and the paintings of Raphael, Vermeer and Durer. Here was the home of Leonard da Vinci's *Mona Lisa*, the most famous painting in the world. It was also a lot smaller than Anthony expected. At the end of the day, the group was silent as it entered the Basilique of Sacre Coeur. This was situated on the summit of Montmartre that overlooked the city. Dozens of candles were lit inside while the choir was singing to the large congregation.

The second day was spent at Versailles, a city five miles northwest of Paris that was mostly a residential community with some industry. But it was world famous as the palace and the gardens of Louis XIV, king of France from 1643 to 1715. It was once a small chateau and then it was enlarged by the chief architects, Louis Le Vau and his successor, Jules Hardouin-Mansart, to house numerous salons and royal apartments. The most famous of the galleries is the Galerie des Glaces, or the Hall of Mirrors. It was completed in 1684 with 17 mirror-filled arches with Pyrenees marble pilasters.

The ceiling paintings portray the history of Louis XIV. Each chandelier can be moved for an unobstructed view of the episodes from the War of Devolution (1667-1668) and the War with Holland (1672-1678). These lighting fixtures are replicas of the original ones that lit up the hall in 1770 for the wedding of Louis XVI and the Archduchess of Austria and Lorraine, Marie-Antoinette.

Only some of the eight classical statues in the hall today are original. The busts of the Roman emperors come from separate royal collections in Europe. A number of other pieces of furnishings are also not originals, except for the remaining andirons that Marie-Antoinette ordered for the fireplace in 1786.

The magnificent fountains are supplied by a water system almost 100 miles long. They include the Fountain of Latona and Parterre; the Fountains of Autumn and Winter; the Fountain of Apollo and the Grand Canal; the Fountain of Enceladus; the Obelisk Fountain; the Fountains of Spring and Summer; the Dragon Fountain and the Fountain of Neptune.

It was the French landscape architect, Andre Le Notre, who laid out the gardens in broad avenues lined with trees, shrubbery, groups of sculpture, ponds and many secluded groves. There are intricately designed flowerbeds lined with bronze vases atop slabs of marble. The palm trees were added in the 19th century.

The gardens were visible from the large windows of the Hall of Mirrors. As Anthony turned back to continue the walking tour, he also saw for the first time that some of the people in the hall were actually dressed in clothes of 50 or 60 years ago. After all that the group tour had seen in the last few days—from the Tower of London to the Notre Dame Cathedral on the Ile de la Cite in the center of Paris—this was a nice touch. Flint made a mental note to include this compliment when he was completing the questionnaire for the group tour.

But now more of the people walking through the Hall of Mirrors were dressed like they were attending a political convention long ago. As one who has visited Walt Disney World any number of times, Anthony was used to seeing actors perform in period costumes. And this was a show by men, women and even children who exhibited a great deal of historic professionalism.

They spoke dozens of languages and were no longer carrying bags with souvenirs purchased in Paris. Since he was not a historian, Anthony Flint had trouble in the beginning as he ascertained what was happening here. He did notice that the air inside the Hall of Mirrors was hot and he could no longer feel any currents of air conditioning. He also saw candles burning in the chandeliers hanging from the ceiling paintings and in the candelabra stationed in the hall.

There was significant change in the next few minutes as Anthony saw nearly a hundred men seated at a long velvet-covered table. He heard a voice callout their names. A man would rise and join in the line that was leading to a small table raised on a dais. It was there that they signed their names to the documents and then returned to the seats at the long table.

It looked and sounded like a ceremony that Flint saw not long ago on the History Channel. He couldn't immediately remember the program. Some of it was a series of old black-and-white photographs. This was all in color and as real as the growing beads of perspiration on his forehead. The whole thing was frustrating and confusing. Anthony hadn't seen Candy in the last half-hour or so. He saw nobody from the group tour. The Hall of Mirrors was filled with people, and yet Anthony Flint was alone. It was something really more powerful than anything with Thomas Jefferson or Robert E. Lee.

Anthony realized it was not 1995 simply because the names of some of the announced countries would not be found on today's maps of the world. It was also clear that no one at the palace could see him. It didn't change matters much for Anthony Flint, but, interesting enough, he took full advantage of the situation. That was when he decided to walk over to the small table and read the documents for himself. He could see the English text. But he also could see the French and German texts. Then when he started to read about the League of Nations, it was quite obvious that the document being signed was one of the most important of the 20th century. And it was popularly known thereafter as the Treaty of Versailles. It represented the hopes of all the people in the Hall of Mirrors and throughout the whole world that Europe would never again become a bloody battlefield.

More delegates signed the Treaty of Versailles, and Anthony Flint was standing close enough to see the signatures on the pages. It was inevitable that there would be words in these documents that would inspire most diplomats. Not even Vladimir Lenin and his Bolshevik takeover in Russia could justly ignore the fascination of peace to a mass population. It was so alluring that Alfred Nobel devoted part of his fortune from the manufacture of mines, torpedoes and other explosives—including nitroglycerin—to awarding those who craft peace in the world during their lifetime.

Czechoslovakia was the last to have its delegates sign the documents in the Hall of Mirrors. The men seated at the long table stood and joined everyone in the hall with cheers and applause for what seemed like an eternity. The time had finally come to return the blessed peacemakers to the capitols of the world and to the governments of the greatest and weakest nations known to man. Each delegate had seen the Promised Land at the Palace of Versailles. Everything in the treaty was expounded in the name of peace. And it was now that Anthony Flint saw Robert E. Lee standing next to President Woodrow Wilson and the American delegates at Versailles.

Lee was again in Paris when 15 nations signed a multilateral peace treaty on August 27, 1929. It was the Kellogg-Brand Pact, sponsored and drafted by U.S. Secretary of State Frank B. Kellogg and Foreign Minister Arrested Brained of France. The Treaty for the Renunciation of War—as it was more formally known—earned Kellogg the Nobel Peace Prize in 1929. This was primarily due to the fact that war was outlawed by the signatories; it was no longer a legitimate act of state. These nations whole-heartedly agreed to settle all international disputes with peaceful means.

During the 1930s, the treaty was absolutely useless for preventing war. It failed to halt the Japanese invasion of Manchuria in 1931 and the armies of Italy from marching into Ethiopia in 1935. The treaty was further discredited by the German occupation of Poland in 1939 and the outbreak of World War II.

All guns onboard the USS *Missouri* were silent on September 2, 1945. But the great battleship was not idle while it was stationed in Tokyo Bay. This was not a massive shelling campaign waiting to commence. It was a time, however, for introspection and prayers of thanks. The orders for the day simply required two copies of the instrument of capitulation on the table. One was bound in leather for the Allies, the other, canvas-bound, for Japan, the Empire of the Sun. The ranking solider and chief of the Japanese imperial staff, Gen. Yoshijiro Umezu, signed his name, and later, Gen. Douglas MacArthur, the future viceroy of Japan.

The setting here was the end to the greatest military conflict in the history of mankind. No one present wanted a World War III. That included Gen. Robert E. Lee, of the Confederate States of America. He saw more firepower on this deck than anything President Jefferson Davis could ever imagine in a thousand years. This was more than enough to stop the combined armies of Grant and Napoleon. But it was not enough for world peace. Lee already knew that he would be attending the signing of the documents in Paris on January 27, 1973, by the delegates of the United States, South Vietnam, North Vietnam and the Provisional Revolutionary Communist Government of South Vietnam. All were favorable to the end of the war on the easternmost part of the Indochinese Peninsula.

The United State Senate actually ratified a separate Treaty of Berlin with Germany on July 2, 1921. But the Treaty of Versailles enacted the terms of surrender that brought World War I to an end. This included, but was not limited to, German coal to France, Belgium and Italy for the next 10 years; restricting the size of the German army and navy with no conscription; the creation of Poland; Alsace and Lorraine restored to France; and a demilitarized zone occupied by the Allies on the west bank of the Rhine River for the next 15 years.

Germany was also required to pay reparations in money to the victorious Allies. It must also admit full responsibility and accept the guilt for the war. This was more than enough to set the stage for the reprisals by Adolph Hitler and the Third Reich in 21 years, and for Keith Flint to become a solider in 31 years.

PART SIX

Chapter 29: Second Man to Mars

After checking in at the Roosevelt Hotel—on the corner of Hollywood and Vine, no less—Flint made certain he was also registered as a panelist for the convention of Sigma Delta Chi, the national society of professional journalists. But the next 48 hours were free to be a tourist in Southern California. So he went to Santa Monica to see the Pacific Ocean for the first time. Then it was on to Sunset Boulevard, Beverly Hills, Rodeo Drive, the Hollywood Bowl, and a walk along the handprints and footprints of famous movie stars in front of Mann's Chinese Theatre.

In Anaheim, the lines at Disneyland seemed to be less hectic, not so long, with the weather cool and a light breeze in the air. It had been raining most of the week but not on this Sunday; it was all sunny skies. And what Flint saw in Disneyland was similar in many respects to Walt Disney World in Florida. It was a smaller theme park, admittedly; and it was not located at all in a sub-tropical climate. Yet Flint was glad to see the same Mickey Mouse hats, the monorail rides, and the same Disney magic that one day would fill theme parks in France, Japan and China.

Now he made it to the waterfront in Long Beach, where the R.M.S. *Queen Mary* and Howard Hughes' *Spruce Goose* shared nearly equal billing on January 14, 1990. The famed luxury liner had sailed over from Southampton, England in 1967, to become a historic hotel and floating museum. But the *Spruce Goose* was purchased in 1980 by the California Areo Club. Which was 33 years after Hughes flew it for one mile for engine and water handling tests.

Inside the domed building that was specially designed to house the giant aircraft, Flint saw what a billionaire aviator and film director could do with proper motivation and a national notoriety. Weighing in at over 170,000 pounds, with a wing span of 320 feet and a tail towering over 80 feet above the floor, it was actually called the H-4 flying boat, a predecessor to the future C-5 cargo plane; but it was made mostly of wood, and intended to carry up to 750 fully equipped troops, or two Sherman class tanks on each flight.

Congress wanted the use of three H-4 aircraft to help win World War II. But in 1947, Hughes was called to Washington, D.C., to explain why he was two years behind schedule. He returned to California during a break in the hearings, and it was then that he flew the damn thing one time. And so all of his attention to detail and insistence on everything being perfect was largely vindicated.

Hughes put the *Spruce Goose* into storage, where it remained from public view until his death in April of 1976. During all that time it was carefully preserved. In fact, the joinery of the laminated wood is so precise, it appears to be one piece instead of the many layers that are actually used.

Flint walked up the several inclined sections of the ramp to reach the entry level and the main deck. Here he could look down the massive length of the fuselage. Then it was up the narrow spiral staircase that leads to the flight deck. He walked past the engineering stations where the many systems of the aircraft were monitored during flight. The instruments are still in place on the tables as they were during the solo flight so many years ago. They are also carefully wrapped in plastic for protection against any layer of dust.

The control wheel was small for such a large airplane, but with it, Hughes easily maneuvered the mammoth hydraulic powered controls. Also near the pilot's seat were the tall power levers to operate the eight Pratt & Whitney R-4360 radial engines. The sound of the H-4 on take-off alone should be sufficient for a separate entry in the annuals of aviation history.

Once he was outside the *Spruce Goose*, Flint stopped to read the various exhibits and displays nearby. He read the caption to the group photograph at the top of the first exhibit: "Astronauts Richard T. Crotty, David O. Kulhman and Floyd B. Calloway hold the Howard Hughes Technology Memorial. It is only one of a few select artifacts planned for NASA's manned mission to Mars."

It was clear to Flint that others standing next to him were actually reading a chronological account of the *Spruce Goose* itself, from construction to exhibition and maintenance. They did not comment about anything relating to a mission to Mars. This was, to them, just another one of the things to see inside the domed building. And as if the tour through the giant aircraft was not enough to satisfy even Howard Hughes himself.

Still, Anthony Flint was reading about the Red Planet and NASA's historic decision to go there. The White House appeared equally impressed and issued the President's statement from the West Wing of the Executive Mansion:

"The journey from Earth to Mars is approximately 119 million miles, and it will take NASA eight to nine months to do it. My guess is, this mission will be the greatest single voyage since the discovery of the New World."

This was not another administration disinterested whether NASA was dead or alive. In fact, the Mars mission was more popular than any of the lunar landings in the last century. As part of his reelection to a second term in office, the President campaigned for NASA to launch a Mars spacecraft with advanced propulsion systems and an escape plan that could be used in an emergency to send the crew back to Earth.

To do so, though, left NASA with the selections of seven astronauts to go to Mars. And because it takes four astronauts nearly all their time to run experiments and keep the Mars command spacecraft operational. That leaves three astronauts to set up the Martian base and run more scientific experiments on the surface.

Another part of the mission was bringing a limited number of artifacts to leave behind at the Ares Vallis landing site. Eliminating what would go was based on weight, size and more political squabblings than a typical Florida election. Yet Hughes Aircraft made the final cut. A company executive said this: "We have a long-standing relationship with NASA and the space shuttle program. This is a fitting tribute to Hughes Aircraft and Howard Hughes, whose legacy as an international pioneer aviator will now reach the surface of the planet Mars."

Like any student building his first science fair project, Hughes Aircraft had the chance to design and manufacture something unique and universal. They chose the Howard Hughes Technology Memorial. It was no bigger than a deck of playing cards, and it certainly weighed a lot less. In Los Angeles many employees believed that the project deserved a tighter focus on space exploration, and probably fewer people behind the drawing board. And then there was the successful effort to siphon a drop of unused fuel from the *Spruce Goose*.

The memorial also included a DNA sample from the remains of the billionaire. Here no explanation was ever made as to how or why this was even available in the first place (or was there more from where that came from?). As the company executive said: "If you wanted to, you could say Howard Hughes is going to Mars. But this is something we know our founder would have liked very much. For one thing, it's highly innovative. So we simply couldn't pass this opportunity up."

To be sure, it was the damndest thing ever. Many times Flint ran a search on his computer to see what he could find under the name of Richard Crotty. The only hit he had was the one on the former county administrator in Orange County, Florida. Yes, the large area that included the City of Orlando and some of the world's most famous theme parks.

So Richard Crotty, the former administrator for Orange County, Florida, was not the man he was looking for; and for that matter, he didn't know who was, really. He could always go back and read his fourth grade science book. This was a fruitless trip down memory lane; and at a time when he really wanted to find an answer.

Hughes Aircraft built the TDRS-D payload for the STS-26 space shuttle flight in 1988. Flint remembered reading a biography on the Los Angeles-based company when he was at the Kennedy Space Center that year, when the countdown was still go for America's first space shuttle launch since the *Challenger* disaster. TDRS was short for Tracking and Data Relay Satellite. In the 1990s, the TDRS system was part of an $81.6 million NASA contract awarded to Hughes. It provided for new satellites, upgraded Ka-band communication services, any necessary modifications to the TDRS ground terminals at White Sands, New Mexico, plus the management, development, integration and testing, shipment, launch support and operations support.

TDRS was NASA's only existing means of continuously communicating with high data rates; it was a capability required by nearly all low Earth-orbiting spacecraft including the space shuttle.

He saw no year or date in what he was reading in the first exhibit. He saw the names of Richard Crotty, and Kulhman, Calloway, and astronauts Michael Amato, Richard Gizankis, Eladio Izquierdo, Jr., and Lowell Thacker.

Then there was the mention of Richard Crotty as the first man who will step foot on Mars. His name would go down in history with more than a footnote, raising the American flag on a sturdy pole, and with a Martian breeze strong enough to flutter the flag. This scene was somewhat reminiscent of the one Neil Armstrong made at Mare Tranquillitatis on July 20, 1969, as the first man on the moon. Except there wasn't a lunar breeze to ruffle Old Glory.

Crotty, according to the exhibit, was a graduate of Purdue University, and was an astronaut at NASA when America's space agency had long passed a critical juncture. It was a time when the space shuttle program ended; it was phased out in favor of hypersonic flights and the technology to fly a spacecraft directly into orbit from a NASA airport runway. It was a new generation of space flight that paid off handsomely.

But Crotty was a family man, the husband of a school teacher at Cypress Elementary School in Orlando and the father of three young daughters. Each of them was a screaming fan for the autographs of some music group of the distant future. Flint was sure of this; his own daughter, a teenager beginning in 2008, had never heard of the group. Period. And it was the one that Flint remembered reading about 18 years ago in Long Beach, California.

The music group was a good example that all of this was happening in the years to come. It was, in 1990, a strong indication of personalities from people and places and things that would change the world. Yet Flint was at a loss to share it with anyone.

At one point that afternoon, Flint decided not to forget to check the other exhibits to see what they had. Most of them featured information on the H-4. How the construction process saved precious metals needed for the war effort; and the wood plane was built to land and take off on water. Other exhibits had profiles on Howard Hughes, Henry Kaiser, his partner in the flying boat project, a co-pilot, Glen Odekrick and a Hughes engineer, Dick Palmer. But it was not to be that he would read anything else about Richard Crotty in Long Beach, California.

When he returned to the Roosevelt Hotel, he rested in his room and later took his seat as a member of the evening's panel discussion. Now how was he going to be effective? He had to put away all these thoughts and be able to participate with renowned journalists from across the United States. It was a very safe bet that none of them perplexed over anything so impossible to explain as Richard Crotty and his destiny to Mars.

The topic for the panel was the 26th anniversary of the historic libel law decided in 1964 by the U.S. Supreme Court. Known as the *New York Times Co. v. Sullivan* case, the nation's highest court clarified and extended the media's protections against libel. This landmark ruling allowed public officials to file a lawsuit for libel; but it had to be proved that there was deliberate lying or extreme recklessness in publishing a story and not ascertaining the truth.

While every citizen had the right to fight defamation of character, it was also true that editors and writers had the right to fair comment and criticism. The Supreme Court called it "uninhibited, robust and wide-open" debate and said it was protected under the First Amendment. In 1967, the high court extended its decision to also include public figures.

When the brochures for the California convention arrived in his mail, Flint could see that this was the making of a good debate. Especially for the journalists from Alabama, where the *Times* was sued in 1960 by Sullivan, a police commissioner in Montgomery. Sullivan's department was faulted by the *Times* for its actions against followers of the Rev. Martin Luther King, Jr. He was awarded $500,000 for his troubles in State court. Yet the Supreme Court reversed the judgement, finding no malicious intent on the part of the *New York Times*.

But Anthony flew home not really knowing if he was any good that night at the Roosevelt Hotel. He was still thinking that a pattern was forming when he visited the *Spruce Goose* and read the first exhibit inside the domed building. The name of Richard Crotty had appeared again since 1964, and that was 26 years after he saw it in his fourth grade science book. Now he didn't know when he would see it again.

Chapter 30: Andrew and Jack "Murph the Surf" Murphy

A caller on a Miami radio station:

"I feel there's lots of training on how to survive a hurricane. I think that anything like this you never know the actual impact until you know the area. Every area in Florida is logistically different, the people's needs are different—depending on the time of year. On any kind of disaster like that, all these factors play in. Whether there's food or shelter. Whether the kids are in school.

"The thing that made the biggest impact on what I saw was the National Guard and their locations. With the M-16s the people did not give them any lip. People were talking back to the regular law enforcement officers. I don't want to over-dramatize this, but it was not a matter of pointing to make a left turn and the person doing it.

"The vehicles on the road were all smashed up. In the areas that I was in. Most of the things I saw around the water areas were trees overturned. Going farther another mile or so, you saw damage to roofs, satellite dishes, mobile homes, sheds, and different things like that.

"Then all of a sudden you're in it. You're in the main path. Once you get in that area, all you see is devastation everywhere you look. We saw people going every different way. They come up to your vehicle when you stop and ask questions. At every intersection the tempers down there were outrageous.

"Horns were blowing, there were sirens—you were overwhelmed by it."

Three days after Hurricane Andrew slammed across South Florida on August 24, 1992, the impact from one of nature's most terrifying storms was startling: phone calls peaking at 4.7 million per hour, overwhelming Southern Bell, price gouging rampant as tuna fish sells for $8 a can, a gallon of water $15. Or even $200.

People needed everything that was coming in at the South Florida Relief Center in West Palm Beach. Anthony Flint saw the rows of tables and chairs with dozens of phones ringing constantly. But it seemed nearly everyone was busy manning the conveyor belts. It was almost a steady process: sending boxes of supplies from the large trucks to the smaller vehicles that would soon travel into the hardest hit areas farther south.

Flint had joined a convey that formed hours earlier in Tampa, and the headquarters for the Kash 'N' Karry food stores. It was there in the lighted parking lot that the Salvation Army and the American Red Cross joined seven semis loaded with food. Also in the convey was a good friend of Anthony's, Greg First, public relations director for the Citrus Regional Blood Bank in Lakeland, Florida. And a new friend that year, Kurt Paquette, a staff reporter with the *Tampa Tribune*.

Anthony knew Kurt was still young and the Tribune big enough to tame ambitious reporters for their entire career. Kurt had already covered Hurricane Hugo in 1989; his newspaper articles highlighted the estimated damages at $7 billion to the homes and businesses of North and South Carolina.

Bad weather really got Dan Rather started back in 1962, when the winds and the rain came howling across the coast of Texas. Weather forecasters called it Hurricane Carla. It was the most powerful tropical system to hit the Lone Star State in over 40 years. But, admittedly, Rather's broadcasts on the JFK assassination, Vietnam and Watergate also impressed CBS News.

Traffic was stalled for 15 miles in one area. In Kendal, south of Miami, hundreds of trees, large and small, littered the streets. This was a common dumping ground and workplace for the cleanup crews. They maneuvered front-end loaders, making trips back and forth, and depositing branches and storm derbies in growing piles. It was really slow-going on Saturday when a heavy thunderstorm blanketed the neighborhoods with rain nobody surely expected to see so soon.

Anthony could see a Bloomingdale's store and a Pizza Hut shattered almost to the point of complete annihilation. In Miami he saw some of the more prominent skyscrapers with glass missing from the highest floors in the buildings. He saw abandoned cars, some left under the overpass, and darkened traffic lights and signs missing along the interstate. But the long line of traffic continued to move on I-95.

The devastation was far worse in Homestead. Everyone could see the endless streets with mobile homes turned into uninhabitable structures with no roofs. Flint imagined a truly massive reclamation project; everything would have to be rebuilt as far as he could see. The same was true for Homestead

Air Force Base; the Pentagon would have no choice.

Anthony watched a National Guard helicopter circle a shopping center in various stages of waste. The landing in the parking area quickly whipped up a dust cloud that drifted toward a fleet of silver tanker trucks. Each was carrying thousands of gallons of "Zephyrhills Spring Water."

Now a sea of water jugs was clearly spotted at one end of the parking area. This surrounded the tent pitched by the Salvation Army Sharing Center; it looked like it was in the middle of an urban war zone. Inside the tent a health care provider found time to stop and tell Flint:

"We have about nine units set up in the area from seven in the morning until seven in the evening. Yesterday was the first day. We're getting more people today. It's really sad to hear so many things have been destroyed by the storm."

"How many volunteers do you have?" Flint asked.

The young woman pauses as she watches the soldiers jumping out from the National Guard helicopter. They carried weapons and ran to positions to secure the stores in the shopping center from any looting. "We can always use more help," she finished with tears in her eyes.

For the weeks and months to come, and for years after, the full impact from Andrew was always grim: the most destructive hurricane in U.S. history. The cause of death for 23 Americans and three more in the Bahamas. And an estimated $26.5 billion in damages, with the vast majority due to the high winds that crossed South Florida.

Another caller on a Miami radio station:

"You're really hampering things when you go down there sight-seeing. It's really a headache to hold up those convoys and hold up the traffic. If you don't absolutely have to—especially in the devastated areas—don't go down there just to check it out. Watch it on television.

"The temptation is there, and I understand that. I was thinking I wish I had brought a video camera with me. I could show this to my grandchildren fifty years from now. They wouldn't believe this. But think about it this way. How would you like it if Hurricane Andrew swept through your neighborhood? You are out there with everything you own scattered across the front lawn? And people come by with video cameras to tape you for their personal hurricane home movies? So keep that in mind."

Flint remembered probably the best descriptions of utter destruction from Robert E. Lee. The General had taken time to view many of the collodion photographs of George N. Barnard, who followed Sherman on his devastating Civil War campaigns through Georgia and the Carolinas. Even with the passage of time, Lee's recollections remained vivid:

The iron wheels and axles neatly lined up along a trackless roadbed, which was all that remained from the ordinance train of John Bell Hood. The Confederate General blew it up on his retreat from Sherman.

A peaceful forest scene, but one that plainly exhibited the bones and skull of the horse belonging to the fallen Union Gen. James B. McPherson.

The battlefield of New Hope Church, Georgia, with acres of broken, torn and twisted trees and hastily thrown up breastworks.

The last 15 photographs from the Barnard portfolio included scenes in Savannah, Georgia, and in Colombia, Charleston, and Fort Sumter, South Carolina. Lee said he saw mostly ruined buildings. Absent was any sign of active warfare, or military occupation, or the face of a single solider. The photographs, for the most part, revealed a stark record of the aftermath.

Jack Roland Murphy was another force that impacted South Florida, alerting law enforcement agencies in Miami Beach during the turbulent decade of the 1960s. In 1968, he was convicted of attempted robbery of $50,000 in jewels from Ava Gabor. That same year he was found guilty of first-degree murder of a young secretary, whose body was found in a river near Hollywood, Florida.

At the same time, he was equally famous as a tennis pro, a movie stunt man, a national surfing champion that gave him his moniker, "Murf the Surf," and as the mastermind behind the infamous heist of the fabled Star of India, the world's largest sapphire.

It was located in the American Museum of Natural History in New York City for half a century. The sapphire was part of a collection of gems donated in 1900 by the financier, J. Pierpont Morgan. In October, 1964, thieves invaded the museum's vast Morgan Gem Hall. They shattered the glass in the gem cases. Then they looted the joint, bagging the 563-carat Star, the 100-carat DeLong Ruby, the 14-carat Eagle Diamond, the 116-carat Midnight Sapphire, and at least 20 other priceless jewels.

The Star was as big as a golf ball, formed some 2 billion years ago and discovered in Sri Lanka more than 300 years ago. However, the museum was not a very safe place. The old security alarm system had once been connected to the jewel cases but was turned off to save electricity. Guards used to lock themselves in the gem hall, but that, too, was eliminated to save some money.

Three men, Roger Clark, Allen Kuhn and Jack Murphy, became the prime suspects in the celebrated case. Clark was picked up in New York with $1,500 cash in his wallet. Officials arrested Kuhn and Murphy several hours later at a U.S. commissioner's office in Miami. The trio had made repeated trips to the museum to examine and snap pictures of the jewel cases in the gem hall. A violinist, Murphy also attended concerts during his stay in New York.

Two pairs of dirty white tennis sneakers were found in the hotel room of the suspects. They matched shoe prints on a desk blotter next to a window in the museum that was used for entry by the thieves. The gems were eventually recovered from a locker at a Trailways Bus Depot in downtown Miami.

Sometime after his release from prison in 1984 from the correctional institute in Zephyrhills, Florida, Jack Roland Murphy, a.k.a., "Murf the Surf," walked toward a lectern at the First Baptist Church in Orlando. He was introduced by the Senior Pastor, Jim Henry, who watched a large crowd come into the building's sanctuary located at 3000 South John Young Parkway.

Anthony Flint was in the audience and recorded parts of Murphy's testimonial:

"They put me in prison in New York City. And my life changed from the sunshine and the boats and the bikinis. The fellow that was in the cell on one side of me had just been indicted for 17 mob-related murders. The fellow in the other cell beside me had just killed the black revolutionary leader, Malcolm X.

"Spent 25 months in prison there. Went back to Miami. One year later I was back in prison. This time it was a little different ball park. They put me in a van one night and put two pairs of handcuffs on me. They had a chain attached to those handcuffs, and it was wrapped around my waist and padlocked, and it went down to two pairs of shackles around my ankles. And in the back of that van we drove for nine hours. When it stopped the doors opened and uniformed guards reached in and they pulled me out.

"In this State we have thirty prisons. And when you mess up big, they send you to Florida State Prison. That's where Ted Bundy lives. Thirteen hundred men locked up. And I walked in the back door of that building with all those chains wrapped around me—I looked like Houdini.

"Where did I go wrong! I had a good education. I had all the opportunities that a person would want. Wondering if I could do that 20-year sentence for burglary. Because if I got over that, then I was going to do the life sentence that I had to do for armed robbery. Then I was going to do another life sentence for first degree murder.

"My eyes focused in the bright lights on guard towers, with machine guns and rifles aimed down on us. Cyclone fences with razor wire, and attack dogs running up and down those fences.

"I ended up there because I was with the wrong crowd at the wrong place at the wrong time. It's kinda like a guy sitting in the backseat of a car. It doesn't matter who's driving; if that car goes into a ditch, you all get hurt.

"I noticed this: when those losers—those prisoners that the world had given up on—when they walked down that aisle in chapel and asked Jesus Christ to come into their lives, when they stood up, the lights (in their eyes) would start coming on. Maybe gradually, slowly—and I would watch them for months at a time.

"And up there at Florida State Prison the thing that impressed me was the champions that came in. Guys like Roger Stauback (Heisman Trophy winner with two Super Bowl titles). And karate champions, race car champions, basketball champions—guys with the reputations for years as being in the winner's circle. They would come into prison and tell us the important role that God plays in a champion's life. And I wanted to be a part of that.

"So I took a chance on it. Sounded good to me. You don't have to tell a guy with 20 years and two life sentences that he's made a mess of his life. And that he needs some help.

"I walked down the aisle of the chapel to ask Jesus Christ to be my personal savior. Not in some sort of emotional sweat, or some sort of weak and wobbling way—like I needed a crutch.

"I want you to know this: God knows you. He's got a plan for your life. You get serious with him, he'll get serious with you. It's a two-way street. If you do as Jesus commands you to do, your life will change. The people who do as Jesus commands them to do—there's something different about them. There's a different power in their lives, a different gusto. There's a different richness in their lives.

"It's the answer. It's the power. The glory. If you'll talk to God, and if you'll read his words so he can talk back to you, God will lift your life up out of the ditch, out of the wreckage, out of the quicksand, and he'll put you on solid ground.

"I was supposed to die in prison. The Parole Board wasn't going to look at my case until I served 30 years. They were going to make an example of me. I stopped looking at the lawyers, the guards, the fences, and I started getting up in the morning and looking up. My life started working differently.

"When the Parole Board was reviewing my case, they were looking at the evidence. Of a man's life that God was managing. They looked at the letters from sixty or seventy prominent citizens of Central Florida. They looked at the letter from the mayor of Orlando, the letter from the sheriff of Orange County, Florida, the letter from the Florida House of Representatives. They said this man is doing God's business.

"You need to ask Jesus Christ to come into your life. Be your manager. Be your Lord. Be your Savior. Be your helper. Be your guide. You need that. We're not here to play games tonight."

Chapter 31: Steven E. Ambrose at the University of New Orleans

It was Anthony's decision to find a nationally renowned historian who would also serve as a source of authority, and hopefully, one that was indisputable and who would be the last word on the subjects of Thomas Jefferson, Robert E. Lee and Daniel Boone. This would be for himself, really, and not for his many critics or any members of his family living in four states.

He found Steven E. Ambrose at the University of New Orleans. Here was a teacher, author and historian who named the family dogs after members of the Lewis & Clark expedition, and who was a consultant for the World War II movie *Saving Private Ryan* starring Tom Hanks and directed by Steven Speilberg. Ambrose also founded the National D-Day Museum in New Orleans, which opened its doors on June 6, 2000, the 56th anniversary of the Normandy invasion.

This man was a prolific writer of more than 30 books, including *Undaunted Courage,* an epic about Lewis and Clark. His novel joined the ranks of other best-sellers on American history like Joseph Ellis' *Founding Brothers*, David McCullough's *John Adams* and Walter Isaacson's *Benjamin Franklin: An American Life.*

He would not be influenced by any of Anthony's columns published in *The Orlando Sentinel.* Ambrose would also shun all other forms of persuasion that ranged from palm readers and crystal balls to the voodoo cults and the pirate lore that was so popular in these parts of Louisiana. He was all about facts. To hear him justify it, the best way to get to the bottom of this thing was simply to meet it head-on.

A meeting with Anthony Flint was scheduled by his secretary and some archival work was assigned ahead of time to his staff. However, he wanted no publicity from it, and the public relations office at the University of New Orleans did not issue any press releases.

Thomas Jefferson was the topic of discussion because Flint said he had more conversations with him and fewer contacts with Lee and Boone. Jefferson was also defensive and insecure about his personal reputation and sounded disappointed to Flint that his shortcomings would receive so much attention. Jefferson remained proud of his writings, and that should be enough to inspire subsequent generations all over the world for centuries to come.

"He thought abolition of slavery might be accomplished by the young men of the next generation," Ambrose explained. Young men like Meriwether Lewis and William Clark. "They were more qualified to bring the American Revolution to its idealistic conclusion...."

"Because," Flint interrupted, "the next generation had, quote, 'sucked in the principles of liberty as if it were their mother's milk.'" Jefferson had told him that more than once.

Ambrose nodded his head and continued. "Few of us entirely escape our times and places. Thomas Jefferson did not achieve greatness in his personal life. He had a slave as mistress. He lied about it. He once tried to bribe a hostile reporter. His war record was not good. He was a spendthrift, always deeply in debt. He never freed his slaves."

Both men agreed that Jefferson knew slavery was wrong and that he was wrong in profiting from the institution, but apparently could see no way to relinquish it in his lifetime.

Even at his magnificent estate at Monticello, Ambrose said, "Jefferson had slaves who were superb artisans, shoemakers, masons, carpenters, cooks. But like every bigot, he never said, after seeking a skilled African craftsman at work or enjoying the fruits of his labor, 'Maybe I'm wrong.' He ignored the words of his fellow revolutionary John Adams, who said that the Revolution would never be complete until the slaves were free."

Then how was it possible that America has produced such a remarkable icon as Thomas Jefferson?

"Jefferson's range of knowledge was astonishing. Science in general. Flora and fauna specifically. Geography. Fossils. Classic literature. Politics, state by state, county by county, international affairs. He loved music and playing the violin. He wrote countless letters about his philosophy, observations of people and places. In his official correspondence, Jefferson maintained a level of eloquence not since equaled. "

Steven Ambrose paused as he turned and looked out his office window like he was peering back through the mists of time. He was remembering a lifetime of research and writing that devoted his life to the history of America. "I've spent much of my professional life studying presidents and generals, reading their letters, examining their orders to subordinates, making an attempt to judge them. None match Jefferson," he said. And in spite of all of his rare abilities, Jefferson was not a hero. "His greatest achievements were words."

Jefferson was the author of the Declaration of Independence. He wrote: "We hold these truths to be self-evident, that all men are created equal." These words were more revolutionary than anything written by Robespierre, Marx or Lenin. "Jefferson, by his words, gave us aspirations. Washington, through his actions, showed us what was possible. Lincoln's courage turned both into realty."

Ambrose explained that Jefferson, Washington, Adams and the other great men of their day established a new nation. It survived the struggles of the early years and then the Civil War and later the civil rights moment. This was no small feat, and yet things have tarnished it.

"Slavery and discrimination cloud our minds in the most extraordinary ways, including a blanket judgment today against American slave owners in the 18th and 19th centuries. That the masters should be judged as lacking in the scope of their minds and hearts is fair, indeed must be insisted upon, but that doesn't mean we should judge the whole of them only by this part."

It was true that Americans in great numbers are rediscovering their founding fathers, warts and all. Amborse said he was a visiting professor at the University of Wisconsin in 1996 when he learned that the History Club there had dropped the writings of Thomas Jefferson from its required reading list.

"He was a slave-holder," was the reason why. Then in the late 1990s the George Washington Elementary School in New Orleans was renamed the Charles Richard Drew Elementary School, after the developer of blood-banking. The reason why was: "Washington was a slave-holder."

Ambrose was still angry about this, and he told Flint how Washington pledged his life, his fortune and his sacred honor for the American Revolution. And what do you think would have happened to him had he been captured by the British Army?

"I'll tell you. He would have been brought to London, tried, found guilty of treason, ordered executed, and then drawn and quartered. Do you know what that means? He would have had one arm tied to one horse, the other arm to another horse, one leg to yet another horse, and the other leg to a fourth. Then the four horses would have been simultaneously whipped and started off at a gallop, one going north, another south, another east and the fourth to the west."

Now the office of Steven Ambrose was filled with silence from his gruff voice. Then Ambrose continued with a quiet tone when he said: "That is what Washington risked to establish your freedom and mine."

"Thomas Jefferson was a man who was always the head of the table no matter where he sat. Those who got to dine with him always recalled his charm, wit, insights, queries, explanations, gossip, curiosity, and above all else his laughter," Ambrose said.

He also quoted John Quincy Adams and his observations in 1785: "Spent the evening with Mr. Jefferson. You can never be an hour in the man's company without something of the marvelous." And even Abigail Adams wrote of him: "He is one of the choice ones of the earth."

Jefferson read more, and he also wrote with more productivity and skill than any other president, except perhaps, Theodore Roosevelt. But Ambrose said he had no positive idea what to do with or about the treatment of Native Americans. "He handed that problem over to his grandchildren, and theirs."

He also had no idea what to do about women's rights. "It is not as if the subject never came up. Abigail Adams, at one time Jefferson's close friend, raised it. But Jefferson's attitude toward women was at one with that of the white men of his age."

Ambrose didn't mind all the publicity surrounding the newspaper columns by Anthony Flint. It was good that America was reading more and learning again about its past. But how many would ever have the same chance as Anthony Flint? He was able to discuss Jefferson with Steven Ambrose in such detail that it was obvious this was no joke and Anthony was no fraud. He told him that Jefferson discussed a letter written on June 24, 1826, and that was ten days before John Adams and Thomas Jefferson died on the same day. The former President was declining an invitation to be in Washington for the 50th anniversary of the Declaration of Independence.

Jefferson told Flint: "All eyes are opened, or opening to the rights of man. The general spread of the light of science has already laid open to every view the palpable truth that the mass of mankind has not been born with saddles on their backs, nor a favored few booted and spurred, ready to ride them."

Ambrose added that Jefferson died with the hope that future America would bring to fruition the promise of equality. " For Jefferson, that was the logic of his words, the essence of the American spirit. He may not have been a great man in his actions, or in his leadership. But in his political thought, he justified that hope."

Steven Ambrose never asked why it was that Thomas Jefferson was speaking to Anthony Flint. But he did explore moments in history when the advice from the inner circles of confidants would not be enough. The leaders of men would reach out, somehow, for respect, reassurance and even inspiration.

As George Washington's second term as President was coming to an end, King George III of England said: "If Washington goes back to his farm, he will be the greatest character of his age." Ambrose explained that Washington refused any efforts to make him the first king of the United States. He also strongly believed that no one should serve more than two terms in the White House. And perhaps the king's statement was made after several walks down the corridors at Windsor Castle. When there was time to contemplate the portraits of the monarchy. Maybe it was unspoken advice from this unexpected source that convinced King George to grudgingly complement his former enemy in the American Revolutionary War.

It was said that General George C. Patton was silent soon after the capture of Sicily in World War II. He stood and observed the ancient ruins and the medieval castles. Patton was a gifted student of history and classical literature. And perhaps it was the general himself who found a contact with the past that was a reassurance that strengthened his inner soul. Later he led his soldiers in the march across France to the Rhine River and into Germany and Austria.

Adolph Hitler visited the Invalides in Paris in June of 1940, the soldiers' home built by King Louis XIV of France and also housing the tomb of Napoleon Bonaparte. Perhaps the Fuehrer was seeking a sign, a voice, a vision or some kind of inspiration from this great historic figure. He certainly was thrilled by the whole thing as he later told his long-time photographer, Heinrich Hoffmann: "That was the greatest and finest moment of my life."

Then it was a visitor who came to Virginia and to the steps of Monticello in 1993—156 years after the death of Thomas Jefferson. Perhaps this was a trip for all the personal insights and political wisdom that one man could muster from a single place. But it was unforgettable to William Jefferson Clinton who was soon to be inaugurated as the 42nd President of the United States.

Steven Ambrose said a young engineer from West Point rented a cottage in 1832 in St. Louis. The landlord was the son of William Clark, then in declining health. But this was the Clark who was joined by Thomas Jefferson with Meriwether Lewis to form the great Lewis & Clark Expedition of 1803. Ambrose said the name of the new tenant was Robert E. Lee. But he did not say how long he stayed.

It was Jefferson who told Flint that Steven Ambrose died on October 13, 2002, at the age of 66. A public memorial was held at the National D-Day Museum in New Orleans. The speakers included the first President George Bush and film director Steven Speilberg.

Jefferson never commented to Flint about anything said about him by the great historian.

Chapter 32: The General at Asheville, North Carolina

In the banquet hall the ceiling arches rise 70 feet above the floor. The room itself was especially designed to display five 16th century Flemish tapestries that illustrate the lively and perilous love affair of Venus and Mars. There is also the large family crest high above the triple fireplace that includes the flags of the great European powers in 1492 when Christopher Columbus discovered America. Located on the opposite wall of the hall, a scene from Wagner's opera, *Tannhauser.* Also, over the entrance to the hall, statues of Joan of Arc and St. Louis and the Latin motto between them that reads: "Give us peace in our time, Lord." And throughout the banquet hall was a collection of replica flags of the thirteen original colonies and the flags of the American Revolutionary War.

Then there was the library with classical-baroque detailing, walnut paneling, a black marble fireplace and the ceiling canvas, *The Chariot of Aurora*, which was brought here from the Pisani Palace in Venice, Italy. The library contains over 10,000 volumes and has a total collection that is over 23,000 books. The shelves contain classic literature, art, history, architecture, and landscape gardening.

The bowling alley was installed by Burnswick-Balke-Collendere Company in 1895. Each lane was laid with hard maple and pine wood, and the bowling balls were made of wood and varied in size based on the different games played over a century ago.

A swimming pool was built indoor, and so was the gymnasium and 17 dressing rooms with separate hallways for ladies and gentlemen. There was also the stable with a carriage house and a repair room, blanket room, saddle room and harness room. For reasons that included pleasure as well as transportation.

At one point in the 4-hour tour, the scale of construction seemed incredibly monumental. Most of the mansion called Biltmore House was built between the years of 1890 and 1895. A brick factory and a woodworking factory were built nearby for the hundreds of workers on the estate. So was a three-mile railroad spur to bring supplies up from the small town of Asheville, North Carolina. That made it possible to celebrate the first Christmas in grand style: a 30-foot tree decorated in the Banquet Hall with presents for the children of all the employees. And enough mistletoe, holly and dinner for 350 people. A tradition which set the precedent for everything enjoyed here by each new generation.

Like Anthony Flint and his wife Candy, who, during the second year of their marriage in 1993, had formed part of the most recent group to make its way through Biltmore House. A great mansion with 255-rooms and needing 80 servants to run this household of the late 1890s. It had walk-in refrigeration, electricity, advanced plumbing, central heating and bedford limestone from Indiana. The architect, Richard Morris Hunt, was world famous in the nineteenth century, having also designed the base for the Statue of Liberty. Hunt used the 16th century chateaux in the Loire Valley of France, the Chateau de Blois, Chenonceaux and Chambord as prototypes for Biltmore House.

They all saw the preeminent gardens that were equally a part of Biltmore House. As it should be, formally landscaped in the 200 acres that immediately surround the mansion. This was primarily on the recommendations of a man whose name was Frederick Law Olmsted, whose most notable accomplishments had been the landscaping of Central Park in New York City.

It was quite evident by the light of the mid-day sun shining down and reflecting in the triple formal pools of the Italian Garden. The symmetrical designs date back to the 16th century; but it was all part of the tour down winding gravel paths with flowering shrubs, Japanese cut-leaf maples, and dogwoods along the way. Every bit of it provided an annual show of Nature's successive colors from spring to summer.

The Azalea Garden, for example, contained the most complete collection of native azaleas in the world. It was, by 1940, a prized collection of specimens from New Hampshire, Florida, Michigan and Texas; and Asiatic and hybrid azaleas, choice metasequoia and exceptional magnolias.

Flint was one of many in the group that appreciated the 3,000 roses of the foremost variety in the Rose Garden. The conservatory and the greenhouses were also in this area, providing the estate with cut flowers, plants and growing ferns, cacti, orchids and other bedding plants. The larger specimens included palm trees, banana trees and schefflera.

Across the way from Biltmore House was the pine grove forests on the grounds of Biltmore Estate. All of it became part of the first comprehensive plan for forestry conservation in the Western Hemisphere. Much supervision was needed for the extensive plantings to come, the establishment of experimental areas and the lumbering of the large tracts west of the French Broad River. Other land from the estate was sold and became part of the Pisgah National Forest and included Mount Pisgah on the horizon.

Most of Biltmore Estate was originally woodland that had been slashed, burned, overgrazed and was badly eroded, with few remaining scrub trees. The remarkable results in managed forest and farmland over the next 100 years are still be studied by the U.S. Forestry Service. No wonder Biltmore Estate was one of the few National Historic landmarks that pays all its property taxes and was completely self-supporting. It was also one of the largest employers in the Asheville area.

One of the revenues used by the privately owned mansion and estate was the wine sales from the Biltmore Estate Winery. In May of 1985, a 90,000 square foot facility is opened to the public in buildings that were originally the Biltmore dairy business. Located in the renovated and expanded facilities was state-of-the-art wine-making equipment and featured in the welcome center, stained glass windows from the New York City home of William H. Vanderbilt.

His father had borrowed $100 from his mother to begin a small ferry business. He soon had a fleet of steamships stationed in Staten Island, New York. This was an unbeatable advantage over sailing ships, and so it was the start of the Cornelius Vanderbilt fortune. The press was already calling him the "Commodore" in recognition of Vanderbilt's iron will and unflappable determination.

The kind of success seen by the tourists when they enter the Billiard Room at Biltmore House. It was paneled in oak but generously covered by hanging paintings on sports and theater by artists like Landseer, Reynolds, Atkinson, Stubbs and the Spanish painter, Ignacio Zuloago Y. Zabaleta, whose *Rosita* hung on the left side. And everybody saw the oak tables and the leather settees and chairs made in 1895. What they didn't expect to see was a smoking room and gun room. This was entered through doors hidden by the paneling of the fireplace wall.

Flint remembered he first saw something move in the background while standing in the gun room; he was not sure. For one thing, they would all see 70,000 objects of one sort or another inside the mansion at the end of the tour. And since photography of any kind was prohibited at Biltmore House, one's memories of the day could only be reinforced with the purchase of books or post cards at the gift stores on the grounds of the estate. So this was usually the way it was with so much to see.

There was even a Halloween Room in the downstairs tour of the mansion. It was painted in 1926 by the houseguests who were preparing for a dance. Each guest designed decorations for a section of the room, and it took three weeks to complete.

But this was not a ghost. It was a translucent figure of a man that Flint could see walking through walls, tables and even moving up in the line of tourists now in the servant's dining room. Clearly it was a white illumination of a man he had seen before and, clearly, no one else was seeing him now. They did not hear him, either.

Flint did. A strong voice that could easily be used to read to small children or to lead grown men to lay down their lives defending Richmond. But he was not in a military uniform. A black broadcloth suit once worn at his son's wedding in Petersburg. "I am a solider no longer," he told Flint.

Now there was no doubt and no apparent reaction from Flint. He knew for sure that the former General of all armies for the Confederate States of America, Robert Edward Lee, had somehow joined the tour at Biltmore House. But he did begin with an explanation that the Stones River meeting would not be the only one possible between the two men. He offered no explanations then or now why he was really wanting to see Anthony Flint.

The General and the Commodore were compatible in many similar respects. For one thing, both had life-long interests in education. Lee served as superintendent at West Point and later as president of Washington College in Lexington, Virginia. And for his part, Cornelius Vanderbilt's best known financial contribution was to the Central University of the United Methodist Episcopal Church of the South, in Nashville, Tennessee. It was renamed Vanderbilt University in gratitude to the Commodore's gift of $1 million.

Lee commanded a field army of 70,000 men, a combatant in the War Between the States which saw a total loss in death reach 620,000 American lives. And he never had more than one quarter the men Grant had to fight the rebellion in the first place.

Vanderbilt raised the family name from relative obscurity to one associated with great wealth during his lifetime. No small feat for a family with decedents coming to American in the late 17th century, content to follow only in the pursuit of agriculture. But in 1867, Vanderbilt had consolidated his control of the New York Central Railroad and the major railroad lines between New

York and the Great Lakes.

The General also wanted to build a railroad for a proposed line that would connect several parts of Virginia on a north-south route that would act as a new corridor to such states as Maryland and Tennessee. And, of course, Washington College in Lexington, Virginia. Lee even went to Baltimore with a delegation to organize the financing; his speech was warmly received and promptly forgotten.

Lee said President Grant was not surprised by the news. During a visit to the White House on May 1, 1869, Lee talked to Grant for the last time. When the General said he made a presentation before the Baltimore City Council and was turned down, Grant replied: "You and I, General, have had more to do with destroying railroads than with building them."

There were also many incompatibilities in the lives of Lee and Vanderbilt. Lee was always grateful to the trustees of Washington College when they conveyed the new President's House on campus to his wife, Mary, plus an annual annuity of $3,000 for the rest of her life. Lee admitted to Flint that he always wanted a permanent home for his wife "who was helpless."

Mary Lee was the great-granddaughter of Martha Washington, who was married in her family home at Arlington, but who lived to see her husband indicted for treason and her home of 1,100 acres confiscated by the United States government and turned into a Federal cemetery. She even lost her claim to family heirlooms in Arlington when it was occupied by Federal troops. This included a set of china given to her great-grandmother by the Marquis de Lafayette, a punch bowl from Mount Vernon and some camping equipment used by George Washington when he was in the field with the Continental Army. Her life in the end was reduced to being in a wheelchair and spending her time longing for the past.

It was an entirely different story for the family and offspring of Cornelius Vanderbilt. The Commodore built a fabulous residence on Staten Island; his fourth child, William Vanderbilt, founded the Metropolitan Opera House in New York City; and a grandson, George Vanderbilt, purchased land in 1888 for Biltmore Estate on 125,000 acres.

Lee said he was also impressed with Germany's Autobahn and the 40,000 miles of interstate highway system started in the United States by President Eisenhower. Both generals knew the importance of mass transportation in times of war. For Lee, it started in the spring of 1862, the year he used the railroads for warfare by ordering a heavy artillery gun mounted on a flatcar with protective armor. Then he shifted his limited number of troops from point to point during the war and, in effect, making his army mobile and larger than what it was. This strategy would be studied in the military academies of the world for generations to come.

He had no interstate highways or any of the incredible marvels of combat used by the Untied States in the 21st century. Lee had only telegraph lines, scouting reports and the knowledge of the hills, pastures, rivers and forests of the Confederate States of America. Unfortunately for him, most of the Civil War was fought in the South.

Now America has miles upon miles of super roads—and traffic reports every day! Lee seemed happy and proud about this. He could have used traffic reports from helicopters flying high over the Wilderness campaign in 1864; it would have been indescribable as well as indispensable. Flint knew that Grant had thrown immense troops at Lee in dense woods of northern Virginia for 11 months to wear down and destroy the Rebel army.

How Lee could have used even one traffic report to coordinate his great victory at Chancellorsville. He successfully used a series of diversionary attacks to immobilize the bulk of the Union Army of the Potomac, under the command of General Joseph Hooker, and which numbered nearly 130,000 soldiers. Lee also approved a plan by General Thomas "Stonewall" Jackson to lead his entire corps of 28,000 men around the right end of the Union line. Jackson moved ahead of his men and was mistakenly killed by Confederate gunfire; his escort looked like a detachment of Union soldiers forming a surprise counterattack. There was even more confusion in the ranks of the Union army now forced to defend two fronts. Hooker was first indecisive and then withdrew entirely from the field of battle during a heavy rainstorm.

Conditions for transportation of any kind in the time of Lee were usually not very good at all. From Lexington, Virginia, Lee traveled to the annual meetings of the Episcopal Church or the Virginia Educational Association. He had only two choices: 12-hours on a canal boat that went only 54 miles south to Lynchburg and then a connection with an east-west railroad line. The second choice was sometimes 7 to 12 hours, depending on weather and the conditions of the rough mountain road, to ride 23 miles on a stagecoach north to Goshen and then taking another east-west railroad line. Lee to told Flint there was really no good way to go: "It makes but little difference, for whichever route you select, you will wish you had taken the other."

Flint did not know if he would see or hear from him again. The General told him: "How easily I could have been rid of this and be at rest. I had only to ride along the line and all would be over." Lee explained how tempting it was in 1865 to ride in front of his army and draw enemy fire that surely would kill him. A plausible suicide that no future historian could ever confirm. "But it is our duty to live. What will become of the women and children of the South if we are not hear to protect them?" The next thing Lee said was in French: *"Aide toi et Dieu t'aidera"*—Help yourself and God will help you.

Chapter 33: Mike Wallace in Orlando, Florida

Shortly before his retirement as the executive producer of the CBS televison news magazine *60 Minutes*, Don Hewitt wanted to send veteran correspondent Mike Wallace to Florida and interview Anthony Flint and see what was behind all the fuss. Most of the interview would be arranged with the use of the studios at the CBS affiliate in Orlando, WFTV Channel 9 Eyewitness News. Hewitt also budgeted for additional on-location shooting in Tennessee and in Virginia.

Hewitt had become famous in broadcasting years ago as the producer of the Nixon-Kennedy debates of 1960. The first meeting between the two men on live television was in Chicago, and additional debates were broadcast live from Los Angels, Washington, D.C., and New York City. But all of them were historic and politics in America changed so much after that. Now he was hoping the Flint stuff would be his chance to go out with a bang.

> **MIKE WALLACE:** Quote: This area is little-known outside the great State of Tennessee. With a little luck, it proved to be a favorite countryside of Robert Edward Lee. You know, Robert E. Lee. The great Civil War General. In the flesh, or something like that. You can add your complete disbelief now and I would understand.
> (Pause.)
> **ANTHONY FLINT:** That was my column printed in 1991.
> **MIKE WALLACE:** Did you see Robert E. Lee?
> **ANTHONY FLINT:** I believe I did.
> **MIKE WALLACE:** Was he in the flesh or what did you see?
> **ANTHONY FLINT:** I was able to see him.
> **MIKE WALLACE:** Quote: "I fear we are destined to kill and slaughter each other for ages to come," said Robert E. Lee, on that night at Stones River. "May God help the suffering and avert misery from the poor."

ANTHONY FLINT: That's what I remember him saying.

MIKE WALLACE: It was also written by Lee to an unknown correspondent on August 23, 1870. It was contained in the book on the General published in 1930 by Franklin Riley entitled: *General Robert E. Lee After Appomattox.* We had help tracking this down from Washington and Lee University.

ANTHONY FLINT: I have never read that book. In fact, I have two books in my home library on Robert E. Lee and that's it.

MIKE WALLACE: What are you saying?

ANTHONY FLINT: I wrote the column during the first gulf war with Iraq. Lee and even Sherman believed that war is hell and should never be glorified or entered into lightly. I think they would have the same opinion today even if the United States now has the ability to wage war with laser-guided bombs and missiles aimed by satellite.

So here he was again standing in the early evening air north of Murfreesboro, Tennessee. He could see the barren trees along the banks of the river and in the woods; and nearly all the bark and branches glistened from another late-afternoon rain. Then across the open field he could see the picnic pavilion and the restrooms.

Nothing had really changed that much from the moment when he could hear the first sounds of horse's hoofs so many years ago. It was through a wet thicket of saplings over there, advancing over a cover of damp leaves on the ground. And it was here at Stones River National Battlefield that he saw a man and a horse come out of the forests; but they were visible only as a pair of translucent figures and they were heading in his direction.

Back then he knew he had no film left in his pocket camera. It was the one used earlier in the day when he was at the home of Andrew Jackson and was south of Nashville. That afternoon at the Hermitage did not prove nearly so memorable as the evening spent at Stones River.

Everybody with the *60-Minutes* film crew was counting on something happening again that was historic or paranormal or both. They set up cameras with night vision and suggested the same time of the year, and they wanted the place as identical as the conditions were when Flint said he saw General Lee. So the park was closed to the public. Also, they placed Anthony in the parking lot next to his car.

All was uneventful for the next couple of hours. It was Wallace who suggested they finally call it a night. The production equipment was taken down, and it was then that Wallace got in his car to drive back to his hotel in Nashville. He got behind the wheel and started to put the keys in the ignition, but quickly, he realized he was sitting on something in his front seat.

It was a gold-colored Civil War button. He held it in his right hand, and then he turned to look outside his car door window. There was now no one around to talk to him; but he did unlock his car and it had a keyless entry. He also remembered his remark to Flint how it was quiet and remote at Stones River National Battlefield.

Yet he decided to bring the button back with him to New York, and it was CBS News that later contacted the estate of Lee's granddaughter in Upperville, Virginia. They provided the primary research from the deButts-Elly collection of Lee family papers dating from 1794 to 1916.

The startling revelation of this work and the additional assistance from the Library of Congress, the National Archives, the Virginia Historical Society, the duPont Library at Stratford Hall Plantation and the Appomattox Court House National Historical Park was one of universal acclaim.

CBS was told it was a gilt button that was covered with a thin layer of gold. It was identical in every way to the ones on the double-breasted grey dress coat, the one Lee wore in 1865 when he surrendered to Ulysses S. Grant.

> **MIKE WALLACE:** Quote: To see for myself, I went to the home of Thomas Jefferson. It seemed the answer came from the apple trees in the Orchard, the East Front columns of the mansion, the vegetable garden terrace, even from the library where six thousand books once filled the shelves.
> (Another pause.)
> **ANTHONY FLINT:** That was my column printed in 1997.
> **MIKE WALLACE:** Did you see Thomas Jefferson?
> **ANTHONY FLINT:** No.
> **MIKE WALLACE:** You heard his voice?
> **ANTHONY FLINT:** Yes.
> **MIKE WALLACE:** You're sure on that?
> **ANTHONY FLINT:** I believe so.
> **MIKE WALLACE:** Quote: "I am so much immersed in farming and nail making that politicks are entirely banished from my mind," I thought I heard Jefferson say.

ANTHONY FLINT: That's what he said to me.

MIKE WALLACE: Jefferson wrote that in a letter to Henry Remsen on October 30, 1794. It took the help of the Massachusetts Historical Society, the Historical Society of Pennsylvania, the Huntington Library in San Marino, California, and the Thomas Jefferson Memorial Foundation to find the contents of that letter.

ANTHONY FLINT: Did they tell you who Henry Remsen was?

MIKE WALLACE: Does it really matter?

ANTHONY FLINT: I wrote the column during the impeachment hearings of President Clinton. Jefferson wanted to be remembered by scholars and historians for his writings and his architecture. But, like Clinton, Jefferson wanted his private life to himself.

Anthony Flint was standing again along the north terrace walk with the white Chinese railing and the commanding view of the south pavilion across the west lawn at Monticello. He could see some of the outbuildings; and the surrounding countryside of Virginia that fascinated Thomas Jefferson more than a century ago. How it all endured when there was snow and rain and drought, with the mountains as a distant backdrop.

But nothing had really changed that much from the moment when Anthony could first hear the voice so many years ago. It came from many directions, each perfectly mixed in tone and volume. And no one else was present that day who was able to hear it; but he could walk on the estate at Monticello and pretend that nothing was wrong.

Back then Anthony only had the program guide and a pencil to take notes. It was now possible to count on the sophisticated array of audio equipment setup by the *60-Minutes* production crew. This included dish antennas and omni-directional microphones and a bank of audio recorders with extended battery backup. The crew also suggested the same time of the year as Flint's visit in 1993, and they asked the Thomas Jefferson Memorial Foundation to close Monticello to the public.

The rest of the afternoon turned out to be a complete dud. It was Flint who suggested they end this and call it a day. The audio equipment recorded nothing mysterious from the north terrace walk, and it was time to drive back to the hotel rooms that night in Richmond. Then it was agreeable that they would meet briefly with Mike Wallace before getting a good night's rest and the long trip back to New York.

Except it was Wallace who was inquiring about the production truck. He had questions like "Why are they late?" and "Has anybody seen them?" and "Call on the cell phone."

On the way back, the sound crew in the production truck had every intention of getting to their hotel rooms on time. But it all started with the calm voice of a man on the truck's radio. It caught the attention of this group of men who heard it all from the radio stations in the Big Apple and which typically shocked the public and the FCC and still got away with murder.

This was entirely something else—a fine defense from a man who said he was never the father of any children with Sally Hemings. She was his slave, and she was special, and he made sure that all of her offspring would grow up someday to be free from slavery. Furthermore, a President has a public role in the White House and a private life on his estate; therefore, the people of the United States are not intrinsically entitled to examine both.

What was this crap!? It sounded like something from one of those liberal think tanks in Washington.

They immediately began to laugh. The driver shrugged his shoulders and changed the stations, and soon he was turning the radio on and off. But it made no difference. The voice continued to be heard through the speakers in the production truck. It was also a bit scary when the speaker said on more than one occasion that he was the voice of Thomas Jefferson.

MIKE WALLACE: Do you believe in life after death?
ANTHONY FLINT: Yes.
MIKE WALLACE: Is that what this is all about? Some kind of reincarnation?
ANTHONY FLINT: I'm a Christian, not a transcendentalist.
　(Laughter from both men.)
MIKE WALLACE: You appear to be a nice enough fellow. Nothing in your past would ever seem to indicate anything like this. You know, Spielberg, *60-Minutes*; and now you are writing a book.
ANTHONY FLINT: *Ambassador for Life*.
MIKE WALLACE: What's it about?
ANTHONY FLINT: Read the book!
　(More laughter from both men.)

A week or so after the *60-Minutes* broadcast on Anthony Flint, Don Hewitt was home watching the History Channel. Tonight's series on the ghosts of

Gettysburg seemed to be particularly interesting to him and it was well produced. He sat up in his seat as the narrator described one home and then another and still another that was haunted by the Civil War.

In some cases, it was the dead owners, and in one poignant example, it was a little girl who wandered away from her home one night in July of 1863. She was never found alive again. Yet she was seen in and around her homestead years after the deaths of her family and friends. Even the great battlefield itself was not immune to the tales of soldiers who died from their wounds and then walked the grounds for decades to come.

Maybe there was something to this, Hewitt thought. How could Flint know the things he wrote in his column? He wasn't even an amateur historian. And, to his credit, Anthony passed a lie-detector test paid for by CBS News and conducted by the Orlando Police Department. They didn't find anything either in his background in Florida or in Indiana.

The genealogical research found out that Candy Flint had a bloodline on her mother's side that was related back to Daniel Boone. And Beverly Flint, Anthony's mother, was found to be a very distant relative of Hermann Goering, who was the infamous World War II leader of Nazi Germany's air force the Luftwaffe.

Now this was Daniel Boone and Hermann Goering. One led the way to settle the frontier of Kentucky and the other wanted to destroy Europe with the Blitzkrieg. What this all had to do with the price of eggs was anyone's guess at *60-Minutes.*

Chapter 34: The Voyage of Discovery

In 1803, war seemed inevitable between France and England in North America. The prospects of the British threatening occupation of Louisiana found Napoleon Bonaparte looking for cash in a hurry. The French minister of foreign affairs, Charles Maurice de Talleyrand-Perigord, surprised the American minister to France, Robert R. Livingston, and his special envoy, James Monroe, by offering to sell all Louisiana territory under the French flag west of the Mississippi River. It was an all or nothing proposition. The price agreed on was $15 million, with a balance of $3,750,00 paid out to Americans who had claims against France. Then, instead of amending the Constitution, the Louisiana Purchase was ratified under a treaty adopted by the United States Senate.

It remains the largest landmass ever added to the U.S. All the acreage drained by the Mississippi and the Missouri Rivers. The Louisiana Purchase included more than 800,000 square miles of land and was enough territory for the future statehoods of Arkansas, Missouri, Iowa, North Dakota, South Dakota, Nebraska, Oklahoma, and portions of Minnesota, Kansas, Montana, Wyoming, Colorado and Louisiana.

The land had endured as well as anything tended by the tens of thousands of Indians who lived there for hundreds of generations. Far more significant than any subsequent civilization of the white man. It was, even now, bizarre for historians to record that Spain, Russia, France, Great Britain and the young United States all "claimed" the land at one time or another.

Those who were here first hunted the deer, elk, beaver and antelope. Or the massive herds of buffalo on the grasslands of the Great Plains, so needed by each Indian tribe for food and clothing. And where the most effective hunt was one that encircled a buffalo herd and then aiming a spear for a spot just behind the last rib.

At one point in the journals of the Lewis and Clark expedition, Meriwether

Lewis reported on July 10, 1806: "I sincerely believe there were not less than 10,000 buffalo within a circle of 2 miles." But for reasons that included greed and waste, the number of roaming buffalo would drop to less than 250,000 over the next two centuries. And remain protected on a handful of preserves like the National Bison Range in central Montana.

In 2003, it was all part of the Kenal Helicopter Tours, located directly across from the main entrance to the Grand Canyon National Park. As Anthony Flint, his wife, Candy, and their daughter, Alanah, were standing in line, they watched the other helicopters take off and head across the northwestern sky of Arizona that was still partly cloudy. The weather report posted inside the nearby Yavapal Geology Museum called for scattered showers. The report also included the following:

	South Rim	North Rim
High	77	79
Low	51	57

Then there was this note on the bottom: Please be careful as you walk along the rim and don't feed the wildlife. They bite!!!

The flight to the Grand Canyon was exciting. The helicopter, slowly at first, hovered above the ground and then turned to cross over a terrain of tall evergreens. This view changed soon enough as the edge of the Grand Canyon appeared and revealed a spectacular gorge with towering buttes, mesas and valleys. Equally impressive was the Colorado River below, the main instrument of nature that excavated so many exceptionally deep, steep-walled wonders that extend over 270 miles long and nearly 18 miles wide in some places.

The main gorge was interspersed with old lava flows, hills composed of volcanic debris and intrusions of igneous rock. This was much different from the rocks exposed in the canyon walls. The tour guide said this strata was mostly deposited as marine sediment during the long periods of time when the canyon area was the floor of a shallow sea. And it was at the bottom of the canyon where the most ancient rocks—Precambrian schists and gneisses—ranged in age from half a billion to a billion years old.

Several times the helicopter would tilt to one side as a formation would pass by, with evergreens as tall as 17 feet growing along the cliffs. This was when the view was greatly enhanced for everyone in the group and, better still, leaning over to one's side at the same moment to see sights nearly half the age of the earth.

The tour guide said they had flown over Mather Point and now the West Rim. This area was nearly 1,200 feet higher than the southern rim, and it was where Flint was standing early that morning. The daylight was reflected in patterns of color along the layers of rock. At midday, all the colors had changed, and there was a different hue that was not visible at dawn. Even now as the helicopter passed by another formation, one could see a contrast in color and know that it would change again at dusk.

There was a sudden interruption that ended the voice of the tour guide who was also one of the co-pilots. Flint would not hear him again.

His first instinct was to look to the front and see if the second pilot was now talking, or had someone put in an audiocassette tape? The first pilot was still talking. He could also see the empty cassette player. But a second voice was speaking to him with the headphones he put on at the start of the trip. He was listening to the tour guide: Flint remembered he was talking about the Colorado River and the six million years it took to form the Grand Canyon.

But this had nothing to do with the formation of the greatest natural wonder Flint had ever seen in his life. He was not wearing anything that could be construed to be a listening device or a hearing aid. Even the headphones he had on looked just like the ones everybody was wearing during the helicopter tour. And, yes, he followed the speaker cords and saw that they all connected at the same place and, presumably, carried the same voice of the tour guide to each headphone.

So what it was remained a mystery for only seconds longer. The identity of the voice was a man who was no stranger to Flint. He first suggested that Anthony continue looking out the window and pretend that this was not an interruption at all. Also, the question was posed: Did he know the year 2003 was the 200th anniversary of the Louisiana Purchase?

A smile on the face of Anthony Flint. No, that wasn't something that was coming to his attention right this minute! Was there a reason why? Wasn't everything as it should be? Of course, appearances can be deceiving even in the best of circumstances. Yes, that was true. But the voice said this was the best time in quite awhile. But what did that mean?

The voice assumed the day would come when there would be another opportunity to exchange ideas. Besides, few subjects were really discussed the last time and the whole thing produced more questions than answers for the both of them.

Now this was another day for Thomas Jefferson and Anthony Flint.

There was only the voice—just like Jefferson at Monticello 10 years ago. It came through in his headphones with a prefect tone and volume. As Flint looked out his window, he didn't expect to see any source of the voice along the rocky cliffs of the Grand Canyon. The rest of the group showed no signs of confusion. All of them were listening to the tour guide and pointing at the sights below.

His wife noticed only that her husband had become intent but distracted. He was not responding like the typical visitor to the Grand Canyon, although he frequently shut things out when he was writing. She saw that he did not have a pad or pen, and he nodded his head whenever he saw his wife pointing to her headphones. This was just her way of responding to the voice of the tour guide; he was very knowledgeable about the Grand Canyon. But Flint was really listening to Jefferson.

Who was very much interested in the Louisiana Purchase and the two Virginians he appointed to lead "the voyage of discovery" under the command of Meriwether Lewis and William Clark. Not surprisingly, both men had served with the army in the Ohio region and where Clark had been Lewis' commanding officer for a short period of time.

"The object of the mission was to explore the Missouri River, and such principal stream of it, as, by its course and communication with the waters of the Pacific Ocean, whether the Columbia, Oregon, Colorado or any other river may offer the most direct and practicable water communication across this continent for the purpose of commerce," Jefferson said.

Lewis, a 27-year-old army officer, was brought to the White House in 1801 as a personal secretary to Jefferson. Flint knew the former President was a close friend with Lewis' father, George Rogers Clark, who was killed during the Revolutionary War; and the two families had been neighbors for many years in Albemarle County, Virginia.

The President remarked: "Captain Lewis was brave, prudent, habituated to the woods and familiar with Indian manners and character. He was not regularly educated, but he possessed a great mass of accurate observation on all subjects of nature which present themselves here, and will therefore readily select those only in his new route which shall be new."

Jefferson wanted an overland expedition to the Pacific Ocean since the early 1780s. He told Flint he was fascinated by the published account of Alexander Mackenzie, a prominent Canadian fur trader, who crossed the Canadian Rocks to the Pacific in 1793. Jefferson realized it would only be a matter of time before the British found a more promising route farther south into the Louisiana territory.

Yet the only primary map of North America that was available to Lewis and Clark was the one in 1802 by Antoine Soulard. This map correctly showed the head of the Missouri River in the Rocky Mountains. But it was far short of the mark when it came to estimating the scale "over those tremendous mountains."

But Lewis and Clark were skillful and tenacious wilderness explorers. They also prepared themselves with a 45-men roster, also 3,150 pounds of cornmeal, 3,400 pounds of flour, 3,705 pounds of kegged pork and 600 pounds of grease. Jefferson was equally organized and scientific: "Beginning at the month of the Missouri, (they would) take careful observations of latitude and longitude, at all remarkable points on the river, and especially at the mouths of rivers, at rapids, at islands, and other places and objects distinguished by such natural marks and characters of a durable kind."

Jefferson was even proud of the code matrix he tested with Lewis and Clark. Nobody knew if there would come a time when the expedition needed to send secret messages back to Washington. In one case, the keyword known only by the sender and the recipient was "artichoke."

Cutting grass in America was one of the most unassuming achievements that Jefferson had ever seen. It was also one of the most dramatic: hundreds upon hundreds of acres lush with green grass that was cut, fertilized, irrigated, and free of insects and weeds. At the end of World War II, more Americans than ever pushed their lawn mowers on weekends in a growing show of discipline and self-pride. The former President told Flint it was astonishing to him to see how the landscape changed over the last 200 years. What was once a wilderness nation was now a country club of sorts. And most of it was maintained by the lawn mower.

Flint remembered Ralph R. Teetor, the inventor and philanthropist from his hometown of Hagerstown, Indiana. The man who was blind but still managed to pioneer piston ring manufacturing and, at one point in a very productive life, finding the time to tinker with a new type of lawn mower. He sent sketches to his patent attorney on July 3, 1945, describing a contraption he was using to maintain his 10-acre lawn that was also extensive with landscaping.

Family and friends were always visibly nervous whenever the demonstrations included its inventor. He motioned with his hands as he described how the mower worked, bringing his fingers close to the sharp cutting edges but never inflicting any injury.

Jefferson was back to the subject of the Louisiana Purchase. "The river Missouri and the Indians inhabiting it were not as well known as was rendered desirable by their connection with the Mississippi, and consequently with us. It is, however, understood that the country on that river was inhabited by numerous tribes, who furnish great supplies of furs and peltry to the trade of another nation carried on in a high latitude, through an infinite number of portages and lakes, shut up by ice through the long season."

Statesmen in his time were equally impressed with Jefferson's dream of a true continental power stretching from the Atlantic to the Pacific oceans. The Spanish minister to the U.S. in 1802, Carlos Martinez de Yrujo, said the former President, "has been all of his life a man of letters, very speculative and a lover of glory, and it would be possible he might attempt to perpetuate the fame of his administration...by discovering...the way by which the Americans may some day extend their population and their influence up to the costs of the South Sea."

Napoleon Bonaparte, commenting on the Louisiana Purchase in 1803, said, "The sale assures forever the power of the United States, and I have given England a rival who, sooner or later, will humble her pride."

The President told Flint that the expedition by Lewis and Clark lasted 28 months. And in an age without photography, Jefferson was indebted to the artists whose renditions on canvas were primarily inspired by the journals of the two explorers. Painters like Charles M. Russell, of Montana, who painted a portrayal of York, Clark's slave and the only black man to journey with them; Olaf Seltzer, who painted in 1934 a Lewis viewing the Rocky Mountains for the first time on May 26, 1805; and George Catlin, who, in 1832, painted Sioux encampments and scalp dances on the banks of the upper Missouri River; and even Charles Willson Peale, who completed portraits of Lewis and Clark after their heroic return.

Jefferson wanted a complete public record of the expedition and Lewis promised to publish the journals. Lewis even went so far as to make up the contract, but as the President explained to Flint, nothing else happened. The manuscript was not submitted or even one word written, and this, Jefferson emphasized, was due to depression and other personal problems that included heavy drinking and addiction to opium. Lewis was only 35 when his death was attributed as a suicide on October 10, 1809.

It was now up to Clark to get something published that would become the most important part of the expedition's legacy. For Jefferson, the pressed plants, exotic furs, the skeletons and the small animals sent back east were all tantalizing specimens. But the journals and Clark's map were that were really important. In 1814, a book was out that paraphrased the journals, and yet contained none of the scientific observations or drawings. That meant the discoveries of Lewis and Clark, which included descriptions and names later adopted by naturalists, would not become public knowledge for the next 90 years. The Wisconsin State Historical Society published all of the journals in eight volumes in the year 1904.

Anthony Flint never mentioned anything about Thomas Jefferson at the Grand Canyon. There was opportunity in certain moments, but there were also second-thoughts about the whole thing, and, increasingly, whether the President's remarks were actually confidential. Permission was neither granted nor denied. For the record, nothing said to Flint was classified or not already a part of history. Except, of course, that this was the voice of the third President of the United States of America. A fact of unique opportunity for Flint—or some kind of elaborate ruse that would never be uncovered in his lifetime.

A good question would be: who would do this? Another question: why? And by what principal means was Flint able to hear the voice of Jefferson? Twice! In one decade! But that was not time enough to hear it all.

Chapter 35: Steven Spielberg in Hagerstown, Indiana

On the set in Dalton, Indiana, the first day of shooting on the new film by Steven Spielberg. The owners of the old schoolhouse agreed to appear in the crowd scenes in addition to the undisclosed compensation and the use of their property for the next two weeks. But nearly everyone in the area wanted to do something, and so they were asked to bring in their used refrigerators, clothing, hand tools, and plenty of home-cooked food. It was all part of the shoot for the 1964 New Year's Day sale.

It was also the plan that all the interior shots would be filmed in Hollywood on the backlots at Universal Studios. But the schoolhouse would be repainted red and Stohler Landscaping from Hagerstown was contracted to rebuild the baseball field and the playground equipment. They included the big slide and the maypoles out in front of the building.

The old livery stable was being rebuilt pretty much like it looked in the photographs taken in the 1960s. Fred House Construction, also from Hagerstown, signed a contract to build it on the same site, but this time they would only erect the outside walls. The production schedule for next week called for the kids to dress up in their snowsuits and run around this prop like it was the dead of winter. It was up to the production crew to operate the giant fans and blow the fake snow for this scene in front of the cameras.

All of the wiring and conduit and outlets for the set were contracted to Mahoney Electric, again from Hagerstown. And one could count the new accounts opening in the name of Amblin Entertainment with Johnson's Texaco Service, Nettle Creek Pharmacy, Beachler's Fine Furniture, West End Building & Loan Association, Miller's IGA, McCoy's Refuse Service, Abbott's Candy & Gifts and Don Dale Chevrolet.

None of them had ever seen a red cent from Hollywood. Yet one explanation was the economic impact that Amblin Entertainment intended to develop in the local community. This was Spielberg's movie production company, and the towns and the cities that had a hand in the making of one of his pictures would see their credits rolling at the end of the film; and the infusion of money—if only for a while—was not bad at all.

Spielberg's attention to detail was everywhere. They even parked a car on the set just like the one Ledona Henderson had in 1964, the year the air was let out of her tires. In fact, the grandchildren were hired and brought on the set to do the same thing that got their grandparents in so much trouble. It was also something that the movie people found and restored three busses like the ones that brought children to the Dalton schoolhouse when Anthony Flint was in the fourth grade. Each one of them had the words "NETTLE CREEK SCHOOL CORPORATION" painted on the sides.

Back in California, they were working on the set for the 6th grade class and a stage production of Dickens' *A Christmas Carol*. Two crewmembers had excellent accents that portrayed well the Victorian times of London in the year 1843. They were reciting lines from the play while they worked:

FIRST WORKER AS MARLEY'S GHOST: I am here tonight to warn you, that you have yet a chance and hope of escaping my fate.
SECOND WORKER AS SCROOGE: You were always a good friend to me! Thankee!
FIRST WORKER AS MARLEY'S GHOST: You will be haunted by Three Spirits…

Flint sold the movie rights to his forthcoming book to Amblin Entertainment. He had no experience in this but hired the Federico law offices in Hagerstown to read everything in the contract. The firm had drawn up the living will for his parents, which was a judgement made by them and Anthony trusted his parents. Also, the firm had served successfully for years as the legal counsel for Hagerstown; and that was also a judgement that was not distrusted.

The first major issue in the contract was the right of complete and total editorial control. In other words, the movie script may not always follow his book. But he was assured that enough would be used from his interviews with Amblin Entertainment and from his columns printed in *The Orlando Sentinel*. And it was all deemed necessary for production logistics, budget constraints and artistic license that was based on the company's past experience in putting projects on the silver screen.

This one, in particular, would involve expensive special effects. For that, Spielberg and Amblin Entertainment would contract Industrial Light and Magic and the company's founder—George Lucas, to do the heavy lifting in this department. Which was always such a knockout at the box-office anyway.

The other major issue was the one on how much was going to be paid. It worked out well that Anthony would receive a percent of all movie tickets sold and all copies of the movie sold on DVD and a percentage from the broadcast on cable TV. He would not, however, be a part or receive any profit from any sequel. And it was discussed how the film did not lend itself very well with toy merchandising. This was never raised as an objection by Anthony, who didn't want to see a Thomas Jefferson toy with a cheeseburger from McDonalds.

After all was said and done, he learned later that Ben Affleck was signed to star as Robert E. Lee and Jeff Daniels would be the voice of Thomas Jefferson. He had no say in that. But Anthony and Candy Flint agreed to arrange donations to the churches they knew in Orlando, Dade City, Zephyrhills, Land O' Lakes and Wildwood, Florida, and in New Castle, Indiana. A generous donation was also made to the Christian Home and Bible School in Mt. Dora, Florida, the Potter Orphan Home in Bowling Green, Kentucky, and the Dave Thomas Foundation on Adoption.

A proclamation was adopted and made public by the Hagerstown Town Council:

WHEREAS, Steven Spielberg has chosen Hagerstown, Indiana, to be featured in his new major motion picture production, which begins on-location shooting this week in Dalton Township, Indiana; and

WHEREAS, this film production will include friends and family in and from Hagerstown and the great State of Indiana; and

WHEREAS, the Town Council of Hagerstown, Indiana, hereby grants "the Keys to the Town" to Steven Spielberg and to help facilitate his time in our fair community.

NOW, THEREFORE, I, Russell Wampler, President of the Hagerstown Town Council, and on behalf of the citizens of Hagerstown, do hereby extend our official welcome and offer the hand of hospitality and all courtesies to Steven Spielberg.

IN WITNESS WHEREOF, I do hereby set my hand, and cause

the official seal of the Town of Hagerstown to be affixed on this Proclamation.

Hagerstown, Indiana

Russell Wampler

Council President

Attest:

Greg Ozbun

Clerk Treasurer

Every Spielberg film has its own national media sensation. And for Hagerstown, Indiana, that was buying a copy of *People* magazine with a picture of the school superintendent on the front cover. The reason was the school superintendent was once the high school band director, who first met Anthony Flint and his youngest brother in 1972.

The interview of superintendent Backmeyer was accompanied by photographs of the Hagerstown Golden Tiger Marching Show Band and a skinny trombonist named Anthony Flint. The caption read that the young musician really liked the music from the rock group Chicago.

Another photograph showed the superintendent standing in front of the completed renovations for the Hagerstown Elementary School. But it was here that Flint was in the first grade in 1962, where and when he first saw the large mural of the solar system on a wall in the library. The beautiful illustrations easily showed how the planets orbit the sun. It was inspirational for many young children.

But it was not something that would single-handedly launch the imagination of Anthony Flint to soar into overtime. And *People* magazine wanted to find some examples that did.

Would superintendent Joe Backmeyer remember talking about the Civil War with Anthony?

No. That would have been his United States history teacher, Robert Mohlke.

Was he a gifted writer in high school?

Our records show he was a member of the *Paw Print* staff.

What about college?

I understand he was once a candidate for the position of Editor.

All of the above constituted the serious highlights of the article in *People* Magazine. There was not another round of questions or publications with as much interest. Anthony's literary agent pushed a theory that the family had only themselves to blame. The parents weren't divorced, none of the boys went to jail, and no arrests were ever made on anything at anytime. There was simply no tabloid news with this family at all except, of course, the stuff about Anthony Flint and Thomas Jefferson and Robert E. Lee.

Which was the whole reason why Steven Spielberg and Amblin Entertainment had come here in the first place. It was why a production schedule was set for the next three months in the greater Hagerstown area. The immediate effect was judged in terms of basic accommodations for an army that had no soldiers and took no prisoners but was just as powerful.

More than once the movie crew and its director booked all of the banquet rooms at Guy Welliver's Fabulous Smorgasbord for the entire evening. It made for great business and the group avoided seeing themselves eating later that evening on such TV programs like *Inside Edition* and *Entertainment Tonight*. But exclusive interviews and media passes were granted to *The Hagerstown Exponent*. That still left the special editions published by *The Cincinnati Enquirer*, *The Connersville News-Examiner*, *The New Castle Courier Times*, *The Indianapolis Star*, *The Muncie Star*, *The Ball State Daily News*, and the *Richmond Palladium-Item*. (It was this newspaper that featured its historic connection to Daniel Boone. A nephew of the Kentucky frontiersman, Nelson, printed the paper's first edition by using a hand press on January 1, 1831.)

Next it was the Junior-Senior prom at the high school and this year's theme: "Hollywood Nights." Then it was even the Governor of Indiana who appeared in a cameo during the on-location shooting at Dalton. He was the school's custodian, Fred Pope, fixing the broken chain on a little girl's bicycle.

All of this was reported by the local paparazzi of neighbors and friends and family with cameras and recorders purchased from the Wal-Mart Supercenters in New Castle, Richmond and Muncie. The sales reports to the store managers told them how well it was going in the electronics departments. It was also good news how all the Spielberg films on DVD and all the toys based on Spielberg films had repeatedly sold out.

Then the publicity machine hit south in Orlando, Florida, as letters arrived in the mail and the e-mail found its way into Anthony's computer. It was before he even had a chance to cut it off at the pass. He learned how he had "extended" family and friends from as close as across the street and as far away as Okinawa, Brisbane, Australia and even Dunkirk, Indiana. They all happened to be lost aunts or uncles or "Joe Blow, remember me?" and who also happened to need money because of death or taxes or both. He knew he didn't need to respond to it. Anthony did acknowledge his neighbor across the street, who said his friend had become such a bigshot he probably forgot he borrowed the push lawnmower last summer. Flint made up for it by having Sears deliver a new thing to the doorstep of his neighbor—which was funny because the lot was just about as big as the shinny Craftsman riding mower.

Yet the other correspondence was heart-warming like the one from Greg First, of Zephyrhills, Florida, who was now the broadcaster that owned radio station WZPH-FM. He also heard from Pat Herrmann, who worked with him years ago in the news bureau at the Indiana State Capitol Building. Then there was the unexpected call from David Pentecost, a first-chair trombonist in the Hagerstown Golden Tiger Marching Show Band for three straight years. Pentecost was president of his 1972 senior class. He applied and received a congressional appointment to the military academy at West Point. Pentecost was smart enough and devious enough to work for the CIA.

Tonight it was a reunion on the telephone, and then the years seemed to unwind as they reminisced about 1970 and the year when they played together in the high school pit orchestra for *South Pacific*. That was a very hot night in the old gymnasium, but the place was packed to the rafters and everybody left humming "I'm going to wash that man right out of my hair" or something like that.

Soon the movie thing came up and what Pentecost wanted to call the "George Washington slept here factor." David explained it this way: "Every time you stop at a Cracker Barrel Restaurant, somebody will say later: 'Anthony Flint ate here.' Every time you fill up the car, somebody will say: 'Anthony Flint bought premium here.' Every time you do this or that, somebody will say: 'Anthony Flint did this or that here.'"

The laughter brought tears to the eyes of both men.

"Better you than me," his friend added.

A long shot was established on LaMar Road with the film crew and the school bus with the engine running. On the director's cue the bus began to travel down the road and then shortly it pulled over to the side and came to a stop. This would be the point in the final editing when the scene changes to the one inside the bus. Here Bruce Willis is acting the role of the bus driver, Harold Pine. Willis is beginning to open the presents at Christmas time from the kids of the Bell, Heacox, Smith, Manifold, Beeson, Bowman, Messer, Burgess, Stockberger, Hendershot, Dishman, Lindley and Flint families.

Chapter 36: Mr. Boone and the 40-Acre Farm

It makes no difference what year it was when Anthony Flint was on the 40-acre farm or when he was inside the screened shelter that was built where the log cabin was razed in 1984. But it was still time that early morning to see the dew on the grass and to feel the gentle breeze in the trees that shade the backyard and the shelter so well during the hot afternoon of Indiana summer. Flint knew that nearly all of the trees were planted here by his father over the last 20 years. That included the maple and the tulip and the walnut.

This was also a time when he no longer worried who was President of the United States of America; or what political party occupied the Governor's Mansion in Tallahassee, Florida; or even how large the annual spending plan was for the Nettle Creek School Corporation in Hagerstown, Indiana.

But now he started to write his book, first by opening his personal laptop computer and then outlining all the chapters to come. His primary inspiration was Katherine Phil, a college journalism instructor at Ball State University in Muncie, Indiana. She made a trusting admiration that found no prodigy in Flint. But also no good reason to forget him. She said this on February 11, 1974: "Anthony always had interesting stories to write. I really wanted to encourage him to keep on writing and get some help with grammar. Anyone can acquire the technical skills, but not everyone has the story-sense and imagination he had."

Then it was the Guild Press in Indianapolis, Indiana. This was the publishing house that printed the biography on Hagerstown's most famous citizen, and which was authored by his only daughter in 1995. They said this: "We've looked with interest at your proposal for the reporter book *Ambassador for Life*. Clearly, you have the credentials and experience to pen such a book. It has an interesting concept. We really think you should get an agent, one who will be more familiar with the publishers to whom you might send the book."

Still another review came from the Greenwood Literary Associates in Tempe, Arizona. Here the editors and the staff worked with new authors and helped them find agents and publishers. This was usually accomplished by editing or developing plot themes and by submitting solid book proposals. There was even the use of the Internet and on-demand publishers like PublishAmerica and iUniverse who sold books to Amazon.com and Barnes & Nobles bookstores.

The Greenwood Literary Associates said this: "Thanks again for sending us *Ambassador for Life*. It's a fresh and welcome change from the manuscripts we've been receiving lately. We very much like the overall concept of this story. A lot of great historical data shows a solid knowledge of historical events and how they impacted the movement of time through the story. Intrigue is built into the story with contact with characters from the past, such as Thomas Jefferson and Robert E. Lee. These kinds of events have potential to develop into an exciting story about a man who sees and knows things beyond the common use of senses."

Anthony Flint probably wanted to put words down on paper when he was a teenager. He enjoyed watching *The Waltons* television series in the 1970s. John-Boy's book on Walton's Mountain had the same family values and the strong characterizations that Flint wanted to have in his own book someday. Then in college he took a turn at science fiction and wrote a 400-page manuscript. He gave it to his father for safekeeping and when it was promptly put in the vault in the postmaster's office at the Hagerstown Post Office.

Yet no one remembers whatever happened to it. Was the manuscript still locked away in total darkness on the day Keith Flint retired? This sounded like a mystery plot by Edgar Allen Poe. Flint once visited the author's home in Baltimore, Maryland. He walked away always remembering a life cut short by the writer's disastrous addictions to alcohol and drug abuse. This must have been the source of the frightful inspirations that produced his world-famous novels and short stories. If so, nothing in Flint's life would ever resemble in print anything ever written by Edgar Allen Poe.

Ernest Hemingway said an author could never write anything in great detail without first-hand knowledge on the subject. Hemingway's robust life is still immortalized today by the annual festivals in his honor in Key West, Florida. He lived a lifetime filled with near-death experiences as a war correspondent in the Spanish Civil War and in World War II, and as a bullfighting enthusiast, and as a survivor of a 1954 airplane crash in Africa.

It was great stuff for classic books and later several motion pictures from Hollywood.

But Anthony Flint didn't even own a handgun and hadn't fired one since Nixon was in the White House. He also forgot to burn his draft card. He never even saw his name on a ballot for public office like Norman Mailer, who was once a candidate for mayor of New York City. And you always knew someone who found a good book on politics to read; whether there was a scandal in it was considered a bonus.

Religion was controversial but another subject that would sell books. Flint still remembered the letters and e-mail he received in Orlando on his column about the Roman Catholic priests and the child abuse of alter boys. One reader simply mailed a postcard to him that read: "He that is without sin among you, let him cast the first stone."

What was really a hit on *The New York Times* best-seller list during this time in Flint's life was pure fantasy. It even showed up at the box office. It was the books by J.R.R. Tolkien on the *Lord of the Rings*, and it was the books by J.K. Rowling on the *Harry Potter* series.

And so the hardest part of Flint's book would not be his childhood on the 40-acre farm; or nor would it be his career as a syndicated columnist for *The Orlando Sentinel*. It would be his recollections of Thomas Jefferson, Robert E. Lee and the other things he was sure he would have to write. Publishers would see this as just another example of fantasy, and they refused to see it any other way.

It was all part of a growing national escape from news like the war with Iraq. This was definable and profitable to the publishers and agents who were successful enough to tell their authors that more and more readers really wanted to forget about the problems of the world. They no longer needed any troublesome headlines from the Middle East or the Persian Gulf or from the Oval Office of the White House. This was now a mindset that wasn't going away any time soon.

No one was writing a book anymore like Charles Dickens' *Bleak House*. And no publishing house on earth was selling any new books like Upton Sinclair's *The Jungle*. If there was anything like that to be done it was left to the 24-hour cable news shows. They had the time and the channels to cover big business never dreamed possible by Ida Tarbell. Even the local broadcasters found ways to show racism and bigotry and poverty never described in scenes from *Uncle Tom's Cabin* by Harriet Beecher Stowe.

So where was Flint's book in all this? Could he write the thing and still be accepted by his peers? Would he keep his job at the newspaper? How would anyone believe it?

The night Anthony Flint first saw Robert E. Lee would most certainly be a dramatic setting for any writer. All of it, of course, was part of the Spielberg film that was now showing in North America and in Europe. But Flint did not go to the theater to see it because his book was not finished. In no way did he want to be unduly influenced by the depictions made in the film. That was also why he did not write the script or participate in any way with the making of Spielberg's new movie.

He had accepted the challenge that he would write the book himself with as few disruptions as possible. Flint would also do it with no staff and with no ghostwriter. This was a promise made years ago when it was becoming clear that he would have something to write about after all.

Across the table he saw his cat jump up and begin to rub her head against the side of the screen to his laptop computer. Cali was a very loyal pet who was now getting way up in years. She had seen her master come a long way from the days when the family rode around in Orlando in a 1985 Saab 900 I. It had more miles on it than the clunker shown on the Beverly Hillbillies TV show. Now things were going to change even more as her master attempted to write his Great American Novel.

This was also the time when the hacker "DB" e-mailed Flint at the 40-acre farm. He greeted him with apparent joy: <Howdydo, Anthony Flint!> Then he wanted to know about Hagerstown, Indiana.

Flint was interrupted by all this but typed in a quick reply: <My hometown was settled in 1832 by Jacob Ulrich and Jonas Harris on land they owned in Jefferson Township, Indiana.>

DB was also curious about the book that Anthony Flint wanted to write. He informed Flint that he read the Bible, a history book, or his favorite, *Gulliver's Travels*, by the light of the campfire before lying down to sleep on hemlock boughs or dried leaves. His three-sided shelter was covered with brush, and the open side faced the light and the warmth of the campfire. He had plenty of time to read because he often spent several weeks in the wilderness, with only his dog and his horse for company. He preferred reading and hunting alone.

All of this brought back memories for Flint. They mostly centered on the first time he was corresponding with this hacker in Danville, Kentucky. Nothing was ever proved or disproved. DB was free to join the ranks with

Robert E. Lee and Thomas Jefferson. But who was next? Paul Revere? Albert Einstein? Saddam Hussein? And would Anthony Flint live long enough to know for sure?

DB realized that Flint remained skeptical about him, and so he began to tell about the book he wanted published when the War of 1812 began. That was the year when many rumors circulated that the Indians were going to attack the white man. In fact, many tribes were encouraged by the British to fight America's westward expansions. But when members of his family headed down the river for a safer location, the boats capsized, and everything was lost, including the autobiographical manuscript DB had dictated to his grandson.

Talk about the troubles of getting published!

This hacker was also skeptical that the story of his famous life would even sell in today's America. Certainly he had faced danger too many times to tell it all. But it didn't seem nearly as compelling as what DB had seen on television. He was convinced that this all amounted to the greatest single threat to the continued peaceful existence of the United States. It was not the prospect of nuclear weapons in the hands of some Al-Qaeda cell in Iran or Pakistan. Nor were violent video games and the unlimited pornography on the Internet something that DB took lightly. Yet they could not bring the country to total ruination all by themselves. Only television could destroy the moral fabric of the nation's people.

Flint did not know what to think. The prospect that DB or Daniel Boone— or whoever the hell he is—was actually watching television was not something that he could easily accept.

DB wanted to know how it was possible that Americans would go to a deserted island to eat worms or tell a live studio audience that a husband was really a woman who was in love with another man's wife? And it was all something that he saw on television. The hacker even commented on the repeated sightings of female toiletries in television commercials. He never found anything in Kentucky or in Arkansas that was so bewildering and that ever defied explanations. The subject was immediately familiar to every consumer's group protesting in America. To pick up the theme more quickly they would have to turn back the hands of time, and witness a society dependent on the recreational activities of the church and to the leisure reading of books by candlelight.

It was becoming clear to Flint that DB had a keen interest in the journalism of America and was like Robert E. Lee in that respect. DB was fascinated that a congressman would lose his office when a secret affair became public on television. It was all the more scandalous that the poor woman was missing for months and then her body found in a wooded section of a park in the nation's capital. DB could only imagine how television might have covered the abduction of his 13-year-old daughter, Jemima. She was captured by the Indians in 1776, and her canoe was abandoned on the banks of the Kentucky River. Jemima was missing before her father tracked her down in three days. Even his own daring escape from the Shawnee Indians in 1778 would have been something on live television: "On the sixteenth of June, before sunrise, I departed in the most secret manner, and arrived at Boonesborough on the twentieth, after a journey of one hundred and sixty miles—during which I had but one meal."

DB saw no end to the problem. It was his opinion that newspapers faired no better than their counterparts in television and even in radio. It seemed news organizations across the country were guilty in 1996 when a man was falsely accused of being the bomber during the summer Olympic games in Atlanta.

Then there was the young male reporter with *The New York Times*. He was out the door after too many false stories about the war in Iraq and the infamous sniper shootings in Maryland. Two decades earlier it was a female reporter with *The Washington Post* who won a Pulitzer Prize and then gave it up and was fired because she was far from honest with her readers.

And so these journalists closed their notebooks, presumably, because the editors believed they had done the right thing and that media across the country would have it no other way. The possibilities of a book deal with a fat figure or a major motion picture contract in the offing next was always very real. For all parties concerned. This conjured up disbelief and disgust on the part of DB and Anthony Flint.

The last e-mail ever received from DB to Anthony Flint was about the 40-acre farm. He was quite envious that it was still in the hands of the Flint family. It would most likely pass from Keith Flint to the youngest of his three sons, Clark; and then to one or more of the four grandsons, Bryon, Brandon, Eric or Nolan. This line of succession assured Flint ownership through an inheritance for the next 100 years.

It was exactly what DB wanted for his family 200 years ago. He lost his vast land holdings in Kentucky due to taxes and bad luck. That was when he became disillusioned and moved to Missouri, where he built a log cabin for himself and his wife, Rebecca, on the land owned by one of his sons, Daniel

Morgan.

In 1806, a judge ruled that DB was living on his son's farm and not on the land he claimed in 1798. The court's decision took away his land and his life as he knew it in Missouri. It was where he continued to do a lot of hunting and trapping even when he was 69 years old.

<Why did you still want to hunt and trap?> Flint typed on his keyboard.

<My wife was getting old and needed some little coffee and other refreshments, and I had no other way of paying for them but by trapping.>

DB added that he died on September 26, 1820, at age 85; but he still had a head full of hair and all of his teeth.

Chapter 37: At the Hagerstown Public Library

Hagerstown's public library was dedicated during an official ceremony back in 1928. It was after the donation of a gift in the amount of $30,000 from the Teetor family—when Ralph R. Teetor was 38. This was a time when the town's population was approximately 1,200 people, and nearly a hundred of its residents were Teetors.

It was also the year when the electron microscope was invented; and when television sets went on sale for the first time; and when Amelia Earhart became the first woman to fly across the Atlantic Ocean; and when Herbert Hoover was elected President of the United States; and when Mickey Mouse starred in the world's first sound cartoon; and when Congress approved construction of the massive Boulder Dam project in Nevada.

All of this became published in biographies, histories, references, young adult series and mysteries, and copies were ordered and put on the bookshelves at the Hagerstown library. And it was true that the library continued to grow and plan for the future. The review for progress was usually made public during National Library Month in April. This was a good time for the more than 117,000 libraries in the United States. And in Hagerstown, Indiana, the Board of Directors in 1958 noted the addition of the Children's department. Then in 1990, the library was doubled in size by the completion of a $500,000 expansion. Now there was room enough for subscriptions to 110 magazines, 10 newspapers and 34,000 books. But none of the new titles on the shelves quite matched the anomaly of Anthony's first book.

Ambassador for Life never won the Pulitzer Prize or *The Los Angles Times* Book Award or the Francis Parkman Prize or the National Book Award. But 25 years of Anthony's life was included as part of the book that was first made into a major motion picture. It was also clear that what appeared in print was no longer confidential but still controversial; and, again, it was now public. Now his wife, his daughter and the readers would have to decide how much of it was true.

Nevertheless, the first inexplicable events in Chapter 1 helped to shape the rest of Anthony's life. The name of Richard Crotty was long ago a catalyst to him and was never less subtle than its re-emergence in Long Beach, California. And now the astronaut would become famous before his time; he was the first mystery character from a book that was void of any sex or violence.

For that to be fact, *Ambassador for Life* would have to sell in bookstores and on the Internet with dependent themes not always associated with books published for the first time. Thus the encounters with some of the most famous men in American history was about as dependent as they come. That it was either true or false lent the book a certain appeal for publicity.

Flint's publisher told him the notoriety was similar to having an author's reputation dragged through the newspapers and all because his book remains the subject of a very public lawsuit. Or, worse, the book is out, and the author suddenly dies in a plane crash. By having to rely on such extreme ways to sell a book was like finding out what was behind door No #1 or door No #2 on some television game show.

It reminded Anthony when he was a boy and his family was visiting the Church of Christ in Lynn, Indiana. His aunt and uncle were long-time members, and good friends with a couple who also worshipped at the church and lived on a farm a couple of miles in the country. But it was the husband of the couple who was the most memorable with young Anthony, who also was a school bus driver and really a man with a big heart. He always liked to tease Flint and his brothers, and he would hold up both hands and clinch them tightly into fists and say: "Okay, what's it going to be? Death or six months in the hospital?"

There was, in the end, plenty of publicity generated with the first printing of Am*bassador for Life*. The publisher was confident about future editions and even the paperback sales. Editors and staff encouraged Anthony to add new material to his book based on the book reviews generated from across the country.

Here are some of them:

Lee in Tennessee, North Carolina and in Europe:
I had always thought that Lee was something of a stuffed shirt

and in some way responsible for the perhaps avoidable tragedy of the American Civil War. But the Lee who emerges from Anthony Flint's book is more human and genius than we have ever come to know.

—*The Boston Globe*

Jefferson in Virginia, New York City and over the West Rim of the Grand Canyon:

It is a rare blend of history and fiction, a book that speaks well to the patriot and the layman. It should be read throughout America. With one way to bring our nation's history to life, Anthony Flint has cast a spell on a new generation of readers who have yet to uncover the many deeds of a great American.

—*Newsweek*

E-mail from Daniel Boone:

Unknown and unproven, with the mystery of a classic Sherlock Holmes. It is a story that is not elementary at all and for which there are no witnesses and no physical evidence.

—*The Atlanta Constitution*

Richard Crotty on the planet Mars:

Flint is probably the first to have a premonition on what most people, we think, have imagined since the invention of the telescope. But we shall wait and see.

—*The Tampa Tribune*

The Treaty of Versailles:

It brings to life the tragedy and the hope of nations who saw this time as a means to end war in the world forever...whether this really happened to Anthony Flint or not.

—*The Los Angeles Times*

Anthony Flint looked down and saw the Ohio River during his flight from Orlando to Indianapolis. He remembered the spring floods in Lawrenceburg, Indiana, and then in a few minutes he was recalling the old Riverfront Stadium in downtown Cincinnati. The lights from the ball games always reflected upon the river as the waters flowed by on a clear night.

None of the lights shinned brighter than when fans celebrated the World Series championship by the Cincinnati Reds in 1975. It was the "Big Red" machine that won it, with Pete Rose, Johnny Bench, Joe Morgan and Tony Perez.

Now, as the plane flew over the Indianapolis Motor Speedway, Anthony easily viewed the track and remembered his time at the 1986 race. Ironically, he had to move to Florida before he was ever able to find tickets and see "the greatest spectacle in racing." He did it with the help from a Chevrolet dealer in Orlando and who also was a big advertiser with *The Orlando Sentinel.* His sudden change in travel plans was Anthony's door of opportunity in May of that year.

It was also possible to bring two friends from high school with him to Indianapolis, Allen Irvin and Marvin Heacox. Together, they were patient and smart to leave early and survive the horrible traffic that forms a gridlock hours before the start of the race. They even managed to find a place to park; and there was no problem getting to their seats. But he only saw a few laps. The rest of the day was victim to heavy rain; and all the people in the infield who played in the mud!

He got enough of it on videotape, and when he was not dodging some of the idiots who actually got in their trucks and drove around and spun tires that churned the ground up into pure muck. It was a sight to see muddy trucks banging into parked vehicles, a growing crowd cheering them on and more and more people like Anthony running over and filming the mess on their video cameras.

When driving to Hagerstown, he was able to think back to his childhood memories and how special they were to him. He once told his daughter how he dropped the collection plate, always plentiful with coins, on the old wood floor of the church. Anthony also told her how he stood at the end of the lane on the 40-acre farm with his two brothers—bundled up to survive the blowing snow—to wait on Gerald Hunt and the Nettle Creek school bus.

Alanah was too young in the beginning to point out the harsh weather conditions in her daddy's story, and that every school in Indiana would be closed that day! Then one day she made him think about his father and his memories as a child in New Castle, Indiana. Each time there was the Great Depression and how it was always more impossible to succeed than the last reminisce. His old friend in school, "Rusty Kleets," gained more stature through the years than Dr. Albert Schweitzer or Mother Teresa.

Was Keith Flint guilty of exaggerating childhood memories like his oldest son and even his own father who was a World War I army cook? It seemed each generation was destined to have it better, or harder, to hear them tell it.

This was the kind of memories full of family emotion and the kind that are guaranteed to wind up in some version of photography albums or home movies for each future generation. Sadly, though, they are writing down less and less words of remembrance. Flint was different, though. He was a writer.

At the Hagerstown Public Library, several blocks along College Street and Plum Street were roped off by the Hagerstown Police Department. This area was reserved for the EMS vehicles, the TV production trucks, the VIP parking, and room to form the line of people outside the library. They were all fully aware of the overcrowding inside that building. This information was supplied by family, neighbors or friends who emerged with a signed copy of *Ambassador for Life* and who stopped to talk to someone standing in the line.

To meet this challenge, Anthony probably arrived early in the morning when he had the assistance of the library director and his staff. That seemed hours ago. Anthony and the director and the staff in the library that was now nearly 100 years old. Later, when it was noon and time for lunch, he didn't want to stop and eat. Neither did anyone standing in line for this length of time. Every hour brought them closer and closer for the air conditioning as well as purchasing the book. The people visible outside the windows must have been something for the director and his staff to see.

The publisher of Anthony's book was amazed at how big a book signing could be in a small town. Even a telephone call from one house to the next was enough to bring entire families to the Hagerstown public library. One had to account for the local reviews and stories in *The Hagerstown Exponent* and the *Richmond Palladium-Item*, and it was only last summer when the movie was filmed in Dalton and then in Hagerstown. It was so that many of them saw themselves as "extras" and for seconds at a time, in a very popular film that was based on *Ambassador for Life*. Now anyone mentioned in Anthony's book would have the kind of fame that nearly everyone could sit down and read. That was also true with the search for places and people described in the book and made immortal. If LaMar Road was mentioned in the book then it was recalled by that name for years and years to come.

Here's what happened today: the autographs by Anthony Flint proved that his hand writing was much harder to read than it was 30 years ago. But he wanted something that was signed by him and was personal with each book sold at the library. And since friends and neighbors knew they were a part of this book, they only had their own apprehensions or imaginations as to what they were really about to read.

It was something the Class of 1973 never expected in a hundred years. Heck, there were only 100 students who graduated that year and who wanted to be teachers and farmers and medical professionals and loving parents. Some would go on to the universities at Ball State, Purdue, Indiana, and Butler; but one classmate, Jeff Vanderbilt, would move to San Francisco to study cures for cancer. Another classmate, Steve Newton, opened a tennis clinic in West Lafayette, Indiana. And, incredibly, one classmate, Anthony Flint, would write a book despite all the distractions in the world.

Still to come would be the day when a decision would have to be made on whether to write a sequel to *Ambassador for Life*. So Anthony used the best place at home in Orlando, Florida, to setup his laptop computer. That was usually the Florida room with the sliding glass doors, large windows and a view of the Number Three Hole at the Miona Lake Golf and Country Club. It was here that he observed a wide variety of golf swings, golf carts and a few golf balls landing in the backyard. That prompted a few words that he typed on his keyboard for the rest of the afternoon.

And there was another time when this whole business of a sequel was still alive. Anthony was visiting friends in Gainesville, Florida, but he always brought along his laptop because he never wanted to forget any ideas that suddenly came to his mind. That was the Saturday spent at Kanapaha Park and when the time was spent mostly watching his daughter having fun on the playground.

What was so surprising was the lack of any inspiration that Anthony had and would have for the second book. How did he find the words to write the first one? And how did he get his publisher to trust him? And what were all his family and friends really thinking of him now? All good questions which no one who was involved remembers as being answered in the affirmative.

But one thing was for sure and that was when it was five o'clock in the afternoon it was time to autograph his last book at the Hagerstown public library. He had to say goodbye and walk back to his car. And when he had done this, and when he got behind the wheel and fastened his seatbelt and shoulder harness, it was his cell phone that was ringing and it was more inspiration than he ever could handle.

Who could believe it was the voice of Floyd Lacy, talking like he was still seated behind his cluttered desk as the editor of *The Hagerstown*

Exponent? He told Flint he liked the book; Anthony could also hear him pause to light his pipe and then he said: "Don't kill a good thing. Let the first book stand on its own."

Flint had a second call when he was approximately 2 miles from the 40-acre farm. He was just turning off the road that was named in honor of Lacy and was heading down LaMar Road. That was when he had the voice of Ledona Henderson on the line; and it was just like 1964 when he was in the fourth grade at the redbrick schoolhouse in Dalton. She always included a word of encouragement with each conservation she had. Today she was very proud of her former student. The book was really a fine example of what a person could do with his life, she said.

From past experience Flint and his family knew how much had happened in as many times and places as imaginable. With each new revelation it was something to behold and always remember. But they easily concluded that this was not the extent of all the things to come. It was not over yet.

PART SEVEN

Chapter 38: Mars at Last

There was a midsummer sun shining high in a clear sky that was yellow-brown in color. The clouds that were gossamer and blue in the morning had dissipated by now, and the temperature was eight degrees Fahrenheit. This was way up from the low last night of minus 100 degrees Fahrenheit. There was even a breeze that wafted from the west at about eight miles an hour.

The meteorological reports said the weather was perfect for an afternoon drive from the Ares Vallis landing site to an intriguing collection of rocks a few hundred yards away. Astronaut Michael Amato first spotted them on Monday, describing the rocks as possibly conglomerates, or a type of rock that forms over millennia as water rounds pebbles and cobbles and deposits them in a matrix of sand and clay.

"That means there was once liquid water on Mars," Amato said in his initial report to fellow astronauts Richard Crotty, David Kulhman, Floyd Calloway and Richard Gizankis. "It suggests a very different climate, perhaps one where life could have developed. That raises the questions: If life developed, what happened to it; and if not, why not?"

Some of the soil at the site was as fine as flour. But it was all part of a dusty, boulder-strewn landscape sculpted by Martian winds that sometimes reach 100 miles per hour. Yet it was first hued out by cataclysmic floods 2 billion years ago. In fact, the astronauts looked all around them and saw the evidence of water.

It was Gizankis who conducted a series of experiments with magnets and dust particles and showed that iron in the planet's crust was once leached out by groundwater. In Mars orbit it was astronauts Eladio Izquierdo, Jr., and Lowell Thacker who mapped and studied a vast region that was predominately flat and that covered much of the northern hemisphere. They thought this was possibly an extinct seabed or an ancient mudflat.

But all the tests from the payload of scientific equipment on the surface of Mars including, but not limited to, the stereoscopic camera with 24 filters, the Alpha-proton x-ray spectrometer and the atmospheric structure instrument meteorology package failed to detect that there was another life form watching the astronauts from Earth.

Anthony Flint never wrote the greatest story of his life. He would know it when he saw it. But it didn't seem so in the beginning when he was still purchasing tickets for himself and for his wife, Candy, and his daughter, Alanah. He was standing in line at the Visitor's Center at the John F. Kennedy Space Center on the Space Coast of Florida.

Here was where the film presentation was on Mars inside NASA's Imax Theatre. It was built during a time when 80 percent of all Imax theatres opened in the United States during a boom in the late '90s and the early 21st century. The images produced by the large-format movie was always much sharper and clearer than ordinary showings. In fact, the 70mm film that is run horizontally through the projector is nine times larger than the conventional 35mm vertical-projection film.

Some of the people in line ahead of Anthony had probably seen other Imax films on the Titanic, Mount Everest, or even the Imax presentations shown at museums and historical sites in the last 20 years. But nobody would see what Anthony did for the same price of admission.

On the fifth day of man's exploration of Mars the Jet Propulsion Laboratory in Pasadena, California, reported: "We found rocks very high in silicon, which indicates that some crustal materials are like the continental crust on Earth." This was gratifying to the astronauts at the Ares Vallis landing site. They were surrounded by a countryside of large and small rocks, angular and rounded rocks, and dark and bright rocks, stretching to the horizon. And everybody wanted a variety of rocks to process and study.

There was a growing consensus that what deposited many of the rocks at Ares Vallis was a flood whose volume may have equaled all of the water that fills the Great Lakes of North America. And any one of the rocks out there could have evidence of fossil remains.

So where was all the water on Mars? The Jet Propulsion Laboratory was joined by leading scientists from around the world that said the Martian water is frozen at the poles or frozen underground. But life cannot exist without liquid water. And no water means no life on Mars.

"There may have been life on Mars," Astronaut Calloway said to a high school convocation in Alabama nearly three months before his historic flight to the Red Planet. "The only way to know for sure would be to go look for yourself."

But it was the first President Bush who said the United States should land a man on Mars by 2019. That year marked the 50th anniversary of Neil Armstrong's first step on the moon. The second President Bush said America ought to return to the moon in 2015 and then a decade later send a mission to Mars. Yet it would take NASA longer than that to see and hear Richard Crotty on the Martian surface.

It was night on the planet Mars after 24 hours and 37 minutes of day. A band of stars arched through the heavens and twinkled brightly above the Valles Marineris canyon. A place which would stretch from San Francisco to New York if it was ever located on Earth; and it is the longest such valley known to exist in the solar system.

The moons of Phobos and Deimos appear just over the distant horizon of a jagged mountain. Phobos is the bigger of the two moons. The mountain was actually the Martian volcano Olympus Mons, with the clouds drifting across its towering summits. Olympus Mons is the largest known volcano in the solar system. It rises a staggering 75,000 feet above the surface and is two and a half times the height of Mt. Everest in the Himalayas of south central Asia.

In the first few minutes of the movie, after the liftoff from Florida, there was the International Space Station. It was in orbit high above the old Barbery Coast of north Africa and almost certainly visible to most of Egypt, Libya, Tunisia, Algeria and Morocco even in broad daylight. The International Space Station was actually the staging point for all of the spaceflight systems needed for the voyage to Mars. It was here that everything was outfitted and sent on its way for the next seven months to travel a distance of 119 million miles.

Don't forget, the announcer added, this all had to work again to bring the astronauts back home to earth. Which was another seven months to travel an additional 119 million miles.

Anthony Flint's enjoyment of the Imax film was complete and was the source of quite unexpected inspiration. He could see everything on the domed screen and hear the sounds of the mission as if he was really standing at the Ares Vallis landing site. Then imagine how he felt when he no longer had the safe confines of his seat in the theatre.

To be sure, he could still see and hear everything. This included all the excitement and the applause from the capacity audience in the theatre. Then he thought he saw the earth in space; and the moon and the distant sun. It was all happening to him and when he could no longer see anything now except a new neighborhood of stars.

Other elements soon entered in from time to time. Before too long it was possible to see an amazing transformation in time and space. Such as his ability to live and breathe without a spacesuit. He could feel the wind of Mars on his face. And no longer was the perspiration on his back the result of any sub-tropical heat in Florida.

The astronauts felt a stong wind on the tenth day of the manned surface exploration at the Ares Vallis landing site. But it was nothing like it was going to be in the approaching Martian dust storm season. This was bigger and louder than anything experienced during the Dust Bowl of the 1930s in the southern Great Plains of the United States. The Martian dust storm season covered the whole planet. Period.

Already dark, gently sloping dunes formed about ten feet long and are composed of both fine and course materials that have been shaped by the wind. They are crescent-shaped and called barchanoid dunes, which are as common at Ares Vallis as they are on Earth.

The astronauts saw the dryness of Mars in these windblown dunes. And with the surrounding rocky plain. Astronaut Kulhman joked that if you added blue skies and flowing water it would make Ares Vallis look like the training sites NASA had them visit in Iceland and in the State of Washington. But it was a phenomenon on Mars that required airborne sand to act as an abrasive of nature. On Earth it was running water that eroded and gorged rocks into shape.

"I have one regret," Richard Crotty reported to Mission Control at the end of the tenth day. "I would have loved to see a big old cloud of dust rolling up from that horizon. I tell you that would have been something."

Flint always wished he would live long enough to see the first colonization of Mars. But he was old enough to walk on the surface of the Red Planet with Richard Crotty. And with all of the astronauts at Ares Vallis, here and now, the presence of his company was not a thing that was made a part of the official flight records at the Lyndon B. Johnson Space Flight Center.

Remember that he could see them, but they did not know anything about Anthony Flint. This was something that he alone could appreciate and understand with any degree of expertise. After all, he was the one with the visions of Robert E. Lee; and he was a friend of Thomas Jefferson; and he was the one with e-mail from Daniel Boone. So he was the one.

Anthony knew that today there was something wrong inside the spacecraft at the Ares Vallis landing site. It was a blue wire, and somehow it was disconnected. The astronauts could not make repairs without another excursion on the surface of Mars. Then they could easily reach it by opening the small door on the outside panel.

After more than an hour Flint could hear the communications about something called a laser altimeter. It was used in navigation and was especially critical when linking with the astronauts orbiting Mars.

"Um, you may have a problem there," replied Mission Control in Houston. "Don't feel too bad. We have spent so much time looking at this that we nicked named it the Bermuda Triangle."

Blame it on the wild Martian temperatures that probably caused the wire to snap or the soldering point to crack. The polar nights can get as cold as minus 200 degrees Fahrenheit and while the summer days south of the equator can get as hot as 80 degrees Fahrenheit. Which means everything in-between can be equally inhospitable. And when it comes to the wind and the sand, this can become a double jeopardy. Nobody at NASA wanted the astronauts back in their spacesuits and on the surface of the planet—especially when consuming limited air and time to pursue a solution to the problem. It still wasn't clear what cut the blue wire to the laser altimeter. Everyone hoped something could be bypassed or a redundancy found that would resuscitate the damn thing.

So it was to be that Flint reached his hand inside the spacecraft and fastened the broken wire good enough to make a solid connection. Then a couple of hours for Mission Control to wonder what the hell happened and then the liftoff into the Martian skies. None of NASA's instruments told the story of Anthony Flint and his intervention at the Ares Vallis landing site. But he saw the ascension of the astronauts into space, as it turns out. The glory of it filled his eyes with tears of joy; and briefly, as the spacecraft roared up into the thinning atmospheres of Mars, it was like watching Columbus discover the New World.

Mars was no longer a place that was found only in science fiction books or used as some kind of futuristic metaphor. The footsteps of Man are now the most important impressions every made in the fine sand at Ares Vallis. It was likely the most historical moment ever for the planet Mars.

But this was not the end for Anthony Flint. What would the astronauts think if they knew there was a stowaway on the long mission home to Earth?

The provisions of food and water and clothing were never a requirement for this passenger of mystery. It was also true that his secret was always safe with him.

This was never part of any Imax presentation with any theatre in the world. Yet the next turn-of-events was certainly a bargain because the room in the State House in Philadelphia was cool and comfortable. It was unlike the usual summer heat that was often excessively hot and steamy in July; or the daily storms pelting rain in the city with a good measure of thunder and lighting. Even the pesky black flies were not present to bite through silk hose, which tormented nearly everyone present.

Anthony Flint was now standing next to the President of the Continental Congress, John Hancock. Here was a man who lived in a mansion in Boston and was one of the richest men in all of Massachusetts. His life, as he knew it, would never be the same again. But Hancock was not intimidated as he signed the document before him. It was one of the greatest papers ever conceived by man, and that was after 80 editorial changes, mostly minor. Hancock was the first to pen his name on it. Also, his signature appeared as the largest. Flint did not hear that day whether this was really done to spite King George III of England, who clearly could read it without putting on his spectacles.

Charles Thomson, the Secretary of the Congress, signed his name next. Then it would be another month before nearly all of the 56 delegates signed a copy elegantly engrossed on a sheet of parchment. A new representative for New Hampshire, Matthew Thornton, added his name in November, although he was not a member when the document was passed by Congress on July 4, 1776. At eleven o'clock that morning the debate was closed and the vote taken. The last to fix his name to all of this was Thomas McKean, of Delaware, in January of 1777. Then the whole world would come to know the signatures of men like Benjamin Franklin, John Adams, Samuel Chase, George Wythe, Richard Henry Lee, Oliver Wolcott, Elbridge Gerry, Benjamin Rush and Thomas Jefferson. He wrote his name legible at lower center on this paper the American colonies called the Declaration of Independence.

Anthony Flint also realized that, sure enough, there would be a room in a parlor with a small table in the corner and a larger one in the center. Officers who were mostly silent in the room included Lieutenant Colonel Charles Marshall, a grandson of Chief Justice John Marshall; Brevet Brigadier General Orville E. Badcock; Brigadier General Lawrence Williams; Brigadier General Seth Williams, a captain and former adjutant at West Point; and Colonel Ely

S. Parker, a Seneca Indian and chief of his tribe.

The general of the most powerful army the world had ever seen lit a cigar and puffed on it as he wrote down the generous terms for surrender. He got up from the center table and brought the draft over to the man who put down his broad-rimmed military hat and riding gauntlets on the table in the corner. This was a general who needed his reading glasses, who wiped them off and perched them on his nose. He nodded and gave an inward sigh of relief after reading the entire document.

This general was more than tempted to look outside on Palm Sunday, April 9, 1865, sometime after one o'clock in the afternoon. He gazed to the northeast but could not see the shattered remnants of his Army of Northern Virginia, or where his men remained in defensive positions a mile away. They would hear this hour that they would keep their swords and pistols and baggage, and the private horses to work the farm fields back home for food. But they were surrounded and outnumbered by a victorious army six times their size. And all of the soldiers were holding their weapons at their sides now. It was very good that every soul out there would not die in any continuing artillery fire or musketry.

Robert E. Lee and Ulysses S. Grant at the Wilmer McLean house in the village of Appomattox Court House would be next for Anthony Flint.

The End

Everything was not known in 2054, the year the Indiana General Assembly approved a state historic site on the 40-acre farm. It was also the 100th anniversary of the birth of Anthony Flint. To commemorate both events, all of the family's children and grand-children attended the dedication ceremonies and unveiled the bronze plaque posted off LaMar Road. There was time spent that centennial year in the new museum that was erected on the site of the old red poll barn. But it was always unanimous to promote the farm in Dalton Township as was done with the James Whitcomb Riley home in Greenfield; or the Ernie Pyle State Historic site in Dana; or the Indianapolis homes of Booth Tarkington and Kurt Vonnegut; or the Brookville home of Lew Wallace, an Indiana lawyer, the Governor of the New Mexico Territory, an major general in the Civil War, a judge in the Lincoln conspirators trial and the author of *Ben-Hur*.

No place had quite the appeal as the 40-acre farm. The model of the Empire State Building was on loan from the Thomas Jefferson Foundation. It was understandable that anybody in America who read the notes had justification to question the ink handwriting. The museum had them all where people could see them in the best interactive exhibits possible. It was also a matter of debate in everyone's mind at Monticello to explain how Jefferson's writings now included the world's most famous skyscraper; and on paper manufactured nearly a century after his death.

Other exhibits on loan from the duPont Library at Stratford Hall Plantation was the correspondence of Robert E. Lee. It included President Woodrow Wilson, General Douglas MacArthur and President Jimmy Carter, and the implications were not lost on those who found the letters in the files that were previously not recorded. Nobody on staff could explain it; this was a mystery for historians, the Pentagon and the growing number of Lee's descendants. But did this have anything to do with Anthony Flint?

Remember that the newspaper columns by him had their first publications in *The Orlando Sentinel*, and then syndicated across the country. The readership had a mix of those who were skeptical, loyal, confrontational and even indifferent. Yet that could not be expected to explain it all.

Notes

Chapter 1: First Man to Mars

Beauchamp, Wilbur L., *Science is Learning*. Scott, Foresman and Co. Chicago. 1961.

Chapter 2: James Warren Jones

Sanders, Douglas and Wells, David, "Sect Leader Was Quiet, Loner As Child In Indiana," *The Cincinnati Enquirer*, Nov. 21, 1978.

Sanders, Douglas, "Chrysler Begins Richmond Plant Site Work," *The Cincinnati Enquirer*, Nov. 17, 1978.

Sanders, Douglas, "Indiana Landowners Scrap Land, Water Plan," *The Cincinnati Enquirer*, Nov. 24, 1977.

Sanders, Douglas, "Teacher Strike Ends," *The Cincinnati Enquirer*, Jan. 26, 1979.

www.religioustolerance.org (The People's Temple, Led by James Warren "Jim" Jones).

www.apolloguide.com (Guyana Tragedy: The Story of Jim Jones).

Chapter 4: Watergate

Bernstein, Carl and Woodward, Bob, *All the President's Men*, Simon and Schuster, New York, 1974.

Sanders, Douglas, "Brill Tells How He Got Nixon's Picture," *The Ball State Daily News*, Oct. 24, 1974.

Sanders, Douglas; Interview with G. Gordon Liddy. WDCF-AM, Brewer Broadcasting Corp., 1984.

Sanders, Douglas, "Dennis Speaks on Watergate Role," *The Ball State Daily News*, Feb. 6, 1975.

www.nixonfoundation.org (Funeral services of President Nixon).

Chapter 5: Dickens at Dalton

Dickens, Charles, *A Christmas Carol*. TOR Associates, New York, 1988.

Sanders, Douglas, "Transformation Of An Abandoned School," *The Hagerstown Exponent*, Sept. 4, 1974.
Wilbur Wright Birthplace and Interpretive Center, *Centennial of Flight Festival: Commemorative Issue*, Millville, Indiana, 2003.

Chapter 6: The General at Stones River, Tennessee
Flood, Charles Bracelen, *Lee: The Last Years*, Houghton Mifflin Co., Boston, 1981.

Chapter 8: Mr Sulu, Ann Landers and the Rev. Rex Humbard
CNN.com (Ann Landers/Easther Pauline Lederer)
DeGeorge, Gail, *The Making of a Blockbuster: How Wayne Huizenga Built a Sports and Entertainment Empire from Trash, Grit and Videotape*, John Wiley & Sons, New York, 1996.
Sanders, Douglas; Interview with Ann Landers. WDCF-AM, Brewer Broadcasting Corp., 1986.
Sanders, Douglas; Interview with Rev. Rex Humbard. WDCF-AM, Brewer Broadcasting Corp., Nov. 7, 1985.
www.startrek.com (Star Trek Timeline).

Chapter 9: Exponent
Lacy, Floyd C., "Ralph R. Teetor Dies At 91," *The Hagerstown Exponent*, Feb. 17, 1982.
Sanders, Douglas, "School Board Okays Master Contract, But Delay On Architect," *The Hagerstown Exponent*, Dec. 16, 1981.
Sanders, Douglas, "$8,685.00," *The Hagerstown Exponent*, Dec. 9, 1981.

Chapter 10: The Fire on Merritt Island
Adams, Peter, "Engle, Truly Arrive Eager; Orbiter 'More Than Ready,'" Today, Nov. 3, 1981.
Dudley, Bruce "Reagan: Teachers Should Be First Citizens in Space," The Tampa Tribune, Aug. 28, 1984.
Radio Advertising Bureau (RAB), Consumer Profiles: Vital Tourism Marketing Data on 86 Demographic Groups, RAB Yearbook, 1983.
Sanders, Douglas, *Shuttle: A Press Guide to the John F. Kennedy Space Center*. Ball State University. 1985.
Schbecoff, Philip "Strain of Human Activity Biggest Refuge Risk," *The New York Times*, May 31, 1984.

Skene, Neil "Shuttle Safe 'Back Where It Belongs,'" *The St. Petersburg Times*, Feb. 12, 1984.

Chapter 11: Band
"Glenn Miller Died in 1944 But Melodies Linger On," *The Indianapolis Star*, 1973.
Guy Lombardo and his Royal Canadians in Concert, Columbia Artists Theatricals Corp., New York, 1972.
Sanders, Douglas, "Chicago Feels 'Apolitical Blues,' Good Time Music at State Fair," *The Ball State Daily News*, Sept. 11, 1975.
Smith, Gretchen, "Lombardo's 'Sweetest Music' Gives Fans Easy Listening," *The Richmond Palladium-Item*, April 16, 1973.

Chapter 12: Jimmy Carter and George C. Wallace
Bayh, Marvella, with Kotz, Mary Lynn, *Marvella: A Personal Journey*, Harcourt Brace Jovanovich, New York, 1979.
Sanders, Douglas, "Carter Speaks at Notre Dame's Center," *The Ball State Daily News*, Oct. 11, 1976.
Sanders, Douglas, "Carters Attract Tourists, Media From Around Nation to Plains," *The Ball State Daily News*, March 15, 1977.
Sanders, Douglas, Interview with Father Theodore Hesburgh. WDCF-AM, Brewer Broadcasting Corp., 1986.
Sanders, Douglas, "Wallace Opens Fourth Indiana Campaign," *The Ball State Daily News*, Feb. 12, 1976.
www.pbs.org (America's Most Honored: Father Theodore Hesburgh).

Chapter 14: The Bellamy Brothers
Sanders, Douglas; Interview with David and Howard Bellamy. WDCF-AM, Brewer Broadcasting Corp., 1983.

Chapter 15: Post Office
Sanders, Douglas, "Blue River & Western to be Operational This Summer," *The Hagerstown Exponent*, June 26, 1974.

Chapter 16: USS *Cony*
Barnard, George N., *Photographic Views of Sherman's Campaign*, Dover Publications, New York, 1997.
Donovan, Robert J., *PT-109: John F. Kennedy in World War II*, McGraw-Hill Book Co, New York, 1961.

Moore, Sandy, "Military Service a Labor of Love for Chester Sanders," *The New Castle Courier-Times*, Nov. 10, 2001.

"UN Naval Air, Cruisers Bomb Rails, Coastline," Pacific S & S, October, 1951.

Chapter 17: At the Indiana Statehouse

Sanders, Douglas; Herrmann, Pat, "Legislators Begin Work in the 99th General Assembly," *The Ball State Daily News*, Nov. 6, 1976.

Sanders, Douglas, "Bowen Discusses State Budget," *The Ball State Daily News*, Jan. 9, 1976.

Sanders, Douglas, "IU's Benson Honored by Indiana General Assembly," *The Ball State Daily News*, March 24, 1977.

Sanders, Douglas; Pat Herrmann, "Women Lobby at State Capitol," *The Ball State Daily News*, Jan. 19, 1976.

Sanders, Douglas, "Pari-Mutuel Betting Bill Passes House, Senate; Bowen's Veto Expected," *The Ball State Daily News,* Feb. 5, 1976.

Sanders, Douglas; de la Bastide, Ken, "Candidate Discusses Marijuana, Pari-Mutuel Betting," *The Ball State Daily News*, April 15, 1976.

Yencer, Rick, "Editors of Ball State Paper Vote to Strike," *The Muncie Star*, April 21, 1975.

Chapter 18: Orville Redenbacher

Sanders, Douglas; Interview with Orville Redenbacher. WDCF-AM, Brewer Broadcasting Corp., Oct. 25, 1985.

www.coolquize.com (Orville Redenbacher).

www.waltdisneyworld.com (Disney's Contemporary Resort-Kingdom Magic Travel).

Chapter 19: Monticello

Bear, James A. Jr., and Nichols, Frederick D., *Monticello*. Thomas Jefferson Memorial Foundation. Monticello. 1993.

McCullough, David, *John Adams*, Simon & Schuster, New York, 2001.

"Museum Should Include Tragic Space Shuttle History," T*he Daily Commercial*, Sept. 2, 2003. www.monticello.org (Monticello).

Steinberg, Jennifer, "Last Voyage of the Slave Ship Henrietta Marie," *National Geographic*, August, 2002.

www.melfisher.org (Mel Fisher Maritime Museum)

Chapter 20: Houston

Emery, Edwin, "The Press and America: An Interpretative History of the Mass Media," Prentice-Hall, Englewood, Ca., 1972.

Sabluis, Thomas, "A Down-to-the-Wire Delay," The Orlando Sentinel, Nov. 5, 1981.

www.finpipe.com (High Yield or "Junk" Bonds).

www.science.ksc.gov/shuttle (Enterprise OV-101).

Chapter 21: Billie Jean King and Julian Bond

Sanders, Douglas; Interview with Billie Jean King. WDCF-AM, Brewer Broadcasting Corp., 1983.

Sanders, Douglas; Interview with Julian Bond. WDCF-AM, Brewer Broadcasting Corp., 1987.

www.education.yahoo.com (Billie Jean King).

www.education.yahoo.com (Julian Bond).

www.wic.org (Billie Jean King).

Chapter 22: New York City

Bond, L. E., *Statue of Liberty: Beacon of Promise*. Albion Publishing Group, Santa Barbara, Ca. 1992.

Harris, Bill, *The World Trade Center: a Tribute*. Salamander Books Ltd., London, 2001.

Isaacson, Walter, *Benjamin Franklin: An American Life*, Simon & Schuster, New York, 2003.

McCullough, David, *John Adams*, Simon & Schuster, New York, 2001.

Chapter 23: Pope John Paul II

Sanders, Douglas; Broadcasts of the Miami Papa Visit. WDCF-AM, Brewer Broadcasting Corp., 1987

www.boeing.com (Air Force One).

Chapter 24: Dave Thomas in Lakeland, Florida

Peltier, Michael, "Wendy's Founder Tops Menu at Chamber Meet," *The Lakeland Ledger*, Jan. 15, 1994.

Peltier, Michael, "Thomas Serves Up Homespun Humor," *The Lakeland Ledger*, Jan. 21, 1994.

The Associated Press, "Wendy's Expects Thousands at Viewing for Dave Thomas," Jan. 10, 2002.

Thomas, Dave, with Beyma, Ron, *Dave Says 'Well Done!' The Common Guy's Guide to Everyday Success*, Zondervan Publishing House., Grand Rapids, 1994.

Chapter 25: Death Row
Sanders, Douglas; Interviews with Ernest Lee Miller and William Riley Jent. WDCF-AM, Brewer Broadcasting Corp., 1986.

Chapter 26: Deed to Daniel
McCarthy, Pat, *Daniel Boone: Frontier Legend*, Enslow Publishers, Inc., Berkeley Heights, New Jersey, 2000.
The Associated Press, "Trails Replace Deadly Road," July 18, 2002.

Chapter 27: Astronaut James B. Irvin
Sanders, Douglas; Interview with Astronaut James B. Irvin. WDCF-AM, Brewer Broadcasting Corp., Sept. 11, 1985.

Chapter 28: The Treaty of Versailles
Bendiner, Elmer, *A Time for Angels—The Tragicomic History of the League of Nations*, Alfred Knop, New York, 1975.
Flood, Charles Bracelen, *Lee: The Last Years*, Houghton Mifflin Co., Boston, 1981.
Klingaman, William, *The Year Our World Began*, Harper & Row, New York, 1989.
Manchester, William, *American Caesar: Douglas MacArthur, 1880-1964*, Dell Publishing, New York, 1978.
Meyer, Daniel, *Versailles*, Editions d'Art Lys, Paris, 1995.
Starke, J.G., *The Commonwealth in International Affairs: Essays on the Australian Constitution*, The Law Book Co., Sydney, 1952.
The Louvre: The Museum; The Collections; The New Spaces; Connaisance des Arts, Paris, 1993.

Chapter 29: Second Man to Mars
Bennet, Howard, "Hypersonic Flight Under Study," The Tampa Tribune, May 18, 1984.
Emery, Edwin, "The Press and America: An Interpretative History of the Mass Media," Prentice-Hall, Englewood, Ca., 1972.
Moore, Patrick, *New Guide to the Moon*, W. W. Norton & Co. New York, 1976.

"Return to Mars," National Geographic, August, 1998.
www.aafo.com (Spruce Goose).
www.qadas.com (NASA Awards $81.6 Million Contract to Hughes).

Chapter 30: Andrew and Jack "Murf the Surf" Murphy

Barnard, George N., *Photographic Views of Sherman's Campaign*, Dover Publications, New York. 1977.
Rather, Dan with Herskowitz, Mickey, "The Camera Never Blinks," William Morrow & Co. New York, 1977.
Sanders, Douglas; Jack Murphy. WDCF-AM, Brewer Broadcasting Corporation.
"The Night they Stole The Star of India," Life, pp 77-80. Nov. 13, 1964.
www.noaa.gov (Hurricane Andrew).
www.noaa.gov (Hurricane Hugo).
www.noaa.gov (Hurricane Carla).

Chapter 31: Steven E. Ambrose at the University of New Orleans

Ambrose, Steven E., "Flawed Founding Fathers," Smithsonian, November, 2002.
Jones, Landon Y., "Iron Will (William Clark after the Lewis & Clark Expedition)," Smithsonian, August, 2002.

Chapter 32: The General at Ashville, North Carolina

Biltmore Estate: A National Historic Landmark. The Biltmore Co., Ashville, N.C. 1991.
Flood, Charles Bracelen, *Lee: The Last Years*, Houghton Mifflin Co., Boston, 1981.

Chapter 33: Mike Wallace in Orlando, Florida

Bear, James A. Jr., and Nichols, Frederick D., *Monticello*. Thomas Jefferson Memorial Foundation. Monticello. 1993.
Flood, Charles Bracelen, *Lee: The Last Years*, Houghton Mifflin Co., Boston, 1981.

Chapter 34: The Voyage of Discovery

Ambrose, Stephen E., *Lewis & Clark: Voyage of Discovery*, National Geographic Society.
Schmidt, Jeremy and Thomas, *The Saga of Lewis & Clark into the Uncharted West*, Tehabi Books, Inc., 1999.

Teetor, Marjorie Meyer, *One Man's Vision: The Life of Automotive Pioneer Ralph R. Teetor*, Guild Press Of Indianapolis, 1995.

Chapter 35: Steven Spielberg in Hagerstown, Indiana
Dickens, Charles, *A Christmas Carol*. TOR Associates, New York, 1988.
Sanders, Douglas, "Transformation Of An Abandoned School," *The Hagerstown Exponent*, Sept. 4, 1974.

Chapter 36: Mr Boone and the 40-Acre Farm
McCarthy, Pat, *Daniel Boone: Frontier Legend*, Enslow Publishers, Inc., Berkeley Heights, New Jersey, 2000.

Chapter 37: At the Hagerstown Public Library
Teetor, Charles, *Charley Teetor's Hometown: The Story of an Indiana Family, Their Village, and the Industrial Revolution*, Westernesse Press, Amagansett, New York, 1994.

Chapter 38: Mars at Last
Flood, Charles Bracelen, *Lee: The Last Years*, Houghton Mifflin Co., Boston, 1981.
Frisinger, Cathy, "Imax Format Reaches for New Heights," *Knight Ridder Newspapers*, April 20, 2003.
McCullough, David, *John Adams*, Simon & Schuster, New York, 2001.
"Return to Mars," *National Geographic*, August, 1998.

Bibliography

Allen, Joseph; Martin, Russell, *Entering Space: An Astronaut's Odyssey*, Stewart, Tabori & Chang, New York, 1984.

Alsop, Joseph, *FDR: A Centennial Remembrance*, Thames & Hudson Limited, London, 1982.

Arnold, James E., *The Hermitage: Home of Andrew Jackson*, The Ladies Hermitage Association, 1967.

Barnard, George N., *Photographic Views of Sherman's Campaign*, Dover Publications, New York, 1997.

Bayh, Marvella, with Kotz, Mary Lynn, *Marvella: A Personal Journey*, Harcourt Brace Jovanovich, New York, 1979.

Bear, James A. Jr., and Nichols, Frederick D., *Monticello*. Thomas Jefferson Memorial Foundation. Monticello. 1993.

Beauchamp, Wilbur L., *Science is Learning*. Scott, Foresman and Co. Chicago. 1961.

Bendiner, Elmer, *A Time for Angels—The Tragicomic History of the League of Nations*, Alfred Knop, New York, 1975.

Bernstein, Carl and Woodward, Bob, *All the President's Men*, Simon and Schuster, New York, 1974.

Bond, L. E., *Statue of Liberty: Beacon of Promise*. Albion Publishing Group, Santa Barbara, Ca. 1992.

Dickens, Charles, *A Christmas Carol*. TOR Associates, New York, 1988.

DeGeorge, Gail, *The Making of a Blockbuster: How Wayne Huizenga Built a Sports and Entertainment Empire from Trash, Grit and Videotape*, John Wiley & Sons, New York, 1996.

Donovan, Robert J., *PT-109: John F. Kennedy in World War II*, McGraw-Hill Book Co, New York, 1961.

Dowdey, Clifford, *The Seven Days: The Emergency of Robert E. Lee*, The Fairfax Press, New York, 1978.

Emery, Edwin, "The Press and America: An Interpretative History of the Mass Media," Prentice-Hall, Englewood, Ca., 1972.

Flood, Charles Bracelen, *Lee: The Last Years*, Houghton Mifflin Co., Boston, 1981.

Franklin D. Roosevelt's Little White and Museum, Georgia Department of Natural Resources, Recreation and Historic Sites Division, Atlanta, 2003.

Guy Lombardo and his Royal Canadians in Concert, Columbia Artists Theatricals Corp., New York, 1972.

Harris, Bill, *The World Trade Center: a Tribute*. Salamander Books Ltd., London, 2001.

Isaacson, Walter, *Benjamin Franklin: An American Life*, Simon & Schuster, New York, 2003.

Kerrod, Robin, *The Illustrated History of NASA*, Gallery Books, New York, 1987.

Klingaman, William, *The Year Our World Began*, Harper & Row, New York, 1989.

McCarthy, Pat, *Daniel Boone: Frontier Legend*, Enslow Publishers, Inc., Berkeley Heights, New Jersey, 2000.

McCullough, David, *John Adams*, Simon & Schuster, New York, 2001.

Meredith, Roy, *Mathew Brady's Portrait of an Era*, Houghton Mifflin Co., Boston, 1981.

Meyer, Daniel, *Versailles*, Editions d'Art Lys, Paris, 1995.

Moore, Patrick, *New Guide to the Moon*, W. W. Norton & Co. New York, 1976.

Rather, Dan with Herskowitz, Mickey, *The Camera Never Blinks*,,William Morrow & Co. New York, 1977.

Schmidt, Jeremy and Thomas, *The Saga of Lewis & Clark into the Uncharted West*, Tehabi Books, Inc., 1999.

Starke, J.G., *The Commonwealth in International Affairs: Essays on the Australian Constitution*, The Law Book Co., Sydney, 1952.

Teetor, Marjorie Meyer, *One Man's Vision: The Life of Automotive Pioneer Ralph R. Teetor*, Guild Press Of Indianapolis, 1995.

The Louvre: The Museum; The Collections; The New Spaces; Connaisance des Arts, Paris, 1993.

Thomas, Dave, with Beyma, Ron, *Dave Says 'Well Done!' The Common Guy's Guide to Everyday Success*, Zondervan Publishing House., Grand Rapids, 1994.

Wilbur Wright Birthplace and Interpretive Center, *Centennial of Flight Festival: Commemorative Issue*, Millville, Indiana, 2003.

Yetter, George H., *Williamsburg Before and After: The Rebirth of Virginia's Colonial Capital*. The Colonial Williamsburg Foundation. 1988.

Printed in the United States
21485LVS00004B/163-165